PRAISE FOR THE SH/

"*Shards of History* and its sequel, *Fractured Days*, are terrifically entertaining reads from beginning to end clearly establishing and demonstrating author Rebecca Roland's consummate skills as an original and entertaining storyteller that will leave her enthusiastic readers looking forward to more novels featuring Malia and her world. Very highly recommended as enduringly popular addition to community library Fantasy Fiction collections."

— Midwest Book Review

"I whole-heartedly recommend Fractured Days to anyone who likes fantasy and strong female characters. Definitely another 5 star book from Rebecca Roland."

—*Purrfectly Bookish*

"*Five out of five stars!*—One of the most beautifully written novels I have ever read. Suspenseful, entrapping, and simply . . . well, let's just say that *Shards of History* reminds us of why we love books in the first place."

—Good Choice Reading

"Fast-paced, high-stakes drama in a fresh fantasy world. Rebecca Roland is a newcomer to watch!"

—James Maxey, author of *Greatshadow: The Dragon Apocalypse.*

"A must for any fantasy reader. Prepare to be taken by storm with Rebecca Roland fever."

—*Plasma Frequency Magazine*

"A passionate tale that will engage both young adults and more weathered fantasy readers."

— *NewMyths.com*

Other Titles by Rebecca Roland

Shards of History Series:
Shards of History
Fractured Days
Shattered Fates

Short Stories:
The King of Ash and Bones
featuring a story from the Shards of History series

The Necromancer's Inheritence Series:
The Graveyard Girl
The Necromancer's Return
The Necromancer's Book of Magic

SHATTERED FATES

Shards of History, Book Three

REBECCA ROLAND

World Weaver Press

SHATTERED FATES

Published by World Weaver Press, LLC
Albuquerque, New Mexico
www.WorldWeaverPress.com

Edited by Sarena Ulibarri
Cover designed by World Weaver Press

ISBN-10: 0-997788887
ISBN-13: 978-0997788884

Also available as an ebook.

For Mom. I'll love you always.

ACKNOWLEDGMENTS

The act of writing might be a lonely endeavor, but the act of seeing a book through to publication--much less a series--takes an enormous amount of effort and help.

Several years ago, Eileen Wiedbrauk saw something special in *Shards of History*, making it the first novel to be published with World Weaver Press. Sarena Ulibarri saw something special in it, too, and in *Fractured Days* and *Shattered Fates*. I am glad that the series found a home with World Weaver Press, and it was both a pleasure and an honor to work with everyone there.

The series began as a short story at the Odyssey Writing Workshop back in 2007. Thank you, Ronya McCool, for saying "novel" while I was thinking it, too. Susan Abel Sullivan was an early cheerleader for the series and has been a first reader for every novel. Beth Cato once again came to the rescue as beta reader and offered insightful comments that made *Shattered Fates* a much better story.

I want to thank my husband, Nate Roland, for being supportive over the years. He sends my books out into the world and talks about my writing to everyone. And finally, I want to thank my son, Miles, for bringing joy and new perspective to my life. Nate and Miles, you're the best.

SHATTERED FATES

CHAPTER ONE

A dragon's shadow passed over Malia. She fell into a crouch, heart thumping fast, blood roaring in her ears, mouth gone dry.

"Aru!" she shouted, alerting the winged Jegudun. Already in the air, he let out a piercing series of whistles that echoed off the cliff walls. Other Jeguduns poured out of the nearby cave homes that dotted the cliffs to join him as he swept through the air toward the dragon.

Aru, like other Jeguduns, was the size of a young human with a similar body shape, although stocky and fur-covered. Massive wings spread from his back and shoulders, covered with red-brown feathers that glimmered like polished dark wood in the bright sunlight. Cream-colored fur covered his head and wolfish snout, and his ears lay back against his head as he strained to rise as quickly as possible.

Malia grabbed Ankti's hand and hauled her toward the Big River. Malia was responsible for the former servant, having brought her this far to keep her safe from the Maddion who had enslaved her and kept Malia prisoner, and she was not about to let anything happen to the other woman.

"Rasmus!" she called to her friend. "To the river!"

The sound of his name broke through the immobility that had struck him when the dragon arrived, and he ran after Malia and Ankti.

The dragon circled like an eagle searching for prey. An empty saddle sat on her back. That, along with the pusing red glow of her sides and the familiar sinuous curve of her neck, marked her as the same beast Malia and Ankti had ridden to escape the Maddion and their mountain. But the Maddion and their dragons couldn't penetrate the magic barrier that covered and protected the valley, which could only mean one thing.

Malia stumbled into the river, followed by Ankti and Rasmus. She gasped at the coolness of the river, and gooseflesh broke out along her arms.

"The dragon shouldn't be in the valley," she said. "The dragon shouldn't be able to get through the barrier."

"Then the barrier must be gone," Rasmus said.

Malia squinted at the sky. Not that she could have seen the barrier if it had been there. She hadn't seen it since she and the Jeguduns had repaired it, bringing the shards of it together to protect them all against the Maddion and their dragons.

"How can it be gone?" she asked.

"I wish I knew," he said.

"At least in the river we'll be safe from the dragon's fire. If it comes to that."

All they had to do was dive under the water if the beast approached. A short ways upriver, Tuvin's Falls roared over the cliffs that surrounded the Taakwa Valley, feeding the Big River. Droplets sparkled in sunlight like beads of silver.

Rasmus nodded. His gaze flickered to Ankti, who clung to Malia's arm and watched the dragon. She still wore the clothes of a Maddion man, which she'd used as a disguise, but she'd lost her cap at some point, and her long, dark curls lay plastered against her head. Although her skin was brown, like the Taakwa, there were numerous details that marked her as an Outsider.

"Who is this?" he asked, his brows drawing down. As a former exile, Rasmus held less animosity toward strangers than most Taakwa, but it was hard to completely rid oneself of lifelong prejudices.

"This is Ankti of—" She bit off the rest because she didn't know. Ankti spoke her own language, and the Maddion's language, and perhaps others, but she didn't speak the language of the Taakwa and so couldn't tell Malia where she was from. "She was a Maddion slave. We both escaped last night. That dragon," she said, nodding at the beast in the air, "was how we left the Maddion's mountains."

At her name, the other woman looked at them. She spoke rapidly and used her arms to indicate a large dome or bowl over them.

Malia shook her head. "It's gone. I don't know why, but it's gone."

Ankti bit at her lower lip and swallowed hard, her anxious gaze returning to the skies.

"She was supposed to be safe here," Malia said to Rasmus. "We all are. I don't understand. Did something happen while I was gone?" She'd left the valley at least half a moon ago in search of the *mutara*, who had been staying with the Maddion, and who had held the cure to Malia's magic-induced memory loss, which had slowly been eating away at more of her mind.

"Nothing I know of. I thought all was well until *this*," he said, gesturing at the dragon, a few droplets of water falling from his fingers.

The beast let out a roar loud enough to vibrate behind Malia's sternum. She cringed, ready to duck her head underwater if need be, and Ankti trembled.

The dragon circled lower, whipping her head around to follow Aru as he flew behind her and beneath her, distracting her while the other Jeguduns rushed to join him. Even in the brilliant sunlight, the dragon's sides pulsed bright orange as she inhaled, fading when she exhaled, and growing brighter each time as she prepared to let her fire loose upon Aru. Malia grabbed Ankti's arm and squeezed.

With the dragon's next breath, she let out a stream of fire as Aru passed beneath her. Malia hissed and clutched Ankti's arm even tighter. Ankti muttered a few rapid-fire words, clutching her free hand to her chest.

It looked like the flames engulfed Aru, but the Jegudun dove out of their reach, wings tight around him like a raptor diving for a meal. Then he snapped his wings out to slow down. Malia sagged and let out the breath she'd been holding.

The first Jeguduns rushed past him, letting out growls and whistles as they shot toward the dragon. The beast rose, but the smaller Jeguduns were more nimble. She snapped at one who darted in front of her, but two others hooked their talons into her belly. The dragon let out a scream that felt like sharp claws scraping through Malia's head, and she winced.

Two more Jeguduns landed on the dragon's back. Her head darted behind her to bite at them, but when they let go and dropped, another dove past, tearing at the dragon's neck. Even on the ground, Malia could make out the spray of red. The dragon bit half-heartedly at another Jegudun, then her body went slack and began to tumble toward the earth.

The Jeguduns scattered as the beast fell. She landed about a hundred paces from the river, the sound like that of a large, heavy gourd splitting open.

Ankti jerked free and stumbled out of the river. She stood on the bank and shouted in the dragon's direction, shaking her fist. She picked up a rock and threw it with a grunt, coming close to hitting the beast, and threw another, and another. She let out one more yell and then merely stood, her chest rising and falling rapidly with her ragged breathing.

Rasmus watched her with his mouth parted. "She's expressive, isn't she?" he muttered.

"She has a lot to be angry about," Malia said. She climbed out of the water, letting out a tiny cry as the air hit her cool, wet skin.

"I didn't say she shouldn't," he said, following.

Aru landed nearby, while the other Jeguduns landed near the dragon. One of them apparently took a cue from Ankti and tossed a rock at the beast, but it remained still.

"Aru," Malia said. She ran to the Jegudun and fell to her knees beside him. "Are you hurt?"

He shook his head, but a quick shudder passed through his body. He smelled of fur and bird, the familiar scent of Jegudun, but also a little of brimstone from his close pass to the dragon.

"Let me check you over," Malia muttered. She gave him a once-over and, reassured he was truly fine, pulled him tight for a hug. "You're very brave, you know that?"

He let out a trill that turned into a pleased rumble deep in his chest. When he pulled back, his lips were curled back, showing his sharp teeth. Once, Malia would have been terrified of the show of teeth, but she knew now it was a Jegudun smile.

His smile faded, though, and he looked up, sweeping his hands much as Ankti did and trilling sadly as his pointed ears drooped slightly.

"Any idea what happened to the barrier?" Malia asked.

He shook his head.

Her hand went to her neck, seeking comfort in the necklace she'd worn for seasons, but found only her bare skin. She'd worn one feather when she began training as her village's next clan mother, and then she'd added the one Tuvin had given her when he'd died at the hands of her late husband. But she'd lost the memory Tuvin had stored in his feather, and then she'd given the other back to her mother when she had determined she couldn't resume the training because of her faulty memory. Losing all of her recent memories had been the price she'd paid for restoring the barrier, which was now simply gone. And then the *mutara* had restored those memories last night, before she and Ankti escaped.

Something tickled her mind, like when a Jegudun asked to share a memory with her, but she had let go of Aru, and as far as she knew, the Jeguduns could only share memories or magic when in contact with a Taakwa, one of her people. Her forehead creased. "Was that you?" she asked him.

His bushy brows drew down and he slowly shook his head.

"What happened?" Rasmus asked.

"I don't know." She hoped the strange sensation wasn't a sign that she still had a problem with her memories. The *mutara* had promised she'd be fixed, that her mind would be as it was before.

She ran her hands over her wet clothes. She wore the same skirt and tunic she'd had on when she had set out from the valley nearly a full moon ago. They were dingy and scratchy and probably smelled rank despite her dip in the river. Her hands hesitated over her hips where she had worn beads since her first bleeding. She didn't recall seeing her hip beads when she'd grabbed her belt and dagger before fleeing the cave where she'd been imprisoned. Her hip beads showed which clan she belonged to, and when she'd married, her late husband Dalibor's clan beads had been intertwined with hers. More recently, she'd worn black mourning beads among her own. Perhaps the Maddion had thrown them away, thinking them silly baubles. Without her hip beads and without her necklace, she felt as exposed to the world as the valley was vulnerable to the Maddion without its barrier.

"Malia, what's wrong?" Rasmus asked.

"Nothing," she said quickly. "I need to get to my grandmother and let her know I'm back and I'm well. She's an exile, like you were."

"I know. Enuwal filled me in when he passed through a couple of days ago."

"How was Enuwal?" He'd been healing from a broken leg when she'd left.

"Worried about you."

She flinched. "I left without saying anything to him. He would have tried to stop me. Was he… did he walk well? He shouldn't be walking so much. He broke his leg not long ago."

"He had a fine walking stick. He seemed to do well with that. He's a healer, Malia, he knows how much he should and shouldn't do."

"For anyone but himself, yes. He's the worst at following his own advice. Did he say how my grandmother was doing?"

"Only that she worried about you, too." He paused. "That must have been strange, realizing she was alive after all this time."

"No stranger than anything else that's happened since this past summer." She turned to Ankti and hesitated. "Aru, can you share memories with Ankti the way you can share them with Taakwa?"

He shook his head.

Malia sighed. It wouldn't have been ideal, but they could have communicated better. "We'll take care of you, Ankti," she said. She pointed west. "We're going to my grandmother's. We'll find clothes for you, and whatever else you need, and we'll figure out how to get you home."

Ankti followed the direction she pointed, bit her lip, and gazed toward the Maddion mountains. "Chanwa," she said softly. Then she pointed south and said something sadly.

"Ah," Malia said. "That must be home for you." And Chanwa was the woman who was supposed to have escaped with them. She was the wife of the Most Worthy, and she'd stayed behind to keep her husband occupied while Malia and Ankti escaped. Anger stirred in the pit of her stomach as she thought of the Maddion, but Chanwa had been different. She suspected Chanwa was dead, or soon would be. The Maddion did not hold much respect for women, and a woman who defied them probably would not fare well.

"I'll grab some food to get us through the walk," Rasmus said.

"Good idea," Malia said.

He trotted off to where a rope ladder hung from one of the ledges along the cliffs.

Malia turned to Aru. "Why don't you go home and get some rest? You've had far too much excitement for one day."

He nodded, let out a tired chirrup and launched into the air, slowly flying in the same general direction Malia and the others would head. Ankti watched him go, her brows furrowed. This was probably the first time she'd been close to a Jegudun, but unlike the deep-rooted fear the Taakwa had held toward them for generations, she seemed simply curious.

More Jeguduns emerged from their cave homes and circled around the dead dragon. They chirped and whistled and waved their arms as they spoke. A dozen or so worked on building a pyre around the dragon. Its bones would soon join those already dotting the valley from the Dragon War.

Rasmus soon returned with a travel sac slung across his torso and two waterskins. He handed one to Malia. "You'll have to share with Ankti. I didn't have another."

She nodded. "Thank you for the supplies."

There was no bridge nearby since Taakwa didn't live close to the cliffs and Jeguduns didn't need a bridge. Malia, Rasmus, and Ankti were soaked again and shivering by the time they reached the other side of the Big River, but the wet clothes were soon refreshing under the hot sun, and they dried quickly anyway. Malia would be glad to see her clothes go and never lay eyes on them again.

She led them along the forest's edge to take advantage of the shade, but she wanted to stay close to the cliffs rather than cut straight through the woods. She felt safer close to the cliffs where the Jeguduns lived. She kept glancing at the sky even though she wouldn't have been able to see the barrier if it was there.

Part of the forest stood charred, evidence of the Dragon War. After the war, fallen Maddion were burned in pyres in discrete locations, but the dragons were too large to move, and so had been burned where they fell. Their bones didn't burn, so delicate wing bones and large, curving ribs and vertebrae marked where they had died.

Rasmus walked a step behind as Taakwa tradition dictated. At first, Ankti walked behind him, with her head down, but Malia gestured for the other woman to walk beside her. Ankti glanced at Rasmus, who smiled and indicated she should walk ahead of him. She took her place cautiously beside Malia. After a while, Ankti held her head high and gazed around her as if taking in every detail.

Rasmus had helped Malia convince their people that the Jeguduns, long thought of as their enemies, were actually their allies when the Maddion attacked the summer before. As an exile, he was not allowed to live among the Taakwa. He'd been falsely accused of murder, had his head shorn and his clothes taken, and been sent out alone into the woods. Like some other exiles, he'd taken up residence among the Jeguduns, and more recently, he'd been trying to reestablish himself with his old village.

Malia filled Rasmus in on what had happened to her from the time she left the valley to that day. She told him about siphoning off a bit of the barrier to form one around herself. She told him about the four Jeguduns who caught up with her and who died when they were attacked by dragons, her guilt and grief as sharp as the day it happened. She told him of her capture, her imprisonment, and her meeting with the *mutara*.

"What happened to the *mutara*?" he asked when she finished.

"She changed. She became... Dalibor."

"What?" he said, stopping.

She and Ankti stopped, too. They stood beneath the shade of a mature pine tree, the smell of its sap sharp in the air. A squirrel ran along one of its branches, chattering angrily at them as if to say, *How dare you stop beneath* my *tree.*

"The *mutara* is Dalibor?" Rasmus asked.

She shook her head. "The *mutara* only looks like him. But it was unnerving." Unnerving, to say the least, that the *mutara* had chosen the form of her late husband. He hadn't trusted her or the Jeguduns the summer before when the Maddion threatened the valley, and in a rage had attacked her when she had tried bringing the Jeguduns and Taakwa together against the Maddion. She'd been left with no choice but to kill him in defending herself. The memory still left a sour taste in her mouth and a twist of guilt in her heart.

That same odd sensation tickled the back of her mind. She scratched her head as if that could make it go away. It pulled harder at her, and this time it definitely came from a direction—the northwest. She pushed it away, and the sensation faded. She began walking again, and the other two fell into step with her.

"You were lucky to survive," Rasmus said.

"I know. It was a foolish decision, leaving the valley. I would swear never to do it again, to live out my life blissfully beneath the barrier, but the future has become uncertain yet again." Her teeth clenched. "I should have asked the *mutara* to destroy all of the Maddion instead of restore my memories. We'll never be rid of them at this point."

"Hmm," he said.

"Oh, out with it."

Ankti arched a brow at Malia's harsh tone.

"It's just… that's a bit of a harsh statement," he said. "Would you truly have wanted them all dead? Women and men, old and young, infants?"

She sighed. "Clan mother take you and your reasonable response."

They stopped to rest beside a stream shortly after the sun passed its zenith. Cicadas droned lazily in the tall grass beyond the forest. Malia sat with her back against a thick fir tree, the scent of it filling her nostrils, and closed her eyes. The stream gurgled over rocks, and Rasmus and Ankti were so still that she could pretend she was alone out here, with nothing more pressing than to give in to the utter fatigue that threatened to drag her body under. A nice nap in the shade on a warm day sounded so very good…

She had almost fallen asleep when the faint tug pulled at her mind again. Her eyes flew open, but nobody touched her. Ankti kneeled beside the stream, washing her face, and Rasmus had moved a few paces away, looking back in the direction they'd come from. It didn't feel like a Jegudun. It felt like that first time the *mutara* moved around inside her mind, pushing at the fog that had been eating away at her memories. This time she had the distinct impression that the presence, at least the physical source of it, was moving more west than north, and putting quite a bit of distance between them, almost desperately. She pushed at the unwanted presence.

And it pushed back.

CHAPTER TWO

Malia let out a startled cry when the presence pushed against her. In an instant, the presence was like a bubble forming in her mind, pushing against her skull, and growing until it nearly burst. Then it withdrew, just as quick.

"Malia?" Rasmus asked. His hand was on the dagger he wore on a belt, and he glanced around.

Malia found herself standing. She must have leaped to her feet when that presence reacted to her.

Ankti had also shot to her feet and looked around them, then up.

"It's all right," Malia said, her speeding heart gradually slowing. "I just—" What? Experienced another person in her mind? After all she'd gone through, that would worry Rasmus too much, especially if she mentioned it felt like the *mutara*. She wanted to find out more before bringing this up with anybody. "I fell asleep and had a nightmare."

"Oh." His shoulders relaxed and his hand fell from the dagger. Ankti frowned and crossed her arms. She glanced up one more time before nodding.

"We should get a move on," Malia said.

She would have preferred a longer rest, but the sooner she found

Enuwal and got to her grandmother's home, the better she'd feel. The skies remained empty save for birds and a few scant clouds. There was no possibility that the Maddion knew about the barrier. Unless they had something to do with it. She urged her tired legs on.

The burnt areas and dragon bones grew farther apart and then disappeared altogether as they walked. The fighting hadn't come out in this direction, where the valley was sparsely populated, but had spread toward the center. So although her grandmother Rina had heard much about the fighting, and had seen some in the distance, the Dragon War hadn't directly touched her.

Malia didn't seek the presence, and it didn't push against her, but it was there, hovering in the background with all of her other concerns. The difference was, her normal concerns didn't give off a hint of anger and frustration as the presence did. It clouded all her other thoughts, enfusing them with a dark, sour tinge. She still had the feeling that it moved away, and she hoped it moved so far that they couldn't feel one another any longer.

Her grandmother had talked about a price to pay for making a deal with the *mutara*. The *mutara* was a powerful being who could create massive change all at once, such as when he cured the Maddion of the illness that had threatened to wipe them all out. Was this it, then? Were they doomed to a lifelong connection to one another? It didn't seem like an outcome he would enjoy, but maybe he received more of her thoughts than she did of his. Maybe he enjoyed a voyeuristic existence. But then he shouldn't be angry, or frustrated. She tried to shake loose the endless loop of thoughts. Rina would know. She'd help.

In the mid-afternoon, a Jegudun approached from the western sky, recognizable as Aru once he got close enough. He landed nearby, hopping a couple of times to gain his balance, and waddled to meet them. Jeguduns were so graceful in the air, and so clumsy on the ground, like a toddler figuring out how to walk. She hid a grin as she imagined a much smaller and younger Aru taking his first steps with huge, awkward wings behind him. He carried a bulging travel sac, which he handed to Malia, and a water skin.

"Thank you," she said. "Rasmus grabbed some supplies for us, but this is welcome. Did you get any rest at all?"

He nodded and flashed his teeth in a grin. He stood taller and did look a bit better, but there was still a tightness around his eyes that suggested he had rested only as much as he absolutely needed.

Malia balanced the travel sac on her thigh as she split the contents between herself, Ankti, and Rasmus: dried, salty strips of venison, shelled pecans, bread filled with chopped nuts and dried blueberries and cherries, and a few of the bitter beans like those Aru had given her when she'd traveled from the valley to the Maddion. She brightened when she found them.

"These will give us some energy," she said, handing a few to Rasmus. "It doesn't take long before you feel it. They don't taste very good, though."

Ankti smiled when she took hers and said, "Cafaba."

Malia picked up one and repeated, "Cafaba." Ankti nodded, her smiled widening. Malia chewed on it, washing down the bitter taste with water. She began walking, nibbling on food along the way.

"Did you tell my grandmother we were on our way?" she asked Aru as he fell into step with them. Malia slowed their pace so he could keep up.

He nodded.

"How much farther? I haven't approached from this direction."

He pointed to the sun, then mimed it setting.

"Shortly after sunset?" she asked.

He nodded, then used two fingers to show a person walking, wagging them quickly back and forth.

Rasmus chuckled. "I don't think *any* of us can walk that fast."

Aru shrugged and gave them a wolfish, toothy grin.

Malia nodded. There was nothing to do other than put one foot in front of the other, then.

As they ate and walked, they passed the time by exchanging the names of their food. Then they began naming clothes, body parts like eyes, ears, nose, then the grass, the trees, dirt, the sky, clouds, an eagle when one soared past, a doe who poked her head out of the shadows briefly to study them, and anything else they came across. Malia was glad for the distraction from worrying about the presence in her mind.

Ankti laughed at Malia's pronunciation of 'butterfly' in her language, and the sound echoed off the nearby cliffs. She immediately stopped, shaking her head and speaking rapidly, a frown forming deep lines.

Malia wasn't sure why the sound of her own laughter made Ankti upset, but she let the language lessons go. Aru had taken to the air a while back, flying ahead of them until he'd disappeared. He could tolerate walking with them for only so long.

They continued in silence. Malia tentatively reached for the presence. Maybe if she moved slowly, she could free herself completely, like slipping out of the house at night without waking others. She pulled her mind from it little by little, picturing it anchored in one place as she tiptoed away. The connection between them stretched and thinned like a strand of clay being pulled apart. Malia held her breath and pulled a little more. Almost there. Almost separated…

The connection rebounded and jerked them together hard enough that pain reverberated through her skull. Malia cried out and put a hand to her head, but the pain was already fading. And, the connection was still there, with unmistakable ire wafting from the presence.

"What happened?" Rasmus asked.

Malia dropped her hand. "Too many aches and pains, I guess. All that time as a prisoner is making it challenging for me to walk this far."

He frowned. "You're not having more problems with your

memory, are you?"

"Not at all. Those are all restored." But she had a new set of problems, thanks to the *mutara*.

Although her legs were so tired they were numb, she set a fast pace, especially as the sun neared the horizon. A few black boulders dotted the grassy plains between the forest and the cliffs, and the forest crept back from the cliffs the farther they walked. The first time Malia had reached her grandmother's home, she'd crossed a field of black boulders in a storm, and Enuwal had broken his leg. This time they wouldn't have to do anything so drastic.

The sun touched the horizon and was quickly slipping beyond when Aru returned, this time bearing three dark lanterns hanging from a chain held in one hand, and a tinder-box in the other.

Rasmus set to work igniting a fire. "Too bad that nasty dragon isn't around to lend its fire," he muttered. He had a flame burning quickly and lit each of the lanterns. The smell of burning oil wafted from them, and light poured out of carvings shaped like the crescent moon, or stars, or squiggles that looked like fern heads.

Aru took to the air again, leaving the lanterns with them, and Malia led them closer to the cliffs. The last sliver of sun fell behind the horizon, and the stars began to twinkle to life in earnest. Malia couldn't even think beyond keeping her legs moving and concentrating on the ground in front of her so she wouldn't step into a divot or on a rock. It wouldn't do to hurt herself just before she reached her grandmother's home. She focused on how good it would feel when Rina would hug her in greeting, the smell of wild roses enveloping her. And she would see Enuwal again, and feel his arms around her, too. If he wasn't too angry with her, that is.

Malia wasn't sure how much time had passed when another lantern appeared in the distance. It bobbled quickly as it made its way to them.

As they drew together, the light revealed a tall, slim figure wearing tunic and pants and walking with a stick nearly as tall as him. The lantern light cast long shadows across his face, but it was clearly Enuwal.

Malia stopped a stride from him, and he stopped, too. His face was impossible to read in the lantern light. Her pulse sped, and tendrils of doubt wound their way through her. He might be furious with her for leaving without a word, and she couldn't blame him if he were.

"I'm sorry," she said. "I couldn't tell you what I was going to do. You would have found some way to keep me in the valley."

"That's right," he said, his voice calm and not at all angry. But she knew him well enough to detect the slight strain. Then, hopefully, "Did it work?"

"Yes. My memories returned to me, and my mind is whole."

His shoulders sagged in relief. "I can't decide if you were brave or foolish for what you did. Resourceful, definitely."

"Probably a little of both." She took a step forward. "Enuwal," she said, pleading in that single word.

He sighed and closed the distance between them. He set his lantern and walking stick down, then took her lantern and placed it beside his, his movements deliberate although there was the faintest quiver in his arms, and pulled her into a tight embrace.

Malia sank into him. He smelled of herbs and sweat, and he felt thinner. "I'm sorry. I think I might have to keep saying I'm sorry for a long time."

"I forgive you, Malia. And if the situation had been reversed, I'm certain I would have done the same." His hold on her tightened. "I can't believe you went outside the valley alone."

"Aru was with me."

"You could have been hurt. Or killed."

She almost had been, but she kept that to herself for the moment, too. She didn't want anything to spoil this closeness. "I dreamed about this," she murmured against his shoulder.

"Me, too." He meant it. The warmth in his voice was genuine.

But he held himself a little stiffly. It might have been his leg. Maybe it hurt him, especially if he'd been walking such a long way looking for her or for any news of her. Or maybe he didn't fully forgive her. Or he couldn't quite let go of his anger at her leaving without a word. She needed a moment alone with him, to talk to him about it. But she had guests, and Ankti was just as tired as she was. She pulled away, keeping her fingers touching Enuwal's, but then he pulled his hand free, breaking their connection completely. He grabbed his walking stick and leaned on it.

Malia grabbed both of their lanterns to give her hands something to do. She gave him his and said, "Enuwal, this is Ankti. She was a Maddion slave who escaped with me."

His eyes widened. "I guess you have a lot to tell us."

She nodded. "Ankti, this is Enuwal of Posalo."

Ankti raised her head. "Enuwal," she said carefully, nodding once.

His gaze fell to Malia's waist then. "Your beads?"

"Gone," she said with a sigh. Her hand went again to her bare neck and then fell by her side. "I feel so out of sorts." The presence in her mind stirred uncomfortably as if it felt the same way.

"Then let's get to Rina's. You'll feel better once you see her."

"Yes."

She grabbed her lantern and led the way, Ankti on one side, Enuwal a half-step behind her on the other side, and Rasmus a couple of strides behind them. Enuwal wore his long, dark hair in a braid, as men did when they had completed five days of fasting and trials, leaving boyhood behind. Rasmus's hair, on the other hand, was short, tufts covering his ears and the back of his neck. He'd been growing it out ever since his exile was lifted, but it would be a long time before he could braid it again.

When they reached the cliffs where Rina lived, a rope ladder hung from the ledge, and torches burned from their sconces high above, the sight a warm welcome.

They doused their lanterns, and Malia was the first up the ladder, with Ankti behind her. When she reached the ledge, a rich, strong feminine voice said, “Hand me your lantern.”

Malia smiled. “Rina,” she said. She scrambled onto the ledge and threw her arms around her grandmother. Her arms somehow managed to be soft and strong, and she smelled of wild roses. She squeezed Malia tight enough to emit an “oomph” from her. Then she stepped back, keeping her hands on Malia’s shoulders.

“You foolish girl,” she said. “Don’t you ever do anything like that again.”

“I’m sorry.” It seemed she really would be apologizing for a while. “Are you well?”

“Well enough, now that you’re back. So, was it worth terrifying your poor, old grandmother? Are your memories restored?”

She smiled a little. There was nothing poor nor old about her grandmother, despite the shock of short, white hair crowning her head. “They are.”

Rina’s lips thinned. “Praise the clan mother,” she said quietly.

Malia sobered. Her grandmother had probably not uttered those words since Malia was a small child.

She helped Ankti onto the ledge, made the introductions, and followed her grandmother inside where a couple of lanterns hung from the granite ceiling, casting a warm glow over the room. The hearth in the far wall was cold.

A pool carved into the stone wall took up one corner. Water trickled down the wall and into the pool, and water constantly drained out of it at the bottom. A stone lip held the water in. Shelves lined the walls, holding baskets, blankets, plates and bowls and utensils, cooking pots, and an assortment of other items. Thick rugs woven in Taakwa geometric patterns in blue, red, black, brown, and white covered the floor. Malia took off her shoes and left them beside the door. She let out a little sigh as her tired feet sank into the plush rugs.

“Where is Ziku?” Malia asked. Rina had lived with the elderly

Jegudun for quite some time.

"Asleep. He's been doing that a lot more lately." The corners of Rina's mouth turned down for a moment. "He'll be glad to see you in the morning, though. Are you hungry? Would you rather clean up? Sleep? I'm sure you're exhausted."

"Ankti, are you hungry?" She mimed eating.

Ankti shook her head. She swayed a little on her feet.

"I think we just want to sleep. Tomorrow is time enough to clean up and eat a proper meal."

Rina nodded. "Very well."

"Yes. Did Aru tell you about the barrier?"

She sighed. "He did."

"Any idea what happened to it?"

A pained look crossed her face, and she hesitated. "Malia, do you remember when I said that the *mutara* always has a price?"

"Yes."

"Do you know what the price was for returning your memories?"

"Well, the *mutara* turned into Dalibor." But her grandmother's words sent her thoughts tumbling in a different direction.

The *mutara* had said, *All will be as it was before.* She thought it referred only to her memories and her mind, but what if it referred to something else as well? What if it referred to the time right before Malia worked the magic that made her lose her memories? If that was the case, then that was when the Maddion had destroyed the barrier. Her blood turned to ice.

The barrier was gone because of her.

CHAPTER THREE

In the morning, Rina insisted they eat and clean up before having any sort of discussion. "Nobody can think very well on an empty stomach or while scratching at skin that hasn't seen soap in days," she said.

Ankti, as their guest, bathed first. Ziku and Rina remained in their private room while Ankti cleaned up in the pool. Malia sat on the ledge with Enuwal, a mug of warm tea in her hands and the cold granite behind her. It would warm up soon enough when the sun came up. She stretched her sore legs out, glad that at least for that day, she didn't have to go anywhere unless it was absolutely necessary. A covered basket sat beside her with a small shovel inside. If she did anything, she might look for clay to make a bowl, a plate, a small figure, anything to get her fingers moving and help align her scattered thoughts.

Although Enuwal sat beside her, he maintained a gap between them. Before, they might have sat with their legs touching, or brush fingertips when he handed her a mug of tea, but he was keeping to himself as if he wore an invisible barrier around him.

Rasmus had gone for a walk. He strolled south along the edge of the field of boulders, stopping from time to time as if he were inspecting them. They were like pebbled, dark skin in the field of grass, and they reminded Malia of badly puckered burn scars.

"I shouldn't have left," she said, staring into her mug of tea. Her reflection stared back at her in the golden brown liquid. She sipped, and the strong, bitter taste helped her emerge from the mugginess of hard sleep. "The *mutara* took the barrier as payment for restoring my memories."

"You didn't know that would happen," Enuwal said. He sat with his legs stretched out, too, and held his own mug of tea. "You can't tell me that if you'd known the price you would have still gone through with it."

"I wouldn't have. But Rina warned me about the *mutara*. I should have listened." She leaned her head against the stone and sighed. The presence was in her mind again, more noticeable than the previous day. It sat like a lump in her head and in her thoughts, pulsing like a second heartbeat. And she could have sworn it was closer than it had been the day before, like it was moving toward the valley. *Just go away*, she thought at it. But it remained, and it loomed, and it felt like it would keep coming.

She straightened. "What price did the Maddion pay for their cure? They burned their scrolls. I understand they were important to them, but without them they can survive. They don't have to worry about their enemies pouring into their homes and enslaving them, or butchering them. Why is it that they paid a lower price than I did?" Her hands gripped the mug so tight she feared it might shatter. "Because my request was selfish, that's why. Of *course* they would want to help their dying and their sick. I only wanted to help myself."

Enuwal's knuckles whitened as he tightened his grip on his mug. He gave her a sharp look. "The *mutara* took advantage of your mental state and your desperation. I don't call that selfishness."

She took a deep breath. "I think there's another price I'm paying."

He sat straighter. "What is it? What else did that thing do to you?"

"I think the *mutara* is still here somehow." She raised a hand to her head, almost expecting to feel a lump where the presence sat. "It feels like there's someone else in here with me. I tried pushing him away yesterday, but I don't think I can sever the connection. And I think he tried pulling away too, but couldn't."

"Dragon flames take him," Enuwal said. "Is he hurting you?"

She shook her head. "Not intentionally. But when I try to pull away from him, it's… uncomfortable."

The blanket hanging over the door rustled, and Ankti stepped out. She wore a skirt borrowed from Rina, belted to help hold it up, and a tunic that hung a bit loose on her frame. The shoes she'd borrowed fit her well, though. Her wet curls hung halfway down her back. She raised a hand to her hair and asked a question.

Malia realized she'd been clenching her teeth and gripping the mug tight. She forced herself to relax and smile at the other woman. "I'll help you with your hair."

"What about what you just told me?" Enuwal asked.

"We'll talk later."

She went inside and dug through the baskets until she found a comb. She sat behind Ankti and carefully ran it through Ankti's curls, trying her best not to snag the tangles, and soon had them all out. She sat back on her heels, contemplating what to do with Ankti's hair. Taakwa girls wore their hair down before they wore beads, and women wore their hair in a large knot at the nape of their necks. Neither would be proper for Ankti because she wasn't Taakwa.

She ended up making a twist on either side of Ankti's head from her crown to the nape of her neck and tying it off with a leather strap, leaving some curls to hang free below the strap. "That should do," she said. "It looks nice, and it'll keep your hair out of the way. What do you think?"

Ankti reached behind her and gingerly felt it. She turned with a smile. "Thank you," she said carefully.

"You're welcome."

Ankti stayed inside while Malia cleaned up. They exchanged words again as Malia soaked in the warm water. Soap. Skirt. Tunic.

Hair. Comb. Hearth. The lesson eased some of the tight anxiety in Malia's chest over the unwelcome presence in her mind and Enuwal's coolness. Rina joined them in the room and in the lesson as she prepared porridge with dried fruit and nuts and a touch of honey. By the time Malia dried off and dressed, her stomach was growling at the smell of breakfast, and some of the tension had eased.

"Malia," Rina said. "I have something for you." She reached into a basket and pulled out a few strands of red beads interspersed with a strand of black. "I saw that you didn't have yours anymore, and I thought you might want them. When I left Taakwa life behind, I actually missed the weight of them on my hips."

Malia took them. The beads were tiny and cool and rattled like windblown leaves. "Thank you," she said. "I did miss them."

Her grandmother pursed her lips. "I know you had problems with Dalibor, to put it mildly, but I know you wanted to go through a proper mourning period."

"Well, it was more like my mother wanted me to go through a proper mourning period, and there's no arguing with her." She shrugged. "But I'll wear them. It's not like I could marry anyone right now, not with the barrier being gone and our futures uncertain." Her voice caught at the end as the realization hit her; she'd never be able to marry Enuwal so long as the valley was vulnerable to the Maddion.

She slipped the beads around her waist, tied them off, and sighed. They did not weigh much, but their presence did settle some of the fluttering that had been plaguing her stomach and mind. Her hand went to her bare neck. The missing necklace would take some getting used to.

Rina called Enuwal inside. He entered with Rasmus behind him. Enuwal glanced at the hip beads, then met her gaze and nodded with a thin smile. He knew how much the beads would mean to her, even those that indicated she was in mourning.

Rina went into the other room to help Ziku out. An ache went through Malia's heart as the elderly Jegudun made his way slowly into the main room and settled against some pillows with a groan. The fur around his mouth was white, and most of the fur around his head was as well. His eyes were milky white and unfocused. His hands, ending in sharp, short talons, were steady when he took a bowl of porridge, though, and his folded wings rose in exact apexes behind him. Still, he looked more frail than before Malia had left the valley, and that hadn't been all that long ago.

Huge wings beat the air outside, and talons scrabbled at the ledge. A moment later, Aru walked in and trilled a greeting at everyone. He took a bowl of porridge from Rina and sat beside Ziku. They all settled into the task of eating, with a few murmured comments about the deliciousness of the breakfast and how the day might turn out.

Rasmus and Enuwal helped Rina clean up after the meal. Then Malia settled back against the pillows and said, "We need to talk about the barrier now."

Rina nodded. "Yes."

She took a deep breath. "It seems the *mutara* took it when he returned my memories." She waited for angry looks or words, but instead, everyone waited for her to go on. Her hands clenched together in her lap. She would almost rather that *somebody* was as mad at her as she was at herself. "So we're worse off than we were during the Dragon War. At least the shattered remnants of the barrier were still around. But now we have to erect an entirely new one."

Aru chirruped and waved his hands rapidly, shaking his head.

"It will work like it did the first time, won't it?" Malia said.

He let out a frustrated little growl, making the fur around his mouth flutter. Ziku raised his head, his ears swiveling. Rina reached over and patted the back of his fur-covered hand.

"I'm here, love."

He let out a trill and grasped Rina's hand. Rina closed her eyes, and a moment later they began moving under her eyelids as if she were dreaming, as Ziku shared a memory with her.

Ankti watched with a crease between her brows and pursed lips.

"Ziku is sharing memories with her," Malia said to Ankti. She pointed from her head to Ankti's. A moment later, Ankti's eyes widened, and she nodded understanding.

Rina opened her eyes and kept her hand in Ziku's. "He showed me the first time they erected the barrier. There were so many Jeguduns and Taakwa. Many more than are alive today. The Dragon War depleted our numbers, and I don't know that there were as many of us before that anyway."

"So there aren't enough of us to replace the barrier?" Rasmus said.

Aru shook his head and trilled sadly.

"What about half the size it was?" Enuwal asked.

Aru canted his head to one side, considered, and nodded.

"But that would mean fitting all of the Taakwa and Jeguduns into half the space they're used to," Rina said. "That would mean potentially giving up half the valley to somebody else to live in and tend. And that would also mean stricter population control so we didn't stress our resources."

"The valley makes a good boundary right now," Malia said. "It's easy to stay within the barrier because we can see where it ends—or rather, where it used to end. The cliffs give an extra layer of protection from Outsiders and the Maddion. But if we only protected half the valley, the Maddion could put men and dragons just outside and bide their time. Or make us watch as they destroyed part of our former home. Or gave it away. And remember how they blocked the falls before and the Big River dwindled? They could still affect us even without coming through the barrier."

"Smaller land will make people feel cramped," Rasmus said. "It will strain our food sources and our tempers."

"Yes," Enuwal said. "I don't like this at all."

Malia bit at the inside of her cheek. Ankti's head was tilted to one side, her forehead creased. She might not understand the words, but she was trying hard to follow the tone of the conversation.

"We could always leave the valley and start a new life somewhere else," Malia said.

Rasmus shook his head. "We'd be vulnerable to the Maddion, and I doubt they'd just forget about us."

"And not everyone would be willing to leave," Enuwal said. "Or capable."

She sighed. "If there aren't enough of us to erect a new barrier, then there certainly aren't enough of us to wage a new war against a healthy Maddion army. Unless anyone has any other suggestions?"

Aru shook his head and looked down. The muscles in Rasmus's jaw jumped. Enuwal looked down at his clasped hands.

Malia couldn't believe it had come to this. Stay and fight, stay and cram together into half the space and fight at some point, leave and fight. If only the Maddion would be happy they were alive and leave everybody alone. She thought again of how she should have used her request for destroying the Maddion once and for all, and not for restoring her memories. The presence in her mind loomed, growing again like a bubble until her head throbbed with the pressure. She laid a hand on her scalp, wincing at the pain.

"Malia?" Enuwal asked. "What's wrong? Is it the *mutara*?"

"The *mutara*?" Rina said. "What's going on?"

She sighed. "I feel this… presence in my mind. I'm certain it's the *mutara*."

Everybody started talking at once. Rina raised her hands, and they all quieted. "Please, let her explain." She turned to Malia, brows drawn down.

"I can tell where he is, more or less. He was moving away from the valley, but I could swear he's closer now." Everybody was watching her intently, as if expecting her to suddenly sprout wings and fly away. "I tried pushing him away and pulling free. I can almost do it, but then he snaps back. I think he's tried, too. I don't think he planned this."

"So it's a surprise to him, too?" Rasmus said. "Wonderful."

"Why would he be coming here?" Enuwal asked. "You said he

looks like Dalibor now. Do you think he wants something from you?"

"I don't know. He took that form specifically to irritate me. Maybe he's headed here to do something about this connection."

"Like what?"

She bit at her lower lip. "I wish I knew."

"I can think of one certain way to sever this connection," Rasmus said. "And he might be thinking the same."

Aru let out a little growl, his talons protracting, and his sharp teeth showing.

Malia's insides twisted around one another. She hadn't even considered the fact that the *mutara* might be on his way here to kill her. She thought he might just need contact with her to break the connection, the way the Jeguduns needed contact with Taakwa to make their magic work.

"We should get ready for when he gets here," Enuwal said.

"You can't fight this being," Rina said. "You'll only get yourselves killed."

"So we just give her up? Let him hurt her or kill her?"

"One of us can offer him a trade, a change, the chance for him to use his most powerful magic again," Rina said.

"I won't let anybody sacrifice themselves for me," Malia said. "I'll face him on my own. In fact, this might be our chance to ask him to reverse what he did." She straightened. "He can replace the barrier and take my memories back."

"No," Enuwal said. "You can't do that."

"I can, and I should. I'm the one who placed the entire valley in danger, so I should be the one to make this sacrifice, not any of you."

Enuwal began to speak, but Rasmus spoke over him. "She's got a point." He raised a hand to cut off further protests. "I'm not saying I like this, but it would be the best solution. We could protect the valley again before the Maddion ever discover that we're vulnerable."

"We shouldn't make this decision hastily," Enwual said.

"I see no other way," Malia said. "When he gets here, I'll have him reverse it all."

Aru chirruped sadly.

"I know," Malia said. "It was a long journey only to end up exactly where we began." She glanced at Ankti. "Only, we saved one person. I think that makes the journey worth it."

Enuwal stood abruptly and limped out to the ledge. The rope ladder snapped as it unfurled and creaked a moment later.

"He'll come to understand that it's the only solution," Rina said, laying a hand over Malia's. "And I can't say that I blame him. I hate to see you suffering, and I hate the idea of losing you to this magic again. But you're doing the right thing. That doesn't mean I have to like it, and neither does he."

"I like it least of all," she said.

"Of course."

Malia stood. "I'm going to find him and talk to him."

"When do you think the *mutara* will arrive?"

"I don't know. He's getting closer all the time. Later today, maybe."

Rina grimaced. "So little time."

Malia's hand went to her bare neck. All of her plans had changed. She would never be a clan mother, never have a family, never live in peace. Her hand fell away. A hot wave of anger surged through her. If the Maddion had just kept to themselves or treated other people decently, this would never have happened. Instead, they rode over anyone in their way on their quest to dominate.

The early morning sun was bright and hot already. The rope was rough beneath her hands as she climbed down the ladder.

The forest stood beyond the field of black boulders, with a few copses in either direction along the narrow plains beside the cliffs. To the north, near the Jeguduns' cliff homes, grew small crops of corn, squash, beans, husk tomatoes, and a few other vegetables. A pair of Jeguduns worked among the rows, pulling weeds or checking the plants. Enuwal had gone south and stood beneath a pair of fir trees with his back to her, his walking stick in one hand. She hastened in his direction.

His shoulders bunched beneath his tunic as she neared him. "I would really rather be alone right now," he said, his voice thick.

She stood a good two paces from him. If it was anybody else, she would have silently left, but Enuwal wasn't one to get angry often, and not so angry that it rolled off him like heat from the sun, and not at her. Not for volunteering to do what had to be done for the sake of the Taakwa and the Jegudnns.

"Are you really so angry with me that you can't bear to even look at me?"

He said nothing, his shoulders as hard and broad and impenetrable as the cliffs surrounding the valley.

"You've been distant ever since I came back," she said. "I suppose I can't blame you. You must have been terrified when you found me gone, and angry, and you have every right to feel that way. But we probably don't have much time left at all, and I'd rather we spend it together than with this strange chasm between us."

He half turned, his eyes red-rimmed and hidden in the tree's shadow. "Do you trust me, Malia?"

"Of course," she said, taking a step closer to him. "I trust you with my life, with my heart." She stopped a stride from him, uncertain if she was welcome any closer.

"You took Aru with you outside the valley rather than wait for me. My leg had nearly healed. I could have gone with you, Malia, and then you wouldn't have risked the Maddion capturing both you and a Jegudun. But you left me behind."

"It had nothing to do with trust and everything to do with haste. I didn't know how long the *mutara* would stay with the Maddion, or how long what was left of my mind would stay with *me*. I couldn't wait for your leg to heal, and that would have been too much to ask of you when it had. It's a long journey."

He raised his head, finally meeting her gaze. "You didn't want me to take care of you, either. If you had stayed in the valley, you would have rather had the Jeguduns care for you as your memories faded altogether."

Her brows drew down. "That had nothing to do with trust either. I told you before, I didn't want to hold you back from caring for other sick or injured Taakwa. You can't spend the rest of my life tending me. I could live a long time in a physically healthy body with a fading mind."

"You had a deal with the Jeguduns," he said. "For when your decline reached a critical point."

"Aru—" she began. His eyes, searching her face intently, shifted to certainty, and he gave a little nod. Her lips thinned. "Aru never let you know. You guessed."

"That's why you didn't want me to take care of you."

"You're a healer. It's not in you to let people die. Or help them along if they wish it."

"Of course not." He didn't quite yell. He took a deep breath and spoke more calmly. "Of course not," he said again. "It's not my inclination. But the fact that you didn't even bring it up with me… it tells me you don't trust me, not completely."

"I didn't want to burden you with that task."

"You didn't even *ask*, Malia. You didn't even give me the chance to help you make that decision. You didn't give me the chance to help at all. You took so much upon yourself when you repaired the barrier, and then when you restored your memories. It's all right to ask for help, to need help. It's all right to rely on others."

A breeze picked up, making the tree limbs dance and whisper. A strand of hair came loose from the twist of hair at the nape of her neck. She tucked it behind her ear.

Enuwal took a step forward. They were close enough now that she could make out the faint, familiar smell of herbs that always clung to him. "When people love one another, they do all they can for each other," he said. "When you left without a word, I felt as if you were pushing me away."

A deep ache sliced through her. "I never meant for you to feel that way. I love you, Enuwal. I wanted to spare you the worst pain. I thought I was doing the right thing. I really did. But all I did was destroy everything I sacrificed in the Dragon War." Her body and her legs shook. Unshed tears burned behind her eyelids. "I messed up everything. I'm sorry. I'm so very sorry."

He pulled her close, even closer than the previous night when they greeted each other for the first time since she'd left. She shook as she held him, as he held her. He murmured against her ear, his warm breath caressing her skin. She had no idea what he actually said, only that his voice soothed her. *This* was what she'd been hoping for when she came back to him. But because of her deal with the *mutara*, this wasn't going to last long at all.

Enuwal pulled back enough to look down at her with his warm, brown eyes. His lips curved into a smile, and he began to speak, but then his gaze flickered beyond her shoulder. His face hardened, disbelief and fear and anger flashing across in quick succession.

Malia whirled. The *mutara* stood a few paces away. He looked exactly as he had when she last saw him. The taughtness of his muscles, the thin line of his mouth, the sharp hook of his nose all looked exactly like her late husband, Dalibor. Only the swirling red-orange of his eyes was different.

He held a dagger in one hand. Before Malia could get a hand on her own dagger, hanging from a belt at her waist, he leaped at her with a silent snarl, his blade raised.

CHAPTER FOUR

Chanwa wrapped her arms around herself and paced the small cell, trying to keep warm. She still wore her disguise, consisting of a man's woolen tunic and pants, and a cap to cover her fine hair, but the cold within the cavern was as deep and sharp as a blade. She felt as though she'd never get warm again.

She had no idea how much time had passed since she had watched the dragon carry Ankti and the Taakwa woman away. Moments after they'd gone, her husband Muvumo had arrived, followed by his personal guard, Delkis. She'd been expecting him to have his dragon burn her or for him to order Delkis to kill her, or for him to throw her off the stone wall surrounding the mesa to crash to the steep, stony ground below. The changer, or *mutara* as the Taakwa woman had called him, had leaped off the wall earlier and disappeared into the forest, but she had a feeling her body wouldn't fare anywhere near as well as his must have.

Instead, Muvumo had dragged her into the prisoner's cavern and thrown her into a cell. He'd left a torch burning somewhere in the hall so that faint light spilled through the small, barred square opening in the heavy wooden door. It was her only company. That, and the waste bucket in one corner. The place reeked of urine and feces and sweat and the sour stench of fear. And she'd been there since.

Her stomach grumbled. Traitorous belly, wanting food when there were important matters going on outside this cell, like whether or not Ankti had made it to the safety of the Taakwa Valley. Chanwa wasn't sure how the changer had planned to make it so she could safely enter the valley along with Ankti. She supposed she'd never know at this point.

Heavy footsteps approached rapidly. She froze, ears straining. Two pairs of footsteps. One definitely belonged to Muvumo; she'd know that authoritative, rapid-fire pattern anywhere. She shuddered, then raised her chin. Whatever her fate, she'd face it bravely. The Maddion men liked to boast about how brave they were. Well, she'd show them the women were just as brave.

The light coming through the small square in the door brightened. A shadow fell across it, and a key turned in the lock. The door opened, and Delkis stepped in first, carrying a torch. The smell of burning oil chased away the fouler stenches of the cell. He kept his face impassive, impossible to read, as hard and cold as the stone around her. A leather belt slung low around his hips carried a dagger on his left, and a short axe on his right. Either would be suitable for carrying out an execution order, should it come to that. Chanwa took a deep breath and clasped her hands together before her to hide their trembling.

Muvumo stepped in next. He was a handsome man, and young, although the events of his short stint as Most Worthy had taken its toll. Dark half-circles marred the skin beneath his eyes, and his forehead seemed permanently creased in worry or frustration or anger—or some combination thereof. His light brown hair was twisted into thick ropes, all of it tied behind him, reminding her of a bear's ruff. And, even in the dim light, his pupils were wide. He was still using the kasi powder, then. He had sworn to give it up once he'd found a cure for the illness that had been killing all of the

Maddion, but it was hard to give up flights on the white dragon once someone had experienced it.

She kneeled and pressed her forehead to the cold, damp stone floor. "Most Worthy," she said, her voice tiny and echoing in the space. She flinched inwardly at the sound.

"Get up," he said.

She stood, biting back a groan as her knees, hips, and back protested against the deep cold, and clasped her hands before her again.

"I'm giving you one last chance," he said. "You will come home with me, you will speak of this *incident* to no one, and you will be a proper and obedient wife. You will bear me sons, or you will go to live among the unmentionables. You will treat the servants as servants, and not as confidants. If you take one as a lover, that's fine, but you will treat her always as your servant, and not as a friend or equal in any way. And you will write no more. Ever. Do you understand?"

She flinched at the harshness in his tone. It took her a moment to realize he wasn't immediately condemning her to death. Why would he give her one more chance? Did he care for her that much? No, more likely it was because the illness had taken so many lives that a young woman of childbearing age couldn't simply be thrown away.

The muscles around his jaw tensed, and he held himself rigidly. Was he afraid she'd refuse and force him to execute her? Could it be that he cared for her more than she thought? He *had* read her scrolls. He denied her to write anymore, but maybe he was simply saying that in front of Delkis to keep up pretenses. He had been touched by her scrolls, she could tell. He had kept them when he could have—and should have—destroyed them.

There was no guarantee she could bear him sons, or bear him children at all. Some women couldn't. But she didn't think it was the right moment for pointing that out. And the way he spoke of the servants, as if they were nothing more than furniture, incapable of feeling or caring, made her fingers twitch, wanting to curl into fists. If Ankti had been caught, he would be using that information against her. Her hands relaxed. At least Ankti was safe. *Ankti was safe.*

A part of her wanted to shout at Muvumo and deny him treating her like chattel. But he *would* kill her. If he swore it in front of Delkis, he meant it, no matter whether he cared for her or not. If she died, it would do no good for anybody. Not for Ankti, and certainly not for her people or the other women who kept their rage and despair in check as she did. She took a deep breath.

"If I don't agree to this?" she asked.

His eyes narrowed. "Then you will die."

Delkis's clothes rustled as he laid a hand on the short axe. He kept a steady, unblinking gaze on her, much like a lizard sitting on a sunny rock, intent on a fly.

Her rage turned to a hard knot in her throat. "Very well," she said. "I will return home with you, and I will be an obedient wife." Her stomach curdled as she spoke the words, but some of the tension fled Muvumo's body. If he still cared for her, things might not be so bad. She still had her scrolls, after all. He told her she couldn't write, but she could read, and she had the history of the women in her family.

"Delkis will take you home, then," he said. "I have matters to attend to." He left before she could say anything. Not that she was quite sure *what* to say.

"Come, my lady Chanwa." Delkis let his hand fall from the handle of his short axe. He stepped aside, allowing her to leave the cell. He slammed the cell door shut, the sharp report echoing, and she flinched. Then he led her down the cave.

The torch was the only light until they neared the entrance where several torches sat in sconces on the walls. It was night, and the air was cool and smelled of pine. Chanwa shivered. She was out of her cell, but still cold. Even her anger with Muvumo burned like ice on her skin.

Delkis's dragon waited for them on the mesa. Her sides glowed red like embers in a hearth when she inhaled, and faded when she exhaled. The smell of brimstone and charred meat hung about her. She fidgeted, her claws tapping a dull staccato in the packed dirt of the mesa. Odd, that. Perhaps Delkis had left her hungry just in case Muvumo had decided to feed Chanwa to the beast.

The dragon wore a double saddle, and when Delkis approached, clicking his tongue, she raised her head. He scratched beneath her chin, and she leaned into it, a rumble coming from deep in her chest.

High above them, the glowing sides of Muvumo's dragon marked his passage. He flew higher than the topmost mesa, toward the peak of the mountain. All that waited up there was a small brick guardhouse that could shelter a dozen or so men, and the dragons' roosts. As Most Worthy, he had no need to spend time in the guardhouse. Chanwa frowned after him.

Delkis climbed into the saddle and helped Chanwa up, jerking a little too hard on her arm. She bit her lip as a burning pain shot through her shoulder. She wouldn't give him the satisfaction of hearing her cry out. She strapped her legs to the saddle, and before she could straighten and grab a hold of the pommel before her, the beast lurched and was in the air. She bit back another yelp as her torso jerked, a new pain blooming in her spine. Her hands finally found the pommel, and she hung on tight.

They soared away from the sheer mountains, and down. Torches lined the stairs at regular intervals, those farthest away twinkling like fireflies, but few lights shone from inside homes. It was late, then. Chanwa wondered what business Muvumo had to attend to. He wasn't stopping at the unmentionables' cavern, and he'd flown beyond the scroll cavern. Perhaps whomever supplied him with kasi powder was spending the night in the guardhouse. It couldn't be a matter of anyone challenging him for his place as Most Worthy, otherwise Delkis would be with him.

Or, maybe he wanted to work on his scrolls. The men would be frantic to fill the scroll cavern again with their thoughts and their knowledge, and those in the guardhouse often complained of boredom. Surely they'd spend part of their night with quill scratching on vellum as they waited for the dawn, and Muvumo could build good will toward them while working on his own. Better than sitting in the empty, echoing scroll cavern, and apparently he was in no hurry to return home with her.

She raised her voice to be heard over the rush of wind and said, "Where does the Most Worthy go?"

"If he wanted you to know, he would have told you," Delkis said over his shoulder.

She bit back a retort. Before the changer came, she could have spoken out against such treatment, but Muvumo would not tolerate her outspokenness now.

Her hands tightened on the pommel. The women's scrolls, few though they were, and hidden, held plenty of valuable knowledge, too. And when Muvumo was poring over the scrolls in search of a cure for the illness, she could have helped, as could have the few other women who knew their letters.

She had received an opportunity from the changer and done nothing with it. No, that wasn't true. She had saved Ankti. Now she was supposed to go home and pretend she had never yearned for something more with Ankti or for her people, or acknowledge her scrolls. At least she had her scrolls, her mother's, her grandmother's, and more that were passed down, unlike the men who had lost them all for the changer's magic to work. The women in her family didn't have opportunities to write often, but they made it count.

Delkis guided the dragon to the lower residential mesa for a relatively smooth landing. He let himself out of the saddle and stepped away. Chanwa almost ordered him to return to the beast's side and help her down, but there was a flash of anger in his eyes before he carefully smoothed his expression again, and there was tension in his body. She wouldn't be surprised to discover that he had argued with Muvumo against giving her another chance. Her fingers fumbled at the straps, and they soon had her free. Her legs wobbled but held when she slid down.

Delkis led the way down the stairs. Bright light spilled out of one home. A midwife hurried up the stairs, followed by a girl who was her apprentice, the girl carrying a satchel bulging with supplies. A woman's cry came out of the brightly lit home. The midwife muttered as she passed, "Fool thinks light will drive away the cries of pain. She needs darkness to soothe her, like the babe in her womb."

Delkis frowned and took a step after the midwife as if he'd reprimand her. Chanwa stumbled and grabbed at the stone wall for support. "I'm awfully tired," she said, yawning. Delkis turned his frown on her, and she ducked her head, afraid she might have overdone it. But it worked. He left the midwife alone and continued down the stairs to the only home with a white sheet covering the door. Faint light glowed around the door covering's edges.

"I'll wait out here," he said, taking up a position near the door.

"If the Most Worthy needs you, you should go to him," she said.

"He asked me to stay here."

"Oh."

Inside she found a basin of warm water scented with lavender. She cleaned herself and changed into one of her gowns. The undergarments were soft and warm, the dress itself light and flowing and the color of new leaves in the spring. She found a bit of bread and fish wrapped near the hearth to keep warm and wolfed it down, chasing it with some wine. The tension melted from her as she finished the meal. She was home, for whatever that was worth.

Tapestries depicting dragons in flight and battle scenes covered the walls in the main room. In the bedroom, the tapestries showed hatchlings and mountain meadows. Chanwa had insisted on the gentler depictions in the room where they would repose. She didn't want to stare at blood and death when she was trying to sleep or rest. A crossbow and long axe hung crossed in an X over the hearth. Those were Muvumo's battle weapons. He'd used them in the war with the

Taakwa and Jeguduns the summer before, and he carried them in training.

Despite the lingering heat from the day and the fire that had burned in the hearth earlier, Chanwa still carried a deep chill, as if the cold from the cells had seeped into her and followed her. It was too quiet. Outside, Delkis didn't so much as shift his feet or sniff. There was no crackling fire in the hearth. There was no Muvumo talking gruffly about his day. There was no Ankti going about her tasks, casting a smile at Chanwa whenever they were alone. She gulped down the last of her wine.

She hesitated, listening for approaching footsteps outside, and when she heard nothing, she searched her chests in the bedroom. Two had false bottoms that held her scrolls. Muvumo had moved the scrolls to the scroll cavern. She didn't think he'd return them, but she sagged to the floor in disappointment anyway when she found them empty. He said she couldn't write any more, but surely she could read them, could feel the well-worn vellum beneath her fingertips and breathe in the smell of old parchment.

Men's voices drifted from outside. She quickly shut the chests and went to the front room in time to hear Muvumo say something about the dragon queen just before he ducked inside, allowing the white door covering to fall behind him. He carried a large sack filled with… something. Outside, footsteps hurried up the stone steps. Apparently, Delkis had been dismissed for the night.

She dipped her head and said, "Welcome home, Most Worthy. Can I get you some wine? Something to eat?" She clenched her teeth and kept her head down.

"No," he said, dropping the sack on the large rug that covered most of the stone floor. It didn't sound heavy. "But you can stoke the fire."

She lifted her head. "Are you cold?"

"You're supposed to obey, not ask stupid questions."

She flinched. He had not been so harsh with her before. "I am sorry, Most Worthy." She placed more wood in the hearth and stoked the fire, coaxing the embers until it caught. Maybe the fire would drive away the icy feeling deep inside her.

"Is there anything else I can do?" she asked once a fire burned cheerily in the hearth.

"Yes. You can take this and put it in the fire." He pulled a scroll from the sack and handed it to her.

Surprised, she took it, turning it over in her hands before realizing it was one of hers. Her scalp tingled like a thousand ants were biting it, and the sensation slowly spread down through her arms and torso and legs. She could hardly breathe. She couldn't move. The flames in the hearth grew larger until they filled her entire vision. They roared in her ears. Her scrolls. Her history. Her link to the women in her family. She couldn't throw them in the fire.

"Chanwa, I gave you an order. Either do it now, or I'll strike you down for your disobedience."

She blinked. Everything came back into focus. For one moment, the urge to grab his long axe from the wall and swing it, burying the blade in his head, was so strong that she could see the spray of blood and smell its sharp tang. Every muscle in her body bunched, and she shifted her weight in that direction. Muvumo might be larger and stronger and carry weapons on his belt, but she'd have surprise on her side.

His eyes narrowed, and she realized she'd missed her chance, just like that. His pupils were huge, making his eyes look nearly black, and his face was flushed. He flinched. He'd taken more kasi powder since speaking with her in the cell. He might very well kill himself with it if he kept this up. Before, she would have gently brought up her concern. Now, she hoped the kasi powder *would* kill him. She hoped something, or someone, did. She hoped she could play a part in his death. She thought he had saved her because he cared for her, at least in part, but if he truly cared for her, he wouldn't make her do this. He had saved her only to use her for bearing children, but until then it seemed he planned on tormenting her, starting with this demand. The chill inside her gave way beneath the onslaught of rage. Her hand tightened around the scroll, crinkling the precious document.

She tossed her scroll into the fire. It crackled and ate it up greedily. She took out another and another and threw them into the fire. She swore she could feel the collected rage of her mother and grandmother and the other women who had penned words pouring through her. Her own rage ate at her greedily. It ate at the numbness, at the bone deep chill she'd felt in the cell. It ate at a lifetime of bowing her head and keeping her words to herself.

When she threw the last scroll into the fire, she was burning from the inside out.

CHAPTER FIVE

The sharp smell of lightning strike filled the air as the *mutara* leaped toward Malia, his hands raised and outlined by a glow that matched his narrowed, red-orange eyes. The power that poured off him was stronger even than that which she used to repair the barrier last summer. She stood no chance against him. She drew her dagger anyway. She wouldn't go down without a fight.

There was movement in the periphery of her vision, and Enuwal stepped forward, raising his walking stick, his face twisted in a snarl directed at the *mutara.*

"No, he'll kill you, too," she cried out. She ran forward, putting herself between Enuwal and the *mutara.*

The *mutara's* steps slowed, and his attention flickered between her and Enuwal behind her. "You would do anything to protect him." He grimaced. "The thought of losing him… gah, so painful."

The smell of magic filled her nostrils and burned in her lungs like smoke from a fire. The world jerked and spun. She flung her arms out as if crossing a narrow log across a rushing river. The *mutara* was in her mind. Blood roared in her ears. She became acutely aware of every heartbeat, every breath. The *mutara* was in her veins, a part of her as much as her own flesh. Every moment, every memory, every carress, every emotion was laid bare to him as much as it was to her.

She felt like a small child again, with a parent looming over her and a knowing glint in their eye as they discovered her in the midst of doing something she shouldn't.

An image flashed through her mind of a little girl, slim and olive-skinned, wearing a dress covered with a pattern of flowers, with thick, dark hair and eyes the deep gray of a stormy sky. Love accompanied that image, bone deep and sharp with loss, like an old wound, purportedly healed, being ripped open again and laid bare.

The *mutara's* heart sped to match hers, and his breathing grew faster, more shallow. He stood a mere stride length from her, arms at his sides as the red-orange nimbus faded from them. He stood as frozen to his spot as she was to hers.

A wide, deep, aching loneliness overwhelmed Malia. She felt as though she stood at the edge of a vast canyon, so deep that the bottom was hidden in shadow even though the sun was out. She could have screamed for days, and nobody would answer. She could have run in any direction for days and never encountered another person. The emptiness stretched out below, and ahead, and behind, endless in every direction. She gasped at the deep gash it left in her, as deep as the canyon at her feet, and filled to overflowing with an aching loneliness.

Then it shifted, and she put her arms out again for her balance. But it wasn't the world that was shifting, or even her body; it was her mind and her heart.

Instead of a deep, empty canyon, her experience was the valley, and the sky above, and they were filled with the love she held for her people and for the Jeguduns. But just beneath that was the ever-present fear that dragons would darken the sky, and the Maddion would kill all the people and Jeguduns she loved, and their blood would soak into the ground, and they would all disappear from the earth, their memories fading quickly, until in a few generations, it would be as if they had never existed at all.

The world shifted again, and her stomach lurched. She fell

forward, landing on hands and knees, her dagger disappearing in the tall, thick grass. She scrabbled back until she reached Enuwal, her breath coming in ragged gasps. She held her dagger in front of her.

The *mutara* remained where he was. His chest rose and fell quickly, and his eyes swirled fast enough to make her dizzy. She lowered her gaze to his chin.

The smell of lightning strike faded, the burning fading from her lungs, but her heart fluttered on. Enuwal shifted behind her.

"Stay where you are," she said to him.

The *mutara's* lips thinned. "I haven't moved toward you, have I?" He slid his dagger back into its sheath.

She opened her mouth to say, *I wasn't talking to you*, then closed it. "Why did you try to kill me? Why are you in my head?" She slowly climbed to her feet, keeping her own dagger at the ready. "And why in the name of the clan mother did you take away the barrier in exchange for fixing my mind?" Her voice rose on every word until her shout echoed off the cliff wall. In the distance, a Jegudun stepped onto a ledge and looked their way. She waved a hand dismissively. The last thing she needed was someone else getting involved here and possibly getting hurt.

Enuwal planted his walking stick on the ground and used it to help himself to his feet. "He looks just like Dalibor," he breathed.

"He's not Dalibor," she said. "He's much worse than Dalibor ever was." To the *mutara* she said, "You have to replace the barrier. Reverse what you did to me so you can replace it."

"It's not that easy."

"He even *sounds* like Dalibor," Enuwal said. He took a step forward, one hand going to the dagger he wore on his belt. Typically he used it for cutting plants or digging out herbs, but he kept it sharp.

"Don't," Malia said. "He could kill you easily if he wanted, before you even took another step forward." Which begged the question, why had he started for her with every intention of killing her, only to stop?

"Why can't you make things right?" she said to the *mutara*. "Why can't you just reverse what you did?"

"Why would you want that?" the *mutara* asked. "Your mind is whole. Before, there was a gray fog slowly eating it."

"Because I didn't know you'd put all of us at risk," she said through clenched teeth. "Because the barrier will save hundreds of lives." A large, dark shadow in the distant sky soared over the treetops. She flinched before realizing it wasn't a dragon, it was a Jegudun.

A flicker of fear passed over the *mutara's* face, quickly smoothed over. "You should have thought of that before asking for a change."

"You tricked me," she said, her hand tightening on the dagger. "It wasn't a fair deal. You cure the Maddion of the disease killing them, and all they had to do was burn their scrolls. You repair my mind, but then you leave my people and the Jeguduns at risk."

A slow smile curved his mouth. "The Maddion aren't done feeling the repercussions of their decision."

"I don't care. Fix. The. Barrier."

The smile disappeared, and the air crackled, raising the hairs along her arms. "I am not some simple magician performing tricks. This is true magic, and very old, and not easily manipulated."

She didn't understand what a magician was. The rest of his meaning caught up to her a moment later. "Not easily manipulated? You mean you need a price this time around, too? Fine, name it. But no tricks this time. Tell me what you truly mean."

"Malia," Enuwal said. "You can't do this. You can't promise something else to him. Look at the mess he's caused already. You're already willing to take back a broken mind. You shouldn't have to give back anything else."

The *mutara* remained silent, his eyes still narrowed. Malia began to pick out subtle differences between him and Dalibor. Her late husband had been an exceptional hunter, and moved as such—

stealthily, with great purpose to his movements, and a patience he never exhibited when it came to her. But the *mutara* was like a coiled snake, angry and threatened and ready to strike if she moved the wrong way. His muscles bunched, his jaw twitched, and his weight shifted forward slightly.

"Tell me," the *mutara* finally said. "Have you been feeling anything... unusual? A presence in your mind perhaps?"

"You know I have," she said. "Another one of your games, spying on me. I suppose it's because I let you into my mind so you could fix it, now you think you can come in any time you want." He had seen and experienced every moment in her heart and mind. Nothing had been kept private from him. Her cheeks warmed. Nobody should be allowed such access to another person, not without their permission.

"Is it because you allowed me into your mind to fix it? Yes. Is it because I am playing games on you? No. I certainly didn't want it." He clasped his hands behind his back and began pacing, another un-Dalibor-like thing to do. Dalibor never paced; he prowled silently. "This magic between your people and the Jeguduns has gone on for how long?"

She hesitated at the sudden change in subject. "Ah... I don't exactly know. A Jegudun would be better capable of answering that. What does this have to do with anything?"

"There's a symbiosis of magic between your people and the Jeguduns," he said as he paced.

"You've said that before," she said. "I don't know what symbiosis means, though."

"It means you have a mutually beneficial relationship." Stride, stride, stride, turn and repeat. "It means your people's magic enhances their magic. They use that magic to protect themselves and your people as well through the barrier."

"That's right," she said, wondering where he was going with this line of thought. Jeguduns could do magic on their own, but they could exert only enough force to bend a skinny tree branch. But when a Taakwa came into contact with a Jegudun, that person could boost the Jegudun's magic, and the Jegudun could rip an entire tree from the ground and fling it into the air like a huge arrow. Not to mention the magic used when a Jegudun shared a memory directly with a Taakwa.

The *mutara* quit pacing and let out a frustrated breath. "The magic inside you—inside all of your people—connects with the magic in anybody else you work with. When your ancestors made the barrier with the Jeguduns generations ago, it made a permanent connection between your people and the Jeguduns. That's what the Taakwa's power really does. It connects with and uses others' powers."

His words ran like ice through her veins. "So you mean—"

"Yes, Malia. There is now a connection between us."

"That's why you were intent on killing me," she said. "To break that connection. But why did you stop?"

"This has never happened to me before. And, if your power boosts the Jeguduns' magic, it might do the same for mine."

Enuwal's hands balled into fists. "You greedy, selfish, piece of dragon shit."

The *mutara* turned his red-orange eyes on Enuwal. The faint smell of lightning strike swelled. "Watch your words. Even if I wanted to, I can't retreat very far from her now because this connection keeps pulling me back. I would suspect your Jegudun friends feel much the same when they try to get too far."

"But they leave the valley to trade," Malia said. She felt as though she stood half inside herself and half out, watching all of this happen to somebody else, her voice coming from both within her and from without.

"They can leave, yes, but they will always feel a pull bringing them back. Trust me," the *mutara* added with a grimace. "The pull might be subtle, but it's there. You don't think it would have been easier for them to leave long ago? Let you live within your barrier and just go?"

"They stayed to protect us," Enuwal said. Malia nodded agreement.

The *mutara* snickered. "Perhaps. Or perhaps it's a story they tell you and themselves to make them feel as if they have a choice in the matter."

His words were like a cold, heavy stone in the pit of Malia's stomach. "How is this a beneficial relationship like you said, then? It's like we take and take, and what do we give back?"

"More power." His voice rumbled, and she could have sworn the ground trembled slightly beneath her. Malia took a step back, pulling Enuwal with her.

"How can we break this connection?" Enuwal asked.

Malia sighed. "I've tried already, and I believe he has, too."

The *mutara* nodded. "There's no way to pull completely free. Which is why you'll have to come along with me."

She stiffened. She'd lowered the dagger to her side, but half-raised it again now. "I'm not going anywhere with you."

The air crackled. The *mutara* tensed. Enuwal moved closer to her, and she swallowed hard. She couldn't stop the *mutara* if he decided to grab her and go, but that didn't mean she had to make it easy for him. After a while, some of his tension eased. "We'll see," he said.

"I need to speak with Rina," Malia said to Enuwal. "And Aru. This is all too much for the two of us to deal with." She turned to the *mutara*. She bit back the harsh command she was about to make. It was easy to hate him, to direct her fear and worries at him, to be angry with him. She might have given in to the anger and the hate, but she couldn't forget the vast emptiness, and the way it slashed through her. He might have seen all that was in her heart, but she had seen some of what was in his, too. "Why don't you come with us? You could rest, have some tea or something to eat."

Enuwal furrowed his brows, giving her an intense, questioning look. She ignored him. She would try to explain things to him later.

The *mutara* hesitated. For a moment, the pull between them

strengthened, and images flashed in Malia's mind of a hidden waterfall, solitude, restless peace interrupted by dragons and men forcefully dragging her away. Then the presence in her mind shoved itself away and she staggered as if he'd physically pushed her.

She grabbed Enuwal's arm. He steadied her. "What did you do to her?" he asked.

"No, no, it wasn't him. It was just... I saw something, that's all." The world steadied, and the presence retreated far away.

Malia had seen something similar before when a Jegudun had shared a memory with her of those who had followed the Maddion to the *mutara's* hiding place. They had pulled out what they thought was an old man, frail and weak, not realizing how powerful the *mutara* was.

He looked at her strangely now, head canted to one side, the swirl of his eyes slowing. She had the feeling he was trying his best to shut her out. Theirs was a two-way connection. He could enter her mind, but she could do the same to *his*. It left her light-headed.

"It's kind of you to ask," he said wryly.

"I wouldn't presume to drag you against your will," she said.

He was silent for a long moment. Then, "Lead the way, Malia of the Taakwa people."

She resheathed her dagger. She kept Enuwal close beside her for a change, her hand tightly holding his while the *mutara* walked several paces behind them. Her back prickled as if the being kept a weapon trained on her the entire time.

The presence in her mind was closer, more there, more a part of her, more *comfortable* than it had been before the *mutara* arrived. Was this what he meant when he said the Jegudun couldn't go far from the Taakwa for long? Was this what he meant by the desire to always return home? Because as much as she distrusted the *mutara*, she didn't want him to leave now that he'd arrived. Her hand tightened around Enuwal's. It wasn't the feeling she'd had when she was a newly braided woman and had been drawn to one of the young men in her village, and it wasn't the mature love she felt for Enuwal. It was simply a desire to be close to the *mutara*, perhaps in much the same way she desired working on pottery. It calmed her. It made something click together inside her and make her feel whole.

"I'll go first," Malia said when they reached the rope ladder. She climbed hastily and hurried inside before anyone could come out to the ledge and see who followed her.

Rina and Ankti were bent over a piece of thick vellum decorated with a detailed painting of a scene from valley life, namely that of Jeguduns and Taakwa tending a large field of corn, squash, and beans, and more Jeguduns flying low in the air with Tuvin's Falls in the background. Rina would point to the picture and speak a word, and Ankti would repeat, and then it was Ankti's turn to point and speak a word in her language and Rina to repeat it. The smell of dough lingered in the air, and water trickled down the stone wall to the pool.

In the corner, Rasmus sat cross-legged, repairing a rend in a tunic, his large fingers moving deftly with the slim bone needle and thread.

"The *mutara* is here," Malia said without preamble.

Rina looked up with her mouth agape. Ankti glanced at the doorway, fear flickering across her features. Rasmus dropped the mending and leaped to his feet, his hand going to the dagger hanging from his belt. Malia raised her hands.

"He's not here to kill me." *Not anymore.* "It's a long explanation. He's on his way up."

"*Here?*" Rina asked.

"I… didn't know where else to go, and I need you to hear this, too."

Rina stood, shaking her head. "No, that's all right." She clasped her hands together, wringing them, and glanced at the back room where Ziku rested.

"I really don't think he will hurt us," Malia said. *Not yet, at least.*

"I most certainly won't hurt anyone," the *mutara* said from the doorway.

Ankti muttered something, but held her ground. Rina straightened, only the faint quiver in her hand giving away her fear, and Rasmus tensed, his hand still resting on his dagger.

"Where's Enuwal?" Malia asked. The image of the *mutara* shoving him off the rope ladder flashed through her mind, and she rose on her toes, trying to peer past him.

The *mutara* stepped aside, and Enuwal walked in. Malia eased down. He hurried across the room and stood beside her. "He's already tried hurting Malia," he said.

Rina and Rasmus both stepped between her and the *mutara*. "Then you need to leave," Rina told the *mutara*. Rasmus pulled his dagger free. The air grew heavy, hushed, like a storm was suddenly moving in, pressing against Malia.

Malia laid a hand on both of them. "He hasn't hurt me. Please, I need your help figuring out what to do. He's told us… quite a bit. The most important thing right now is finding a way we can keep the valley safe from the Maddion. Please."

Rasmus slowly slid his dagger back into its sheath. Rina let out a shuddering breath. Malia's hands fell to her sides. The air shifted, eased, and the feeling of an impending storm dissipated.

"Well, isn't anyone going to invite me in?" the *mutara* asked with a hint of amusement, although the tightness around his eyes gave away his wariness.

"Oh, come in already," Malia said.

Rina arched a brow but merely said, "Yes, do come in."

He inclined his head. "Thank you."

Rina gestured to the pillows. The *mutara* settled against some. The others slowly sat, looking as ill at ease as if they shared the room with a hungry cougar.

"He looks very Taakwa," Rina said as if the *mutara* wasn't in the room.

"He looks exactly like Dalibor," Rasmus said. "Except for the eyes, of course."

Malia choked back a laugh. She had a feeling that if she started, she wouldn't be able to stop. "Can we talk about the reason he's here?"

"Of course," Rina said.

Malia hesitated, then asked the *mutara*, "Would you like some tea or water?"

A slow smile spread across his face. "No, thank you. I don't require sustenance as you do."

"Very well. I believe I need some, though."

While Rina bustled around the hearth, preparing hot water for tea, Malia told them what she had learned from the *mutara*. When she got to the part about their magic keeping a hold on the Jeguduns, Rina went still. By then she was sitting, holding a mug of tea. Rina stared down into it. Then she looked at the bedroom again where Ziku rested.

"So we're not much better than the Maddion," she said quietly. "Holding them here. They could have gone far away and put plenty of distance between themselves and the Maddion, but they can't, not without us."

"It's not like we knew this would happen," Malia said. "Even the *mutara* didn't know it would happen when he worked his magic on me."

The *mutara* grimaced. "I really despise that term. *Mutara*. It sounds like an expletive every time you use it."

"I'd say it rather is," Rasmus muttered.

The *mutara's* eyes narrowed, and the swirling red-orange quickened. The air crackled.

"What shall we call you, then?" Malia asked quickly. "With the Maddion you went by Sersha. Would you like us to call you that?"

"No, let's go with a new name for my new form. I'll go by Cian this time," he said.

"Cian. Very well."

Ankti spoke, gesturing at the *mutara*—at Cian—and then at Malia. Cian nodded in understanding.

"You know her language," Malia said. "What did she say?"

"She wants to know what we talked about, and whether there is any news about the Maddion or the woman she left behind."

Malia waited for more, then said, "Aren't you going to tell her?"

"I'm not a translator," he said with a growl.

The presence in her mind shifted. She opened her mouth to warn him against whatever he was thinking of doing when he added, "But I think I can adjust a few things so that you understand her."

"What do you mean by 'adjust a few things'?" she asked. "I thought you couldn't reverse my memory loss and repair the barrier. So how can you do something to make me understand her?"

He shrugged. "That's a fairly simple process in comparison to restoring your barrier. There's not much power in that. Do you recall when I could open and shut the lock on your cell door? Or even when I repaired your broken leg? Those are simple changes. They don't require a change on my part, or a price on yours."

"And what's the catch?" Enuwal asked.

"No catch."

Malia caught Ankti's gaze. It would be nice to speak with the other woman, not only to get to know her better, but to find out what she knew about the Maddion and about the outside world, especially since it seemed that Cian couldn't help them replace the barrier. She needed to figure out a different way to keep her people and the Jeguduns safe. There was much to gain and little to lose. Unless Cian was lying, of course. But he said the magic would be like that he used to work the locks in the Maddion prison, and that had seemed simple enough.

"I don't believe him," Enuwal said.

"I'll do it," Malia said.

"Malia," he began.

"She's made up her mind," Rina said.

He sat back, his lips in a thin line. "I don't think he should be messing with your mind any more than he already has."

"I don't care for it either, but I think the benefits outweigh the risks." She nodded at Cian. "What do you need me to do?"

"Nothing in particular."

The presence in her mind stirred, and she bit back a startled cry even though she'd been expecting it. She closed her eyes, because everybody's concerned gaze on her was distracting.

She smelled lightning strike again. The magic burned in her lungs like sharp, cold air in the midst of winter. The air grew heavy around her, pressing on her, making her ears feel as if they wanted to pop, like when she had flown on dragonback. The hairs along her arms raised, as did those along the nape of her neck. She had trouble drawing a full breath.

She didn't feel pain, exactly. When she learned lineages from her mother, her village's clan mother, she also learned how to keep track of them all by imagining a large map. This family tied into that one, but not this one, and so on. The map was huge, but she could easily navigate it and, as part of a clan mother's task, arrange a marriage between two suitable people, which was a vital task given how secluded the Taakwa lived.

Now it felt like the presence—Cian—carved new maps in her mind. She felt as though she were expanding within her skin and might break free if he went much further. She wanted to tell him it was enough, to stop, but she couldn't speak; she could hardly breathe. She heard voices from far away, as if she were underwater. She reached a hand out. *Stop, please stop.* This was going to kill her if it went on.

And then it *did* stop. She sprawled on one of the blankets on the floor. Enuwal spoke her name, and then his warm hands were on her, helping her turn over.

She was breathing fast as if she'd sprinted up a hill, and her heart was speeding along. She turned her wide eyes to Enuwal's, and her pulse and breathing started to slow.

"That felt… awful," she croaked.

Enuwal turned to Cian. "You made it sound like it would be easy, and you said there was no catch. You almost killed her."

"I never said it would be easy for *her*. It was easy for *me*, though. And no, there's no catch." He nodded at Ankti.

The other woman kneeled beside Malia, her forehead creased with lines. "Are you all right? Did he hurt you?" she asked.

"Oh," Malia said in Ankti's language. "It worked. Praise the clan mother, it worked."

CHAPTER SIX

In the morning, Chanwa sent for her sisters.

She hadn't spoken with them much since she'd married Muvumo. They were busy with their children, and caring for family or friends with the illness. And, Chanwa had never felt very close with them, not like she'd felt with her mother. They were good Maddion women who kept quiet and bore children on a regular basis. Chanwa's oldest sister, Nyda, had four children, and her next oldest sister, Prali, had two with a third on the way. Each of them had two daughters. As far as she knew, they hadn't written anything since they were children and might not be teaching letters to their daughters. But they were family, and they were all she had left with Ankti gone.

A servant prepared tea and fried quail eggs with greens and onions. Muvumo gulped down his tea and food. He had a slight tremor when he reached for his tea, and dark half-circles marred the skin beneath his eyes. Chanwa ate sedately, seated on a comfortable pillow at the low, long wooden table as if she hadn't destroyed her most precious possessions the night before. There was a soreness between her legs that she hadn't felt since her first night as a married woman, and pressure behind her nose and eyes as she held back tears. Muvumo had seen fit last night to take her back fully as his wife once she'd burned her writing.

Muvumo stood when she was only halfway through and said, "Good day." With that, he was gone, the door covering rustling in the wake of his passage. His footsteps joined others traveling up and down the stone stairs. Conversations drifted by, and in the far distance, a dragon roared.

Chanwa sat back and let out a sigh of relief. The servant, an older woman with plenty of wrinkles in her fair skin, bustled around, cleaning up. She had the look of the northern people who lived deep in craggy mountains, like the Maddion. But unlike the Maddion, they had no dragons, and so were ill prepared to defend themselves when a raiding party found them. The woman had a permanent stoop in her shoulders, and a few strands of gray hair had escaped the cloth covering her head. Chanwa was amazed the tiny woman could heft a basket of dirty clothes as she was doing at the moment, and not grunt at the exertion. She bit back an offer to help. The Maddion did not help servants, no matter that they might be elders deserving respect. This wiry woman would not only decline, but would most likely report such a thing to Muvumo, which would not help Chanwa.

"My lady Chanwa, I'll be back shortly once I've delivered these to the laundry. Don't fret yourself over the dishes. I'll take care of them next." Her voice was surprisingly deep for such a tiny woman, and held a strong accent.

"Take your time." She sipped her tea.

The servant left, and she was alone. She studied the crossbow and long axe over the hearth for a long time. The Maddion men took what they wanted with no qualms as to the amount of blood shed or the lives destroyed. It was time that ended. She needed a different sort of fight, one in which any woman or child or sympathetic man could participate and make an impact. She didn't think for one moment that her fight wouldn't result in spilled blood, but if things changed for the better, it would be worth the sacrifice.

She was still sitting and contemplating when the servant returned. "Would you put some more water on?" Chanwa asked. "My sisters should be along shortly."

"Of course." She dipped her already bent head and got to work.

Chanwa went into the other room and cleaned up with the basin of water the old woman had left for her. She dabbed lavender scented oil on her neck and wrists and put on one of her finest dresses. The underdress was cream colored while the dress itself began as a faint rose color around the neckline and shoulders, gradually deepening to crimson at the hem that swirled around her ankles. It had a high waist and long sleeves that billowed slightly at her wrists. Tiny roses had been sewn around the collar, the hems on the sleeves, and the hem at the bottom. She brushed out her cornsilk gold hair herself, rather than calling for the servant to help her, until it fell down her back in long waves.

As wife of the Most Worthy, she had access to many of the jewels captured during raids. She rarely wore any, though, because she couldn't help but think of the people the jewels used to belong to and wonder if they had been killed or captured, or if they had escaped with their lives but not with their belongings. She claimed she preferred a simpler look whenever Muvumo asked about them.

But now she pulled out her selection and decided on a heavy, teardrop-shaped necklace made of turquoise, with progressively smaller bits of hanging turquoise leading up to the clasp. The stone sat cool against her skin, nestled on top of her breastbone just above her heart. She wanted to remind her sisters of her status. Much as she despised it, it might come in useful when she tried to persuade them to her cause.

A familiar voice drifted from the main room. Chanwa took a deep breath, nodded, and raised her chin. She went into the main room and found Nyda with her youngest child, a little girl toddling around, exploring the nooks and crannies of the room, stopping every so often to reach down and bury her fingers in the deep, soft rug and giggle.

Nyda had dark hair and dark eyes, and where Chanwa was slight, she was all curves and softness, especially after having had four children. Her eyes crinkled as she smiled. She carried a small bundle of cloth tied with a ribbon.

"Chanwa, my dearest, how are you?" Her gaze flickered to Chanwa's belly and back up again.

She swallowed the bitterness at the unasked question. It was one Maddion women became familiar with. "I'm well."

The door covering rustled, and Prali stepped in. Like Chanwa, she was slight, save for her belly, which was heavy with child. Her face was flushed, and she walked with the waddling gait of expectant mothers near their time.

"Hello, Chanwa," she said, brushing back a strand of light hair. She wore her hair in an elaborate braid that crowned her head, with a few loose curls hanging down. Her dress was the green of new grass in the spring, and matched her eyes. Prali had always been the most put-together of all of them.

"Here, sit." Chanwa set up several of her most comfortable pillows for Prali and let her sister lean on her as she eased to the ground. Prali let out a sigh and sank into the pillows.

Chanwa saw both of her sisters settled in with cups of tea, then dismissed the servant. Fear flashed across the older woman's face. As she'd suspected, Muvumo must have given her orders to report to him on everything Chanwa said and did. She smiled.

"You have work to do, and we're only going to sit around gossiping and complaining. You may go."

The woman dipped her head and left, her lips in a thin line.

"Whatever happened to the other girl?" Nyda asked, sipping her tea. "The young, pretty one. Did you send her away, or did Muvumo become displeased with her?"

Chanwa brought her cup to her mouth to hide the ache the casual question brought. "I dismissed her." It was as much of the truth as she was willing to share.

Prali nodded. "It's better to have ugly, old ones around."

"That's not a nice thing to say."

She crinkled her nose. "What? They're servants."

"They're people."

Nyda's lips thinned. "Someone's as prickly as a hungry dragon."

Chanwa bit back her retort. She needed their help, and admonishing them like they were little children wouldn't help. She decided to start over and smiled. "Prali, how are you feeling?"

She grimaced. "I can hardly sleep, I make water all the time, and I'm worried I'll have a third girl."

"Do you recall Tangie?" Nyda asked.

Chanwa and Prali nodded. Tangie was the eldest sister of one of their childhood friends. "She doesn't live far from me," Chanwa said.

"Well, she's is in the same predicament. She's due with her third any day, and her husband has already said he would send her to the unmentionables if she didn't bear him a son." She absently swirled her tea, her brow creased.

"I think she's already laboring," Chanwa said, recalling the midwife from last night and the echoing cry.

Prali sighed. "Well, Elter hasn't threatened me with that, but he would certainly be furious if he had another daughter." She raised an eyebrow. "What about you, Chanwa? Any signs of new life?"

"Not yet," she said.

"Don't pester her," Nyda said. "It's not polite, and it doesn't help." She must have read something in Chanwa's expression earlier. She handed the bundle to Chanwa. "Speaking of, though, I brought this for you."

Something solid was beneath the cloth. Chanwa frowned as she untied the ribbon, letting the cloth fall away to reveal a carved wooden figure of a man with a disproportionately huge erection.

Prali snickered. "It's what every man imagines he looks like."

Chanwa joined in with their laughter, but hers faded quickly as the movement reminded her of the soreness between her legs. "What is it for?"

Nyda leaned forward, her dark eyes sparkling. "A friend gave it to me. She was having trouble conceiving until someone gave it to *her*. And I didn't conceive my first until she gave it to me. And now, four children later…" She shrugged. Her gaze shifted to the corner where her daughter sat with her doll, walking the toy around and humming a lullaby to herself.

Chanwa didn't want to tell them that until recently she'd been taking a tea that would keep her from conceiving. When the illness had been striking people, the last thing she wanted was to be expecting a child and perhaps come down with the illness herself, or give birth to a baby who might contract it. And now, she couldn't imagine bearing Muvumo's child. Not when he saw her as hardly better than a warm body in which to plant his seed.

"I didn't mean to upset you," Nyda said quickly. "I just thought it would help."

"No, it's very thoughtful of you." Chanwa wrapped the figure in the cloth and set it aside. "But that's sort of the reason I asked you both here."

Her sisters exchanged a knowing glance. "What is it?" Nyda asked.

Chanwa took a deep breath. They were her sisters. They wouldn't run off to Muvumo and report this conversation. They would, at worst, chastise her and leave, and perhaps avoid her for a long time.

She told them about the changer, about asking for help with making things better for Maddion women, about how Muvumo found her scrolls and accepted them initially only to have her burn them later. Her sisters gasped and grew wide-eyed when she mentioned that. She left out anything to do with Ankti. It felt too personal and too raw to share with them just yet.

"You're lucky to be alive," Prali said.

"See, that shouldn't be so," Chanwa said. "Things have to change." When their mother was occupied, Nyda used to help teach Chanwa her letters. Sometimes they'd sneak away into the forest and use sticks to write in the dirt before wiping it all away. Nyda wrote an entire story on the hillside one time. It lasted for only moments when she was through, only long enough for Chanwa to read before Nyda erased it all. She still recalled the story of a brave little girl riding on dragonback. "Have either one of you taught your daughters their letters?"

Nyda's little girl picked up a wooden spoon and began banging it against the low wooden table. She grinned at them and banged faster. Nyda said, "It's too dangerous. And to what purpose? They'll only grow up to get married and be kept home and have children anyway and have no use for any of it." Bitterness crept into her voice.

"It's more than that," Chanwa said. "Women and girls have the right to learn, too. And we shouldn't be treated as property to be destroyed or given away when we're not serving someone else's purpose."

Nyda shuddered and glanced at the white door covering. "You're talking about things that could get all of us killed. Or taken away from our children."

"I have an idea. It wouldn't get anyone killed—" except for maybe Chanwa, but she was willing to make that sacrifice "—and it would certainly get the men's attention."

"No, thank you," Prali said, struggling to rise. "Nyda, get off your bum and help me up."

Chanwa jumped to her feet first and pulled Prali up. "I know you're scared," she began. "But just hear me out."

A wail cut her off, rising as if someone pulled the still-beating heart from that person. Chanwa went still. Wails of grief had been common during the illness. Had the changer fooled them? Was it back? Her heart sped as she raced to the door. Footsteps hurried down the stairs outside, and the wail came again. Feminine. Exhausted. And it came from the depths of whoever uttered it, as if she dredged her very spirit out and set it free with that cry.

She pulled the door covering aside. Another wail came from the stairs above, this time an infant. Tangie's husband, Jehan, was storming down the stairs two at a time, a squirming, crying bundle in his arms. His face was bright red, though whether from anger or exertion or both Chanwa couldn't tell. He was a large man, gone soft in the middle as they tended to when they stopped riding out on dragons.

Another figure stumbled down the stairs after him, holding onto the stone wall for support. Tangie, wearing a gown stained with blood from the waist down. Chanwa's veins turned icy. She stepped into the middle of the stairs.

"What is this, Jehan?" she asked.

He ran down another couple of stairs before coming to a stop, whipping his head up and narrowing his eyes at her. "Get out of the way."

"Is that your newborn? My heartfelt congratulations on your growing family."

"I said *get*."

Tangie fell to her knees. She cried out and dragged herself up. The midwife was hurrying down the stairs while her apprentice stood just outside Tangie's home, wringing her hands. More people had been coming down the stairs beyond her, but at the sight below them, turned hastily around. Nyda and Prali stood in the doorway, silently watching.

"Let me see your baby," Chanwa said, climbing one stair. Her heart thumped crazily beneath the heavy turquoise necklace, but her voice was surprisingly cool and calm.

He swung an arm back as if to strike her. She straightened, held her ground despite the trembling in her belly, and said, "I don't think the Most Worthy would be pleased *at all* if he came home to find a bruise on me."

His arm dropped. "I wasn't going to hit you. I need to be on my way."

"To the drowning pool?"

Everybody froze. Even the midwife, still quite a few steps above them, stopped in midstride, her mouth agape. Everybody knew of the rarely used pool where one could go to privately and quietly drown a malformed infant, but nobody spoke of it. And sometimes people used the pool to drown babies who were perfectly healthy, the only problem being that they were girls.

Jehan's jaw twitched. He couldn't quite meet her gaze. "There's something wrong with the babe."

"Nothing's wrong," Tangie gasped behind him. "Save that it's a girl."

Chanwa called up to the midwife. "Is there anything wrong with the baby?"

Her gaze flickered between Chanwa and Jehan. Her tongue darted out, licked her lips. She was clearly weighing the cost of angering a man versus angering the wife of the Most Worthy. "Nothing's wrong, my lady Chanwa. He's mad the babe weren't a boy."

His face scrunched up into a furious sneer. "I told her she'd better have a boy this time. Even before she conceived, she knew. She claimed she took steps to make sure it was a boy."

"Do you know how many babies died of the illness?" Chanwa asked quietly. "Or indirectly because their mothers died? Or their wet nurses?"

"What does that have to do with anything?"

"One hundred and sixty-six babies died," she said. "And that's only infants. Then there were the children, and the men, and the women. Yet you are alive, and so is your wife, and so are your children. All three of them now. But you would throw one away when so many have lost their entire families?"

"I need a boy," he said, hitting his chest with one hand. "I need a boy to carry on my family's honor."

"The Maddion need more people to repopulate. Who do you expect infant boys to procreate with? This little girl," she said with a nod at the squalling infant, whose cries were becoming alarmingly weak, "is the future of our people. What a great sacrifice you make, providing our people with three healthy children. The Most Worthy would be most pleased to hear of it, I'm sure. What he would *not* be pleased to hear is of a healthy baby dying. There has been enough death for our people already."

His chest rose and fell rapidly. His gaze darted from her to Prali and Nyda, her little girl clinging to her skirts, hovering in the doorway trying not to look horrified, to his wife crumpled on the stairs behind him, sobbing. Finally he returned his attention to her.

"The Most Worthy would hear of this, eh?" he asked. "He'd hear of my noble sacrifice?"

"Absolutely," she said, her voice like ice. *Noble sacrifice, indeed. Bah.*

He turned and trudged up the stairs. He didn't even spare a glance for Tangie, but when he reached the midwife, he jerked his head toward his wife. "Help her up, would you?"

Chanwa hurried up the stairs. The sharp tang of blood filled the air. She got her hands under one of Tangie's arms, and the midwife got her hands under the other. Together they hauled Tangie to her feet and helped her up the stairs.

"Thank you," Tangie gasped. "Thank you so much. He was going to *kill* her." Her voice was rising.

"Shh," Chanwa said. "It's all right now."

"And he was going to send me to the unmentionables," she said in a hushed voice. Her eyes, the color of a washed-out winter morning sky, were wide and brimming with tears. "He was going to take me from my other babies."

Chanwa's teeth clenched. "I'll see to it that he doesn't."

Prali and Nyda came up behind them. Together, they all saw Tangie back into her home. They bustled around, putting out clean sheets, seeing her changed into clean clothes and nursing the baby. They fixed a meal for the two girls as they played with Nyda's little one, and they sent the apprentice to the laundry with the bloodied blankets and clothes. A servant, who had been run off by Jehan earlier, came back and took over the duties. Chanwa took her leave, her sisters following close behind.

Prali's eyes were wide. She rubbed her belly absently and looked up and down the stairs. A runner was high above them, delivering a message or running an errand. Otherwise, they were alone.

Nyda held onto her little girl's hand, looking down at her. The faintest tremor went through Nyda, though whether it was from fear or anger, she couldn't tell. "What's your plan, Chanwa?" she asked.

CHAPTER SEVEN

Muvumo stood beside his dragon at the top of the mountain, watching his men on dragonback wheel and dip in formation overhead. Sweat trickled down his spine from his time in the saddle, leading his men through their drills, practicing defensive maneuvers, and firing crossbows at the targets set up along the mountainpeak. His entire body ached from so much time on dragonback, but it felt good to be in the air again, to work on synchronicity with his men until he practically knew what they were thinking. His heart swelled as he considered how perfect it all was.

And then his heart fluttered uncomfortably, followed by a quick constriction of his chest, and then an abrupt release. He let out a little gasp and laid a hand on his dragon's warm side. He gave her a pat, acting as if that was his intention all along in case anybody was watching. Heart flutters were normal while taking kasi powder. Maybe he'd been taking it too often. Maybe he'd cut back. Instead of taking a sniff after lunch, he'd put it off until late afternoon, give his heart a break. He no longer needed so much now that he didn't have to search for a cure to the illness that had been killing the Maddion.

In the air, two groups of dragons broke apart and headed straight for one another as if they would crash headfirst. At the last moment, the dragons tipped their wings, and they passed within a few hands' breadths of one another. It was like watching a dance, tightly choreographed and perfect in every way. Maddion life was returning to normal. Normalcy was the main reason he took Chanwa back. As Most Worthy, he needed a wife and sons.

But there was still a flare of defiance in Chanwa. It had shone briefly in her eyes a couple of times. He'd made a mistake when he didn't destroy her scrolls the moment he discovered them. He'd coddled her too much, given her too much freedom. She'd taken that freedom and used it to write—which was ridiculous and utterly useless for a woman—and to form a friendship with that servant. And more than friendship, yes. He didn't care if Chanwa took a woman and servant as a lover, but to treat a servant as equal to her was just as ridiculous as her writing.

She couldn't hide her pining for the servant. She needed to focus her energy on getting pregnant with his child and carrying a healthy son. The most important thing for the Maddion right now was to rebuild and repopulate, and so he needed to ensure she was obedient, not only for her sake as the future mother of his children, but for the sake of the Maddion. She had to understand that. And that brought him to why a group of men were coming in for a landing to speak with him.

He stood on the eastern side of the mountain. Here, it sloped down at a much gentler angle compared to the sheer granite walls where the Jeguduns had built the Maddions' homes long ago. Behind him, at the very top of the mountain, stood the guardhouse: a brick structure with thick walls, a massive hearth inside, and space enough to easily hold two dozen men if need be. There were always at least half a dozen men staying in the house at all times, and sometimes more, keeping an eye on their surroundings. On a clear day, a man could see to the mountains far in the west and north, and to the south where the Taakwa Valley lay hidden beyond the rolling hills and grassy plains.

Tall grasses covered the mountain, dotted with white daises, fiercely blue salvia, and red-orange paintbrushes that reminded him far too much of the changer's eyes. A large portion of the mountain's slope had been cut into large steps leading down. The uppermost steps were covered with grasses, but some Maddion men oversaw servants working on those farther down where greens, onions, garlic, corn, squash, carrots, and other crops had been planted. The air was cooler up here and smelled of pine and fir, which covered the parts of the mountain not devoted to the crops, along with aspen and spruce. In the distance, more mountains rose, purple in shadow from the clouds.

Delkis stepped up beside him, his neck craned to take in the two groups overhead. "They look magnificent."

"That they do."

The men he'd summoned approached. They all wore long wool tunics and pants in various shades of tan, brown, rust, and orange, like a collection of fall leaves, and their tunics were belted with various colored sashes that marked their standing among the men. None wore the purple sash of a Peerless warrior, one of the most coveted. And none other than Muvumo wore a white sash. They went down on their knees and bent their foreheads to the ground in a proper greeting, saying, "Most Worthy."

"Rise," he said.

They stood. The one in the lead, Sanchar, was one of the most promising warriors. Muvumo was considering having him train to become a Peerless, the most elite of the fighters and those who were leading the drills in the sky right now. He walked with a bounce that suggested plenty of energy held in reserve, like a young wolf eager for a hunt. And for now, at least, he looked upon Muvumo with respect. In a few seasons, though, he might become a threat to Muvumo's position unless he was appeased with a promotion.

"Sanchar," Muvumo said. "Are your men prepared?"

He nodded. "Yes, Most Worthy. We have divided into pairs and will search the entire area outside our mountains for the Taakwa woman and the servant."

"Very good." He was sure the Taakwa prisoner had made it back to the cowardly safety of her valley, but the servant might have gone her own way, back to her people. "When can you leave?"

"Immediately."

"Then good hunting. And remember, bring them both back alive."

"Yes, Most Worthy." He turned and barked out orders to the other men. Soon they were on their dragons, breaking into pairs, and flying in different directions. Muvumo watched them until they disappeared.

"Most Worthy," Delkis began in a low voice even though none stood close enough to overhear, "there have been more problems with the dragons."

His heart fluttered painfully again. "What is it this time?"

"I found five corpses on the ledge, just a short while ago, all younglings. I used my dragon to pull them over into the woods and hide them, but… there are only so many dead I can hide before other Maddion start to notice."

Muvumo absently patted his beast's side, her hide warm and dry. A faint, deep rumble began deep in her chest. "This started after the changer left."

Delkis nodded. "Do you think it has to do with her?"

"I don't know. What I *do* know is even while the Maddion were dying off or killed in the war last summer, the dragons' numbers have remained the same."

"Save for those killed in the war."

Muvumo nodded. "Save for those."

"So there are far more dragons than we need."

"For the moment."

Delkis frowned. "They could be culling their own numbers."

"Or they could be ill. What if the sickness plaguing us has now turned to them?"

His eyes widened. "That would be… unimaginably horrible. But the changer didn't say anything about the dragons, did she?"

"No. I don't trust her, though." If she'd transferred the illness to the dragons… if they would now start falling ill, then soon the Maddion would be without their mounts. Their hunting, their travels, their fighting would all have to change. Without their dragons, they'd be vulnerable. They'd have to leave the mountain. The idea left a funny sensation in his stomach, like riding a dragon that took an unexpected drop.

"How do we find out more, then?" Delkis asked.

Muvumo scanned the air where the two squads were going through their final formations for the day. "Who are the best at caring for the dragons? Who has the best rapport with them?"

"I can think of a half dozen, easily."

"Then pick those you trust the most and go into the dragons' roosts. Check them over. Make note of anything at all out of the ordinary. And make sure the men find the dragons' queen. If there's something wrong with her, there could be something wrong with all the dragons." His hands curled into fists. "If only we still had our scrolls, we could find out more, find out if this has happened before. I know there have been problems, usually when there is a change in queens."

"How long has the current one been in charge?"

"I'm not sure," Muvumo said. "Again, if I had the scrolls, I could easily find that information. I've read it, but I never bothered memorizing it because I thought it would always be there." There was a heavy emptiness in him at all of that lost knowledge.

"When do you want this done, Most Worthy?"

"Soon. But use discretion."

Delkis nodded. "It will be done." He walked away.

Muvumo laid a hand against his dragon, breathing deep the smells of brimstone and pine, and turned his face to the warm sun. By next summer, he fully expected to have an infant son, and for all the trouble his people had recently gone through to be nothing but a memory, including the trouble caused by that servant Chanwa had taken a liking to.

The more he thought about it, the more certain he became that the servant must have goaded Chanwa into her behavior, and all so the woman could escape. She'd used Chanwa and turned her against her husband. Well, he'd see that she got what was coming to her.

CHAPTER EIGHT

"This is wonderful," Ankti said. "But are you sure you weren't hurt when the *mutara* gave you my language?"

They walked through waist high grass still wet from the afternoon rain. The air was heavy with lingering moisture and heat and filled with the smell of damp earth, sage, and lavender. Rays of sunlight cut through dark clouds in the distance where sheets of rain fell. A half dozen Jegudun younglings played in the distance, diving and swooping after one another, occasionally letting out a whistle or shriek or squawk. As fast as adult Jeguduns were, the younglings were speedier and more daring, and reminded Malia of swallows dipping and darting in the air.

"I wasn't permanently hurt," Malia said. "Although it felt bad while he did it. But it's worth it. As much as I enjoyed our lessons, I wasn't learning fast enough." It was strange, hearing a new language come from her mouth and understanding it so easily. It felt like that knowledge had always been there, had always been a part of her even though it had only been planted there earlier that day. She would have been concerned with what else Cian could plant in her mind if it wasn't for the fact that her new grasp of Ankti's language came with such unforgettable pain.

"I won't be letting the *mutara* touch my mind." Ankti raised a hand quickly. "Not that I'm questioning your choice."

"No, I understand. By the way, he doesn't care for the term *mutara*. He prefers the name Cian. This time around, at any rate."

His presence was always there in her mind, like being in a room where someone worked silently behind her. He was unseen and unheard, but unmistakably there, like the heavy air before a storm.

"Ah," Ankti said. "He called himself Sersha when he was with the Maddion and was a woman. I do not know what he called himself when he was an old man before that."

A Jegudun youngling shrieked in the distance. An adult, watching from one of the ledges, called out a series of chirps and whistles. The younglings' flight slowed and, one by one, they landed on various ledges, shaking off their wings. Their movements seemed reluctant, even from this distance, like little children called back to the village as dusk fell when they were in the midst of an exciting game. For all of the outward differences between the Taakwa and Jeguduns, they were essentially the same. Yet the Taakwa and the Maddion, who resembled one another more, couldn't be farther apart in those things that mattered most.

Malia filled Ankti in on what Cian had told her about the symbiotic magic and how he was uncertain what would happen to her whenever he changed again. She talked about her ancestors helping the Jeguduns and how that act tied them all together for subsequent generations.

"I had no idea that creating the barrier in the first place would bind the Jeguduns to us," Malia said when she finished. "It seems like they left one type of enslavement for another."

Ankti walked in silence for a while. She plucked a strand of grass and began tying it in knots. Their shadows stretched long beside and behind them. "Even if your ancestors knew this would happen," she finally said, "Do you think they would have forced the Jeguduns into making the decision to help them?"

"No," she said without hesitation.

"And if they didn't know, then you cannot blame yourself or them for this symbiosis. Besides, it kept your people *and* theirs safe for a long time. Even if the Jeguduns had been able to leave and settle elsewhere, that would not have guaranteed their safety, believe me." She grimaced. "I come from a place far south and west of here, and the Maddion still found me and took me. They have few limits with their dragons."

"I've been thinking about that, actually. Rather than try to replace the barrier, perhaps we should remove the threat altogether."

"Do you mean, kill them? Some are innocent." Anguish flashed across her face.

"Yes, I know," Malia said gently. "I was thinking more along the lines of removing the dragons. Without them, the Maddion are significantly weakened. They might even have to give up the mountain as a home and go somewhere else, preferably far from here."

Ankti took in a sharp breath. "It's hard to kill a dragon, much less all of them. What did you have in mind?"

"That's also what I wanted to speak to you about. Where do they keep their dragons? How many are there? When are they most active, least active? We need to know everything that you know about them."

Ankti gazed northwest, as if she could see beyond the cliffs and the distance to the Maddions' mountain. Her mouth drew down, and her chin, a slight cleft in the center, trembled momentarily. Then she took a deep breath.

"I don't suppose my lady Chanwa is still alive," she said sadly.

Malia stopped and laid a hand on Ankti's arm. "I am truly sorry. What she did was brave, and it showed how much she loved you."

Unshed tears glimmered in Ankti's eyes. She wiped at them angrily with the back of her hand and resumed walking, this time at a quicker pace. "For her, and for the others like her, I will help you. For the slaves, I will help you. But I do not like the thought of innocents dying. Most of their women are not much better off than the slaves, and their younger children are innocent. The older ones… they have learned to hate by then."

"Destroying the dragons should keep the innocent ones safe."

She nodded. "Their dragons roost atop the mountain in an extensive cave system. Those who actively serve the Maddion remain close to the entrances. Those who are tending hatchlings or are breeding stay deeper in the caves." A smile tugged at her mouth. "What I find amusing is that their mounts are all female, and the dragons are ruled by a queen. They are the larger dragons, while the males are smaller and do not even breathe fire. The Maddion have little respect for their women and yet rely on females to carry them." Her grin faded. "I do not know how many dragons there are. At least enough females to serve every fighting Maddion man, and that is several hundred, plus those tending hatchlings, plus their mates, although there are not as many males. They only keep those who produce strong offspring and kill the rest."

Malia nodded, allowing the information to sink in. "How many ways in and out of their caverns? Are there exits that would allow them to escape the caverns, or are the entrances fairly close to one another?"

"That I do not know. I only know that much because I overheard it, because the Maddion see us as part of their surroundings, like a tapestry or a table," she said bitterly. "The men do not speak of the details of the dragon caves, and the women don't know. There are a handful of men who take turns living out of a home on top of the mountain. They keep watch over the dragons and hatchlings, and I'm sure they also keep watch over the other side of the mountain in case anyone should be foolish enough to approach."

Malia chewed at her lower lip. "You said the dragons are ruled by a queen. Don't they obey the Maddion, though?"

"They do. But from what I understand, they do as their queen does. But I don't know if she serves the Maddion against her will, or if they have a mutually beneficial relationship, or if she chooses to serve them, or if they recompense her… I do know, from what I observed, that the dragons have plenty of ground to hunt because nobody wants to live or travel near the Maddion. So there's no competition for large game." She shook her head. "Sorry. I don't think I'm very helpful."

"No, you've been informative. Perhaps a couple of Jeguduns could get close enough to find out more. If we're able to decimate their dragons, they would be unable to fight or raid, and they would essentially be stuck on the mountain and forced to adapt or find another place to live. And then *we* would be the ones with the advantage, what with the Jeguduns living close to us."

An idea began coiling in her head like clay becoming a piece of pottery. She slowed, following the idea as it unfurled and started to take shape.

A flash of anger that didn't belong to her jolted the idea out of her head. She stopped, whirling, unsure what just happened.

Cian. Wherever he was, he was angry with someone. And highly irritated. His emotion poured into her, driving her to pace in a circle as she tried to tease out what belonged to her and what belonged to him. Ankti was speaking, but it was difficult to make out her words because her own thoughts were swirling through her head along with Cian's emotions.

She looked toward Rina's. She and Ankti had come a long way, so she couldn't make out any details at all. Another surge of anger went through her. And then the impression of *who* Cian was angry with.

Enuwal.

And if Cian was that angry, he might strike Enuwal down.

She broke into a run.

CHAPTER NINE

Malia's legs wobbled as she ran. Cian's rising anger was like a storm building in her head, driving her on. Damp grass slapped at her legs and tugged at her skirt. Her lungs soon burned, but she kept running anyway.

Ankti caught up with her quickly, breathing easily, her legs striding smoothly. "What is it? What's wrong?" she asked.

"Cian. Enuwal," was all she could manage.

"I'll go ahead," Ankti said. She pulled ahead, long strides eating up the ground. She was amazingly graceful, like a deer bounding through the grass. Even if Malia had her usual health, she couldn't have matched the other woman's grace.

Her shadow ran ahead of her, hopping and limping along. Her breathing was heavy, labored. A painful stitch ran along her side. She pushed on.

Ankti became a smaller figure in the distance as two other, even smaller figures came into focus, standing at the base of the cliffs. One leaned on a walking stick. Raised voices came faintly across the distance. Cian stepped forward, but Enuwal held his ground.

No, no, no, thought Malia. *You fool, forget about your pride and stand down. Whatever you're arguing about, it's not worth it.*

Cian took another step forward. He was too close to Enuwal.

Malia did the only thing she could. She found his presence in her mind, and she yanked.

His head snapped around in her direction. Enuwal raised the walking stick. Not high, but clearly he was thinking about swinging it around. Malia's heart jumped into her throat. Cian would kill Enuwal if he swung that stick.

But then Ankti was there, pushing the stick down. She positioned herself between the two of them, guiding Enuwal back, creating more space between the two men. Malia slowed to a jog. Praise the clan mother, but she had a feeling that Ankti had just saved Enuwal's life.

Enuwal hurried to her, his brow furrowed. "Malia," he said.

She clutched his arms and sagged against him. Her legs couldn't hold her up a moment longer. She sank to the damp ground. He sat beside her, brows creasing even more. "What is it? What's wrong?"

"Don't. Antagonize him," she gasped. "He'll kill you. What were you… arguing about anyway?"

His mouth turned down, and a muscle in his jaw twitched. "Is that why you ran here? Could you hear us?"

She shook her head. "Felt his anger."

Enuwal looked over his shoulder. Cian stood in the same place, arms crossed. Ankti stood near him, her muscles bunched as if she expected she'd have to jump in their direction at any moment. He turned back to her. Some darker emotion crossed his face quickly before concern returned.

"I'm fine," she said, her breathing and heart slowing gradually. "Just fatigue easily. I was in a cell with a broken leg for a while, remember?"

"Of course. Is that all? Did he hurt you?"

"No. But I was afraid he'd hurt *you*. What were you arguing about?"

He glanced over his shoulder again. Cian raised his chin. "Go on, tell her," he said.

Enuwal couldn't quite meet her gaze. "I asked him if he could change the connection between the two of you. I offered him whatever he wanted in return."

"Oh," she breathed. "Don't make any deals with him." She glanced at the clear sky where the barrier used to be. "It's not worth it. And I don't think anything can sever this connection. Unless I die, and I don't think you want that."

He grimaced. "Of course not."

"But why did the two of you start shouting? Just because he couldn't do what you asked?"

His gaze slid away. Cian smirked, then strode forward. Ankti followed at a distance.

"He couldn't bear to hear the truth," Cian said.

"Shut up," Enuwal said.

"He twists his words," Malia said. "Whatever he said, you can't believe it."

"Oh, but it *was* the truth," Cian said. "I don't need a special connection with him to know."

Enuwal flinched. He straightened, grabbing his walking stick as he did so. "I told you to shut up."

The air crackled, and the tiny hairs along Malia's arm stood. "Stop it," she said. "Both of you." She struggled to her feet and held onto Enuwal's arm for support.

Cian nodded once at Enuwal. "He hates that you and I have such a strong connection."

Enuwal's free hand balled into a fist. His chest rose and fell quickly. Malia tightened her grip on his arm. "He's goading you," she said. "Believe me, it's not like I want this connection."

"His magic is useless," Enuwal said. "He can't do a thing without somebody wanting it of him. He can't undo what he's done. Between us and the Jeguduns, we can do more than he can. He's practically impotent."

A snarl crossed Cian's face before smoothing out, and the air crackled even more. "Would you like to know how Malia *really* feels about you?"

She took a step forward, slicing her hand through the air. "Stop," she said, the word originating deep inside her and barreling out, echoing off the cliffs, and sending shivers down her arms, down her spine, making her warm all over. The air vibrated and thrummed, reminding her of the times she had connected with a Jegudun to boost their magic.

Enuwal turned to her, his eyes wide. Ankti murmured a few words, taking a step back. Cian's mouth opened and closed quickly. Then the corners of his mouth turned up in a sly grin.

"Well, that was interesting," he said. "You borrowed some of my power."

Wonderful. Just what she needed. She could borrow his power and do… what? What good did it do her? She couldn't single-handedly create a brand new barrier, not if he couldn't.

But maybe there was something she could do against the dragons. Maybe she could use the power somehow to destroy them. She needed to find out the limits of what she could borrow from Cian.

The western sky burned a bright red-orange, like Cian's eyes. The last of the rain clouds were gone, leaving behind wispy ghosts of themselves. A short way down the cliffs, a Jegudun emerged, letting out a long whistle. An answering whistle came from the distant woods, and moments later three younglings burst out of the cover of the trees, zooming home as quickly as they could, no doubt for dinner. For their sake, for her people's sake, she needed to find out what she could do with this power. She needed to find a way to stop the dragons, and thereby stop the Maddion.

"First thing tomorrow morning," she said to Cian, "you and I are going to start working on this. I want to know what I can do with your borrowed power."

He frowned. "You assume I want to help."

She hesitated. She'd messed everything up. She had to do whatever it took to make it right, even if it broke her heart. Even if it broke Enuwal's. That hurt her more than the idea of her own pain, causing him any more anguish. But she wanted him safe, and her people, and the Jeguduns. She would do anything for that. "I'll give you what you want," she said quickly, before she could change her mind. "I'll leave the valley with you once I know the dragons are taken care of and my people and the Jeguduns are safe from the

Maddion."

"Malia, no," Enuwal said.

The swirling red-orange of Cian's eyes quickened. "I'll help you, then, and you'll come with me."

"Yes," she said. She couldn't believe she was agreeing to this. She couldn't believe she'd leave her home behind, with only this… *thing* for company. Soon she'd be as mad as him. But her people would be safe at last, not to mention all of those living within a dragon's flight from the Maddion. "Yes, I'll go with you after you help me." She raised one finger. "And only *if* you can help me. If you don't help, I don't go with you."

"Deal," Cian said.

The last fire of the sunset faded to a deep purple hue, calm, quiet, peaceful. Enuwal let out a curse and turned, striding away with a limp, his walking stick hitting the ground hard with each step.

She felt sick to her stomach. Part of her wanted to flee to a dark corner, or to her grandmother's arms, and pine over the fact that, should things go well, she'd be leaving behind everyone she knew. But she wasn't the only one hurting.

Footsteps scuffed against the stone overhead, and then Rina called down, "Dinner is ready."

Malia turned to Ankti. "You go up and eat. Let her know, if you can, that I'll be in later. I'm going after Enuwal." She briefly filled in Ankti on what she'd agreed to, and the other woman's eyes widened.

"Malia," she said, that one word holding admonishment and sadness.

"I know," she said. "But I don't think I can do this without Cian's help."

Cian looked far too pleased with himself. Her lips thinned, and she held back a retort for him. Instead, she hurried after Enuwal, who had already put quite a bit of distance between them. Her legs shook, but they held.

"Enuwal," she called. He walked faster. "Enuwal, please wait." She caught up to him and laid a hand on his arm, but he slipped away and kept walking. She straightened, added a sternness to her voice that she'd learned from her mother, and said, "Don't make me chase you down again. It's disrespectful."

He stopped, an outline in the dark gray that preceded full night. He'd led them to the edge of the field of black rocks between the cliffs and the forest. In the near dark, the large rocks were like the pebbled skin of a giant reptile. A warm breeze rustled the grass, the blades whispering to one another.

"I'm sorry," he said without turning around. "I just had to get away from him. I just—" His shoulders bunched, and he lowered his head.

She approached slowly and laid a hand on his arm again. "I know you hate the thought of my leaving. I do, too. But I see no other way to get him to help, and I see no way we can win this without him."

He stiffened. "I do hate that, yes, but he said—" He broke off and looked away.

"What? What else did he say? Because you know better than to put any stock in it. He's looking to create problems, to create chaos."

He let out a breath. "Well, he certainly achieved that."

She moved around to face him. His profile revealed a straight nose, a chin that receded slightly, a gently sloping forehead. His eyes glittered in the dark. In sunlight, they would be a warm, dark brown, like the earth after a rain. Lines fanned out from them, creased even deeper than usual.

"The only reason I agreed to leave," Malia said, "was to save the Taakwa, including you, and my mother and Vedran, and my grandmother, and all the others. And to save the Jeguduns. It is long past time that we stop living in isolation and fear. And besides, it was my selfish desire that left us all vulnerable, so it's only right that I do this."

He turned to her, forehead creasing. "Is this some sort of punishment you think you owe yourself? Because if that's all it is, then we can find some other way. You did what any other person in the same situation would do. You had a strand of hope, and you followed it. It's not your fault that the *mutara* deceived you."

"Cian," she corrected automatically.

His brows drew down, and his eyes narrowed. "But that's not the only reason you'll leave with him, is it? This connection means something to you."

"What? No, it doesn't, only that it's an unwanted tie between us."

"Do you know why he didn't kill you after all?"

"He has more power if he has this connection with me."

Enuwal shook his head. "He won't admit it because he's twisted and inhuman, but he feels something for you, Malia, beyond this unanticipated connection. He's been in your mind, and he liked what he saw, what he felt. He can't wait to have you to himself."

Her stomach knotted, twisting, and bile rose in her throat. "No. He doesn't care for anyone but himself."

"He told me that he's been inside you in the way that matters most. He told me that even after a lifetime together, I would never know you as intimately as he knows you."

"He knows nothing," she hissed. "He knows none of the things that matter. He might have seen up here," she said, pointing to her head, "but he doesn't understand the first thing about what I hold in here," she finished, pressing her palm over her heart. She grabbed Enuwal's hand and pressed it against her breastbone, her heart thumping rapidly beneath. "But you do. You understand."

"Malia, if you leave with him, you won't be you for very long. Being around something like that will change you, and not for the better."

"I know. But I don't see any other way. Do you?"

He said nothing, but pulled her close, nearly crushing her. His lips came down on hers, and he kissed her as if he were a starving man, and she returned the kiss just as hungrily. She pressed herself as close to him as she could.

But as close to him as she might get, she had to admit, she didn't know what truly went through his mind, not the way she knew Cian. With a muffled growl, she pulled free. "We should get back before Rina worries."

She walked off without waiting for Enuwal. She cursed the day she'd agreed to let Cian fix her mind. She cursed the day she let him in.

CHAPTER TEN

Chanwa lay curled on her side, with Muvumo snoring behind her, his seed still wet on her thighs. She clenched herself tight, as if she could hold in the seething anger through sheer force. He was her husband, he could take her when he chose. But he'd also had that old woman servant throw out her tea, the one that kept her from getting with child.

The fertility figurine her sister Nyda had given her was tucked away in the bottom of one of her chests, clothes folded neatly atop it. She never put much stock in such symbols, but now she wished she'd thrown the silly thing out. Her gaze kept going to its hiding spot.

If she ended up with child, whether she had a daughter or son, their choices would be limited. A daughter would grow up to marry and have children, if she was lucky. Her growth in knowledge would be stunted, and she would have to watch as any brothers left to do adventuresome things and learn just as Chanwa had done. If she wasn't lucky, she would end up as an unmentionable, used by the men for whatever they desired.

If she had a son, he would be pushed to become a warrior, especially with the Most Worthy as his father. He would have to be constantly on guard against anyone who might want to harm him in order to harm his father. He would have to toughen up according to the unspoken rules among the Maddion men. If he somehow couldn't train as a warrior, he would always be looked upon as a disappointment and as less than a man and be relegated to training as a healer, or in agriculture, or as a guard. Any show of affection on his part would be seen as weakness, and so he would continue the cycle of treating his sons harshly and forcing his daughters to be silent and obedient.

Muvumo's snores reached a crescendo. He turned over, away from her, and soon his breathing deepened and light snoring began again.

Chanwa eased to her feet, watching him to make sure he didn't wake. It was early, but she had plied him with plenty of wine, and she'd taken a more enthusiastic approach to their postprandial activities. The kasi powder, which typically kept him awake, or sleeping fitfully, had not been evident before their meal, nor after, when he preferred taking a snort. He'd already dismissed Delkis, so he wasn't planning on going anywhere. Tonight, it seemed he would sleep the sleep of the well sated. Better for her. She cleaned herself up, grabbed a covered basket sitting in one corner, and tiptoed out to the main room where the old woman was just finishing her cleaning. The lines around the woman's mouth deepened.

"You should be lying down," she said, "and letting the Most Worthy's seed take."

"And you should keep your opinions to yourself," she snapped. "Remember your place." She winced inwardly at her harsh tone, but the woman was clearly one of Muvumo's spies.

The old woman dipped her head. "My deepest apologies, my lady Chanwa. I only have your best interests in mind."

She bit back a retort and slipped her feet into her shoes. The old woman perked up. "Where are you going?"

"To visit a friend."

"I shall go with you."

Chanwa took her time looking around the room. The floor had been meticulously swept, the thick rug shaken out, the table cleaned until it shined, and the dishes washed and put away. The fire in the hearth was dying, and two lanterns hung from the ceiling, casting dim light through the room. Night fell early in the mountains, even in the summer. A vase on the table held fresh daisies in vibrant white and yellow, with tall bluebells in the center. Despite all of that, the room was cold and lifeless so long as Ankti was missing. Chanwa pushed aside the sharp ache. There was much to be done tonight, and she had to be careful. She gave the old woman a smile she didn't feel.

"That would be most helpful," Chanwa said. "You can carry this for me." She handed the basket over.

The old woman grunted in surprise as she took the basket. It held two skeins of Muvumo's finest wine, a new set of clothes for Tangie's baby, dolls for her other two girls, a small leather sac filled with beads and buttons and other trinkets for the girls to play with, and a small wooden rattle. Chanwa set a brisk pace, not pausing to see how closely the old woman followed.

Torches burned at regular intervals along the stone stairway, casting half circles of light upon the way. Each door yielded a different aroma as people finished up their evening meals, from *sprinko*, which was goat meat rubbed with spices and cooked all day, to river trout and roasted corn, to roasted venison or venison stews. With the dragons' help, they never had much trouble procuring meat. As she neared Tangie's, she could hear the wail of a hungry baby. A couple of messengers raced up and down the stone steps, their feet hardly making a sound as they padded along.

Bird song rose from the nearby pine trees, although it was momentarily drowned out by a sudden increase in the intensity of the baby's cry. Babies often did not seem to care for twilight or early evening, and neither did the very old and infirm. Chanwa wondered if they could sense something that the rest of them didn't know about the daily ritual of darkness overtaking the world, or if there was a more mundane explanation for the pattern.

Chanwa reached the doorway, covered by a dark green, heavy sheet, and waited for the old woman to come panting up the stairs after. She nodded once at the servant who took a couple of deep breaths, hoisted the basket onto one bony hip, and called into the home, "My lady Chanwa, wife of the Most Worthy, has come with gifts for the new babe and its mother."

She noticed how the old woman referred to the baby as 'its' rather than 'her.' Had the baby been a boy, Chanwa was certain she would have used the proper pronoun. Even the servants learned to distance themselves from girls, to view them as less. Her teeth clenched, but she held her tongue.

The door covering rustled, and the oldest girl, no taller than Chanwa's waist, peeked out. "Come in, my lady Chanwa," she said in a quiet voice, holding the cloth aside.

She entered, the old woman right behind her. Lanterns lit the room as did the fire blazing in the hearth. Something simmered in the kettle hanging over it, and to one side of the fire lay a flat object wrapped in corn leaves. Judging by the scent of fish, river trout and some sort of vegetable stew was for dinner.

Tangie sat back against pillows, the midwife sitting on her heels next to her. Tangie held the baby to her breast, quiet at last.

The midwife ducked her head at Chanwa. "The baby has been having trouble latching, but she seems to be doing well now."

Tangie smiled wearily, dark half circles beneath her eyes. "I'm sure you heard her protests. She's had a rougher time adjusting to the world than her sisters did."

The old servant sniffed, crinkling up her nose, but said nothing. Chanwa frowned at her and took the basket. She set it beside Tangie. "A gift for your husband and you, for the baby, and for your daughters."

At that, the two girls brightened. "Mama, what's in there for us?" asked the oldest. The middle hid behind her older sister, seemingly torn between the presence of so many adults and the prospect of a gift.

Tangie rustled through the basket with one hand while holding the baby with the other. "It can't possibly be these two dolls," she said with a slight grin.

The middle girl squealed, then bit her lower lip as her older sister shushed her with a nervous glance at Chanwa. Chanwa smiled at them. "It's all right to be excited. Go ahead, take them out."

The girls took the dolls from their mother and disappeared into the other room where the sounds of pretend play soon emerged.

"As everything seems to be going well," the midwife said, "I'll take my leave." She stood, gathered her things in a small basket, and nodded to Chanwa. "My lady Chanwa." She turned to Tangie and gave her a small nod. "Send a messenger if you need anything. Good night, ladies." She left with a rustling of the door cover.

"And wine," Tangie said, taking out the skeins carefully and setting them aside. "How lovely. Thank you. When Jehan returns tonight, I'm sure he'll enjoy some." She cast her gaze down.

The only thing that kept a man out during the evening meal, unless he was a young apprentice, was the unmentionables. Most men did not touch their pregnant wives, and they couldn't for the first moon or so after women gave birth, although some ignored that and attempted to impregnant their wives again as soon as possible.

"Here," Chanwa said, reaching into the basket. "One more thing." She pulled out the rattle. "This belonged to my sisters and then to me." Baby items were often used to convey written messages between women who could read. A tiny slip of paper could be rolled up tight and slipped into the rattle's handle, for example.

Tangie took it from her, sadness fleeting across her face before she smiled. "Ah, a rattle for the baby. Do you think the baby is ready for a toy?" she asked, carefully meeting her gaze.

She nodded, blood roaring in her ears. This was the main reason she'd come to visit Tangie tonight, to deliver this rattle and her message. "Why, she could play with it this very night once she's done nursing."

The old woman covered a yawn with her hand, looking around the room.

Tangie sighed and looked down at the nursing baby, whose eyes were drifting shut. "It feels like starting over with each one, and yet feels familiar at the same time. And it makes time do funny things, like stand still or go too fast, or feel like it turns back or jumps ahead. I don't know if I'm ready for this."

"I have no children yet," Chanwa said. "But one thing I always hear parents say is that you're never ready. You must simply move ahead and put your trust in your capabilities." Her heart was pounding so hard she was sure the servant could hear and would wonder why such an innocent conversation was making Chanwa so anxious.

Tangie smiled. "Then move ahead we shall. Thank you for the gifts and the advice. I'll make sure to share your wise words with others." And that sharing would begin tonight, the word spreading quickly among the women. "Would you like to stay for supper?"

"No, thank you. You have a full house and busy hands. I'll take my leave and return tomorrow night to see how she enjoys the rattle."

"Good night, my lady Chanwa."

"Good night."

She left, letting the door covering fall behind her so that the old woman had to hurry and grab it before it fell against her. The nearest torch popped and flared bright for a moment, the fiery orange putting her in mind of the changer. She wondered what sort of trouble he was up to now, and how far away he was from the Maddion, which then put her in mind of Ankti. She quickly shoved away thoughts of the other woman. She needed to focus on tomorrow night. Things were happening fast. Part of her shrank from it, but part of her embraced it. If she was to take advantage of the recent changes, it had to happen soon, otherwise her people would fall back into the same old roles.

She didn't need the changer. She had herself, and the other women, and men who wanted more for their sisters, mothers, daughters, wives. Tangie would spread the word, and by tomorrow night, things would be vastly different for the Maddion.

CHAPTER ELEVEN

Malia stood on the narrow, grassy plain just below Rina's home as the lingering clouds turned fiery shades of pink and red in the setting sun's light. Two days in a row, afternoon showers had come, leaving the earth damp and the air smelling sharply of petrichor and, more faintly, the unique smell of Jeguduns as well.

Cian was nowhere to be found, praise the clan mother. She'd spent the entire day making sure he and Enuwal never encountered one another, and Cian had spent the night... somewhere. She didn't care, although because of her connection with him, she knew he'd remained in the valley. She only hoped he wasn't searching out other Taakwa and trying to make trouble.

Enuwal stood just behind her, holding onto his walking stick but not leaning on it, and Ankti next to her. Rina was a small figure on the ledge above. She hadn't wanted to leave Ziku, who seemed to daily be failing a little bit more. A pang went through Malia. Her grandmother had so much to worry about as it was, she didn't need to add the fear of a Maddion attack to that.

Malia cleared her throat and addressed the Jeguduns. "First of all, thank you all for offering to do such a dangerous task."

She cast a glance at Aru, who carefully met her gaze with his green eyes, dark as the pines after a rain. His tufted ears pricked forward, and he held his body tense, ready. He was doing this to assuage his guilt over helping her leave the valley in the first place to find Cian. Not that he would admit to that. She had tried talking him out of this, telling him he'd helped enough already, but he was stubborn.

"Remember what your scouts let us know earlier today, that there are dragons and Maddion systematically searching the plains between here and their mountains."

The Jeguduns nodded in reply, one letting out a low trill. It seemed the Maddion were searching for something, and she could only assume it was for her or Ankti, or both. Their stolen dragon had never returned home, so the Maddion might eventually think Malia was safe beneath the barrier and Ankti far away with the beast. She could only hope so, and that they'd give up soon. The Maddion had no reason to believe the barrier was gone, but she didn't want them getting near enough to ever find out.

"You all know the mountain well, so I leave it to you to position yourselves accordingly, but your lives are more important than the information. If you can't get close enough to study the dragons' roost, then find out whatever you can and come back safe. Even confirming the times they come and go, and whether the Maddion visit the dragons' roost will help us plan. And if you think to be brave and get too close—" Here she cast another glance at Aru, who shifted his gaze away. "Then remember that your capture will alert the Maddion to our interest in them, and any element of surprise will be gone."

Aru and the other Jeguduns wore travel sacs slung across their bodies, carrying food and water.

"Any questions?" she asked them. They shook their heads, feet shifting, wings shuffling behind them.

She turned to Enuwal. "Anything else I should add?"

His lips thinned. "I can't think of a thing."

To Ankti, she said, "They know what to do. Is there anything else at all you think they should know? Has anything major changed since they last gathered information on the Maddion?"

"Only that their scrolls are gone," she said. "And they're no longer ill. But the structures of their lives are the same, and they're such creatures of habit that I'm sure their routine is exactly what it was before. They do know about the guardhouse, right?"

Malia nodded. "They'll go in under cover of night, when the dragons aren't active. There aren't traps or anything, are there?"

She shook her head. "If anyone manages to scale the stone to reach their homes, they can raise the alarm and have men and dragons helping them within moments. If anyone tries to attack the guardhouse, the same goes. They are well prepared, and practice often. They don't scour the woods, though, at least not more than a cursory check. They don't fear that many people would be able to approach through the woods, at least not enough to pose a threat to them. Your Jegudun friends should be fine."

Despite the assurance that all would most likely be well, Malia's stomach knotted. "That's it, then."

She got on one knee and pulled Aru into a hug, so far as his massive folded wings would allow. He let out a little squawk of surprise but quickly returned the hug, the soft fur around his face tickling her cheek.

"Don't be brave," she said. "Just gather what information you can, then get out of there." She stood.

Aru adjusted the travel pack, nodded once at her, and then gave her a quick, toothy grin before trilling and whistling to the others. One by one, they took to the air, their massive wings stirring the grasses around them and making the blades dance, and tugging at Malia's hair. They rose higher until they were small specks in the sky, hardly discernible from birds of prey, and then they flew toward the Maddion.

Their departure left behind a hollow feeling to go along with the knots in Malia's stomach. Her friends risked much to bring them more information. And yet she couldn't simply tell Taakwa or Jeguduns to attack the dragons without knowing as much as they possibly could.

"They'll be fine," Enuwal said.

She hesitantly reached for him, then pulled her hand back,

clasping both of them behind her. Her hip beads shifted and clinked together. One hand twitched, wanting to rise to her neck, but there was no necklace there for her to grab onto.

The world was gray, save for the sliver of orange in the west. The Jeguduns would reach the mountains while it was still dark, and they should have plenty of time to infiltrate the forest and find hiding places in the foothills before day broke.

"I'll go up and help Rina with dinner," Ankti said. She retreated to the rope ladder and climbed hastily.

The moment between her and Enuwal stretched, like a clay strand that might break at any time. His weight shifted, and she had a feeling he was going to walk off alone, or follow Ankti, and then their chance to talk would be gone.

"Rasmus went back home, then?" she asked, silently berating herself for asking such an obvious question.

A flicker of a smile crossed Enuwal's face. "He left earlier. He said he brought you safely back to Rina, and there were things he needed to do." He paused. "He met a woman, last fall during the harvest festival."

"He went to his village." That was more of a surprised statement than a question, but Enuwal nodded anyway. Rasmus had been an exile for a long time, like Rina, and had settled in among the Jeguduns, but when the Maddion had camped just outside their valley last summer, he'd risked his life by trying to warn the Taakwa about them. As an exile, he wasn't allowed to interact with any Taakwa. Things had changed following the war, though, and some of the old laws had become obsolete.

"He did," Enuwal said. "And that murder he was exiled for? He found the true murderer during the harvest festival last fall. His exile was formally forgiven by the clan mother."

"And yet he still lives with the Jeguduns."

It was full night, making it hard to read the smaller movements of Enuwal's face, but she was certain he grimaced. "It's hard to return to the old way of life after so long. And… there are those who still mistrust him. Mostly those who still mistrust the Jeguduns. It sounds as if they weaved some story about how he used magic to convince people that the other man was the murderer."

Malia sighed. "When will people stop doubting?" She imagined they were like her late husband. He didn't trust the Jeguduns at all, not even when she assured him he could. He had rather believed her mad, or under the influence of magic, than trust them. Or her. Funny how that still sent a little stab of anger through her after all this time. She shook her head. "Never mind. Tell me more about this woman he met."

She fell into an easy walk, and Enuwal walked a half-stride behind her. His walking stick made a dull *thump* each time it hit the ground, which wasn't often. Today, at least, it seemed Enuwal hardly needed it. They had to go inside soon, but she wanted to savor this moment with him. She wanted to pretend there was no impending struggle to destroy the dragons, or a promise that she would leave the valley with Cian.

As if even that passing thought was enough to garner his attention, he shifted in her mind, drawing her away from the easy walk, from the tall grass brushing against her legs and skirt, from Enuwal's presence. She pushed his presence aside, hoping he picked up on her irritation as his interruption.

"Her name is Jetati," Enuwal said. "She's the clan mother's daughter."

"Oof," Malia said.

This won a chuckle from Enuwal.

"So if he married her," she said, "he'd have to move back to his old village. With those who still don't trust him."

He nodded, somber. "That's why he still lives with the Jeguduns. In the spring, several young braided men from his old village were to stay with him and the Jeguduns, to see how they live and to exchange ideas. Rasmus said it was a success, and the clan mother has approved another such venture."

"Has the clan mother approved of his marriage to her daughter? Is it even possible?" One of the clan mother's main purposes was the track lineages in order to avoid people marrying if they were too closely related, an important task in an enclosed valley such as theirs.

"It *is* possible," he said. "But she hasn't approved it yet. Of course, she hasn't denied it, either. It sounds like she wants time to allow some of the villagers to cool down, and to make sure her daughter really wants the match."

Malia sighed. "I hope, for their sake, that she makes that decision soon. Waiting is hard."

He nodded. "It's the hardest part of healing, whether for physical injuries or injuries of the spirit."

Full night had fallen, although light from the stars and the moon lent enough of a glow so they could see their way. Still, it wouldn't do if one of them tripped and broke a leg. Again.

"We should go up," she said. "Or Rina might get worried."

"And dinner might get cold."

She smiled, and he returned the smile, lines crinkling around his mouth and eyes. Malia closed the gap between them and laid her hand lightly on his arm. This was the way it used to be between them. Comfortable, warm. It felt as though they were the only two people in the entire valley. The world stretched away far beyond them in all directions, but there was no one else, just Enuwal, and his dark eyes, and the warmth of him so close, and the smell of herbs and fresh-turned earth and the faint, unique smell that belonged to him alone. She leaned closer to him, and he leaned toward her, and dipped his head, and—

Cian's presence leaped to the forefront of her mind. She yelped and pulled back, the interruption as abrupt as someone putting an ice cold hand on her bare back. Her free hand clenched, and a little ball of anger quickly formed in her belly, growing and rising. If he didn't want to experience a loving moment between her and Enuwal, then he could just do his best to ignore it.

But that wasn't it. There was something else... surprise, uncertainty.

"What is it?" Enuwal asked, frowning.

She didn't know. But then she saw a light bobbing in the distance at a steady pace. Somebody was walking toward them. "There's somebody coming."

Enuwal turned, back straight, standing casually, although he kept himself between her and the newcomers. Malia laid a hand on his arm. "There are only two of them. And they're Taakwa. No need to worry."

And yet, who would come all the way out here? Only somebody looking for them. Did they look for Rina? Rasmus's village had forgiven his exile. Perhaps her mother, Selu's clan mother, had decided to forgive Rina's and had sent messengers. Malia bit her lower lip. She could only imagine the choice words her grandmother might say to that. Rina had carved out a life with the Jeguduns in much the same way they'd carved out comfortable homes from the cliffs.

Both figures were tall, solid, and wore pants. Men, then. One had a familiar, loping stride, one that could easily break into a run, or as a boy, chase her down or try to keep away from her during games. A smile spread across her face, and she ran toward her brother.

"Vedran," she called out.

The figure with the lantern broke into a run as well, meeting her halfway between the two little groups. When she had first woken from the long sleep that had overtaken her after she'd used magic to repair the barrier, it had been as if he'd grown overnight. She had recalled him as a boy. An older boy, yes, but still a boy. But he had greeted her as a braided man, taller and wider and more muscular than she had known.

She was half-afraid he'd again undergone a similar, disconcerting change, but no, he was much the same as when she'd last seen him. He didn't even seem to have grown any more, although one more growth spurt awaited him at some point. He wore a plain tunic and pants, carried a bow and quiver strapped to his back, and wore a belt around his waist that held a dagger. A dragon's claw hung from a leather strap around his neck, earned during the Dragon War. He also wore a wide grin that made him look like a boy again.

He set down the lantern and grabbed her and spun her around, making her momentarily dizzy, before setting her down. "I couldn't quite believe it until I saw you," he said. "You're really back, and safe."

"How did you know?" she asked.

"Rina sent a Jegudun with a message the moment you returned."

Of course. Malia thought she'd heard Rina say something along those lines, but she'd had so many other worries at the time. Rina would have wanted to assure Vedran and her mother that Malia was fine. A little stab of guilt went through her. She'd been so consumed by the barrier, and by Cian and the Maddion that she hadn't thought to ask if Rina had sent a message, or suggest doing so herself.

Vedran looked past her shoulder. "Enuwal, it's good to see you up and about."

"Good to see you, Vedran," he replied behind her. "Who came with you?"

"Ah," he began, glancing at Malia and then away. "There's a long explanation. And a good one. It's Andrij."

"Andrij?" Malia said. Dalibor's brother had accompanied Vedran. For what purpose? He loathed her and blamed her for Dalibor's death. True, she *had* killed Dalibor, but only because he was trying to kill her and she'd had no other choice. The lightness she'd felt when she recognized Vedran turned to a heavy stone in the pit of her stomach. "Why did you bring him?"

"He'll tell you. Honestly, Malia, it's all right." He lowered his voice. "I wouldn't have brought him if it was going to be a problem."

Andrij had the same hooked nose as Dalibor, and looked very similar through the face, but he was a little slimmer, a little shorter. He emerged from the night into the circle of light cast by Vedran's lantern. Malia tensed.

Andrij wore a tunic and pants much like Vedran's, and also had a bow and quiver slung over his back. His belt held two daggers, and with a jolt she realized one of them had been Dalibor's. She hadn't noticed before, when he'd confronted her in their home village of Selu, because the magic-induced fog had been affecting her memory back then. Like Vedran, he wore a dragon's claw on a leather strap around his neck.

He met her gaze, but there was nothing challenging about it, no anger tightening his mouth or the skin around his eyes. His shoulders were tense, though. He gave her a slow nod. "Good evening, Malia." He turned to Enuwal. "Enuwal."

"This is a surprise, Andrij," she said.

"I know."

Silence stretched between them all. An owl called mournfully from the distant woods. Something small scurried in the grass nearby. Her heart thumped hard against her breastbone. "There's something I must tell you," she said in a hurry. "Before we talk of anything else."

Enuwal shifted a little closer to her. She took a deep breath, nodding once at the small sign of support.

"What is it?" Vedran asked.

"Do you know of the *mutara*?" she asked Andrij.

His eyes narrowed, and he nodded. "A powerful being that can bring about great changes."

"Yes." She clasped her hands together. "When he works magic, he changes, too. And, well… he's not really the person whose appearance he takes on, he just *looks* like them. And he happens to look like… he's taken on the appearance of… Dalibor." She held her breath.

Andrij took in a sharp breath. "You're saying that some magical being has taken on the appearance of my late brother."

"Yes." Deafening silence stretched out.

"The *mutara* is a story that clan mothers use to scare their villagers, much the same way parents use the story of spirits to keep their children from running off places they don't want them to go."

"It's not a story," she said, exasperation clear in her voice.

"Malia," Enuwal said gently. "They've traveled a long ways, and they're tired. Why don't we show them to Rina's, and we can discuss this more later?"

Her hands clenched. She wanted to discuss it *now*, but Enuwal was right. Pushing Andrij to believe her right now would be like trying to push the Big River back up the falls and out of the valley.

"Yes," she said. "I'm sure they could use food and some rest."

Andrij's shoulders relaxed. Vedran nodded. "Thank you," he said.

She led them to the rope ladder. She insisted Vedran and Andrij go ahead as they were guests. While they climbed, she spoke quietly to Enuwal.

"He seems… not as angry as I was expecting. Although I'm bothered that he doesn't believe me about Cian."

He nodded. "He just needs time to adjust to what you told him."

"What do you suppose changed?"

Enuwal shrugged. "I'm sure we'll find out."

She climbed up next, then helped Enuwal when he reached the top. She pulled the ladder up. Enuwal said, "What about our, uh, other guest? Not that he needs to come up. He can stay out in the woods for all I care, but I hate the thought of him caterwauling to be let up in the middle of the night."

One corner of her mouth twitched at the idea of Cian standing at the base of the cliffs, looking up and calling out for the ladder so he could come up like some wandering pet. "He'll find a way up here if he wants."

"Oh," Enuwal said.

Inside, warm light spilled from the hearth and from lanterns hanging from the ceiling. Rina was smiling, one arm still around Vedran as she directed Andrij to put his travel pack and Vedran's in one corner, and where to find the bowls and utensils and cups. Enuwal helped gather what they needed, and Malia made sure there were enough pillows. Vedran and Andrij served themselves first, and soon the smell of trout and onions and potatoes filled the space.

Rina went into the other room and returned a few moments later with Ziku leaning on her arm. The Jegudun took small, shuffling steps, his back bent, but his milky white eyes were sharp, and he trilled a greeting at their guests.

Vedran greeted the Jegudun enthusiastically, and Andrij more carefully. Andrij had been one of those who still didn't quite trust the Jeguduns. But surely he could trust Ziku, who obviously couldn't hurt anyone unless they happened to get within easy range of his talons.

"Malia," Rina said. "Our other guest is waiting in the other room. I thought it best if you made the introductions."

"Of course."

Ankti sat on her heels in one corner of the room. There were thick rugs covering the stone floor, and a plush sleeping mat near the hearth with pillows piled around it, and Ziku's faint outline on it. The room smelled of Jegudun and herbs and woodsmoke and wild roses.

Ankti's eyes were wide. "There are new people here."

"My brother and my late husband's brother," Malia said. "I'll introduce you."

Her lips thinned.

"It will be all right." Malia held out a hand. "Come."

Ankti's hand was slim and cool and strong as she took Malia's and stood. Malia led her to the main room and made the introductions.

Vedran gave Ankti a quick, warm smile and a nod. Andrij's eyes narrowed, and his jaw tensed.

"An Outsider?" he asked.

"A guest," Rina said. "*My* guest, in *my* house. If you don't care for her, then feel free to leave."

Andrij bowed his head. "My apologies." He looked up. "You said she was a Maddion servant? I only wonder at the wisdom of giving shelter to her when the Maddion may come looking for her."

"Would you leave her outside the valley, alone?" Malia snapped. "Recaptured, beaten, raped, killed? Torn apart by dragons?"

He flinched. "Of course not."

"Old thoughts are difficult to get rid of," Enuwal said. "We were all raised to fear Outsiders, and for good reason, as it turned out, but there's no need, not for Ankti."

Malia exchanged a quick glance with him. *Thank you*, she mouthed.

Rina clapped her hands together once. "Let's get down to important business. Eating."

Soon they were all sitting in a circle, the only sounds that of wooden utensils thunking against wooden bowls, and eating, and a few words of appreciation for the food. Malia watched Andrij out of the corner of her eye, wondering what he was about. When Malia had last been in Selu, his wife had been expecting their first child. She should have had the baby by now. So what was he doing here? She hoped nothing had happened to his wife and child. A spasm of sadness went through her as she considered that possibility.

When they had finished eating, Vedran went out to the ledge to wash the dishes. Malia settled back against her pillows and asked, "Andrij, how is your wife?"

His face softened. "She's well, thank you. She had our baby about a moon ago. A little girl."

"That's wonderful." Relief flooded her. So his wife and child were fine, then. "I have to ask... what brought you out here?"

He took a deep breath. Both of his hands clasped his mug, a little tea sloshing inside. He looked inside the mug as if it held the answer to her question.

Rina stood with a small groan. "I have to help Ziku to bed. Come on, dear." She helped Ziku to his feet, and together they went into the other room.

Andrij looked up. An ember popped in the hearth, and water trickled endlessly down the stone and into the pool. "This isn't easy for me," he began. He sighed. "When my daughter was born, a lot of things changed. People tell you that they change, but you never know how until you're holding your child in your arms. When I looked at her, she reminded me of Dalibor. I remember when he was born. He was tiny, and squalled a lot, and I thought he made a horrible little brother."

Enuwal snorted. Andrij inclined his head. Ankti sat quietly in a corner, watching them all silently. Malia would have to explain all of this to her later, although, sharp as she was, she was probably picking up the gist of it right now. Malia finished her tea, waiting, her hands clasped around the mug. She sat as still as she could, waiting for Andrij to get to the point.

He continued, "I thought about my brother a lot while I held my daughter that first night, and the next, and the next. She's a calm baby. Only cries when she's hungry or wet. Dalibor… was never easy. Not as a baby, not as a little boy, and certainly not as a man."

Malia looked into her empty cup. She recalled the time Dalibor had thrown her pottery, shattering it, and then held her against the wall. He had been jealous because she'd made the piece to thank Enuwal for all he'd done to help her while she'd been ill when she was younger. Back then, she hadn't felt anything more than appreciation for Enuwal. Maybe… maybe a little more, if she was honest with herself, but nothing would have ever come from it. She had been devoted to Dalibor, and to her role as training to be her village's next clan mother. The pottery was a way of telling Enuwal good-bye, and leaving that part of her life behind her for good. It was easy to see that now, looking back on it.

But Dalibor had destroyed her work, and her trust. Then he destroyed her life when he killed the Jegudun named Tuvin, and he tried to destroy her reputation when he told the gathered Taakwa that the Jeguduns had manipulated her mind. He had torn down a lot, much the same way the Maddion had torn down the barrier.

"Malia," Andrij said. She looked up and met his gaze. "I came here to apologize to you. I blamed you for Dalibor's death when it was his own anger that led him to his choices. You were only defending yourself. You were right about him, and about the Jeguduns."

Much of the heaviness in her chest lifted, just like that. "Thank you," she said. "Apology accepted."

Andrij let out a breath. "That was… not as hard as I thought it would be."

"Apologies usually aren't," Enuwal said.

The blanket hanging over the door rustled, and Vedran ducked inside, carrying a stack of clean dishes. He looked around and grinned. "We're all friends, then. Good." He put the dishes away on the shelves.

Rina emerged from the other room. "Ziku is resting. Did you all have a good talk?"

Malia nodded. "We did."

"Excellent. I abhor misunderstandings."

Vedran straightened from where he finished stacking dishes. "Malia, there's something else I need to tell you."

"And there's something I need to tell you and Andrij," she said, thinking of Cian. She tugged at his presence, checking where he was. Close. In the forest. She had the sense of him watching the light spilling around the door covering. There was a flash of something else, something deeper that he strived to keep her from seeing. A deep, aching loneliness. For a moment she stood at the edge of that endless canyon, the wind howling and tugging at her skirt, her hair, at her, almost urging her to take a step into the great nothingness before her. Her heart quickened. Being out in the woods alone while they sat up here, cozy and well fed, couldn't have helped that sensation. He shouldn't be alone.

Cian shifted, moved in her direction. No, Andrij couldn't see him until she'd had a chance to explain. She didn't mean for him to come to them. She pushed him away frantically, forgetting how doing so before resulted in an unpleasant reciprocation until it came, reflected off him and rebounding in her skull.

"Ugh," she said, pressing a hand against her throbbing head. "Andrij, the *mutara*—"she began.

There was a soft scrape of stone outside, then the rustle of the blanket over the door. She knew the moment Cian entered because Andrij's eyes widened, and he stood, tremulous fear, and worse, hope, crossing his face.

Then Andrij's face darkened, brows drawing down, lips rising in an angry sneer as his hand went to his dagger. "You're not Dalibor," he said.

He pulled his dagger free.

CHAPTER TWELVE

After dinner, Chanwa retreated to their private room on the pretense of doing needlework while Muvumo remained in the front, writing in his new scrolls, filling in old information and adding new information at the same time. His quill scratched at vellum, the smell of ink and oil from the lanterns filling the air along with the fading scent of woodsmoke. The old servant was long gone after whispering about all Chanwa had done that day. The woman thought she was being sneaky, but Chanwa's hearing was good enough to pick up what she said in the other room. Chanwa hoped her bones ached in the cold mountain night as she made her way to the servants' quarters.

Muvumo had dismissed Delkis for the night once he had sat down to dinner, which meant he was staying in again. Fortunate for her plans, but not for her body. He seemed to be doing what most men did when they wanted to see their wives heavy with child, and that meant he planned to take her daily until she could prove his seed had taken.

It was getting late when a tiny rustle of paper told her that he was getting out the kasi powder. He must plan to stay up all night writing. That would not do at all. Her gaze went to the chest where the fertility carving hid beneath her clothes, and she shrank into herself at the thought of him touching her again. But if she couldn't leave later, the others might grow too fearful without her presence.

She tossed the needlework aside and snuffed the lanterns so the only light came through the door to the other room.

"Muvumo," she called out. "It's getting late."

He grunted in reply, and the scratch of quill against vellum continued. She clenched her teeth so hard that her jaw ached.

"The bedroll is chilly," she called out.

"Then stoke the fire in the hearth," he replied.

She took a deep breath. She had been cold toward him, so of course he'd be cold toward her. It was time to make him think she was caving in. "There *is* a fire I'd like to stoke," she said. "But it's not in the hearth."

The scratch of quill against vellum stopped. A long silence answered, and after a while Chanwa thought he would ignore her and go on writing, but then came the sound of sand against vellum and the capping of the ink followed by rustling as he put things away. The lights dimmed, plunging the room into near darkness. His footsteps entered the room, his breathing ragged as he stood in the doorway, an outline against the main room's darkness.

She was glad for the night that hid her face. If he could see it, she was sure her hatred for him would be evident in the tightness of her jaw, her narrowed eyes, the tension underlying her entire body. She forced herself to take a deep breath, to let the coiled muscles ease into fluidity, to soften her voice. All she had to do was get through this little part of the night, and then things would be different.

"I am eager to have a son for you," she said, surprised at how calm she sounded.

His ragged breathing quickened. "I knew you would come around." He stepped into the room.

She endured his touch, which was thankfully fleeting. When it was over, he sprawled beside her, his breathing slow and deep as he sank into sleep. Meanwhile, her mind spun as fast as the legs of a messenger boy up and down the stairs.

When he had settled into a deep slumber, she eased quietly to her feet. She cleaned herself up, then put on a thicker underdress she'd laid out earlier, with a heavier dress over that. The clothes were more suitable for the middle of autumn rather than late summer, but nights got cold in the mountain at any time of year. She dug through his discarded garments carefully in the dark until her fingers found the rolled up little paper containing his kasi powder. It felt full. She tucked it into a small pocket in her dress. Then her feet went into her slippers, and she padded out to the main room to wait.

An owl hooted in the distance, and crickets chirped, otherwise all was still. Even the guards were silent. Chanwa leaned her head against the cold stone beside the door. She was relying on so many others to make this work. Any one of them could grow scared and not follow through, and could she blame them? Her own heart felt as though it resided in her throat, pounding fast.

What if the others didn't follow through? She could head back into the bedroom and lie beside her husband and sink into the oblivion of her life. Or she could leave. She wouldn't get far before Muvumo found her, and then she would die, but at least she would die fighting the best way she could, and maybe that would spur people to action.

Something scraped against stone above her. She straightened. She hardly breathed, her ears straining for another sound.

It wasn't long before it came. More scraping, a thud, a violent curse, a moan. Footsteps hurried up, past Chanwa's door, and more approached from far above. Voices rose and fell, but the words were hard to make out. After a while, footsteps slowly neared, then passed her door as low voices discussed a guard who'd hit his head and was having a hard time coming around. The nearest healer lived below, close to the Most Worthy but a bit of a distance from the nearest mesa where dragons landed and took off.

She counted steps in her mind, and when she thought the guards had reached the healer's, she poked her head out and looked down. The stairs were empty.

This is it. She rushed up the stairs, wondering if she'd be the only one to show up. But as she passed one home, a slight figure slipped out and joined her silently on the stairs. Another emerged, and another, until a line of women hurried up the stairs with her, silent as ghosts, silent as they'd been for so many generations. *Silent no more*, she thought with grim satisfaction.

The steps in front of Tangie's home were dark and clear, but Chanwa knew that only moments ago, small trinkets and toys had been left on the step as if by a forgetful child, and the nearest torch had died, which would have made it hard for any passing guard to see the small dangers. Tangie had done her part by spreading the news that tonight was the night for them to gather. Her life was on such tenuous hold that Chanwa had insisted she remain home with her children.

When she reached the mesa, quite a few women were already there. Some were carrying food into the large cavern that opened onto the mesa. Normally the cavern was home to apprentice boys who saddled dragons, but Tangie had also made sure that their schedules were messed up tonight and that no boys were staying in the cavern. It would serve as their storage for food and water, and as a place where they could relieve their bodily functions.

On the other side of the mesa, a half dozen servants had gathered. Three Maddion women were finishing with the ropes they'd tied to the waists of some of the other women. They looked to Chanwa. She nodded.

They threw the ropes over the stone wall. The ropes unfurled with slight hisses. The first three servants climbed hastily over the wall and descended into the darkness below while the women braced themselves. The other three servants soon went over the wall as well, all of them on their various routes to the Taakwa Valley to deliver Chanwa's message. Normally the servants wouldn't dare escape because the Maddion could overtake them so easily on their dragons. But the Maddion wouldn't be going anywhere.

She hoped the Taakwa would help. They wanted nothing more than to be left alone, but she had promised that if things changed for the Maddion, they wouldn't have to fear her people anymore. Of course, they could simply remain beneath their barrier and stay out of this altogether, but they had helped the Jeguduns a long time ago. She hoped they felt the same urge to help the Maddion women, especially as they had so much respect for their own women.

The women quickly set the ropes aside, and Chanwa arranged all of them around the mesa. Far above her, more women were settling on *that* mesa. Some of the unmentionables joined them, although others were too scared to do so and remained safely hidden with the servants. Chanwa was glad for those who showed, and did not blame those who hid in the least.

Soon the space was filled, with women sitting beside one another as tight as the stitches on a tapestry, allowing no space for a dragon to land. Chanwa took a seat at the front of the group, facing the stairs that led down. That would be the direction her husband would come from. He would be furious. This might be her last night alive. But if the others could hold strong, it would be worth it. The Maddion couldn't kill all of their women.

A cool hand fell on her shoulder, and she startled. Her sister Nyda sat behind her. Her hand tightened on Chanwa's shoulder, and she smiled grimly, nodding once. Chanwa returned the nod. Prali remained home. She was too close to delivering her baby to be out here. A few other women had to pass because of much the same reason, but nearly every woman had turned out. The Maddion men would certainly be in for a surprise when the sun rose over the mountains.

Chanwa and the other women remained quiet. Even the small children and infants with their mothers were silent, as if they understood the weight of what they were all doing. The night air was chilly, and Chanwa was glad she had worn her heavier clothes. Even then, she shivered at times. She fought against the feeling that what they were doing was silly. She fought against the fear rising like hot flames from a dragon's belly. She fought against the worry that the other women would grow too scared, or too bored, and leave. She fought against boredom herself, fingers fiddling with her heavy dress. She didn't dare speak with her sister Nyda or any other women around her because she didn't want them to hear the fear and doubt that would surely make itself known in her voice.

The guards emerged from the healer's home far below, tiny specks against the torch light. Chanwa stirred, as did the other women in front of the group who could see the figures in the distant torchlight.

"Have courage," she whispered to those around her. They passed the message along, their whispers like the pounding and hissing in her ears as her heart sped.

Nyda snaked a hand forward and squeezed hers once. "I never thought my little sister would grow into such a leader," she said.

"Well, I had an older sister who was *very* good at telling her siblings what to do. I learned from her."

"Rascal."

The half dozen or so guards climbed about halfway up before the one leading them froze. *That's it. He must have seen us. Here we go.* Chanwa's mouth went dry.

The guards hurried up the stairs, taking two at a time in places. As they drew near, the leader's face became clear in the dim torchlight. He was older, with a receding hairline turning gray around his temples, and a heavy brow drawn down. His hair was worn in long, twisted ropes, although they were thinner than those of a young man. Like the men behind him, he wore a bright pink sash tied around his waist, marking him as a guardsman. He wore a short axe on one hip and a long blade on the other. Most guards also wore a dagger strapped to their legs beneath their pants, and usually hid a bevy of other weapons on their persons.

This one reached into a pouch on his belt and pulled out something small that twinkled briefly in the dim light. A dragon claw. She went cold all the way to her bones. It was a weapon that could fit in his hand. If he made a fist, short, sharp blades would protrude between his fingers and out from beneath the base of his pinky finger. It was the preferred weapon of those who like grappling with their enemies. Or of men who enjoyed backhanding with it. Chanwa had witnessed that once as a child. A man had backhanded an unmentionable who had teased him, leaving three deep, red gashes in her cheek and across her eye. After that she'd been considered damaged and given over to the dragons. Her deep chill turned to a fiery pool of anger that heated her blood.

He stood on a step below Chanwa, but it still gave him plenty of height over her. "What is this foolishness?" he said.

Chanwa considered standing so she could look him in the eye, but then she'd make herself vulnerable to either an attack or him separating her from the others. Instead, she linked arms with the women on either side of her, and they did the same, until the women were all holding tight to one another. She craned her neck to meet his gaze.

"If the Maddion men wish to ride their dragons again, then they will listen and attend to our requests."

He sputtered, then laughed, the sound echoing off the rock towering above them. Then his laughter cut off. He brandished his fist, the blades of the dragon's claw glinting. He leaned over, close enough that Chanwa could smell the rank sweat coming off of him, and said, "You will all disperse and return home this instant if you know what's good for you."

She didn't blink or flinch. "No," she said.

She could sense the anger rising from the women around her and behind her. They'd all held it in check for a lifetime. It flowed now, a tension that filled the air. Behind her, Nyda shook, but it wasn't the faint shake of fear; it was the heavier shudder of anger, of the anticipation before a battle.

The guard pulled back, his arm rising to bring the blade down. Chanwa remained still and said, "I hardly think the Most Worthy would appreciate you hitting his wife, and certainly not with a device that could maim me, especially when I might be carrying his son." There was some time before she'd know whether she was with child or not, but this brute wouldn't know that.

He hesitated, then dropped his arm at his side. "Speaking of the Most Worthy, I doubt he knows you're out here, my lady Chanwa." He spoke her name with distaste, as if naming a Taakwa or Jegudun who was a particular nuisance. "I'd better let him know."

"You'd better do that," she said.

That gave him pause. The lines around his mouth deepened, and his eyes narrowed. "Watch them," he said to one of the other guards, then left all of them but one behind while he trotted down the stairs.

Nyda's hand crept forward and squeezed Chanwa's shoulder again. She felt strangely calm now that the confrontation with Muvumo was about to happen. She'd imagined it going a number of different ways, but the only thing she was certain of was that it would all turn out somehow different than anything she could have imagined or prepared for.

A light spilled from her home. There was no shouting, no clanging of weapons, no sign of any kind of rage, but of course Muvumo would be angry. She wondered if he would try to take a pinch of kasi powder before coming out to deal with them, and whether he had another stash hidden somewhere.

And then she didn't have time to wonder any more. He strode out, shadowed by the light spilling from her home, outlining his familiar figure. One guard hurried after him as he took the stairs one at a time. He didn't run, like the guards had, but his strides covered the distance quickly nonetheless. The other guard ran down the stairs, presumably to fetch Delkis.

Muvumo stopped on the stair immediately before her, making her look up at him. His face was unreadable in the night's shadows, but his shoulders were tense, and his fingers twitched once. He wore his belt with his short axe and dagger hanging from it. Chanwa swallowed the knot in her throat. What she and the other women were doing was more powerful than those weapons. She straightened and met his gaze. She would not break the silence first. That was a trick Muvumo liked to use on people when he questioned them.

Delkis emerged from a home far down the stairs, still hastily strapping on his belt. The guard followed, carrying a crossbow and quiver. Delkis finished putting himself together and took the crossbow from the guard, pulling ahead of the other man easily. He joined Muvumo, hardly breathing hard at all, and glared at Chanwa. She returned his glare with a calm look even though her heart thudded along.

"What is this?" Muvumo finally asked.

A tiny victory. He had broken the silence first. "We have gathered here because we want the Maddion men to hear us. We are tired of being treated as chattel, as inferior, as servants, as whores, as ghosts. We demand to be treated as equal members of the Maddion people. We demand fair treatment, the chance to make decisions for ourselves, an education equal to that of boys and young men, the right to choose whether to live with family or alone or with a partner, and the right to keep our bodies to ourselves if we so choose."

Silence answered. Even the animals of the forest were quiet, as if waiting for Muvumo's reply. There was no wind through the trees, no cough to break the moment. All was still.

Muvumo shifted, and the faint light from a nearby torch glinted off his eyes, which were so dark they looked to be nothing but pupil. A vein throbbed in his neck, pulsing rapidly. Chanwa took a deep breath. Every nerve in her body tingled with anticipation as she waited to see if he'd pull his dagger free and bury it in her, or swing his short axe into her. He couldn't kill them all, she reminded herself. But he might kill her. The women had instructions to carry on if he did. Those sitting on either side of her tightened their grip on her. They were linked arm to arm like fibers woven on a tapestry. She could have sworn they even breathed in together, and out together. Nothing—and no one—could break them.

"Do you remember what I told you about complete obedience?" he finally asked. His voice was low, rumbling, like the growl of a ravenous bear who had been disturbed while eating.

"I do."

He turned to the guard who had spoken with Chanwa. "Bring me a servant. Any one will do."

Most servants lived in a series of rooms carved into the mountain, but this was above them. The guard stepped forward. Chanwa pulled the women on either side of her closer. Behind her and around her, they all shifted until they formed a wall of flesh made of hundreds of women. The guard hesitated.

"I would have to climb over them," he said.

"A few broken bones and scratches are the least of their worries right now," Muvumo said.

Metal scraped on stone behind Chanwa, first in one spot, then another, and another. The guard's gaze flickered back and forth. She didn't look behind her, but she knew if she did, she'd see some hunting spears, some crossbows, some daggers, and a variety of other blades raised and waiting. The guards couldn't plow through the women fast enough to avoid being hurt, and the guards couldn't fight all of them.

Delkis stepped between Muvumo and the women, raising his nocked crossbow to aim directly at Chanwa's heart. At this close range, that arrow would probably go through her and at least one more person behind her. She swallowed hard.

The guards also brandished their weapons, pushing close to Muvumo and Delkis, their attention darting among all of the women on the mesa.

"Stand back," Muvumo said. "I don't need all of this fuss to protect me from women."

The guards seemed only too eager to back away. Delkis stood a moment longer, then lowered his weapon and stood beside Muvumo. He didn't take his eyes off Chanwa, though, and he kept the crossbow ready to fire.

"Go through the homes," Muvumo said. "Find a servant."

The guard gestured for a couple of others to follow. They immediately split up and began going into homes. A few protests drifted out as the guards went through home after home. A couple of people poked their heads out, but Muvumo sent another guard to send them back inside.

Sometimes a servant would stay in someone's home to help care for children or infants or the infirm, but tonight those who were asked to stay were told to mention that they were ill themselves and to insist on being sent to the main living quarters for the servants. There shouldn't be any servants for the guards to find. Still, Chanwa's grip on the other women tightened, and her palms grew sweaty as she waited, her body tensing a little more with each home that the guards darted into.

After the last home, at the far bottom of the stairs, the guards trotted up. "There are no servants, Most Worthy," one said.

Muvumo turned to her. His jaw twitched. His hands curled into fists. She met his gaze and held it. She would not let any of the women depending on her see any fear, and she certainly wouldn't let this man see it, either.

He raised his head and let out a series of piercing whistles that tore through the night sky. Chills ran down Chanwa's spine and through her arms. He couldn't call down his dragon. The beast had nowhere to land. Unless he planned to kill them all using her. But she'd been relying on the fact that he couldn't kill all of them, not when they were trying to rebuild their people. But what if the kasi powder had made him mad? What if he wasn't thinking clearly at all? A thousand other thoughts ran through her mind. A few women murmured behind her, and they began to stir. They might panic and break up the group, running for home.

"Have courage," she said, her voice echoing off the stone rising high above them. "We are brave. Remember all we've been through. Remember all our mothers and grandmothers have been through. Remember that we do this for ourselves and our daughters and our granddaughters."

The guard sneered at her. "We'll see how brave you are before a dragon."

"How brave are *you* before seated women?" called someone behind Chanwa.

He frowned. "Who said that?"

"Maybe your wife," muttered one of the other guards. A couple of them snickered.

The women had found a new source of bravery. That was good, because far above them came the beat of massive dragon wings. Her mouth went dry. How far would Muvumo take this? How far would she let it go? She had believed her life would be the only one in true danger. She never considered Muvumo's anger might urge him to do something like call down his dragon on all of them. Despite the chilly night air, sweat popped out along her forehead and under her arms. *Hold steady*, she told herself.

The dragon emerged out of the darkness, her side pulsing a bright orange as she inhaled and fading as she exhaled. She circled lower, her head snaking back and forth as she realized her landing spot was filled with people. She pulled up and circled nearby.

Muvumo climbed down the stairs. He spoke in a hushed tone with Delkis, gesturing at the dragon, then at the mesa. Delkis looked at the dragon and shook his head vehemently. Their voices raised, but Chanwa couldn't quite catch what they were saying. She felt like leaping up and shouting at them. *Just listen to us, you stubborn bunch of dumb bears.* Would Muvumo truly rather kill them all than talk? Would he see them dead rather than compromise one bit?

She hoped the servants were well on their way to the Taakwa Valley to bring help. She hoped Ankti was already there, safe beneath the barrier. She hoped Ankti would always remember Chanwa fondly even though other members of the Maddion had treated her so poorly.

Muvumo's hand sliced through the air. A guard ran to their home and returned shortly with vellum, ink, and a quill. Muvumo scribbled something on the vellum, hastily spread sand over it, and tied it with the white sash taken from around his waist, adding a small stone to the package. He whirled and whistled sharply to his beast. The dragon circled, dropped lower. Chanwa's breath hitched.

The dragon dove over them. A few women shrieked, ducking their heads. Chanwa waited for the dragon's sides to brighten, for the flames to come pouring out of her mouth.

The beast passed them. Muvumo tossed his message high in the air. The dragon caught it in her claws and banked, then beat her wings to carry her up, toward the mountaintop.

One woman let out a hysterical laugh. Chanwa's heart beat in her throat. No flames. Just Muvumo sending a message to the guardhouse on the mountaintop. What would he have them do? They couldn't remove all the women on the mesas. They couldn't know about the servants she'd sent out, could they?

Muvumo stood over her. "I'm sending out the men stationed at the guardhouse. They are going to look for your Ankti and bring her back." He leaned down and lowered his voice. "I will rip her open on these steps and let her blood flow down them. I will let her cries echo off the mountain. I will make you bathe in her blood." He straightened. "Then, we will hear your demands."

He strode down the steps, followed by Delkis and all the guards save for three who moved down a small distance, as if there was an invisible buffer between them and the women on the mesa. Wave after wave of shaking passed through Chanwa. She should have killed him one of these nights. She should have escaped. A dragon roared high above them, and several answered. She thought of the servants she'd sent to the Taakwa.

"No, my husband," she said quietly after his retreating form. "It will be *your* blood that will flow down these steps."

CHAPTER THIRTEEN

The air crackled and pressed against Malia, making it hard for her to breathe. Andrij had to feel it, too, but he ignored it, ignored the swirling red-orange warning in Cian's eyes, the way he crouched, empty-handed but no less dangerous.

She jumped between Andrij and Cian, holding her hands out to Cian, because he could keep his temper much better than Andrij could. "Give me a chance to explain," she said to Cian. "He doesn't know what's going on. Why don't you go back down?"

"You know this *thing*, Malia?" Andrij asked behind her.

Enuwal got to his feet, and Rina rose, more slowly. They positioned themselves between Andrij and Malia. Ankti stood, her eyes wide and flickering between Cian, Malia, and Andrij. Vedran laid a hand lightly on Andrij's arm, but he jerked it free and moved aside.

Cian bristled at the word 'thing,' but quickly recovered. The swirling of his eyes slowed, and a grin spread across his face. "Didn't she tell you? I'm the *mutara*." He said it bitterly, and yet with relish, as if he both despised the term and enjoyed the fear it provoked. "She asked that I cure her of her memory loss, and then I took this form."

"Malia, how could you?" Andrij asked.

"I didn't ask him for *that*," she said, throwing an angry glance at

Cian. "He's teasing you. Cruelty is his specialty."

Cian's grin faltered, and a sweeping wave of anger burned through her, followed by a dizzying stand at the edge of the precipice. Swaying over darkness… falling… She shook her head. She was here, in this home, with solid stone and rugs beneath her feet.

"He took this form to be cruel to me," she continued. "And now he's using it to be cruel to you."

"Why is he even here?" Andrij asked.

Before she could reply, Cian said, "Malia and I have a special bond now."

Enuwal winced as if struck by a dagger. Vedran gaped open-mouthed at her. Rina pursed her lips and narrowed her eyes, glaring at Cian as if he were a child caught being naughty and not some powerful being. A host of emotions passed over Andrij's face, ending with his mouth turned down at the corners, and his jaw twitching. Ankti watched silently.

"That's not quite true," Malia said.

Andrij shook his head. "You have the audacity to take my brother's form," he said to Cian. "I will kill you for that."

He leaped forward, pushing Enuwal aside. Enuwal stumbled and went down on one knee. Vedran raced forward. Andrij held the dagger low and ready. Malia tensed, frozen in place because there was nowhere to go in this little space, and she didn't want anybody else getting hurt.

Cian shoved her aside. She fell against some shelves, dishes clattering to the floor, and a line of pain blooming along her side from the shelf's hard edge. The smell of magic burned in her nostrils, and the air drummed against her, pressure building in her head and her ears until it was painful.

She shoved the discomfort aside and stood just as Vedran tackled Andrij, sending both of them to the floor. Malia's heart stuttered. If Andrij accidentally stabbed Vedran with that dagger… blood roared in her ears.

Vedran snatched the dagger free from Andrij and scrambled back. Malia shoved Cian out to the ledge. His red-orange eyes swirled in the darkness, leaving bright flashes behind her eyelids whenever she blinked.

"You should go," she said to him.

"You called me."

She shook her head. "I did not."

Movement in the corner of her vision, and Enuwal stood just in the doorway. The sounds of scuffling came from inside, and the light spilling onto the ledge flickered as Vedran sought to keep Andrij from going out.

"You were thinking about me," Cian said. "It's why I came. I thought you might need help."

Enuwal shifted, his face hidden in darkness, but she thought she saw a quick spasm of pain cross. "I was thinking of how to explain you to him," she said through gritted teeth. "If you were truly in my head, you'd know that. Stop twisting the truth."

A grunt came from inside, then Andrij hurtled out, Vedran right behind him. Andrij's narrowed eyes focused on Cian. He had a dagger in his hand, Dalibor's this time. He would never be able to kill Cian, but Cian would surely kill him, and Malia couldn't let that happen, especially not when Andrij had a newborn daughter to take care of. She started forward, Enuwal moving to intercept Andrij, too.

She was going to push Cian off the ledge. She'd seen him leap from a much higher distance in the Maddion's mountains. He might be angry with her for such a thing, but he'd survive. But Andrij moved faster than she thought him capable of, with eyes only for Cian, and he shoved her aside in his haste and anger.

She took a step back to catch herself, and then another. Her second foot landed on only air, and over the edge she went.

Somebody shouted her name. A hand reached for her. Enuwal's face flashed above her as he nearly fell himself trying to grab her hand, her ankle, anything, but she was gone that fast, the air already rushing past her. She didn't have time for fear, or perhaps because of all the times she'd flown in Jegudun memories, falling didn't scare her. Maybe the moment right before she hit the ground, it would.

The smell of magic burned a path through her nostrils and into her lungs just before a jolt of magic struck her body. She caught a glimpse of Cian's red-orange eyes blazing brighter and larger, nearly swallowing her vision. The jolt sent a tingling through her, a buzzing that made her dizzy. But she was slowing down. The cliff face, which had been a blur passing her, came to a stop. She hovered in the air.

She was halfway between Rina's ledge and the ground. The buzzing flowed through her body, and she knew she could either go up, or down. This was better than flying. She'd never been so strong, so in control. She moved smoothly away from the rock cliff and came to a stop. She moved to the rock cliff, close enough to touch it. She turned in a small circle, taking in the valley, stretching out before her in the dark, the stars scattered overhead as if some great being had been playing with bone dice lit from within and let them lay where they had fallen. She could fly, on her own. But this was borrowed power, and she didn't know how long her control would last, so she eased herself down, her feet touching the ground lightly.

Faces peered over the ledge. "Malia!" Enuwal shouted.

She waved an arm. "I'm fine," she called up.

"Something's wrong with you," Vedran shouted, fear tinging his voice.

"No, really, I'm fine."

"Your eyes," he called down. "They're glowing."

She dropped her arm. She couldn't see herself, and she didn't feel any different, although for a while there she'd been powerful. That had felt… good. Really good. But the tingling was already fading, and the smell of magic was clearing from her lungs with each breath, replaced by the scent of crushed grass and pine and her own sweat.

A figure leaped over the ledge and fell like a boulder. She yelped and jumped out of the way, but at the last moment, Cian slowed and landed as lightly as a cougar jumping down from a tree. Blood stained his tunic.

"You're hurt," she said. "You should have Enuwal look at that."

"I'll be fine. Your healer can't help."

"Is Andrij alive?"

He looked up. "He is. But he'll have a terrible headache when he comes to."

Her shoulders slumped in relief, but her hands balled up into fists. "You knew I didn't want you to come. You *knew*. And yet you came anyway. All you did was stir up trouble."

He met her gaze, the red-orange of his eyes faded a little. "You want to know why I'm like this, don't you." It was a statement, not a question. But still, she hesitated, then nodded. "Then come on," he said.

He took off at a bounding run, straight for the field of black boulders. Malia craned her neck, looking up at the ledge, expecting the ladder to come unfurling and for Enuwal and Vedran to come down. Voices drifted down, Andrij's puncturing everybody else's as it rose.

"No, let me go. I got him once already, did you see?"

Cian stood beside her. She gasped and jumped back, her heart stuttering. "Or, we could stay here, and fend him off," he said. "He came to much more quickly than I anticipated."

There was something underlying Andrij's anger as he shouted. Fear. Just like Vedran, he was scared, and the reason stood beside her. And perhaps she, too, had a little to do with their fear. The best thing, for now, would be to let them calm down.

"Let's go, then," she said.

Cian tut-tutted. "The magic I lent you has worn off already. All your excitement burned it off. Here."

He laid a hand on her arm before she could speak, and the buzzing returned, reaching her fingertips, her toes, vibrating in her head and even in her teeth and verging on the edge of pain. This was not the pleasant experience of sharing memories with the Jeguduns. But then the displeasure gave way to power, and to the feeling she could do anything.

He bounded toward the field of boulders again, and this time, she followed. Her legs were no longer fatigued as they had been ever since she'd escaped the Maddion prison. Instead, each stride carried her over a huge portion of ground, and when she reached the boulders, she leaped from one to another easily, as if skipping across a small stream. Her vision was sharper than it had ever been in the dark, outlining the boulders easily. The pine-scented air rushed past her. She nearly laughed at the simple joy of moving so easily and quickly, but the constant buzzing reminded her of the confused, angry, scared people she was leaving behind, and that the cause of it all was the figure ahead of her. The brief joy fell away, replaced by a hard, cold ball of anger.

Cian reached the forest's edge and waited. She leaped off the last rock and ran to him as the magic he'd lent her faded.

"Is this where you've been disappearing to?" she asked with a nod of her head at the dark woods.

"Yes. The boulder field makes it hard for anyone to follow me."

Her sharper vision was fading along with the buzzing. The woods, which had been more like the forest in late twilight, were dark again.

"There's a place just inside the woods where we can sit," Cian said. He strode toward the trees. When she didn't follow, he stopped. "What's wrong?"

"It was one thing for you to lead the way across the boulder field. I wasn't sure where we were going. But if your place is not far, then I lead the way."

"But you don't know where it is."

"Tell me."

He sighed, then mumbled something that sounded a lot like, "You stubborn Taakwa people and your rules."

She ignored his mumbling and walked past him. Her foot caught on a small rock, and she stumbled. "Light, please," she said, her heart thudding in her throat at the near fall.

He held out a hand, and a light flickered above it, like a fire, but without the snap and hiss of one. It cast enough light for her to see well ahead of her. She picked her way through the forest, at one point finding a pair of bright eyes glaring at her from a bush. The animal chattered angrily, then raced away. A fox, startled from its den.

The smell of pine and fir and forest detritus seemed stronger at night than during the day. She threaded her way among the trees, changing direction every so often when Cian spoke softly.

She made her way carefully down a slope, and then to a stream gurgling among rocks. Cian's light gleamed off the water's surface.

"We're here," he said.

She found a flat spot beside the stream and sat, a handful of leaves rustling beneath her weight. Cian sat near her and set the fire from his hand on top of a rock where it burned silently on.

She waited. Although they sat a few hands' breadths from each other, there might as well have been a bottomless chasm stretching the length of ten men between them, so great was the emptiness coming from Cian. It was a palpable ache, pressing against her heart and making it hard for her to breathe, and making her nauseaous. But still, she waited.

Cian sighed. He picked up a tiny pebble and tossed it into the stream with a *plink*, and tossed in another. *Plonk*. He slouched. With his head turned, and the night hiding his features, he could have been any Taakwa man contemplating his sadness, or a great loss. Malia reached for his arm, then set her hand back in her lap. This was still the *mutara*, no matter what he called himself.

"I had a daughter, once," he began. "Kara was only eight years old—eight winters, if you will—when she became sick," Cian said.

The nausea eased, and the chasm between them shrank. Malia took a deep, grateful breath.

"She became listless," Cian said. "Pale. She was a slim child to began with, and she couldn't afford to lose the weight that she did."

"The wasting illness," Malia said. "My father had it."

He nodded. "I tried all the medicines I could. Those I could afford, at any rate. I tried all the remedies people pressed upon me. I tried spiritual healers from every religion, even though I practiced none myself, and I berated myself for not having any faith. I thought perhaps her illness was punishment from a god or gods."

Malia frowned. "Any god who would punish you for a lack of faith by making your child ill would be no better than the cruelest Maddion." Her stomach was almost settled, her mind almost clear, praise the clan mother. "The Taakwa have no religion. We have no gods. We rely on ourselves, and the wisdom we pass down."

"Yes. In all my time on this earth, I have come to see that that is certainly a wise approach. But at the time, I was looking to blame someone, and the only one I could blame was myself.

"Nothing worked. Some remedies gave temporary relief to her symptoms, and some made her worse. She became a ghost of herself, a wisp of a thing. I grew desperate." He swallowed hard.

His emotions returned, twisting Malia's insides into knots of anxiety and terror. She could smell the sickly sweet aroma of illness. She could feel the frailty of Kara's bones beneath her fingertips the way Cian must have. She could feel his desperation spiraling out of control, making her dizzy.

"I... can't," she gasped. "You... too much."

"My apologies."

The experience fled her, but the scent of illness lingered faintly, as did the discomfort in her belly.

Cian bent his knees and wrapped his arms around them, clasping his hands in a most un-Taakwa-like fashion. That, more than the red-orange of his eyes, reminded her just how strange—how much of an Outsider—he truly was.

"What happened then?" Malia asked. *Something* had turned him into this. His desperation, old that it had been, still tasted of sour fear and boiling anger, and lingered in her mind and heart.

He closed his eyes and let his head fall back. The tip of his braided hair brushed the ground. Then he straightened and met her gaze. His eyes swirled slowly. A tiny tremble passed through him, and an unseen wall stood between them. He must be fighting hard to hold his emotions back from her.

"There was an old woman who lived deep in the woods. She was said to be a witch. My mother had spoken of her when I was a child, and she said *her* mother spoke of the old woman when she was a child, too. The woman had always been old, so far as the stories went. Despite the horrid stories of what she had supposedly done—over the years she was blamed for everything from droughts to stillbirths to deals with demons and to cheating husbands and wives—nobody dared force her to leave. Nobody dared get near her, or speak to her.

Every so often it was thought she had finally died, but then some woodsman or hunter would spy her from afar."

He took a deep, shuddering breath. "I went to her one night, carrying my little girl in my arms. She hardly weighed anything, the illness had ravaged her so. I was shaking from tears, from terror, from desperation. I thought the old woman would laugh at me, or turn me away, or turn me into a toad."

Malia let out a soft snort at the image of Cian becoming a toad.

"I told her what I wanted—a cure for my daughter. She looked Kara over. I dreaded those wrinkled, bony fingers prodding at her, but I didn't know what else to do. Finally she looked at me and said she could cure her, but it would require my taking on a burden that she could no longer carry."

"She was a *mutara*," Malia breathed.

He nodded. "She had been one for such a long time that she couldn't remember who she had been, or how long she had lived. She hadn't practiced magic in generations. She wasn't even sure she could help Kara. She only knew that she had to pass on that which gave her the power."

Malia had witnessed Cian's change from Sersha to his current form. It had been as though something else was alive within him, sharing his skin, and it had writhed just beneath the surface for a moment before he had taken on Dalibor's form.

"She pulled out a blade," he went on. "She cut her hand first, then mine. When she touched her hand to mine, it was like… like the most intimate moments I had with my wife, but so much more powerful. It was like we shared the same skin, the witch and I. I could feel her heartbeat slow, and mine quicken. I could feel the power leaving her, and the life leaving her, and it entered me, and it was like being struck by lightning, again and again." He shuddered.

Malia's cheeks warmed. Some of the memory of that pleasure came through, and it was like Enuwal's kisses, or like the sweeter moments when she and Dalibor had first been married and he'd caressed her body. She ducked her head, pretending to study the stream as she waited for the warmth in her cheeks to fade.

"And then it was pain like I've never known," he continued. "It was claws tearing through me, and not just my body, but *me*, cutting me into pieces and then stitching me back together. It felt as though it went on for days, but I'm certain it lasted only moments. When it was over, the witch was on the floor, breathing her last. She said, 'When you create a change, you will change, every time.' And then she died."

Malia knew the pain Cian spoke of. It was the same pain as when he'd altered her mind so she could understand Ankti. It was the same pain as when he fixed her memories and made her mind whole. Only for him, it had been even more intense.

"I could feel what was wrong with my daughter," he said. "It was within her bones, and affecting her blood. In fact, I could feel many new sensations. But I would sort them out later. At the moment, all I cared about was her. I reached out with the magic and cured her. I *changed* her. I made it so the wasting illness not only left her body, but that it would never return, and neither would any other illness. I could see the terror in her eyes. She shrank away from me, but I ignored it and went on with the magic. She was cured, and then... then I changed for the first time."

He fell quiet, but she knew the story wasn't quite over. There was a sense of gathering, as if he needed courage for the next bit. A small animal rustled in a bush, and the stream gurgled on. The red-orange flame he'd set on the rock burned lower, less brightly.

"Of course, since I worked a major change on her, I also worked one on myself," he said quietly. "And I had been thinking of her, and therefore of my late wife, and so when it was over—"

"You looked like her mother," Malia finished.

He nodded. "She was horrified. She ran from me and told me to stay away from her. I made sure she returned home safely, and then I left. Too many people would have recognized my late wife's appearance.

"Kara went to live in an orphanage, I discovered later. I waited until she was grown, and then I went back. I thought maybe enough time had passed that she wouldn't be scared anymore. She had a husband, children of her own. I looked different because I had worked magic again and again for other people, trying to figure out the intricacies of it. But of course, the eyes give me away every time." He grinned ruefully. "Although, if enough time passes, the, ah, appearance of them becomes normal, and I could pass for a regular person.

"She still wanted nothing to do with me. She was convinced that I had cursed her somehow, and not healed her, and she feared me and loathed me. She cried out for the villagers, and they chased me out of town. She led the charge herself, a sword in one hand, a baby in the other arm. My grandchild. I ran for a long time. I never saw her again." He gazed across the stream to the dark woods on the other side. "I have never spoken of that to anyone. Before now." He turned back to her. "This bond that we share, it is most unexpected, but also… welcome."

Malia had thought him dangerous, cruel, deriving pleasure in the suffering of others, but in reality he came to this through desperation, and because of his love for a daughter long gone. She suddenly wasn't sure who had suffered the most over the generations—him, or those whose lives he had affected. She would have doubted his story, if it wasn't for the raw emotion pouring through her. That was something he couldn't lie about.

"What was in the witch's blood? It's now in yours, I assume. Can you pass it on to whomever you wish?" She raised her hands quickly. "Not that I'm asking for you to share with me. I'm merely curious."

He canted his head to one side. "The magic is in my blood, yes. It is… rather like a disease that one can pass on to another. But I do not keep the magic if I pass it on. I die, as the witch died."

They fell silent. Malia ran her fingertip through the dirt, tracing a flower, then a bird. "Did you ever find your grandchildren? Great-grandchildren?"

"Only to check on them, and only a few times. It was too painful to watch them grow old and pass on. I stopped looking for them after a while. I don't even know if any of my descendents live today."

Again, Malia felt as though she stood at the edge of a deep canyon, the bottom so far away that she would never be able to see it, no matter how bright the sunshine might be, or how sharp her vision. It was a vast, echoing emptiness that held nothing but loneliness. She was the only person around. She could turn and walk for days upon days and never find another living person, or she could step off the ledge and fall…

She gasped, jerking away from the vision.

"I'm sorry," Cian said. "That slipped out."

She dug her fingers into the soil around her. "That's all right." Her heart thumped hard and fast.

"Malia," he began hesitantly, "you've done all you can for your people. Things are under way. You don't have to stay. You can come with me now. I can share my power with you because of this connection we have. It felt good to control your descent through the air, didn't it? You felt strong. You enjoyed it."

She thought of Enuwal's words. *He knows you more intimately than I ever will.* Cian didn't know her body. Even though he looked like Dalibor, he wasn't her late husband, and this… *being* had hardly touched her at all. But he knew the emotions running through her, and he knew the thrill that had gone through her when she'd hovered in the air, taking in the forest and valley stretching out before her, and feeling the borrowed power in her veins, rushing through her. That pleasure was a heat deep in her belly, pooling and spreading to her fingertips, her toes, her scalp. Nobody else had ever made her feel that way.

And she hated Cian for it.

She turned and began walking back toward Rina's. "I have a duty to my people. Perhaps you've forgotten what that's like, since you've cut yourself off from your family and anyone else you might ever care about. Once my duty is taken care of, then I'll go with you, but not before."

She strode along without looking back, but she knew he'd follow. She pulled her thoughts in as tight as she could, but she was afraid he'd still feel how turning down his offer was like a deep, regretful ache pulsing in the back of her mind.

CHAPTER FOURTEEN

Chanwa's brothers had been dead for a while. One died in the war against the Taakwa and Jeguduns the summer before, and the other died from the illness back during the first days of it. She couldn't help but wonder what they would have thought of her protest. Both had been older than her and set in their ways. They believed in their authority over women despite the subtle ways their mother had tried to raise them differently. Her methods had been like setting out pebbles in a rushing river and expecting them to impede the water's flow.

But early this morning, just as the sky was lighting up and the birds were singing riotously in the trees, one woman's brother arrived, bearing a huge basket filled with nuts and dried fruit and bread that, while lumpy and unappetizing in appearance, was actually quite tasty. He slunk into their group, greeted by curious and sometimes hostile stares and hushed whispers, and sat a couple of rows behind Chanwa.

"Oriz!" his sister hissed. "What are you doing here?"

"I brought you something to eat. There's plenty to share."

"Oh… thank you."

Chanwa leaned against her sister Nyda with her legs stretched out before her. It reminded her of when she was little and used to climb into Nyda's lap. Their mother's lap was the best, most comfortable place to be, but when their mother couldn't hold her, Chanwa always went to Nyda.

They all took turns stepping away to relieve themselves, or standing and stretching, or sleeping against one another. It was their second night outside, and their first day had been sunny initially, then damp as a rainstorm barreled its way across the mountain. They'd lost only a couple of people despite it all, and those left only because they were too ill with stomach issues to remain outside. The servants remained in hiding, deep within the caverns of the mountain.

Everyone had to be uncomfortable; Chanwa certainly was. Her body was perpetually chilled, her joints ached, and she hadn't had good sleep in quite some time. But overhearing Oriz and his sister revived her. She shifted her weight against Nyda who sighed but said nothing.

"Why did you bring this?" the sister asked.

"Because… I was worried about you, Bertra."

She chuffed softly. "You never seemed particularly worried about me before. Not when father planned for my marriage to a man three times my age, not when the illness took him and I was his sole caregiver, not when I lost my first baby."

"I was worried then, too." His tone became defensive. "I just… oh, this was a horrible idea."

Shoes scuffed against stone. A couple of people protested. Bertra said, "No, don't go, please stay. I'm angry, is all, and tired, and cranky. Please, Oriz, stay."

Clothes rustled. There was a quiet exclamation. "Oh, you brought sweet wine, too," Bertra said. "Thank you."

The sound of a wineskin cork popping out followed. Bertra quietly shared with those around her. Each woman took a sip and murmured thanks. The wineskin reached Chanwa when it was a little less than half empty. She took a sip, relishing in the warmth that spread down her throat to her belly. She passed the wine to Nyda. For a moment, at least, the bone-deep chill was gone.

The other contents of the basket were divied up and passed around, too. Oriz had brought the best, not stale nuts or moldy bread.

"Did you make this yourself?" Bertra asked.

"Yes." Slightly defensive.

"This is good." Her tone was genuine, and surprised. "When did you learn to make bread?"

Silence, then, "I watched Meera all the time. I loved the way she moved. Everything was so graceful, so purposeful." His voice cracked on the last word.

"I'm sorry, Oriz. I know you loved her."

A deep sigh. "I guess she's the reason I'm here. Or part of it. You are, too."

"Oh?"

Nyda tensed behind Chanwa. She could almost feel the expectant, held breaths of the women around her. They were all listening but pretending that they weren't.

"We were close when we were children," Oriz said. "Do you remember how we'd play together? I always wanted a brother—"

"But you were stuck with me," she finished with a smile in her voice, as if she'd finished the phrase many times before.

He chuckled. "And you always wanted a sister. So I suppose we're even." He sobered. "You were actually quite good at climbing."

"For a girl?"

"For anyone."

Silence, only broken by shallow breaths. Somewhere from the mesa high above them, a baby started crying. Though it was early, dragons circled high overhead near the mountain peak. They didn't appear to be hunting, nor were they younglings playing. They were simply moving, moving, moving, like they wanted to fly away, but something unseen held them back.

"Do you remember," Oriz continued, so quiet that Chanwa strained to hear. "When our father was asleep at night, how I would teach you letters?"

The hush was so loud that it roared in Chanwa's ears like a waterfall. Even the baby had fallen silent.

"Yes," Bertra finally said. "Oriz, you could get in trouble for admitting that."

"No more trouble than you're in already. You were smart, Bertra. *Are* smart. When I left for training that first morning… dragon's breath, but you looked so sad. I was going off to learn, and you had to stay home. I didn't say anything to anyone at the time, but I thought it was so unfair. We shared so much from even before we were born. Our mother's womb, her loss, laughter, tears, scrapes, games. Then it all changed that day. I kept on moving ahead, and you—"

"Didn't," she finished.

"Yes. And I think it's time that you move ahead, Bertra. That's why I'm here. I know I'm not the only man to feel that way. One of us has to be the first to sit with all of you."

"Oriz, I… I don't know what to say. This is the greatest thing that anyone has ever done for me."

Chanwa reached her hand back and squeezed Nyda's. She finally turned around and smiled at her sister. Tears glimmered in Nyda's eyes, but she returned the smile.

"I would say," Nyda whispered, "that she is probably very proud of her brother right now. I know I'm very proud of my sister."

Chanwa swallowed the lump in her throat and blinked rapidly before the tears could properly form. Their sister Prali had visited them the day before, but contractions had sent her home before she could spend much time with them. Prali wouldn't be back. Her husband would never allow her to leave again so long as this protest went on. But Nyda was here. Chanwa was so glad that at least one person who loved her—and whom she loved—sat beside her.

"As I'm proud of mine," Chanwa said.

She looked at something behind Chanwa's shoulders and sobered quickly. "The Most Worthy comes."

Chanwa braced herself and turned around to face her husband.

He strode up the stairs with several guards trailing. The men's clothes look bedraggled, their faces lined and haggard, their shoulders hunched slightly, save for Muvumo. He walked tall, his eyes bright and focused on a spot behind Chanwa, and came to a stop two steps below her. The fingers of his left hand drummed against his leg while his right hand rested on the hilt of his dagger. His fingers tap, tap, tapped away as if reflecting the rapidity of the thoughts flying through his head.

"I was hoping that after spending a couple of nights outside, you would all have come to your senses," he began, his voice carrying and echoing off the stone rising in a sheer wall over them. "Instead, I find a man hiding behind your skirts. Oriz, aren't you one of my own men? A warrior? A dragonrider?"

Chanwa faced Oriz for the first time since he'd sat beside his sister. He was lanky, with wheat-gold hair worn in long, twisted ropes loose around his head. His face was all angles, and the apple of his throat bobbed as he swallowed. His eyes were bright green, like spring grass, and filled with quiet determination. He slowly stood, graceful for someone so tall and spare.

His sister, Bertra, echoed his build. The delicate lines of her bone structure reminded Chanwa of a small thrush, as did the way her hand fluttered up as if she'd yank him back down. He held a hand out to her. *It's all right*, that gesture said. The acid churning in Chanwa's stomach belied that sentiment. Muvumo looked ready to hurt someone, and the most obvious target at the moment was Oriz.

"I am indeed one of your own men, Most Worthy," he said, dipping his head. "I am also brother to Bertra, and I was husband to Meera, who died from the illness. My wife was a bright woman. I could see her frustration at days filled with monotony, at her stunted education. She told me once that she was relieved to have married me because I was one of the few who would have treated her nicely." He swallowed again, his throat bobbing. "Meanwhile, my sister was sent to share a bedroll with a man who could have been our grandfather. He treated her no better than a servant. I've seen bruises on her, and although she never spoke of them, I know they hurt her heart as much, or even more, than they hurt her flesh.

"I agree with our lady Chanwa. The changer gave us a second chance. I think we should spend it on rebuilding our people rather than on vengeance. We've lost enough of our people to the illness and to the war with the Taakwa and Jeguduns. I am ready for a home filled with children and a wife who is content with her life and who doesn't feel stifled."

Muvumo had been breathing rapidly, shallowly, the entire time Oriz had been speaking, his eyes narrowed. But now he took a deeper breath, his chest expanding. It was the inhalation before a burst of action, before a thrown punch, or a thrown weapon, and given how several rows of women filled the space between Muvumo and Oriz, it would be a weapon that would fly, and not his fist.

The deep chill and the aches dissipated as Chanwa rose. If Oriz died, other men who might join them would be discouraged from doing so, and they needed all the help they could get, especially from those who had—on the surface, at least—always gained the most from the Maddions' traditional way of life.

Someone yanked her back just as she reached her feet. A figure hurtled past her. Chanwa reached out and grabbed nothing but air. She noticed only swirling skirts, and the sky and the mountain spinning, and voices rising, and then she was landing on hands that lowered her slowly, and she was shouting for them to let her go and let her fight.

She scrabbled to one knee, gasping, shrugging off the hands. Somebody screamed, and the sound pierced her like a blade. She whirled, preparing to find Oriz dead or dying.

Instead, she found her sister Nyda crumpled on the ground at Muvumo's feet, his dagger in his hand, coated with blood.

Chanwa crawled on her hands and knees, ignoring the hard stone, ignoring the sharp pain, because the sudden pain deep inside was far worse. It yawned like a crevice, and she teetered on the edge, peering into complete darkness.

"Nyda," she gasped when she reached her sister. She brushed back her sister's dark hair and met Nyda's eyes, but her life had flown from them already. Nyda was gone, leaving behind only this body as empty of life as Chanwa's heart was suddenly empty. A wail built from deep inside, like an earthquake building and preparing to shake the earth, but she swallowed it back. Gasping, she slowly pushed herself to her feet and faced Muvumo.

He pointed the dagger at her. A drop of blood hung on the edge, hovering, so perfect and round and so very dark, and then it fell to the stone. Nyda's life, gone to feed the mountain and the madness that resided in it.

"This didn't have to happen," he said. "She attacked me, and I had to choice but to defend myself. What it comes down to is that she died because of this game you're playing. Give it up now, before others get hurt. Come home where you belong, and put this all behind you."

She knew what Nyda would say. *He only cares for you because you might be carrying his child. His* son. *Otherwise, you'd be lying dead on the stairs, too.*

"I am exactly where I belong," she said through gritted teeth. "All of the women behind me? They are my sisters, too. And the men behind me are my brothers. You, however, are a monster."

His eyes narrowed, and he clenched the dagger tight enough to turn his knuckles white. Chanwa braced for him to lunge at her.

But he whirled and hurried down the steps, all the guards but three following. Those that remained behind took up stations a few steps down, keeping their faces carefully averted.

Chanwa sank to the ground beside her sister and gazed toward the Taakwa Valley. Help had to arrive soon. She thought again of her scrolls burning as she ran her hands through Nyda's hair, the tang of blood sharp in the air.

When help *did* arrive, she would see that Muvumo paid for this. She would take the anger burning in her veins and bring it to life, burning him with it as he'd burned her scrolls, as he'd destroyed her sister.

CHAPTER FIFTEEN

The first night out, Aru and the other Jeguduns managed to find a place to hide in the foothills of the Maddion's mountains. Dragons were most active during the day, so he and the others kept hidden and rested that first day, each of them taking turns watching the skies. One group of Maddion scouts went out early, then came back that afternoon, empty-handed so far as he could tell. The way they flew home, slow and easy, suggested they had no idea the barrier was gone. Otherwise, they'd be headed straight for the Most Worthy with their news. The Jeguduns and Taakwa were safe, for one more night at least.

The next night, the Jeguduns went their separate ways, each aiming for a different part of the woods so that, should any of them get caught, the others had a chance to escape. Aru was normally a firm believer in numbers, but they would be safer this way.

He found a spot near the Maddion's homes first and nestled beneath a spruce, between a blueberry bush and a juniper bush, their various smells filling his nostrils, along with the scent of rabbits who had taken shelter in the brush some time during the day. And, when the breeze blew just right, it brought the smell of brimstone and charred meat. Dragons. He shuddered. He would head toward their roost later.

Even as he had volunteered for this, part of him had been screeching in protest. Like all Jeguduns, he carried the collective memories of what had happened to their ancestors when they had been Maddion slaves. His people had carved those homes and stairs and caverns into the mountain, had struggled under the burden of carrying food, water, and other goods to the Maddion, had paid in blood for any transgressions, real or imagined, against their masters. Rage and terror and desperation rolled through him along with the screams, the smell of blood, the roar of dragons, and the roar of men bent on total domination. His nostrils flared and he gave his head a little shake.

He blamed himself in part for allowing Malia to leave the valley. If he'd just told someone else what she was planning, they could have helped him stop her. Then she would have never met the changer, never agreed to the magic that made the barrier disappear.

Never have her mind back.

He sighed. He had envisioned himself a hero. *The Jegudun who saved the heroine of the Dragon War.* What a puffed chest he'd had. He had ignored the lessons of history and instead let his imagined future guide him. But more than that, he wanted to help his friend. Malia had taken a huge risk when she'd befriended Tuvin. At the time, her people feared his people. She created what eventually became a bridge between them.

Focus, he reminded himself again. Fretting would do no good. He needed to make a cursory check on the Maddion, then make his way up the mountain to the dragons' roost. He scooted forward and peered through the brush, expecting to find a minimum number of torches burning along the stairs, and guards and perhaps a few people out, but torches blazed all along the stairway, and on the mesas—

At first he thought there must be some ceremony going on with so many people gathered and so much light. But then he realized that nearly all the people on the mesas were women, and they were sitting quite solemnly. Guards lined the stairs. Were the women under arrest? But it looked like all of the Maddion women, or nearly so, were outside. They couldn't *all* be under arrest.

A white door covering rustled, and the Most Worthy, notable because of his white sash, emerged along with an armed man who must be his personal guard. Several other guards fell in behind him as he led the way up the stairs. All of the men looked a little worse for wear, their shoulders tense, their faces drawn. The Most Worthy stopped a few steps down from the women, and a heated conversation, judging by the movement of his arms and that of the women in front of the crowd on the mesa, ensued. Interestingly, his personal guard remained quite close to him, and several guards stood between him and the women. He *feared* them.

Aru's breathing quickened. The women had staged a protest. The men, save for a few who must have been on the mountaintop when it happened, were grounded. They could go nowhere, not unless the Most Worthy was willing to have their dragons land on their women, and he would never do that, not when their numbers dwindled already.

He chuffed and leaned forward, his talons digging into the soft earth. He couldn't wait until he could fly home and bring everyone the good news.

He still had to observe the dragons. He hesitated. This protest was great news, and it meant the Jeguduns and Taakwa could strike without fearing a mounted Maddion army fighting them. But he had no way of knowing how long it would last. By the time he got back and told them, and they gathered and returned, this could be over. Malia wanted information about the dragons.

But she'd want to know about this, too.

The last time he'd taken the initiative, he'd helped her leave the valley, and it had resulted in the deaths of four Jeguduns who had come looking for them, and Malia's run-in with the changer, which led to the barrier's disappearance. No, this time, he would do exactly as he'd been told. No special heroics, no detours. He'd spend some time observing the dragons, then leave the following night. Whatever was going on with the Maddion, it would either wait or sort itself out.

He put distance between himself and the Maddion's homes before beginning the trek up the mountain. He flew low over the trees when he could. As he neared the dragons' roost, he kept to the ground, scrabbling across loose dirt and small rocks, clinging to trees and brush, making his way to a boulder clinging precariously to a ledge, surrounded by brush that would make a great hiding place and yet allow him to watch the roosts' entrances just overhead.

The breeze changed directions, rustling the branches of pine and spruce and aspen. It also brought the stench of decay.

Aru froze. He raised his head and sniffed the air, picking out pine resin, vegetation rotting on the forest floor, the faint whiff of a bear, and more strongly, the smell of something dead. The smell was nearly overwhelming, which meant there was a lot of dead… whatever they were, or it was something big, like a dragon.

Except, dragons left nothing to waste. They ate their own dead, the savage beasts. So the only reason they might not is if there was something wrong with the dead dragon.

Aru crept toward the smell, stopping every so often to prick his ears and sniff the air. No other large, living creatures were out here with him, and he didn't expect any. Dragon hide was tough, and even if an animal made it through, there was the fire sac to consider. Even a small leak could taint the surrounding meat, and consuming the fire sac's contents could make one very sick, or even kill. Dragons, however, could eat one another without worrying about such things.

And yet, they might have left one of their own here.

At the edge of a small meadow, he stopped. Star and moonlight revealed the large outlines of several dead dragons in the midst of tall summer grass and wildflowers. They weren't younglings, but they weren't adults, either. They were adolescents, and though it was hard to judge for certain, he thought most of them were male.

The stench of decay mingled with that of brimstone, and Aru gagged. He moved quickly from the meadow until the smell ebbed, then made his way higher.

So many dead dragons… he was never sad to see a dead dragon, but what could have done it? There were no marks on them, so they hadn't challenged any mature dragons. As far as he could tell by sniffing the air, there was no disease among them, so no illness had killed them. What could have happened? He headed up the mountain.

Not far away, he found another pile of dead dragons, again adolescents. He wondered how many such piles there were, and if it had anything at all to do with the women's protest.

It took him most of the night, but eventually he found a spot where he could watch the wide, dark openings that led to the dragons' roosts. Like the Jeguduns' homes, they had ledges outside the roost, although much grander in size. There were no collective memories of building those caves or those ledges among the Jeguduns, and so the story went that the dragons had carved them out of the mountain themselves. Aru pulled himself in small and tight and waited to find out what the dragons might have to tell him.

A scuffle came from the huge ledge above. He froze, ears pricked, nostrils flared to pick up whatever clues he could. *The dragons didn't come out at night.* Not to hunt, not to socialize or mate. Grunts and the sound of something scraping along stone echoed. No beasts took to the air. So they weren't out to hunt. What were they doing, then? His heart fluttered like the wings of a hummingbird.

A dark figure appeared at the rim of the ledge, hovering for a moment before it dove off. Aru bit back a squawk that would alert the beast to his hiding place. But it wasn't flying; it was falling. Its flaccid limbs and folded wings told him it was dead and so no harm to him. And yet… given where it would land, it would roll directly toward him.

He fought the urge to fly away. The dragons on the ledge would surely see him if he did. He tried to run parallel to the slope and out of the path the dead dragon's body would take, but his short legs weren't meant for such a pace. He bared his teeth, curses silently streaming through his mind as he waddled along, grasping at tree trunks to help steady him. A few steps along, and he was already panting.

The body hit the ground with a thud somewhere just behind Aru's hiding spot. He paused, one hand on the tree and the other on his knee, panting. He used to pity humans for having no choice but to use their legs to get around, but long legs certainly had their advantage.

Something big crashed through the trees over him. Aru's heart leaped into his throat, and he ran forward. He managed one step before the second dead dragon landed beside him and rolled down the slope. Aru leaped aside, but was pulled up.

His foot and lower leg were pinned between the tree and the dead dragon.

The sound of rushing blood roared in his ears, and his panic was like a hive of humming bees, drowning out any other sounds. He took a deep breath, searched for his most peaceful memory—the first sunrise of spring, three past, where he and the other Jeguduns silently watched the sun emerge from the dark east as they sang in the season—and let it bring calm into him.

He braced himself against the tree and gave an experimental tug. His foot didn't budge. He gave a harder tug, pulling until pain lanced through his leg. Nothing.

Another scrape against the stone ledge above was the only warning before another body dropped nearby. Aru held back a whine, waiting to see if the dead dragon would roll against this one. Branches cracked nearby, then all went still again.

None of the other dead had been found close to the dragons' roosts. Which meant they might come down here and move them at some point. Aru tugged at his leg frantically. The dead dragon shifted, pinning a bit more of his leg against the tree. He bared his teeth and shook his head. No more brute force. He had to think this through.

He'd seen trapped animals gnaw off their own appendages to escape. He grimaced. That idea was wholly unappealing. He couldn't cut down the tree. But he *could* slice at the dead dragon and maybe create enough give to slide his leg free. He just had to make sure he didn't puncture its fire sac.

He made a careful cut with his talon against the beast's abdomen, but the cut was *too* careful and did nothing but nick the dragon's hide. He took a deep breath and cut again, pressing harder this time.

He let out a startled gasp when his talon dove suddenly into the dragon's hide. Warm blood seeped out, and its iron tang filled the air. Aru grimaced and continued to pull his talon through flesh. It was slow going as the hide was so tough, and he was dangerously close to the fire sac.

The cut was about the length of his forearm when something snuffled overhead on the ledge. He froze. He'd been silent in his work, but perhaps the dragon up there could smell the freshly spilled blood.

Large talons scraped against stone, and then wings beat the air. Aru fought his rising panic and tugged at the dead dragon's flesh, his hand and talons awash in blood.

A pungent smell assailed his nostrils. He'd hit the fire sac. Tears filled his eyes as fumes rose from it. He pulled at his leg. The dragon's cut flesh allowed some give, but not enough. He placed his hand, slick with blood, on the tree trunk to brace himself so he could turn from the fumes and breathe and think, but his hand slipped.

That was it. His eyes and nostrils stung as he wiped blood along his leg, reaching as far down as he could and letting the rest dribble down. Wings beat closer overhead. If that dragon landed in the nearby clearing, it could easily spot him. He worked faster, until his leg was slick with the dragon's blood. Then he braced himself and pulled.

His leg didn't budge. He grit his teeth, his eyes swelling shut from the fumes, and pulled again, grunting with the strain. The tree tops swirled and rustled in the dragon's passage, and the beast sniffed at the air. Aru renewed his efforts.

His leg eased out a smidge, the tree bark scraping at his tender flesh as it did so. He bit back a whimper and pulled again. Every pull won him a tiny bit of freedom.

Now he could see the dragon. It was a dark, massive shadow blotting out the stars, and it was slowly making its way down. He pulled hard this time, choking on a yelp as the rest of his leg came free, leaving behind a burning trail of pain from where the bark scraped him.

He fell, panting. He had no time for rest, though, because the dragon was coming in for a landing just up the slope. He got to his legs and fell again. Pinpricks of pain, like thousands of tiny ant bites, raced up and down his recently captured leg, and it simply wouldn't hold him. But he couldn't fly out of here; he'd be spotted instantly. With his eyes stinging and shut from the fumes, he pushed himself to his feet again. One hand reached out blindly and found a tree to steady himself. Then he stumbled down the slope.

He was making noise, but so was the dragon about to land. Its wings were brushing against trees and sending branches whirling against one another. Aru opened his eyes long enough to spot some kind of brush ahead. The fumes from the dead dragon's fire sac still filled his lungs to the point where he couldn't smell anything else. He stumbled into the brush and collapsed, panting hard.

The dragon landed on the slope above. Its feet scraped at the dirt, sending little rocks sliding. It sniffed hard. Normally, it would have smelled Jegudun, but the fumes from the fire sac were so strong they might actually cover Aru's scent. The dragon would pursue a Jegudun, but perhaps not another injured animal. At any rate, Aru was too tired to go on. The pain of a thousand ant bites lingered in his leg.

The dragon fell silent. Aru closed his eyes. He recalled one day as a youngling when he and his friends had gradually flown closer and closer to Tuvin's Falls. Droplets of water covered him on each pass, cooling him on that hot summer day. They whistled and trilled, the sound of their fun echoing off the cliffs. That had been a great day. So simple in its fun, and so beautiful because of its simplicity.

The dragon chuffed, and then wings beat at the air. The beast returned to the roost high above. Aru waited for the worst of his trembling to pass, and then, assured more dragons wouldn't be forthcoming, made his slow, painful way down the slope to a stream where he could clean himself.

CHAPTER SIXTEEN

Rozik led the pitifully small group of scouts on dragonback along the rolling hills and grassy plains that made up the land between the Maddion's mountain home and the Taakwa Valley. The wind rushed past him, tugging at the braided ropes of his hair. The dragon was warm beneath him.

He couldn't believe the women's protest had gone on for so long. The Most Worthy needed to put them in their place, clear the mesas, and allow life to resume. With the illness, many things had changed for the Maddion. He didn't want any more change. He wanted predictability and the comforts of home. Even the dragons must be feeling the disturbance, because they'd been plenty agitated over the past few days, coming and going far more often than usual, and circling the mountain for no apparent reason, like an impatient man pacing.

He and the other riders were spread out, slowly winding their way across the possible routes the escaped servant and Taakwa woman might have taken on their way to the valley. They had been gone a while and most likely had already made it to the safety of the valley, the cowards, but he wasn't in a position to question the Most Worthy.

The sun was halfway between its zenith and the western horizon as

Rozik made yet another pass over the grassy plains. The Taakwa Valley was a dark, wide rift in the distance. Occasionally, several Jeguduns would fly out and approach him or one of his other men, but they never got too close. It was as expected, the filthy creatures reminding them whose valley that was.

His body ached from spending most of the day in the saddle, and he longed to sleep in his own home, on his own bedroll, which he padded with a second one so it was extra soft, and which he unfurled on top of a plush rug his grandmother had made, which made his bedroll even *more* comfortable. Instead, he'd most likely be sleeping on the threadbare mat in the guardhouse on the mountaintop with half a dozen other men, all of whom had begun to annoy him. The belches and farts and ribald jokes reminded him of his days as a very young man, when he was first training to become a warrior. He much preferred gentler, softer company these days.

But that would have to wait, especially if the women hadn't resolved their protest. He sincerely hoped they had given up and when he and his men returned home, the mesas would be empty save for a messenger boy or two. A soft bed and the soft arms of a woman sounded achingly wonderful right now.

He was so lost in his daydream about perhaps even bringing home *two* unmentionables to keep his bedroll warm that he almost didn't notice the movement in the tall grass. And, he might have even dismissed the movement as coming from a deer or some other creature if not for the flash of skin before the figure disappeared again into the tall grass.

He raised one arm and circled it several times. The man nearest him returned the signal and aimed his beast closer to Rozik, flying in a deceptively calm fashion as if they hadn't spotted prey.

Rozik circled back around slowly. Shadows were lengthening, making it a little tricker to spot details in the tall grass. He flew lower, gaze darting as he sought any little thing that didn't belong in the grass.

There. He almost missed it. A figure huddled in the grass, wearing the clothes of a Maddion servant. She'd actually made it quite far. If she'd traveled through the coming night, she probably would have been in the Taakwa Valley by daybreak. Too bad for her that Rozik spotted her first. He brought his dragon lower, circling around. It wouldn't do to land and then have to chase the servant on foot, especially if the servant proved fleet. He'd have to come down practically on top of the woman. He wished he carried a net like the sort they used during hunts for bigger animals, like bison, when they had to carry the flesh back home. Then he could drop it on top of her.

She looked up and glared at him, then took off at a run. Rozik pressed his left leg against his dragon's side to turn her after the servant. The other Maddion urged his dragon ahead of her to box her in. She had nowhere to go, no way to outrun them, but she didn't falter for a moment. Rozik grudgingly admired her for it.

He flew in low, coming upon her quick even though he had the dragon slow down. He unstrapped his legs and brought both of them to one side. He'd have to time his jump well, otherwise the wing might clip him and send him sprawling, or break a bone. He hadn't practiced moving dismounts in a while. The ground seemed to rush up at him, the grass passing in a blur. One hand gripped the pommel and the other the saddle's edge as they came up to the woman. Wait… wait… and *jump.*

The wing passed close enough to tug at his hair and he was falling, and then he was on his feet, his knees bent to cushion the landing, and he rolled. He popped up to his feet, the roll timed perfectly, and tamped down the inner crow of pleasure at a perfect jump. He whirled, and found the woman had turned. The second Maddion was forced to make a sweeping turn to follow her. Rozik sprinted after.

She turned as he caught up to her, a dagger flashing. He jumped aside, fabric ripping. His heart hammered against his breastbone. *She almost stabbed me.* He rushed in and grabbed the arm holding the dagger. He had it out of her hand in a moment and quickly checked for more hidden weapons. She was shouting at him, pummeling him with her other hand. He grabbed that one, too, and used his sash to tie her hands behind her back.

She was olive-skinned, with dark, curly hair that had come free of her head covering. A few lines fanned out from her eyes. She glared. She matched the description of the servant the Most Worthy had sent them out to find. He grinned. Bringing this servant back would most likely crush the women's silly protest, if the Most Worthy was going to use her as an example.

"Where's the Taakwa woman?" he asked.

Silence. A tremble passed through her body, but given the hatred in her expression, it might be from anger rather than fear.

"Things will go better for you if you tell me where she is." He doubted that was true, but if he could bring back *both* of them, he might be able to trade his striped sash in for the deep purple of a Peerless.

She spat on him.

He backhanded her. She staggered but held her ground. He whistled for his dragon. She landed nearby, her massive wings stirring the tall grass. The other rider landed also and hurried to help Rozik pull the woman along and hoist her onto the saddle. The other rider strapped one of her legs in as Rozik took care of the other, then he climbed into the saddle and strapped himself in. The dragon launched into the air, and soon they were speeding to the Maddion's mountain.

The second rider quickly gathered the remaining Maddion, and they all turned for home. The shadows were long, and it was already dark in the deepest crags of the mountain by the time they arrived. The torches lining the stairway burned. The women were still sitting on the mesas.

He made a pass near the Most Worthy's home and called out to the guards. The other men continued to the mountaintop and the guardhouse. He circled around, and on his next pass, the Most Worthy stood outside.

"I have the woman," he called out, the wind snatching at his words. "I'll drop her to you on the next pass."

The moment he freed her, she began wriggling. "You're making it difficult," he said through gritted teeth. "But that's all right. I enjoy a challenge."

To get over the stairway, he would have to guide the dragon so that she was practically at a ninety degree angle to the ground. He grunted as the woman struggled even harder. They neared the stairs, and he kept his left knee digging into his dragon's side. She kept turning, and it was getting awfully hard to keep somewhat upright and hold onto the woman. The stairs were approaching fast, and if he screwed this up, the Most Worthy would be the Most Displeased, and Rozik could say farewell to ever having that purple sash. Time to drop her... *now.*

He dropped her and flew on. She screamed behind him, the sound abruptly cut off. He circled around, his heart pounding.

The guards had her. Rozik had made the delivery. He grinned as he urged his dragon to the mountaintop where the last of the sun's rays glimmered off the stone guardhouse. He would share dinner with the other men, then return to check on the Most Worthy's progress with ending this protest. Things would begin to return to normal tonight, thanks to him.

Chanwa could only watch with hands clenched in her lap as the dragonrider came in with a squirming, human bundle on his saddle. All she could make out, as the figure fell, was that it was a woman dressed in servant's clothes. When Ankti had left, she had been dressed as a man, not wearing a dress as this woman, so it must be one of the servants who had escaped the other night. Her hands unclenched and she reminded herself to breathe as she battled relief and terror simultaneously. It wasn't Ankti, but it *was* someone Muvumo would use against her.

Nyda's dried blood stained the stairs. At first, she couldn't look at the spot, but she forced herself to do so now. She had to remember her sister's courage and sacrifice. She had to remember what Muvumo was capable of. Chanwa closed her eyes. That poor captured servant.

The smell of woodsmoke was sharp in the air, and mingled with the smell of burnt food from one of the homes, presumably the one from which a man's curses emanated. It would have been funny, if only the women weren't sitting outside in protest, if only Nyda hadn't died. If only. But it was a sign that the men were uncomfortable, and that was a good thing. Discomfort forced change.

Now that the sun had set, the air was rapidly growing chilly. She shivered. Not that she wasn't already cold before the sun set. The rage and grief that had come on after Muvumo had killed Nyda had not gone anywhere, but she *had* pushed them aside so she could focus on the needs of the women relying on her. And yes, on the handful of men who had joined them. Most were young, like Bertra's brother, Oriz, but there were a couple of older men, too. In fact, some of the younger men had joined them just after they had carried away Nyda's body. Chanwa should have gone with it, to help prepare it for the pyre, but she was needed here. And there would be no pyre until a dragon could land to carry Nyda's body to the mountaintop. Until then, her body rested in the cold depths of the mountain.

Bertra sat beside Chanwa, her legs drawn up with her dress pulled down over them, and her chin resting on her knees. "What if they found the other servants, too?"

"The others are fine," Chanwa said, opening her eyes. "At least one of them should reach the valley tomorrow." Barring any other unforeseen problems. "We'll get help soon."

Bertra nodded, but she bit at her lower lip, giving away how anxious she felt. She patted Bertra's hand. "Truly, it will all be fine."

Bertra flashed a smile, the tension fleeing her face. They put so much faith into her. Chanwa couldn't let them down. She glanced at the cavern where their food and water supply sat. They'd been out here three nights. She had considered it might take time to convince the men to hear her out, but their supplies were already dwindling at an alarming rate. Without the dragons, none of them could leave to hunt or work the crops. At least during the rainstorms they could gather some water, but their strength would flag without food. And during each night, a small trickle of women left. They had children they worried over, or their own illnesses to tend. She couldn't blame them. And yet, she needed every body she could get to fill the mesa.

Scuffling on the stairs drew her attention. She couldn't make out what they were doing to the servant. The guards' bodies blocked her view.

Muvumo glanced her way and spoke to the guards. The thud of fist against flesh followed, again and again. Chanwa was on her feet before she knew it.

"No," Bertra said. She stood right beside her. "He wants you to leave us. Then he'll have you, and he won't let you back. He knows we're scared, and you're the one holding us here. He knows you're the one giving us strength."

She swallowed the lump in her throat. "But they'll beat her to death."

"We're all beaten if you leave." She kept a hand on Chanwa's arm and turned. "Here, give me that spear." She hefted the hunting spear another woman handed her. "My lady Chanwa, please step back."

"If you kill Muvumo, they'll kill you."

"This is only a warning."

Chanwa moved two steps back. Bertra held her left arm out straight and brought her right arm back with the spear, the shaft held gently between her fingers like a large quill. In one fluid movement, her left arm dropped, her weight shifted, and her right arm came forward, releasing the spear. She pulled Chanwa back into the crowd of women right before it hit the stone stairs beside Muvumo's foot. He whirled, Delkis already shoving his way between the Most Worthy and the crowd on the mesa, but all they would see were the women and a few men sitting and watching.

Muvumo barked an order, and the guards dragged the servant up the stairs behind him as he climbed. Anger lined his face as he stepped over the dried stains where Nyda had bled her life onto stone. Chanwa's deep, bitter cold gave way as rage—hot as a dragon's flames—pushed forward. She shoved it down. Not now. Later.

Muvumo gestured behind him, and Delkis brought the servant forward. She stumbled but caught herself before she fell. Frathiel. She was one who had been born in the mountains, born into service for the Maddion. She met Chanwa's gaze and nodded once, her jaw set in a determined line. She had given nothing away despite the bloody cuts on her face and her eyes, already swelling shut.

"I find it no coincidence that a servant escaped during this little disturbance," Muvumo said. "Did you send her to the Taakwa? Do you really think they'll help you when they live as cowards beneath their barrier? *No one* is coming to help you. Give this up," he said with a wave of his hand at those gathered behind her as if they were bothersome flies.

Despite the cool air, sweat beaded along his forehead, and he couldn't quite stand still, as if he itched all over. So, he didn't have more kasi powder, and neither did anyone below this mesa. Chanwa bit the inside of her cheek to keep from smiling. She brushed a finger over the tiny packet hiding in the inner pocket of her dress.

"If you haven't come to discuss the terms we presented to you, then you are wasting your time and your breath," she said. "However, if you wish to discuss the issues that we have with the way women and servants are currently treated, then we may talk."

His eyes narrowed. "I told you that if you could not return home and be an obedient wife to me, then people would suffer."

"I would say I've already suffered plenty," she said, pointing to her sister's dried blood.

Delkis shifted, his lips thinning. The guards stared ahead impassively, but one of them swallowed hard. Muvumo, however, remained as strained and tight as a crossbow ready to fire. He shoved Frathiel to her knees before him and slipped his dagger free.

"No," Chanwa began, but before she could get any more out, he slid the blade across Frathiel's neck. The servant's mouth opened as blood poured out of the wound, but all that came out was a final sigh. Muvumo let go of her, and she slumped forward, her fresh blood mingling with the dried blood Nyda had left behind.

"This death is on your hands, too," Muvumo said, cleaning his blade on the hem of Frathiel's skirt before sheathing it. "You can stop this any time by dispersing and returning home where you belong." He turned and trotted down the stairs as nonchalantly as if he simply needed to return home to dinner, Delkis at his heels.

Chanwa's stomach churned. "Oh, Frathiel," she whispered.

She prepared to mourn another night. Silently, she wished the other escaped servants a speedy arrival at the Taakwa Valley. She wasn't sure how much longer she could hold out before she either lost her courage altogether or before she couldn't hold herself back any longer from trying to kill her husband.

CHAPTER SEVENTEEN

Malia spent the next few days waiting for Aru and the other Jeguduns to return with information about the Maddion and their dragons. Each day felt like one closer to finding dragons flying over their valley, and Maddion men on the ground with their weapons, and dragon flames burning anyone and anything they could. Vedran and Andrij hunted, bringing back rabbits one day, a turkey the next. They also helped the Jeguduns work their crops, returning home in the evening with sweat sheening their brows and making their tunics cling to their backs.

Enuwal spent his days searching for and collecting herbs. He, too, came back sweaty, with a basket filled to show his progress. Ankti insisted on helping Rina around the house, giving her lessons on her language the whole time, and learning more of the Taakwa language as well.

That left Malia with little to do. She tried making pottery, but each time she tried to make something, whether coils for a bowl or shaping little chunks of clay into a deer or fish or bird, it didn't work. It wasn't that her fingers didn't know what to do, or she'd forgotten how to make something, it was that she couldn't connect with the task. Her mind kept turning to Aru and the Maddion and Cian, and the careful way Rina and her guests and the *mutara* all stayed out of one another's way. It was like a choreographed harvest dance, but with underlying currents of anger rather than joyous expression.

So she gave up on pottery and went for walks instead, breaking out into occasional runs. She found a copse of pine trees and climbed as high as she could on each one until she was breathing hard and dizzy from exertion. She moved and moved and moved until the endless thoughts in her head slowed at last, although they never truly went away.

Enuwal evaded her attempts to talk with him alone, as did Andrij. She had a few exchanges with Vedran about how their mother and their friends were doing back home in Selu, but otherwise they mostly left her alone. Even Cian stayed far away, which was good. Andrij walked around as taut as a strung bow.

She considered finding Cian, or asking him to come to her, but her anger rose like a wall each time, cutting off the idea. Besides, once she saw to it that her people and the Jeguduns were safe, she'd be spending far too much time with him.

Today, the monsoons passed east of them, making the air heavy and sticky and hot. She trudged back to Rina's late in the day, the sun leaving fiery fingers of red, orange, and pink in the western sky. Maybe tonight she'd sleep better than she had been sleeping. She was tired enough.

A pair of Jeguduns flew low, coming in fast from the northeast, headed toward Rina's. News, at last. Malia broke into a jog. Vedran and Andrij jogged toward her from the opposite direction, and they arrived at the rope ladder at the same time. The pair of Jeguduns landed on the ledge above, their trilling and chirping drifting down.

She climbed up first. Neither Jegudun had been any of those she'd sent to the Maddion. Had they been captured? Killed? Was there a Maddion army on the way at this very moment? She couldn't imagine any other reason the pair would have come so quickly to Rina's.

Ankti was pacing the ledge when she reached it and helped Malia up. "What's wrong?" Malia asked.

"I don't know. Rina looks excited, but not upset, so I'm not sure what it could be."

Rina's home smelled like stew and dumplings. Normally, Malia would have been anxious to dig in, especially after a day of so much activity, but her focus turned to the pair of Jeguduns seated against pillows, sipping from mugs. They were still breathing a little fast from their hurried flight.

Enuwal stood on the other end of the room. He straightened when Malia entered. Rina ladled stew into two bowls and handed them to the Jeguduns before preparing more.

Andrij and Vedran hurried in moments later. "They bring news?" Vedran asked.

"They have only just arrived," Rina said.

"Is Aru safe?" Malia asked.

Rina's face softened. "They don't bring news of the Jeguduns who went to the Maddion mountains. They indicated their news could wait a bit. Here," she said, handing a bowl to her. "Sit. Eat. You look like you've run all over the valley today."

Vedran's nose crinkled. "And you smell like it, too."

Malia gave him a friendly punch on his arm, took the bowl and a mug of tea, and settled against some pillows. She ate quickly, hardly listening to the scant conversation drifting through the room as the others compared their day. Rina brought a bowl of stew to the other room and returned moments later, her lips thin and her face more lined than usual. She said nothing, though, as she sat and tucked into her meal.

After the dishes had been gathered, Rina said, "This is Marista," she said, indicating a female Jegudun with feathers that shone like polished cedar, transitioning to light brown fur, and warm, dark, brown eyes that were an awful lot like Enuwal's in both color and the gentleness they held. "And this is Indwen," she added, indicating the other Jegudun, whose dark gray feathers glimmered like silver in some places, his fur a light gray. He reminded Malia of Tuvin, and grief tugged at her heart. "They are messengers and frequent this part of the valley."

Malia nodded at both of them and made introductions all around. Both Jegudun canted their heads when she introduced Ankti, and Marista let out a low, curious trill, exchanging a glance with Indwen.

"What message do you bring?" Malia asked.

Marista chirruped and whistled, got to her feet, and sat closer to Malia. She held out her small hands and waited.

Malia placed her hands in Marista's, whose palms were leathery and warm from holding the bowl. She closed her eyes. Marista's inquiring, polite tug came at her mind, and just as Malia followed along, she wondered what, if anything, Cian would experience as the Jegudun shared a memory with her.

She went from sitting in her grandmother's home to flying in bright, afternoon daylight. A wave of dizziness passed through her as she adjusted to being in Marista's memory. Cian's presence remained attached to hers, silently experiencing all that she did.

The Jegudun was flying just outside the valley near Tuvin's Falls, scanning the grassy plains both near and far. The river that fed the falls had swollen a bit with the recent afternoon rains, and the water roared as it fell far to the valley floor and the Big River below. Malia experienced everything in Marista's memory, including the rushing wind and the scent of sun-warmed grass, the earth, and—

A whiff of something else that shouldn't be up here. Or rather, some*one* else. Marista circled around and, hidden in the tall grasses near the valley's edge, was a man. She trilled to the other nearby Jeguduns, and together they landed near the man, encircling him. Marista's talons emerged, not to attack, but in case she had to defend herself.

She whistled inquisitively toward him. The man slowly stood, revealing threadbare Maddion servant clothes, a gash across one arm caked with dried blood, and eyes wide in terror. Marista immediately drew her talons in. She eased forward, holding out the water sac she'd carried slung across her torso.

The man hesitated, then took it and drank deeply. He spoke rapidly, gesturing back from where he'd come, but Malia didn't understand. It sounded like the Maddion's language, although with a slight accent. Marista gestured for him to follow, and he did so. He started down the narrow, switchbacked trail near the falls, headed to the valley floor.

Marista released Malia from the memory. She blinked a few times, adjusting to being back in Rina's home with pillows behind her back and stone all around, a plush rug beneath her. Cian's presence shifted in her mind, falling back once again.

"Thank you," Malia said to Marista. Then, "A Maddion slave has made it to the valley. He seemed to have a lot to say, but I didn't understand."

Vedran straightened. "Can Ankti experience Jegudun memories?"

She shook her head. "Only Taakwa. She would have to speak with him herself, and then relay his message to me, and then I could tell you all what he said."

"Where is he?" Enuwaul asked.

"Near Tuvin's Falls." She asked Marista where the man was now, and she ran a hand over her head to indicate short hair. "With Rasmus."

"That's a day's trip."

"And I'm worried there might be Maddion in pursuit," Malia said, biting her lower lip. "We might not have much time."

"The best we can do is run tomorrow," Andrij said. "Maybe send a Jegudun ahead and have them guide him to us so we can meet halfway."

"That's an excellent idea," Rina said.

"It is," Malia said. "But there's a way I could get there tonight, and perhaps the rest of you, too."

Enuwal's mouth turned down and he shook his head. "No. It's

one thing for that—for *Cian*—to save you from falling, and it's another entirely for you to ask for him to purposefully embue you with his power so you can get somewhere quickly, when you could arrive under perfectly ordinary means tomorrow."

"That poor man has traveled a long ways already. We can't ask him to travel more simply to meet us halfway. We must go to him."

"I agree," Rina said.

"What?" Enuwal's head swiveled around. He opened his mouth to say more, then shut it.

"Malia has an advantage," she continued. "It's not wrong for her to use it."

"Ankti," Malia said, standing.

Ankti followed her out to the ledge. Voices continued to rise and fall inside as the others argued over Malia's suggestion. She did her best to ignore them as she explained what she'd seen to Ankti.

Ankti's eyes widened at the mention of a Maddion servant. When Malia finished speaking, she asked questions about what he looked like, or if she could parse his name from what he'd said.

Malia shook her head. "He spoke in the Maddion language, which the Jeguduns understand, but they don't have the ability to translate for me. He might have said his name. I don't know. But he didn't come here for a casual chat. He has something urgent to tell us. I think we should go to him tonight, and you can translate. Cian can help us get there. I know he can give me some power to make me much faster. He might be able to do something to help you, too."

She recoiled as if Malia had brought out a poisonous snake, then caught herself. "Perhaps he can. It can be no worse than some things I've been through already." She nodded. "Very well. I'll go with you."

Malia considered the raised voices. "We should go down first."

She and Ankti quickly climbed down. The night air was warm, and crickets were just beginning to chirp in the tall grass. Malia pulled inquiringly at Cian's presence.

Ankti gasped, and Malia turned. Cian was already approaching, his red-orange eyes swirling slowly in the dark. The corners of his mouth were raised in a faint smile.

"I didn't hear him at all," Ankti said.

"I didn't realize he was so close," Malia murmured. He'd kept his emotions well hidden from her. A traitorous little pang went through her. She shouldn't enjoy sharing her raw feelings with someone else, but she had to admit, it was nice sometimes to have someone acknowledge them without having to put them into words. Sometimes words made a mess of things.

"You tagged along when Marista showed me her memory, didn't you."

His smile faded. "I did. I couldn't help it, seeing as how I'm privy to your mind at all times."

"No, no, that was quite all right. But you know there's a Maddion servant who made it to the valley. He seems to have something urgent to tell us. Would you—" She took a deep breath.

"Yes," he said before she could get the words out. "I'll take you." He frowned. "Your urgency is like a battering ram against my head, by the way."

"Oh. My apologies." She did her best to pull her emotions in, imagining them as a tight ball tucked safely in a corner of her person.

"That's better," he said with a sigh.

"Is there a way you could get Ankti there quickly as well?"

He frowned, his forehead creasing. "I can't give her some of my power the way I can with you."

"Are you strong enough to carry me and move fast?" Ankti asked.

"I'm not a pack animal," he said.

Ankti turned to Malia. "He can't, and he just won't admit it. He's not strong enough."

"Hey, now," he said. "I know what you're doing, goading me on so I'll prove you wrong."

"I'll just have to go on believing you're too weak until you prove otherwise, then."

"You said you'd help us if you could," Malia said. "Here's your chance. Unless you want to break your promise and just leave? I'll gladly stay in the valley, and you can go."

His lips thinned, and his eyes narrowed, the red-orange swirling faster. "Very well. When would you like to leave?"

"Give me a few moments," Malia said. She hastened up the rope ladder. As she reached the ledge, Enuwal stepped out, a wedge of light spilling ahead of him. Voices drifted out, but they were calmer now. He helped her up. She let her hand linger in his, but he pulled it free. She pushed aside her disappointment. If only she knew what was going on with him the way she knew what Cian was feeling, this would be so much easier.

"You called him to you," Enuwal said. It was a flat statement in a flat voice, but she couldn't help but hear an undercurrent of accusation. Maybe it was her guilt, putting emphasis where none existed.

"He can help me and Ankti reach the servant tonight. Quickly. Enuwal," she said, swallowing the lump that suddenly formed in her throat. "I want you there, too. Tonight."

"That would take magic, of course," he said. "*His* help."

"Yes. But we're helping all of the Taakwa and the Jeguduns, remember? Aru and the others aren't back yet, and this man might have information that can help us."

"Or maybe he simply escaped and thought he'd find shelter beneath our barrier."

Her hands went up in the air. "Fine. I won't beg for your help. You can stay behind." She moved to go inside. He grabbed her arm, gently.

"Wait," he said. He dropped his hand from her. "Every time I think of Cian, I am filled with rage, for what he did to our valley, for how he needs to stay close to you, for this connection that the two of you have. And I let some of that rage slip out around you, directed toward you. It's not right. I'm sorry, Malia."

"I can understand that. You truly do not have to come if you don't want to."

"Do *you* want me along?"

"Of course." She smiled. "Yours is the voice of reason more often than not."

He let out a soft snort. "Then we are all doomed."

Vedran protested the idea of traveling quickly with Cian's help, but then grudgingly accepted. Andrij, however, adamantly refused to go along with them. "I'll travel by foot, under normal means. And most likely, I'll find you all still there, unless, of course, the *mutara* whisks you all away to the farthest corners of the earth and leaves you there."

"Well," Rina said, rubbing her hands together. "On that cheery note, I'll gather up some things you can all take along with you."

Malia joined her grandmother as the older woman packed dried meat and berries, nuts, and bread into their travel sacs.

"You be sure to be careful," Rina said. "Whether you come back here or you travel on, you be careful."

"Of course. Besides, Cian will watch after me. Maybe. He might decide he's better off if I'm dead after all."

Rina stopped and looked up. "He won't hurt you, and he won't let any harm come to you if he can help it. He cares for you." At Malia's widened eyes, she added, "Oh, not like that. Not the way that Enuwal does. More like Vedran, if he were a self-centered rat. He's forgotten what it's like to have someone in his life. You've reminded him of that."

She sat back on her heels. "So he cares about me, and because of that he wants to take me away from everyone I love?"

"He's been alone for a long time. He hasn't been human in a long time. He's forgotten a lot." She resumed packing.

Malia took two packs and handed three to Vedran. She said a quick good-bye to Rina—Ziku was asleep already and she didn't want to disturb him—and an equally quick good-bye to Andrij. She went down the rope ladder ahead of Vedran and Enuwal. At the bottom, she handed out travel packs.

A wave of emotion passed through Cian, and for Malia it brought back memories of when the Maddion removed the dam they'd made in the river, and a wall of water had come crashing down on her as she and Rasmus were crossing a bridge. Cian's emotions were like that wall of water, towering over her and eager to pull her under and drown her in them. Her stomach coiled, and her heart thudded quickly.

"Cian," she said. "Back away."

The others might have thought she meant physically, but he understood. He pulled his emotions tighter, and the upheavel in her mind and body ebbed. She took a deep breath, quelling the nausea, and said, "Can you give me enough of your power to get me there? And then bring Ankti next?"

"Of course," he said.

"And then bring Enuwal." She didn't trust Cian to bring him last in case Cian took advantage of the moment and, as Andrij had suggested, tried to deposit him in one of the farthest corners of the earth. "And then Vedran."

Cian looked as though he might say something, but all he did was nod. "Are you all ready? This will go rather quickly once it's begun."

She met Ankti's gaze. The other woman nodded. So did Enuwal and Vedran, albeit with tight lips. Vedran's hand hovered near the hilt of his dagger frequently. Enuwal had grabbed his walking stick from its perch at the cliff's base and held onto it with a white-knuckled grip.

Malia took a deep breath. "Let's go, then."

Cian raised a hand. A red-orange flame came to life in his palm, matching the swirling in his eyes. A tiny portion of it danced away and flowed to Malia, with more silently streaming behind it.

She reached for it. The flame was neither cold nor hot as she'd expected, but she could *taste* it, oddly enough. It was cinnamon and summer sky, a lavender filled wind, a spicy pepper hot on her tongue. It flowed into her, tingling up her finger, through her hand, up her arm. It flowed through her, to her other fingers, to her toes, to her scalp.

The red-orange of Cian's eyes dulled, and a hint of normal eyes flickered behind it. Enuwal gasped. "Malia, your eyes," he said.

She had a feeling they were taking on a distinct red-orange hue even though her vision was no different and her eyes felt the same. Cian made a fist, shutting off the flow of power to her. The red-orange of his eyes dulled for a while before brightening again. He had told her that when he went long enough between changes, his eyes returned to normal, so it could mean that the power he'd gained from the changes he'd worked was fading. And, he had to bring three other people quickly across part of the valley.

Power hummed through her, like when the Jeguduns coaxed it out of her when repairing the barrier, but it was all hers.

"Off you go," Cian said.

"Be careful with them," she said. She turned without another word and began walking. She made sure the travel sac fit securely around her torso and broke into a jog.

The borrowed power flowed through her, and her legs moved effortlessly. The soreness and fatigue she'd felt ever since escaping the Maddion prison was simply not there. Her breathing came easily, as if she were strolling through the woods and not gradually increasing her speed.

Her feet moved lightly, silently over the ground. The wind flowed past her face, brushing back her hair. She moved faster. The world blurred around the edges. She moved even faster, and the world blurred more until she could only focus on that which was directly in front of her. And still her legs moved easily and her breathing hardly sped up.

A thrill went through her. This was what Cian felt all the time, or at least when he put his power to work. He could travel the entire world in a couple of days if he chose, maybe less. She couldn't stop the smile that came to her face.

She moved so fast that she had no true sense of time, and so when Tuvin's Falls came into view, her steps faltered. That was *fast.* One last surge of power went through her and she leaped over the wide river, landing lightly on the other side. She slowed to a jog. The moon had hardly moved. Her heart quickened, but not from exertion.

Without the barrier overhead, a constant sense of vulnerability gnawed at her. But with this speed, she could escape an attack at any time. And moreso, it felt good, like the shivers of a loving hand, or a mug of tea and a bite of sweetbread after a long day's work, or sitting beside a hearth during winter's longest night.

Her borrowed power ebbed. She was simply herself once again, not privy to a speed or ease of movement other people had never experienced. She loved her people and the Jeguduns no less. She loved Enuwal and Vedran, her mother and grandmother, and Ankti and her other friends no less. But… the idea of leaving with Cian and all the power he offered once she saw her people safe from the Maddion no longer weighed so heavily on her.

CHAPTER EIGHTEEN

Moments after Malia reached the other side of the river, a blurry figure stopped nearby. It was Cian, holding Ankti in his arms like he might hold a small child. As soon as he stopped, Ankti climbed down, smoothed her skirt, and patted her hair. Some curls had come loose and hung around her face. Her first steps were unsteady, and then straightened as she joined Malia.

Tuvin's Falls roared behind her. The air was warm and damp. Rasmus's home was not far. Light poured out, and a Jegudun landed on the ledge, carrying a basket.

"That was… interesting," Ankti said.

Cian left without a word.

Ankti shook her head and let out a shuddering breath. "That was terrifying. I've never moved so fast, not even on a dragon. I couldn't even breathe. What was it like, running that fast?"

Malia began walking toward Rasmus's home, and Ankti fell into step beside her. "It was a bit exhilarating, I admit. Ah, are my eyes still strange?"

She shook her head. "They look normal again." Her steps quickened. "I wonder if he has any news about Chanwa." She stopped. "But if it's bad news… I don't know. I don't know if I can hear it if Muvumo killed her."

Malia grasped the other woman's hand. "You're not alone. Whatever he has to say about her, I'm with you."

She squeezed Malia's hand. "Thank you."

They were halfway to the bottom of the cliff where Rasmus lived when Enuwal called out behind them. "Malia!"

She turned. Cian was already gone. Enuwal was holding tight to his walking stick with both hands. She met him halfway, pulling him in for a quick embrace.

"You look windblown," she said, tucking a stray strand of hair behind his ear and smiling.

"I'm just glad you're safe. Malia, he's changing you the way he changes situations. What if he gives you too much power?"

She stepped back. "I doubt he'd do that."

"He might make you so much like him that you won't ever be you again."

His words coiled around her heart. He was scared, as they all were, but Cian couldn't change her like that, not unless he gave all of his power to her and died, and she certainly didn't want any part of that.

"That won't happen. I'll still be me."

"It was more than your eyes, Malia. You had this look of anticipation, as if you were happy with what he was about to do to you."

"It was convenient. We're wasting time discussing this when we should be talking to the man who arrived tonight."

She spun and returned to Ankti. Enuwal fell into step just behind her, his footsteps punctuated with the rhythmic thud of the walking stick against the ground.

A blur appeared in the periphery of her vision, and then Vedran was standing there, looking as shaky as Ankti had. Cian's presence stirred in Malia's mind, and then faded. He had brought them all here, but he was going to wait in the woods and let them speak with the escaped servant alone. Probably for the best.

"I feel a little sick," Vedran said. "I never thought I could move that fast."

He joined them, and when they reached the cliff's base, Malia craned her neck and called up to Rasmus.

His head appeared over the ledge a moment later as he looked down. "Watch for the ladder," he called, and then it whistled through the air, unfurling with a snap.

Malia climbed up first. Rasmus waited on the ledge and helped her up. "You got here fast," he said by way of greeting.

"Cian brought us."

"Oh," was all he said. He waited until they all stood on the ledge, then said, "I'm glad she's here," with a nod toward Ankti. "The poor guy still looks terrified, and I have no idea what he's saying."

Malia let Ankti go ahead of her. Inside, a Jegudun sat against some pillows, a mug in both hands, and a man sat near the hearth.

Even while seated, it was obvious that he was a large and very tall man. He wore ragged clothes that looked plain and rough. It was hard to tell whether the tears in the cloth had been there a while, or whether his journey from the Maddion's mountain had ripped them.

He had thick hair the color of deep red clay, more sprouted along his chin and above his lips, and he had bushy eyebrows the same shade. Malia had never seen a man with so much hair before. He reminded her of a bear, albeit a terrified one, given the way he shook and hunched his shoulders.

"Vontor," Ankti said.

His head jerked up, and when he saw her, he stood immediately, the top of his head brushing the ceiling. He pulled Ankti into a hug that made her grunt and then stepped back, speaking rapidly in the Maddion's language. She nodded while guiding him back to the pillows. She handed his mug back to him and urged him to drink, then handed him a bowl filled with nuts and blueberries. She mostly listened, and occasionally said a few words soothingly. He and Ankti spoke quickly in a guttural, harsh language that Malia recognized as the Maddion's.

Malia sat near them, and Enuwal, Vedran, and Rasmus took up their spots behind her. She felt like a clan mother sitting down to discuss important business, backed up by members of her council. A pang of loss went through her as she realized she would never finish her training. Her hand went to her bare neck and then back to her lap. For a while, she'd been hopeful, but now she knew she'd have to leave with Cian when this was all over.

Ankti nodded as Vontor finished speaking and turned to Malia. Her eyes were bright, and her lips quivered as if holding back a smile. Good news about Chanwa, then. Ankti deserved some good news.

"Vontor says he and five other servants left the mountains a few days ago. Chanwa went back to her husband—" Here, her voice faltered. "—and she arranged for a huge distraction to allow Vontor and the others to escape. She and the women gathered at the mesas under the cover of night and filled the spaces so that the dragons can't land. Essentially, they've trapped the men, save for the few who stay at the guardhouse on the mountaintop."

Malia had briefly seen the layout, and so she knew what Ankti spoke of. "So… all of the Maddion women are doing this?"

"Most, it sounds like. The men can't hurt them; these are their wives and mothers and sisters and daughters. And their numbers have dwindled so much, they can't simply execute all those who are participating." Her hands clenched and unclenched in her lap. "It's a risky undertaking for them, though. Chanwa asked the servants to hurry here and beg the Taakwa and Jeguduns for help. She asks that your people and the Jeguduns stand with the women. They are looking to make major changes to their way of life, and they can't do it alone." She leaned forward. "This is what your people and the Jeguduns have been hoping for. Believe me, if the women were allowed a voice, things would certainly be different." She sat back. "Not that I don't think you shouldn't move ahead with finding a way to remove the dragons, but now there are two fronts to this war."

Yes, war. Without an army standing behind her or taking to the skies overhead, Malia kept forgetting. This was war, albeit a different sort. The Maddion women were waging war against their own men, without bloodshed.

She conveyed Ankti's words to the others. Vedran grinned widely. "I wish I could have seen the look on their men's faces when they realized what was happening."

Enuwal's reaction was more tepid, but his smile genuine. "What a clever solution."

"At least *some* of their people have sense," Rasmus said. "I wondered if they had any at all."

Vontor was done eating. He was simply sitting now, staring at the blanket. Or rather, given the haunted nature of his gaze, seeing things she probably couldn't imagine. He'd lived for many seasons as a Maddion slave.

"Do they know about the barrier?" she asked Ankti.

She shook her head. "When he left, they still believed it to be working. I didn't tell him it was gone. He's so hopeful right now, and he feels completely safe for the first time in a very long time. I don't want to take that away just yet."

"Well, let Vontor know that we will put this information to good use. He is welcome to stay with the Taakwa, of course. And the Jeguduns?" The Jegudun, one she didn't know, nodded from where she sat.

Ankti relayed the message and spoke more with Vontor. Malia sat back against her pillows. Now that she'd found out what Vontor had to say, the urgency that had driven her here only grew. His information was days old, and she still hadn't heard from the Jeguduns, but she felt as though with each passing day, the Taakwa and Jeguduns were losing their advantage.

"What are you thinking?" Vedran asked.

She took a deep breath. "We should leave first thing tomorrow morning for the Maddion mountains."

Enuwal echoed her deep breath before asking, "And do what?"

"And add our numbers to their women. Give them support. Their men are unable to fight us right now, but that might not last if the women cannot hold out."

"Who would go?" Rasmus asked. "You're talking about leaving tomorrow, but there are only us few Taakwa here. And Ankti."

"There are plenty of Jeguduns we could muster," she said. "I don't think we have time to wait for a Taakwa army to form, and then lead them across the plains. Too much could change between now and then, and perhaps not to our advantage."

"What could we do?" Vedran asked. "We're but a handful."

"There would be Jeguduns," she said. "And… Cian."

The lines cupping Enuwal's mouth deepened as he frowned. "He's the one who cured them of their illness. What if he helps them again rather than us?"

"He made a deal with me. He'll keep it."

The muscles around his mouth twitched, and his eyes narrowed. He took a long sip from his mug and then looked away. "You'll drown in him," he said quietly.

She thought of the borrowed power flowing through her, and how easily she'd run from Rina's to Rasmus's. She thought of the pleasure it brought her. "No," she said. *Not yet, at any rate.* And once she had seen to her people's safety and left the valley… well, then, it wouldn't matter. Maybe if she drowned in Cian, she wouldn't have to feel the heartache of leaving her people and the Jeguduns and those she loved.

"Could he get us all there at once?" Vedran asked. "Like he did tonight?"

"I'll ask," she said, some relief joining the warring emotions within her. Vedran, praise the clan mother, was always level-headed.

"Er," he added.

Malia arched a brow. "Yes?"

"I'm sure Andrij will want to join us."

"And how will he do that if he wants nothing to do with Cian?"

"He'll want to fight something. Someone. He's been aching to do so for a long time. If we could convince him to tolerate Cian and then point him in the right direction, he could be a big help."

Rasmus nodded. "One more person would be a help."

"Then I'll talk to Cian, and we'll leave tomorrow if he's willing to help get us all there quickly." She settled back against the pillows again. If Cian was agreeable, she'd be returning to the Maddion's mountains tomorrow. A chill went through her.

CHAPTER NINETEEN

Full night had just fallen when Aru made it to the rendevous point in the foothills. Emmata, a Jegudun he'd just met before they'd set out for the Maddion's mountains, was there already. They nodded a silent greeting at one another and settled in to wait, tucked partially beneath a huge boulder that jutted out from the hillside and was protected from casual prying eyes by scrub.

Aru fairly hummed with his news and was eager to share it with someone, but they could not make a sound. The dragons rarely came out at night unless driven to do so by the Maddion, but it was still better to be safe.

The only sounds were that of Aru or Emmata occasionally shifting their weight, or small animals in the brush, or the wind dancing through pine or juniper. The air smelled of summer: sun-warmed earth and grass, wildflowers, pine. They were comforting smells and sounds, and yet Aru's heart fluttered like hummingbird wings and he continuously scanned the star-laden sky.

Coryn joined them next. She pointed uphill and flew her hand through the air. Releven was coming along.

He arrived moments later, sending tiny pebbles skittering down the slope. Aru gave him a stern look and pinned his ears back.

Releven ducked his head, ears drooping. He was probably simply in a hurry to reach them so they could start their journey back home. They were all in a hurry. If they'd seen what Aru had, he couldn't blame them. They had important information to convey, yes, but then there were all the dead dragons. The stench of their rotting corpses still clung to his nostrils.

Emmata ducked out first. She scanned the sky, head raised, nostrils flaring as she sniffed, tufted ears pricked forward as she strained for any sounds that shouldn't be there. She stood that way for what felt like a long moment, then gestured for them to join her.

Aru crawled out next, then Releven and Coryn. They all stood, heads raised, picking up the barrage of odors and sounds from all around them. All was as it should be.

Emmata pointed to herself and then up. She would take off first, and then signal for them to join her. Then together they would dart along the open plains for home.

Home. Aru could be home by dawn, sipping tea from his favorite mug, seated on his ledge while the sun rose and the Jeguduns sang a greeting to the sun.

No, he'd actually be sitting in Rina's home, conveying all he knew. *Then* he could go home. He sighed. Home was still close.

Emmata spread her wings, crouched, and launched into the air, rising higher, higher, higher. She hovered in place, scanning all directions, then gestured for them to join her.

Coryn, then Releven, and finally Aru flew up. Emmata turned for home.

Something prickled along Aru's spine, a sensation that shot up and made his ears stand straight up. Something was wrong.

The night sounds had stopped.

The smell of brimstone and charred meat confirmed his fear. He whistled a warning, folded his wings tight against his body, and dove just as a dragon swiped at him, passing close enough for him to feel the wind of its passage.

He unsnapped his wings to stop his descent and whirled. One dragon slashed at Releven. The Jegudun let out a shrill cry. A second dragon was diving, but Emmata and Coryn were already zipping up and past it to come around and attack. Praise the ancestors, there were no other dragons, but two were bad enough. And their fight could easily draw more beasts.

Aru darted up to help Releven, who was flying much more slowly. Aru chirped and whistled and growled, suggesting the injured Jegudun take cover. Releven shook his head and started to argue with an angry series of whistles, then let out a frustrated growl and headed for a thick cluster of brush instead.

Aru aimed for the belly of the dragon who had injured Releven. They wore no saddles, had no riders, and their sides pulsed brightly and rapidly in the dark as they breathed. Dragons didn't come out at night unless goaded on by their Maddion riders. Again, he wondered if they were sick. If only these two would drop dead from whatever was plaguing them.

The dragon whipped her head around when he neared, but Aru was smaller and faster. He raced past her and tore into her belly with his talons, drawing some blood. She roared, but instead of fighting him, continued on toward the other beast.

Emmata dove for the second dragon as Coryn zipped up behind her. But the first dragon was headed straight for Coryn. Aru whistled a warning as the first dragon's belly brightened and expanded. Coryn altered her path, but the first dragon let loose a stream of fire that caught her. The smell of singed feathers and fur and burning flesh filled the air along with Coryn's dying scream, the sound like a spear through Aru's heart.

He let out a scream that turned to a deep, guttural cry. He attacked the dragon again, this time latching onto her belly and slashing at her over and over. One talon found the perfect spot, tender and fleshy, and ripped the dragon open, spilling her blood and intestines. He let go of her as she plunged to the ground below, landing with a heavy thud.

Aru whirled. The other dragon was bearing down on Emmata as she darted away, close to the ground. She spared a quick glance for Aru and whistled. *Go home, now.* Somebody had to get back to Malia with their information. But he couldn't leave her. Below, Releven was rising. Even injured, he could help them fight off that dragon.

He whistled and chirruped to Releven. *We can help her. Come on.*

Releven answered, *No, we must go before more dragons come. Our information is too important.*

Aru hesitated. Already Emmata was so far gone that they'd have to fly hard to catch up, and Releven wouldn't be able to do so. Releven would need help because of his injuries. And they were right; the Jeguduns and Taakwa needed to know about the Maddion women's protest and that something strange was going on with the dragons.

With a growl, Aru turned and joined Releven as they hurried away from the mountains, flying low. Aru's fury drove him faster. He had to force himself to hold back and wait for Releven.

He wanted to rage, to scream, to slash at something. Instead, he swiped at his eyes as the wind tore at the tears forming there. Blasted dragons. Blasted Maddion.

He smelled the beast just before she dropped onto them. She drove him and Releven into the ground, pinning them both. Aru struggled uselessly against her massive talons and size. He couldn't draw enough breath, not with her on top of him. His struggles slowed as a different sort of darkness creeped along the edges of his vision. Her weight lifted, but not soon enough to stop the blackness creeping over him. He was hefted into the air, and then all was dark.

Dawn was only a hint in the eastern sky when Malia left Rasmus's home and everyone still sleeping. She climbed down the rope ladder and hurried toward the forest. Tall grass, heavy with dew, tugged at her skirt, dampening the hems.

She nudged Cian's presence in her mind. He was close. She stepped into the woods, the air dark and cool and filled with the scent of pine and fir, and the sweetness of wildflowers crushed beneath her feet. Cian melted out of the darkness, his eyes blazing red-orange. They might have been a little less bright than they had been yesterday before he'd brought them all here in a hurry. Or it could be the shade of dawn making them seem so.

"Good morning," she said.

His lips were a thin line. "Good morning."

"Thank you for bringing us all here so quickly last night."

His mouth relaxed. "You are welcome."

She hesitated. This would have felt a little better if she'd had some tea this morning, but she was facing him to ask for another favor without reinforcements of any kind.

He sighed. "I know there's something on your mind, even without the emotions swirling around in there. What is it?"

She filled him in on what Vontor had told them and finished by saying, "We decided to leave today, while we can still take advantage of their immobility."

"It will take a while to reach them, though, unless you send the Jeguduns on ahead."

"Yes. And that's what I want to ask you about."

His brows drew down, and the red-orange of his eyes swirled faster. "You want me to bring you there today and plop you down right in the middle of their civil war."

She stood straighter. "Yes, actually."

He shook his head. "It's one thing to zip you across your valley, but quite another to take you to the heart of the enemy."

"You seem oddly concerned all of a sudden." She thought of Rina's words. She hadn't really believed Cian could actually *care* about her, but perhaps Rina was right.

"Last night, I pushed myself and my powers in ways I'd never done before. I doubted I could do it, to be honest. But I *did*, and it was because of the slight boost that you gave me, the way your people give Jegaduns a boost to their magic. Without it, I could have helped you and perhaps brought one of your fellows quickly, but certainly not the rest. Last night, I was actually… *tired*." His brows crinkled.

"And you don't want your extra little boost of power to go away by dying, is that what you're saying? Well, that's too bad, because we had an agreement that you would help me ensure the safety of my people and the Jegaduns, and only then would I leave with you. If you won't help, then I'm afraid the deal is off."

He was breathing rapidly, his chest rising and falling quickly, just as Dalibor used to do when he got angry. But his hands remained open, relaxed, and there was none of the hate that flashed across Dalibor's face. No, there was only exasperation. Cian might have borrowed Dalibor's appearance, but he had not, praise the clan mother, borrowed his personality whatsoever.

"Very well," Malia said after a long moment of silence had passed. "We shall go without you, then. I'll send the Jegaduns ahead to help as they can, and the rest of us will catch up and face… whatever we'll be facing." She turned on her heel and strode back as the indigo eastern sky began to glow orange at the horizon. Her heart thumped, and she waited for Cian to call her back, but he never did.

Her heart constricted. She'd been so sure he would help. She'd been so sure she could get them all to the Maddion's mountain that day. But now they would face a trek of several days across the plains, and so much could change in that time. Maybe they shouldn't go without Cian's help.

But if the women's protest failed, then Maddion life would return to the way it had always been, and it would only be a matter of time before they realized the barrier was gone and they could swoop into the valley as they saw fit. With Cian's help, they might die out on the plains if they were attacked by the Maddion, or they might die in the mountains, but without him, they would surely die in this valley.

She reached for his presence. He was in the valley, but far from her, his emotions coiled up so tight that she couldn't read them at all. They were on their own, then.

CHAPTER TWENTY

Another night passed on the mesa. Dawn wasn't far away. Chanwa's body had grown used to the constant ache, the constant cold, the gnawing hunger in her belly. They were running out of food. Not just those on the mesa, but everyone. They were rationing the last they had. And still, Muvumo would not listen. Something was going to have to give soon. It was almost palpable, like a tremor in the earth promising a large quake later on. Then things would shift. The world would never be quite the same.

Amazingly, most of the women were still with her, even after all they had witnessed, even after so many nights shivering out here, and days sweating beneath the sun or sitting in the pouring rain. Even after watching Nyda die, and the servant Frathiel, they stayed with her. And, a few more men had joined them.

Chanwa stood and stretched. Her stomach cramped, though whether from hunger or from the stretch or from being still for so long she didn't know. She slowly made her way past sleeping forms and into the cavern where everyone had been relieving themselves. She passed rows of saddles, the smell of leather sharp in the air, and passed the small rooms where boys lived as they were going through their apprenticeships, the smell of leather giving way to the stale smell of sweaty boys. Torches burned at intervals, leading her deeper into the large cavern and to the latrines.

She squatted over one, the smell of urine wafting up. With the usual tasks at a standstill because of the protest, there was nobody tending the latrines with herbs to keep them from smelling unpleasant. Chanwa crinkled her nose. If only their protest accomplished what they wanted, smelly latrines would be the least of her worries.

Her needs taken care of, she began the slow walk back to the mesa. She still did not bleed, and it was past time when it should have begun. She might be with child. Part of her marveled that she could be growing a child. But part of her—*most* of her—filled with dread at what could become of the child.

She scanned the figures as she picked her way through the crowd on the mesa. When she found Bertra and her brother Oriz, she sat beside them.

Bertra was asleep with her head against her brother's shoulder. Her mouth was open, and tiny lines, even in sleep, creased her brow and fanned out from her mouth. The worry was constant for all of them.

Oriz nodded once. "My lady Chanwa," he said quietly. A few snores rose around them, punctuated by an owl calling mournfully in the distant woods.

"How are you doing?" she asked.

"Well enough."

"You're a comfort to your sister."

He pursed his lips, but all he said was, "Thank you, my lady Chanwa."

"What has the talk been like? Do you find that people are strong, or are they faltering?"

"They stand with you. There has been no talk of ending this."

She nodded. Somehow, they still believed in her and in what they were doing. And yet, they couldn't go on at this standstill for much longer.

"We're running out of time," she said. "I don't think the Most Worthy is interested in listening to us. I believe he thinks he can outlast us. We've sacrificed too much to let that happen." Her hands curled tight, nails digging into her palms. Once again she felt the life slipping out of Nyda, smelled the blood—her sister's blood—and felt the gaping hole her death had left behind. "I fear the servants we sent might not have made it. I fear we're waiting for help that's not coming. Do you think you and some of the other men could slip out on dragonback? Find the Taakwa, find the Jeguduns, and urge them to aid us?"

He glanced at his sister's sleeping form. She snorted once, closed her mouth, and her head lolled to the other side. Her mouth promptly fell back open, and she snored on. The corners of his mouth turned up.

"I've come this far," he began. He frowned and studied the guards on the stairs. "They might try to shoot us down."

"I'll arrange a distraction."

"The Jeguduns and Taakwa will definitely try to take us down."

"They will. I'll leave that to you, but perhaps landing a long ways from them and approaching without weapons would help."

He grimaced. "I don't want to lead myself and other men to a slaughter."

"I don't want that either. But we need their help, and we need you to do this. Bertra needs you to do this."

He took a deep breath and nodded. "I'll start talking to the men."

"The sooner you leave, the better." This entire protest hinged on so little right now, like a massive boulder perched precariously on top of a slim rock. Anything that shook the earth would send it falling one way or another.

"Very well, my lady Chanwa. If you would be so kind as to take Bertra? This is the first decent sleep she's had in a while."

"Of course."

She scooted closer and accepted Bertra's sleeping form, letting the other woman's head loll against her shoulder. Although she slept on, she let out a little whimper as if part of her had heard their exchange and didn't want her brother to leave.

Oriz slipped into the darkness, crouched beside another man, and began speaking in a low voice. Chanwa held Bertra up, ignoring the fatigue in her arms, and wondered how long she could hold up those of her people gathered on the mesas.

As an orange glow crept over the mountains, dragons began to call above them, and some took to the air. During the night, the men Oriz had spoken with had crept one by one into the large cavern off the mesa to fetch saddles, hiding them around the mesa's perimeter. All they needed now was Chanwa's signal.

Her plan to keep the guards occupied was simple, but required that people move fast, so before she stood, she spent some time stretching her legs, flexing her feet, twisting her back this way and that. Her stiff spine let out a few pops, and the movement took away some of the chill that had settled into her body over the past few days. The guards ignored her so far as she could tell. Their clothes were rumpled, their mouths downturned, their shoulders hunched. They were men used to riding dragons, used to practicing with their weapons, used to moving constantly. Instead, they'd spent the past few days trapped on one staircase, with dwindling food, and with only brief spurts of action to stimulate their minds. Chanwa hoped it all served to dull their reactions.

She stretched her arms overhead, planting her feet on the ground as she did so. When her arms came down, she pushed herself to standing, as did every other person on the mesa.

She thought to lead the rush down the stairs to block the guards, but others were faster. They streamed past her, bodies that hadn't been washed in days, fueled by frustration.

The guards shouted. Somebody screamed. The sound of flesh hitting stone hard reached her even through the stamping of feet and the shouts. Then the crowd slowed, stopped. She stood a few doorways down from the mesa, past where the first two guards had stood. Her breathing was fast, her heart speeding.

From the mesa came the whistles commanding the dragons to come to them. A few shouts drifted down from the higher mesa.

Then, in the dawn sky, came the beasts. From below, shouts. Muvumo was demanding that he be let through, that the crowd disperse. Nobody moved.

Four dragons landed while the others circled. Within moments, those first four were saddled and in the air with their riders, making room for four more. Soon, there were a dozen in the sky. Oriz flew to the other mesa and had a quick, shouted conversation with those milling around up there. He had to let them know to hold, let them know the plan. When he turned his dragon away, the crowd on the higher mesa had stilled.

Oriz joined the waiting dragons, and together they swooped past, toward the foothills and the plains beyond. A crossbow bolt flew from the stairs below. The nearest dragon in flight easily avoided it, but Chanwa's hands curled into fists. The dragons and their riders disappeared from view as the sun fully rose over the mountains. Robins sang deep in the forest. It was going to be a beautiful day.

There was a flutter in Chanwa's belly. It was far too early for it to be coming from a possible baby, but it reminded her of what her future might hold. A new beginning. Hope.

Oriz and the others would bring help back. This would all be over soon. She shuffled back to the mesa with the others to find her seat and wait.

CHAPTER TWENTY-ONE

It was a long way to walk from the Taakwa Valley to the Maddion's mountains. It hadn't been long since Malia had made this very same walk, and here she was again, headed to the Maddions' mountains. She tried not to think of the distance and the time as she led Enuwal, Vedran, Ankti, and Rasmus away from the valley, away from the roar of the Big River as it plummeted over the cliffs, and away from home. Her travel sac, slung across her torso, was heavy with provisions, as was the waterskin hanging from her belt, but neither were as heavy as her heart.

She'd been sure that Cian would help her. But he remained in the valley, the distance between them a palpable tension with a weight at the end that gradually grew, like pulling a full harvest basket a long ways. She could probably tolerate the growing distance between them. After all, the Jeguduns could fly far from the valley before giving in to the pull that always brought them back. It would be a distraction, though, when she least needed distractions.

Enuwal looked over his shoulder for what had to be the tenth time since they'd left the valley and struck out across the grassy plains. "The Jeguduns will follow shortly?" His walking stick made a rhythmic, gentle thump against the ground.

"They were already gathering when we started our climb," she said. "They should all be ready soon. They'll go ahead of us and assess the situation. If all remains as Vontor described, they'll take action tonight. If the situation has changed, they'll return and let us know."

"And then what?" Vedran, on the other side of her, asked.

"I suppose it depends on exactly how the situation has changed," she said.

"The Jeguduns are sure they can block the dragons in their roost?" Enuwal asked.

"They're relying on their collective memories," she said. "I'd feel much better if Aru and the others had come back." She squinted into the distant sky, hoping to find the Jeguduns' familiar figures heading for them. Instead, a pair of red-railed hawks circled the distant narrow copse of pine trees where she estimated they'd take their break. Clan mother curse it all, but they were wasting *so much time.* She let her frustration ride out, hoping it would give Cian a headache.

"I'm sure Aru is fine," Vedran said.

"They should have been back by now," she said. They might have gotten too close to the dragons' roost. They might have been killed. The women's protest might have ended unfavorably for them, and the Maddion men could all be riding around on dragonback at this very moment, celebrating the Jeguduns' deaths or capture. They could be headed this way, determined to break through the barrier again, or they might have somehow gotten the information that it wasn't there any longer. A shiver passed through her despite the morning sun's heat. "I'm going to walk ahead for a bit."

She put some distance between her and the others, letting her thoughts chase one another as her legs moved. She and the others were halfway to the trees where they'd break for the morning when the beating of hundreds upon hundreds of wings approached behind her. Soon the Jeguduns were passing over, their shadows zipping along the tall grass, shadow and sunlight flickering across Malia. She shaded her eyes with one hand and craned her neck.

A small hand lighted on her shoulder, startling her. Ankti walked beside her, brows drawn down. "You look like you carry something much heavier than that travel pack and waterskins. If you talk about it, that might help."

She sighed. "Part of me thinks we should run and hide, let the Maddion sort themselves out."

"And?" Ankti prompted after a while.

"And... this would have been easier with Cian's help. I was relying on him. I really thought he would... well, I guess I didn't understand him as well as I thought I did. Rina thought he cared about me, but I suppose when you've been alone for so long, you get so that you care for no one but yourself. Maybe he realized his existence would be easier if I died."

Ankti said nothing for a while. In the far distance, a small herd of antelope bounded through the tall grass. Behind them, Vedran murmured something about hunting.

"Perhaps the truth is more complicated than you think," Ankti said. "Perhaps it's harder to let go of sorrow and loneliness after it's become so entrenched in one's being."

Malia recalled the vast canyon, the way it stretched out below without any end in sight, the way its depth and breadth filled her with loneliness, with grief, with rage bordering on the deepest sorrow. She felt as though she could tumble into that canyon and fall forever. That was Cian's experience each day. It sent a pang through her.

"Perhaps," was all she said in reply, though. Ankti's words made her wonder, just how long had she been a Maddion slave? How endless had the days and the nights been for her? She must have thought she'd never leave. She was young and had her whole life ahead of her, and for the longest time, the only promise of her future had been to unwillingly serve others. Malia was not the only one filled with a host of doubts, anger, grief.

When they reached the trees, Malia led them to a shady area beside a stream, one of many tributaries that sprang from the Big River. The air was cool in the shade, and smelled of pine and earth. Malia dipped her hands in the stream, first scrubbing her face and then drinking deep of the cool water. She sat with her back against a pine tree, stretched out her legs, and ate a handful of nuts and a bite of jerky.

Enuwal slowly crouched beside her, holding onto his walking stick for balance. She said, "How's your leg holding up?"

"Better than I anticipated. I think the walking is good for it." He held out his hand, his long, tapered fingers curling around a bunch of blueberries. "I found these a short ways upstream."

She took some, the berries bursting in her mouth, the juice warm and tart and a little sweet. "Thank you."

He offered the rest to Ankti, who took them with a nod and a smile.

"It's strange, being so far outside the valley," he said. "I feel almost naked."

One corner of Malia's mouth turned up. "That's a pleasant image."

He chuckled. "I'm grateful for clothes. Although it would be interesting to face the Maddion with nothing on. They would certainly be distracted for a moment."

"And all of your bits exposed. No, clothes are a necessity for going into a fight."

"The Jeguduns wear none."

"They wear fur and feathers, and claws and teeth. They are better equipped than us. And they have better numbers." She sighed.

Ankti stood, brushing bits of dirt from her skirt. "I'm going to see if I can find more blueberries."

Malia nodded. She recognized the other woman's departure as a way of giving them privacy. Ankti slipped away, upstream.

"This is foolishness," Malia said. "Heading straight into the enemy's home. And yet, waiting in the valley like turkeys in a trap doesn't seem like a much better option." *If only Cian were here.* She almost said it aloud, but that would have been a huge mistake in front of Enuwal. She wanted Cian with them for his power, not for the reasons he tried planting in Enuwal's mind, but Enuwal wouldn't see it that way.

"The valley still seems safe, somehow," he said. "And yet, it's not. No place is safe so long as the Maddion go on as they were, and so long as they have their dragons. While I admire their women for taking a stand, I don't know how they're going to change the Maddion way of life dramatically when their men are used to having the upper hand and enjoy their power. No, our best bet is to rid them of their beasts, and if we can lend our support to their women while we're at it, the better off we'll be."

If only it wouldn't take so long to get there. The power that Cian lent her so she could run fast was temporary, but it could get them all much closer to the Maddion in a short amount of time. Was that really the only reason she wanted Cian around? For his power? His selfishness was rubbing off on her if that was the case.

The truth was, she'd been unbelievably lonely when she had fled Selu, and Dalibor, and Tuvin's death. She had thought the rest of her life would be one of living in exile. That first night had been one of the hardest of her life, and to imagine countless nights like that for Cian made her heart ache. Nobody should go through that, especially when all he'd wanted was to cure his daughter of the wasting illness.

"Malia?" Enuwal said gently, his brow furrowed. "What's wrong?"

She shook her head. "Lost in thought is all." She stood, brushing dirt from her skirt. "We should be going."

He straightened, stifling a groan. "I'll gather the others."

She stepped out of the trees' shade and peered across the vast, grassy plains. They had such a long ways to go. She sighed. Well, nothing to it but to place one foot in front of the other, and eventually they would get there.

Ankti stepped out of the trees, followed by Vedran, Rasmus, and Enuwal. They were ready. Malia was ready. She turned northeast, ready to set off again when a wall came down within her mind, and Cian's unmistakeable presence loomed. Behind her, a voice said, "Aren't you going to wait for us?"

"Cian?" She whirled.

He stood in the shade, his red-orange eyes swirling slowly, with Andrij beside him.

He had come to her after all.

CHAPTER TWENTY-TWO

Oriz's stomach fluttered from the thrill of flying again, and from having given his sister Bertra most of his share of food, but mostly from the fact that he flew away from his home to seek the Taakwa and Jeguduns *on purpose.* He knew it was the right thing to do. The night he joined his sister on the mesa, he'd had every intention of talking her out of the silliness of sitting out there for no good reason, but instead had been overwhelmed by the silent strength he faced. The women might not have raised blades or crossbows to make their point, but they had made it, and by doing something as simple as sitting.

The sun was over the horizon and rising steadily. They were flying fast and would come to the valley by midday if they kept up the pace. He wondered what life might be like if Maddion women had a say in their lives, if they helped make decisions that impacted all of their people. He imagined his sister married to a man near her age, and content with her life, rather than looking like someone being slowly crushed to death by the weight of it all every time he saw her. He wondered what sort of woman he might marry if things were more equal.

He was still daydreaming when a shout rose from one of the other men. In the distance were tiny figures in the air. They could have been a flock of birds, but as they drew closer, the formation and outline shifted to show a sizeable number of Jeguduns flying out to meet them.

Oriz shouted, getting the attention of the closest men. They had never even had time to designate a captain to take charge of their group; they had simply gone tearing off into the dawn. He gave the signal for landing and received perplexed looks in response.

"They won't attack if we're grounded," he shouted, the wind whipping away his words.

A couple of men nodded and immediately flew lower in preparation. Oriz moved closer to the next men and gave the same instructions. It was taking far too long to convey his idea, and meanwhile, the Jeguduns were drawing closer at a frightening rate.

He waved at the others and began landing. Six dragons down. Three more getting ready to land. The last few noticed, at last, and began coming down as well.

Oriz pushed his dragon to land. She found the ground quickly, jarring him and letting out a little growl of her own. His fingers fumbled for the straps holding his legs, and then he half-fell out of the saddle. His legs were shaky, weak from days of doing hardly anything, but they managed to catch him before he tumbled all the way to the ground, and then he was running through the waist-high grass, waving his empty hands at the Jeguduns who were moments from reaching them.

"We do not wish to fight," he yelled. "We want to talk. We need your help." He repeated the words. The Jeguduns bore down on him and the others, claws out, teeth bared, ears flattened back. He repeated the words again, and again, holding up his empty arms. "Please, help us," he cried out as the first of them swooped overhead.

Behind him, a dragon snorted, and another roared, and a man cried out, but not in pain; he sounded startled. Oriz turned and found the Jeguduns flying low over the group, but not attacking. The dragons had their heads up, darting one way and the other as they followed the Jeguduns, but they listened to their riders and did not attack. One of the larger beasts, her sides pulsing bright and then fading in rapid succession, roared, but remained where she was. The Jeguduns passed over them, swept higher, and made a sharp turn. Oriz couldn't help but admire how tightly they held together.

They landed a good distance from the Maddion, save for one who flew closer before landing near Oriz. Her massive wings whipped the grass in different directions before her short legs found the ground. She folded her wings behind her, their apexes like two shields. Her fur was light gray, blending to darker gray feathers. She walked with a rolling gait that might have seemed humorous, except she still had her claws out and her teeth bared. Her tufted ears swiveled, searching for threats. Her eyes shone with intelligence, anger, and… yes, curiosity. Some of the tension in Oriz's body fled. She wasn't going to simply lash out at him.

He kept his hands out before him, open. She glared. He fought the urge to return her challenge. How dare she! But that was the old him, the old way. Instead, he lowered his gaze. His pride was a huge, heavy lump in his throat. He swallowed it down like a lump of stringy, tough meat. For Bertra and the others, he could do this.

"We come to you in peace, to ask for your help," he began. "I know our shared history. I know your people feel much animosity toward us. I and the others with me are here to ask for your forgiveness. Our women have staged a weaponless coup against the Most Worthy and those who would not allow them a better standing among our people. We are at a tipping point, and without the assistance of your people and the Taakwa, I'm afraid things will return to the status quo. We… we humbly beg for your forgiveness, and for your help."

Behind him, one of the men shifted, another sniffed. Their discomfort was palapable. But they had come all this way to ask for help. They simply couldn't demand it. And asking for forgiveness seemed so trite. It couldn't possibly be enough for the Jeguduns to put aside their hatred and help the Maddion. Oriz's face warmed. This had been an idiotic idea. The Jeguduns would surely rip out their throats and—

A warm, soft hand gently took his. He raised his gaze, though he still had to look down because the Jegudun was no taller than a young child. Somehow he had forgotten how small they were when they stood on land. He could have sworn the Jegudun's eyes shimmered with unshed tears, but she looked away, toward the Maddion's mountain home. She took a deep breath, letting it out, and the fur around her mouth fluttered. Then she nodded. She swept her arm around, pointed to herself, and then pointed at the distant mountains.

"You'll help?" he asked, incredulous.

She nodded.

"And the Taakwa?" he asked. "Do you think they would help, too?"

She turned to him with a grimace. He blinked rapidly and realized it wasn't a grimace, but a grin. She nodded, then chirped and trilled and whistled rapidly, gesturing toward the Taakwa Valley. She took a few hopping steps away, spread her wings, then gestured as if to say, *Come on, hurry.*

He ran back to the others. He couldn't help the grin that spread across his face. "Mount up! We have some help."

Muvumo's blood burned hotter than the fire that had destroyed his scrolls and those of his ancestors. He paced the main room inside his home, Delkis standing off to one side. The place was starting to take on the odor of unwashed men and stale bread, of wine and piss. It was unacceptable. He was no animal or beast, he was the Most Worthy. He required servants to tend to him, not fending for himself and scrounging up whatever he could for food. Yet, the servants hid deep within the mountain, and there was no way to get to them with the women blocking the mesas. He could have brought the unmentionables to serve him, but they, too, hid in the mountain, protected by the women on the mesa. Cowards, the lot of them.

He required kasi powder. But his *wife*—in his mind, the word was as sharp as a blade, and as cold—his wife had taken it with her. She must have, because he couldn't find it anywhere, and it had been in the small inner pocket of his tunic the last night she'd spent with him. He let out a little growl. He'd gone through the sweating and the desperation, the nights dreaming of it and the way it would make his heart pound. And then that had worn off, replaced by this hot rage pulsing through him.

"Most Worthy," Delkis began.

"They allowed their *pets* to take off on dragons," he said. "The men they've whipped into doing their bidding. When we've cleared the mesas of this foolishness, those men will die."

"Of course, as they must."

He pulled up short. "Perhaps this strange behavior has something to do with the dragons. Perhaps the two are related. Perhaps the dragons and these men were both exposed to… something."

"Perhaps." But Delkis didn't sound so sure.

Muvumo narrowed his eyes. "What do you think of it?"

He took a deep breath. His wool tunic and pants were rumpled and stained, as were Muvumo's own, as were the guards and all the men who had been stranded by a gaggle of women. Muvumo's hands balled into fists, then relaxed. "Don't hold back, Delkis. Tell me."

"There is something odd going on with the dragons, true. But there is nothing odd going on with those men whatsoever. They simply enjoy their women too much. They enjoy what they find between their women's legs and want to ensure they keep receiving it. In short, they do it because they want to fuck."

Muvumo grunted in response. "They could fuck whomever they want, whenever they want, if they would simply clear the mesas and let life resume as it's meant to be lived."

"Perhaps they actually believe that women should have more rights."

He let out a mirthless laugh. "I'd sooner believe they do this for sex than for some belief that women deserve more than they already get." He resumed pacing. "Do you think the dragons' behavior is a result of the women's behavior, then? Could it be that they sensed the dissent and have been reacting to it all this time?"

Delkis shrugged. "I do not know."

One of the guards popped his head in. "Most Worthy, one of the men from the guardhouse is on dragonback and flying past with a message for you. He seems rather excited." He left before Muvumo could ask whether he meant the good kind of excited or the bad kind of excited.

"Wonderful," Muvumo muttered. "I suppose I should see what crisis has emerged now."

He stepped into the morning sunlight, letting the white door covering fall behind him. Delkis caught it and slipped out smoothly to join him on the stairs.

A dragon, with one of the men from the guardhouse in the saddle, was banking and coming around. He held a scroll weighed with a rock. As he passed, the dragon tilting so they could get near the stairs, he tossed it. The beast's passage created a brief wind that stirred Muvumo's clothes. He caught the well-thrown message and opened it.

Most Worthy,

A pair of dragons brought in two Jegudens this morning. Judging by the blood beneath the dragons' talons, there might have been more who did not survive. But we have two living Jeguduns. Their blood could prove useful in destroying the barrier. We have bound them and are keeping them in the first two cells in the prison. We will tend to their basic needs awaiting further instruction from you.

All glory to you, Most Worthy.

Rozik

Muvumo read it twice more before rolling it up again. Two Jeguduns captured. All they needed was a Taakwa to bleed. And his wife had sent several Maddion to search for help among the Taakwa, which meant if they agreed to help, they would be headed straight for the Maddion.

A wide grin spread across his face. He handed the scroll to Delkis, and when his personal guard looked up, he matched Muvumo's smile.

"Let the Taakwa come to us, then," Muvumo said. "We will be waiting for them, and we will use their blood to destroy the barrier and enter their valley and destroy them and the Jeguduns, once and for all."

CHAPTER TWENTY-THREE

Malia hadn't realized she felt as though she teetered at the brink of a huge, empty chasm until she spotted Cian. She'd been wavering all morning, as if she'd truly stood at the top of the cliffs and felt the pull of that fall. Just tip forward a little, and she would go. Now, she stepped back from that imaginary chasm, cold relief flooding her. Until this moment, she had been certain she was going to her death, and that Cian was allowing her to do so, and worse, that he was *glad* she was doing so.

She took a deep breath of pine-scented air, urging her heart to slow down. Beside her, Enuwal's confused frown turned to anger, deepening the lines around his mouth and eyes. And something else—a flicker of fear—crossed his face as well.

"What is *he* doing here?" Enuwal asked.

"Helping," she said.

"What he feels for you—"

"Is not what *you* feel," she said. "He's just been lonely for a long time, and I'm his only friend. And he's forgotten how to be human." The words held a great weight, as if she'd finally stumbled onto the truth.

Enuwal shook his head. "A *friend?* I don't think that word applies to him. A parasite, yes. An unwanted visitor like a snake in one's bedroll, certainly."

"I didn't say he was doing it right. I only said that's what he's after." The chasm yawned out before her. "He's been quite lonely, like I was when I left Selu and before I found you and Rasmus. You two were the only ones who believed me and who I could trust, at least for a little while. Imagine how that felt, and then imagine that stretching over lifetimes. Is it any wonder he's become so disagreeable?"

Enuwal took her by her shoulders. "He's planning on taking you away. For the rest of your life. How can you call him a friend? How can you be so understanding?"

"I don't like it any more than you do. His loneliness makes it more tolerable. Don't take that from me, please. Give me what comfort I can take."

His lips thinned, and his brown eyes, usually warm as the earth, were dark and shimmered with unshed tears. His fingers dug into her shoulders as if he might pull her closer to him, but then he abruptly released her and limped away.

Malia took a step after him, but again came the sensation that they were running out of time. She turned to Cian instead. He stood in the dappled shadow beneath the pine trees.

"You changed your mind," she said.

He nodded. "Once I realized your stubbornness would keep you going, I decided I should help. Without me, you'd surely get yourself killed, and there's still much more I'd like to know about how my power might work with yours."

She frowned. "Maybe you just tired of the constant pull between us."

"If I wanted the pull gone, Malia, I would have left you to head to your death. I came because I chose to come. Don't make me regret that decision."

Vedran stepped forward. "Andrij, how did you get here?"

Andrij kept a good distance between him and Cian. "I arrived this morning to find you all had left already. I was preparing to follow when he," he said with a jerk of his thumb at Cian, "showed up and asked if I wanted a faster way to reach you. I said yes before I could think it through, and then he grabbed me and—"

Vedran grimaced. "No need to explain. He did that with us last night. It was far faster than I ever wish to travel again."

"And yet, you look as if you'll have that very opportunity again today," Malia said. "Oh, but this is good. We'll all get to the Maddion so much more quickly."

"Malia," Enuwal called out behind her, fear tinging his voice.

She hurried into the sunlight, followed by the others. Enuwal pointed northeast. She shaded her eyes against the bright sun with one hand and squinted.

The Jeguduns that had passed them earlier were returning. And behind them, dragons followed. Her pulse quickened.

"Into the trees," she said. "They might not have seen us." She whirled, pushing Vedran ahead of her. "Go, hurry!"

In the sparse protection offered by the trees, she took a quick count. They were all there. "Cian, is there something you can do to protect us?"

He frowned, his red-orange eyes swirling fast. "The best I can do is camoflouge us all. But should they know we're here, we would be vulnerable to their weapons and the dragons' flames. Well, all of *you* would."

"Do it. Hide us."

His eyes brightened momentarily, and the smell of lightning strike filled the air. The tiny hairs along Malia's arms and at the nape of her neck rose as Cian's magic slid across her.

She stood as still as she could, hardly breathing, watching the figures in the distance rapidly approaching. She snaked out a hand to grab Enuwal's and held tight. He returned the squeeze, his other hand on his walking stick, his gaze riveted to the approaching Jeguduns and dragons. Ankti clutched her hands to her chest, murmuring low. Malia caught snatches of words, like 'protect' and 'safe' and added her own silent pleas to Ankti's.

The wind picked up, rustling the pine needles and boughs, and the stream gurgled along. The pleasant, peaceful sounds were at odds with the danger approaching. The Jegudun's were flying fast, keeping ahead of the dragons.

No, not ahead. They flew *together.* The dragons flew in formation with the Jeguduns, and they weren't attacking.

"Enuwal, do you see that?" she said. "Look at where the dragons are."

"I… they're flying with the Jeguduns. Why aren't they attacking one another? The Jeguduns can't be leading them to the valley, can they?"

"No. Not unless those Maddion are looking for help." She moved forward.

"Malia, wait, what if that's not the situation?" he said.

"There's no reason Jeguduns and Maddion would fly together unless they had reached some sort of truce." She left the trees, Cian's protection skittering across her skin and then falling behind.

She waited in the bright sunlight, heart thumping, with the beginning of a headache thrumming at the base of her skull. Far to the east, high, gray clouds were forming, promising a storm in the afternoon.

The Jeguduns in the lead slowed and flew lower; they'd seen her. She waited, her heart feeling more in her throat than in her chest. Several of them landed nearby, their wings stirring the tall grass. One, a female with dark feathers that blended to gray and then light fur along her torso and her face, walked forward with a rolling gait, her wings folded behind her.

The other Jeguduns spread out and landed, giving plenty of space to the dragons to land, each ridden by a Maddion man. Malia stepped forward to meet the Jegudun.

She pressed a small, fur-covered hand over her heart and bowed her head. Malia returned the gesture. "Are they here to harm us?" she asked.

The Jegudun shook her head. Malia let out a breath and nodded. "Do their women still hold the mesas?"

She gave a wolfish, toothy grin and nodded.

"Wonderful," Malia said.

One of the men climbed down from his beast and slowly approached. He wore the wool tunic and pants common to the Maddion, the tunic tied with a multi-colored sash. He looked to be Malia's age, with dark hair twisted in ropes and tied back with a leather strap. His belt held a dagger but no other weapons, and his hand was nowhere near its hilt. His gaze searched Malia and then the woods behind her. He frowned momentarily, his face quickly wearing a neutral expression.

If she was going to talk to him, she'd need Ankti. But Ankti had been a servant and had escaped, and she wasn't sure how this man would react to her. She took a deep breath and called behind her.

"Cian, would you come out here, please?"

She knew the moment Cian stepped out of the trees because the Maddion's eyes widened, and his breath hitched. He took a half-step back and swallowed hard, the apple of his throat bobbing. Cian let his amusement at the man's discomfort flow freely to her. He joined her.

"Would you please translate?" she asked.

"Why not get Ankti to do it?"

"Because this man might react unfavorably to her. I don't want to put her in danger."

Cian let out a long-suffering sigh but nodded. "Very well."

"How about introductions first?"

She found out the man's name was Oriz. He confirmed that the women were, indeed, still sitting on the mesas and preventing anyone from coming or going, save for him and the dozen men who had quickly taken their leave.

"Ask him what he wants," she said.

Oriz spoke, his gaze darting between Cian and Malia and the woods behind them. Cian said, "They sent several servants to the Taakwa Valley, but when they hadn't heard anything, the Most Worthy's wife sent him and the other men for help. He says a show of support from the Taakwa and the Jeguduns would tip things in their favor, and they could come to a peaceful agreement. He says he's not sure how much longer they can all hold out. The Most

Worthy does not appear willing to listen to their requests or make any compromises. He's worried things might end poorly if you do not help them."

"What sort of help is he thinking of?" she asked.

Cian and Oriz spoke again. Then Cian said wryly, "He seems a bit fuzzy on the details. It seems that all he was thinking of was getting to you, and not much beyond."

"If we arrive, will the dragons attack us?"

A quick exchange, and Cian said, "Yes. They guard the mountain and their roosts against any force that would approach."

She hesitated. There was a certain level of trust they had to give one another in order to work together. And yet… she couldn't help but recall the Dragon War, and the Maddion's vicious attacks, and the fire streaming from dragons, setting the woods and people ablaze. The Maddion had looked upon her as if she were no better than the dirt clinging to their shoes. But this man didn't. He shifted his weight and looked around as if expecting an attack at any moment, but then again, he and his men were severely outnumbered. She might have been hiding a Taakwa army in the narrow woods behind her for all he knew. He had shown quite a bit of trust by leaving his dragon behind and standing before her, making himself vulnerable.

"Tell him we have a plan already." She outlined how they were hoping to shore up the dragons' roost to trap them inside and then join forces with the Maddion women.

Oriz shifted his weight as Cian spoke, slightly shaking his head. He replied, and Cian said, "He's uncomfortable with blocking the dragons in."

She frowned. "There's no other way to ensure our safety from them, is there?"

Oriz's gaze met hers and quickly slid away. He turned abruptly and walked off, joining the other Maddion men. They bent their heads together and spoke in hushed voices, Oriz's hands moving when it was his turn.

"Can you hear them?" Malia asked.

"Of course," Cian replied. "They're discussing something about the dragon queen."

"The dragon *queen*?" She glanced over her shoulder at the woods. They appeared empty, but she could feel the weight of the others watching her, could feel their presence. It reminded her of the childhood stories she'd hear at night when one of her friends would speak of spirits in the forest. Even in the day's warmth, she shivered and turned back around.

"Here they come," he said.

Oriz's expression was guarded. This time, the other Maddion men trailed behind him. Although they remained a few paces behind him, their presence sent the message that this was a united front, that their decision was unanimous. Disappointment coiled in Malia's belly. The Maddion loved their dragons. They would never agree to blockading them in their roost. Oriz began to speak.

Cian listened impassively, giving no clue as to what Oriz was saying. Then he spoke. "They reiterate that they don't feel comfortable blocking their dragons in their roost. They say nothing of the dragon queen, which tells me that they didn't agree on a suggestion there, either."

"So they suggest we do what instead? Show up and let their beasts kill us?"

"They will do their best to control the beasts and give you safe passage."

She held back the derisive snort. That wouldn't do to seal the tenuous alliance between them. She recalled Ankti's words. *They do as their queen does.* So if the dragon queen helped the Taakwa and Jeguduns rather than attacked them, then the other dragons should fall in line. How to convince a dragon to listen, though? She thought they were mindless beasts, willing to serve the Maddion. And perhaps they all were.

"Give us a moment," she said to Oriz. She led Cian a ways away even though she was fairly sure none of them spoke the Taakwa language. She'd take no chances. In a low voice she said, "Do you think you can help me find the dragon queen?"

One brow arched. "I probably could. What would you do with

her?"

They do as their queen does. "I'm not sure… yet. But I don't trust a dozen men to hold back hundreds of dragons."

Cian sighed, a very un-Dalibor like thing. It was still strange to witness different mannerisms on an otherwise familiar body. He said, "It's a good thing I'm helping you, Malia of Selu. You seem determined to get yourself killed."

"This wouldn't be necessary if I hadn't been tricked into allowing the valley's protective barrier to fall."

"Ah, true. It wasn't exactly a trick, though."

"You hid your intentions from me. It was a trick."

He inclined his head, neither agreeing nor disagreeing.

"If we find her," Malia said, "could you help me communicate with her the way you helped me communicate with Ankti?"

"I… have never tried anything quite like that before. I might be able to." He paused. "I probably could. But would you *want* to communicate with a beast like that?"

"I communicate with Jeguduns. I don't see that it could be very much different. It might be easier, if they're as simple-minded as we believe them to be."

"Very well. Shall we tell the others, then? It will take me a while to bring them all to the mountains."

"Yes, we'll tell them. But I don't think you need to use your powers on transportation." She eyed the saddled dragons. "We have a ready source."

"Do you think the others will agree to riding the dragons? Alongside *Maddion*?"

A mirthless grin spread across her face. "It beats being held in a hunting net beneath one of the beasts. If they want to join the fight, they'll ride."

CHAPTER TWENTY-FOUR

Chanwa hardly noticed the guards switching out, one by one, at midday. The sun was overhead and bright, although heavy clouds were rolling in over the mountain peak, promising later rain and respite. The air was hot and still, cicadas droning nearby. The birds had fallen silent as if they, too, were wilting in the heat.

There wasn't much to pass around to eat. Not that Chanwa was very hungry. Her stomach had felt uncomfortable all day, but she didn't know if that was from poor food, heat, worry, or worse. She closed her eyes and tried to forget all about it by thinking of Ankti, but that led to a painful spasm of memories, so she quickly turned her thoughts instead to what life might be like if girls could learn as boys.

Boys learned their letters from their fathers or uncles or grandfathers, but there were few women who could pass on that knowledge. They would have to set up a place for the girls to gather in order to learn, and especially for those who were older so they could catch up to where they should be. She cast her mind back, trying to recall how, exactly, her mother had taught her letters and words, how to string them together and read them, how to write them. The task seemed as imposing as the mountain rising above her.

Footsteps scraped stone. Chanwa opened her eyes. A man stood at the top of the stairs, a girl on the verge of womanhood beside him. His shoulders were hunched, and he kept glancing furtively over his shoulders at the guards down the stairs. The guards looked as wilted as Chanwa felt and didn't seem to have noticed the pair yet.

"I really must speak with my lady Chanwa before my daughter and I join you," the man said to those who sat at the top of the stairs. "We'd be taking a huge risk."

"Are you doing this just for food and water?" asked one of the women sitting before the pair.

"No, of course not," the man hissed.

His daughter met Chanwa's eyes. They were huge in her small face, silently begging. She held her hands behind her back. Chanwa stood and made her way through the crowd.

"Why are you here, then?" she asked the man, although she kept her attention on the girl.

He took a deep breath. "My wife and sons died of the illness. My girl is all I have left. I want good things for her."

Chanwa turned to the girl. "Do you know any letters?"

She shook her head, her wide eyes never leaving Chanwa's.

"Would you like to learn them? And learn more?"

She nodded once.

The man nudged his daughter. "Show her."

The girl brought her hands forward. Those surrounding Chanwa tensed, but then relaxed when all she held was a scroll tied with old string. "It was my mother's."

"Oh," Chanwa breathed. She reached for the proferred scroll.

The man snatched Chanwa's wrist and pulled her forward. Chanwa stumbled past him and the girl and fell on the steps, her face nearly hitting the step stained by Nyda's dried blood. Shouts rose from behind her.

Hands grabbed her and pulled her to her feet. They dragged her down the stairs as guards raced up past her. She jerked at the hands that held her and looked up, fully expecting to find the man who had snatched her.

Muvumo, dressed as a guard, had her. He clamped an arm around her torso and pushed her along.

"Don't fight, or it'll be worse for you," he growled in her ear.

Her blood went cold and then hot. She dug her nails into the arm he held around her chest. He grunted but did not let go.

Her feet stumbled, her hands tried to find purchase, but days in the elements and without proper food had weakened her. In little time they were in the dim interior of her home.

Muvumo shoved her inside. Her foot caught the edge of the thick rug and she fell, catching herself. Pain shot through her wrist. She held in a cry and fought the instinct to rise and fight. She would never win a physical battle against Muvumo. She had to fight him in other ways.

She still carried the kasi powder in the tiny inner pocket of her dress. She clutched it as she crawled forward on hands and knees toward the hearth, her first thought to throw it in the flames and deny him the powder the way he'd denied her her scrolls.

She reached the edge of the rug. Instead of throwing the powder in the hearth, she quickly shoved the tiny packet beneath the lip of the rug. Things were happening too fast to consider why she changed her mind, but some part of her didn't want her to get rid of it, at least not yet.

His hand grabbed the back of her dress and some of her hair, hauling her to her feet as sharp pain blossomed along her scalp. She swayed on her feet, almost falling again when he let go of her. His face was contorted in anger, his eyes unfocused. His hands balled into fists.

"I am with child," she said quickly. "Strike me, and you are striking your unborn son, too."

He focused on her, his hand uncurling slightly. "What?" He shook his head. "You're lying."

She raised her chin. "I have not bled. I have always been regular. There can only be one explanation for it. I am with child."

His eyes narrowed. "I will believe you after I have ascertained that for myself."

His touch had not been welcome before, but this was worse, this unbelieving probing. The only reason she endured it was because it would save her life. When he'd affirmed for himself that she was not bleeding, he moved to search her dress. He found the small, hidden pocket empty, and she silently praised herself for thinking so fast and hiding it. Done with his search, he tossed down a few pillows and gestured to them.

"You shouldn't be out there in your condition," he said. "You should be inside, with good food, rest, and being tended to. If something happens to this child, it will be because of this folly of yours."

She bit back the words that tumbled into her mouth. He blamed her for Nyda's death when it was *his* blade that caused it, and now he would blame her for anything that went wrong with this pregnancy or with this child when it was *his* refusal to listen that put them all in this situation. But pointing that out would do her no good and only infuriate him. She clenched her teeth together so tightly her jaw ached.

"So here is what you will do," he said. "You will go out there and tell those people on the mesas to return home. There will be no consequences if they leave immediately and resume their proper tasks. Then all will be as it was, and we will go on rebuilding our population."

"I will tell them to disperse," she began, and his stance relaxed, "after you have agreed to listen to our terms and allow girls and women to learn their letters, to have authority over their own bodies, and to have more rights."

His fingers curled up, and the muscles in his jaw twitched. "I will not." He raised his chin. "But without you, they will fall apart quickly. Guard," he called out.

One of his men entered. His face was gaunt, and he had dark half circles beneath his eyes, but he stood straight as he said, "Yes, Most Worthy?"

"Find the best food we have for my lady Chanwa. And inform the other guards that she is not to leave this home under any circumstances unless I have given the order."

He nodded once. "Of course." He gave a curious glance at her before leaving, no doubt wondering why, when he had anticipated her punishment, she was instead being treated well.

"After you eat and drink, you will go lie down and rest," Muvumo said. He changed from the guard's clothes to his own.

The door covering rustled, and the man and girl who had coaxed Chanwa away from the safety of those on the mesa stepped in. Both of them went to their knees and pressed their foreheads to the floor. "Most Worthy," they said.

"Rise," he said.

They stood, neither one looking at Chanwa. The man clasped his hands before him. "We fulfilled our task, Most Worthy. I hope you remember us once this has all blown over."

Muvumo nodded once. "Your daughter will be given a good husband, and your son a chance to train with the warriors on dragonback."

"I thought your sons were dead," Chanwa said.

The man flinched. The girl met her gaze for a moment, unshed tears brimming in her eyes, and gave a tiny shake of her head. Chanwa clenched her teeth. She'd been fooled because this man had brought his daughter, and because his desperation had been real.

"Speak with the guards outside," Muvumo said. "They'll give you some food and water to take home."

"Thank you, Most Worthy," the man said. He tugged at his daughter's sleeve when she didn't move, and they slipped outside.

Chanwa took a deep breath, fighting the quivering anger in her belly. "Why don't you have something to eat as well? And get some rest, too."

His eyes narrowed. "Your concern is touching. But thanks to you, I have much work ahead." He left, the white door covering rustling in his passage.

He couldn't tell the people on the mesa to disperse, because if they chose to stay, then he would have no power over them any more. He would lose face with them. Anyone else could easily challenge him for position as Most Worthy.

He couldn't tell them himself because she held immense power. She had to be the one to tell the people on the mesa to go. A wide grin spread across her face, and she settled back against the pillows.

Power was tipping in her favor.

CHAPTER TWENTY-FIVE

As evening fell and shadows slanted across the mountains, one of their neighbors brought dinner for Muvumo and Chanwa. The elderly man said his wife was a decent cook, having picked up a few tricks from the servants over the years. The stew he brought was thin, with only a few root vegetables and chunks of meat, but the bread was fresh and not too lumpy, and there was actually butter to go with it.

He nearly dropped the basket holding the bowl of stew when he got to his knees to bow and press his head to the ground in greeting. Chanwa rescued the basket at the last moment, letting out a small *oomph* at how surprisingly heavy it was. Muvumo barked an order to a guard to take the basket from her, and she gave it up willingly.

The man bowed repeatedly, even on his way out of their home. Muvumo sat with a sigh. He'd pulled the table from where it had been propped against the wall and set it out in the center of the thick rug. He gestured at the table, and the guard set about putting out bowls and cups and serving their food, his movements awkward but sure enough that Chanwa didn't worry—much—that he would spill anything on her. He found a wineskin in the basket and poured some for Muvumo.

Delkis entered and set out his own food, helping himself to wine.

He sat with his back to the hearth, facing the door. He sat almost directly on the kasi powder. The rug was so thick, the little packet had to feel like one of its many natural lumps or threads. A low fire crackled in the space, and for a few moments the only sounds were that of spoons against bowls, and in the distance, dragons roaring.

"How goes it?" Muvumo asked after a while.

Delkis glanced at Chanwa and said, "All remains the same."

The stew was decent, and the bread was good with butter melted in it, but Chanwa's stomach coiled and tightened. She wanted to know what was happening out there. She wanted to join her people on the mesas.

"We have to clear the mesas," Muvumo said. "And without bloodshed, if possible."

"That will be difficult without their instigator telling them to disperse," he said with another glance at her. Her grip on her spoon tightened, but she said nothing. "But I think one more night outside, without her, will weaken their spirits."

"The rains were heavy this afternoon."

Delkis slurped at the stew, nodded. "But brief. They all got soaked, though."

Muvumo stared into his bowl, the stew half-eaten. "Send our best food up to the guards nearest them. Tell them to thoroughly enjoy it in front of those on the mesa, and make sure to send them plenty."

So, he'd make it seem as though they were eating well, that she was taking it easy while they were struggling. She studied her spoon and the tiny piece of meat in the middle of the dark broth and put it back down.

"They can speak of my lady Chanwa," Delkis said. "Have one of the guards bring them news."

She went still.

"Such as?" Muvumo asked.

"Start with the truth. That she's with child. Make it seem as though her maternal drives are affecting her already and she's changed her mind about her little protest. It will be believable, given the way women *do* change their minds so easily."

Her blood roared in her ears, and she could easily imagine herself throwing her bowl of stew at Delkis.

Muvumo snorted. "True enough. Very well. By tomorrow, we will have cleared the mesa. I will make an announcement that no one who leaves voluntarily tonight will be punished. We have work to do, after all, and a people to rebuild." He took a bite of stew and chewed. "It shall be good timing as well, for when those she sent away for help return with Taakwa."

"Yes," Delkis said. "Seeing as we have two captured Jeguduns, a few captured Taakwa will ensure we are able to destroy the barrier protecting them."

Her body went cold. She no longer even pretended to eat, but sat and listened, staring at fat congealing on the stew's surface as it cooled.

"Then many in the valley will die," Muvumo said casually, finishing the last of his stew. "And the rest shall be our servants."

Ankti was in the valley, protected beneath that barrier, as were all of those Taakwa and Jeguduns. Children would die. Babies. Mothers, fathers, siblings. She didn't know how or when they had captured Jeguduns, but she hoped they found a way to escape.

Delkis finished his stew. He glanced at Chanwa, then said, "She's not too delicate to clean up after the meal, especially as it would show her gratitude for the man who brought it."

"And the woman who cooked it," she said before thinking.

Delkis frowned and stood slowly, replacing his short axe on its spot on his belt. "Good evening, Most Worthy," he said, leaving them alone.

"I think you'll settle down once you become larger," Muvumo said. "The fatigue that expectant women claim they feel will overtake you. Becoming a mother will wipe out much of this." He finished with a general wave in her direction and drained the last of his wine.

She scooted to Delkis's vacated spot. "More wine?" she asked. Her finger deftly slid beneath the rug and found the little paper intact. She slipped it out and palmed it.

He nodded and gently pushed his cup to her, paying her little heed.

One nail broke the paper open. With that hand, she held the cup, and with the other, she poured. As she poured the wine into the cup, she also poured all of the powder in as well, the sound of gurgling wine hiding the faint hiss of powder falling. Her heart pounded so fast it sounded like a drum in her ears. She didn't know if he'd be able to taste it, or if it would have a chalky texture, or if he would drink only one sip. She didn't know what that much kasi powder would do to him when he had been taking two and three pinches a day. But there had to be at least several days' worth in the paper, and surely that would make him feel at least a little uncomfortable if not outright immobilize him, and she needed to give the people on the mesa more time so that Oriz might return with help.

She passed him the wine with her eyes downcast and sat back, the empty paper curled in her hand. He sipped, and she waited for a comment, for his hand to reach out and grab her, for any kind of reaction. He sipped again. She held her breath.

"Don't just sit there," he said, bringing the cup to his lips again. "Clean up in here."

She swallowed the knot of rage and hope in her throat and began to clean.

The sun was a ball of melting gold in the west, burning through the last wisps of rain clouds. The air was cool and sharp and smelled of petrichor, brimstone, and on occasion, the whiff of someone unwashed for days. Malia's nose crinkled. She could forgive Oriz's smell easily, but the dragon's smell bothered her. It was the smell of death and destruction.

They flew over the last of the grassy plains, with the foothills and the Maddion's mountain just ahead. During a brief stop for a cold dinner, they had finalized their plans, with Cian interpreting for them. The Taakwa would be deposited on the mesa where they would promise their help to the protestors and let them know that more would be coming. The Maddion men on dragons would hold positions around the mesa, and the Jeguduns would quietly show force through their numbers. A couple of dozen Jeguduns would continue on to the mountain peak to trap the men in the guardhouse and ensure they couldn't clash with the protestors on dragonback.

Cian was the only one not riding a dragon. He had raced off ahead of them, and was somewhere in the dark woods dotting the mountains ahead. His presence was acute in her mind, his concern, and yes, excitement, palpable. She had to push him aside gently so she could focus on her own thoughts and the whirling emotions pouring through her.

She clutched the pommel of the saddle, doing her best to *not* touch Oriz, although he probably would not have minded if she needed a better grip. To her right flew a dragon and a Maddion with Enuwal sitting behind. Enuwal, too, clutched the pommel, sitting upright and stiff. As if he could feel the weight of her gaze, he turned and gave her a short, quick wave. She returned the gesture.

To her left flew a dragon and a Maddion with Vedran riding along. At first he had been stiff and upright as well, but now he sat easily, his lanky young body having adapted to flight on a dragon already. He leaned into the turns and the dips and the rises, and earlier, he'd let out a few encouraging yells, spurring the Maddion to do more daring moves, which had been squashed by a stern-faced Oriz. It had made Malia realize that it would be the youngest among her people and the Maddion who might forge the best alliance between their people. It was something to remember for the future... should she live through this night.

The grassy plains gave way to foothills dotted with scrub pinyon and juniper. The air held the scent of pine and the lingering smell of damp woods and earth. Shadows slanted beneath, the world growing more dark than light.

On Vedran's other side flew a dragon and a Maddion, with Ankti sitting behind the rider. Malia had offered Ankti the chance to stay behind, but she had insisted on coming. When she'd made her presence known, the Maddion men had looked surprised and spoken among themselves. Malia had made sure they knew that Ankti was under her protection. She sat stiff in the saddle, like Enuwal, facing forward, careful not to touch the rider. As much as Malia's nerves coiled tight, Ankti's must be on the very edge.

Her hands tightened on the pommel. She couldn't speak with Oriz even if she wanted to and so had no choice but to hold her thoughts. She didn't like the idea of leaving all those dragons free. She didn't like the idea of the handful of Taakwa landing on the mesa, trapped on the mountain. She preferred finding the dragon queen. And so, before they left, she had told Cian that she wanted to leave the group before they reached the mesa. She shared her nervous energy with Cian, the coiled tension in her belly, the feeling of standing on the edge of a precipice, not knowing what came next.

He sent back such utter and complete calm that she closed her eyes and allowed herself to imagine she was a Jegudun, flying over a piney forest. The wind rushed across her skin, pressing her clothes against her. The setting sun's warmth touched her. Her heart slowed and steadied, and the tightness in her stomach loosened. Her hands on the pommel relaxed.

The dragon lurched up. Malia opened her eyes. They were past the foothills and climbing. Granite rose above them, a fiery pink in the last of the sun's light, and the forest below was dark. There was a meadow ahead, and more forest, and circling high above, near the mountain peak, were dragons. Her breathing hastened.

Cian's presence loomed in her mind, drawing her attention back to the meadow. He stood in the center, his red-orange eyes tiny blazes in the distance. The feeling of power and control washed over her, reminding her of how she'd felt when she fell off the ledge and he had lent her his magic to land safely. He wanted her to jump. Her heart kicked into her throat. It was one thing to accidentally fall off a ledge; it was another altogether to voluntarily leap off a dragon in mid-flight. And yet, she trusted him. His idea of friendship was twisted and selfish, but Rina was right. He cared for her.

She took a deep breath and undid the strap holding her left leg. She hoped they wouldn't suddenly bank to one side or the other.

Then again, Cian could move more quickly than the dragons, and he wouldn't let her fall. He wouldn't let her get hurt.

She undid the strap holding her right leg. Oriz didn't notice her movements until she swung both legs to one side. He spoke rapidly in the Maddion's guttural tongue, twisting around to grab at her.

She kicked the dragon hard on her side. The beast faltered, and Oriz's attention was torn between the dragon and Malia for a moment. Malia jerked out of his grasp and pushed off.

She dropped and swallowed her scream because she didn't want anybody to think Oriz had pushed her off. Enuwal shouted her name. *I am sorry for scaring you*, she thought. She would have a lot of apologizing to do later.

The smell of magic filled the air, and her skin tingled. Her descent slowed. She hadn't quite timed her jump right. She was coming in over the forest, just short of the meadow. But Cian had caught her. She felt as though she were flying. Cian's power hummed through her and ran across her skin like tiny pinpricks. She shivered at the delicious power.

She passed between pine trees, the needles brushing gently against her and leaving their scent on her. She landed lightly on the ground. Her legs wobbled, and she reached out automatically for something to keep her from falling to her knees.

Cian grabbed her and helped her remaing standing. He grinned. "That was quite the ride, wasn't it?"

Malia took a moment to let her stomach settle and said, "Let's go find the dragon queen, shall we?"

CHAPTER TWENTY-SIX

Chanwa finished cleaning the dishes and stacked them on the thick wooden shelves with the other dishes and utensils. The hot water and soap on her skin, the smell of the mild soap, the lifting of the dishes to their places, the gentle thumps and thuds of settling them in their places all reminded her of Ankti and the wide, hollow space in the middle of her heart. Whenever she couldn't help, she had watched the other woman's graceful movements, had exchanged a smile when possible, had allowed herself to dream of time alone with Ankti.

Muvumo let out a strangled little groan. Chanwa drew herself out of her tangled thoughts. He sat against the pillows at the table, his cup empty. He'd had all the wine, and all the kasi powder, unless it had clumped together at the bottom. Maybe the noise he'd let out was one of surprised anger at finding his precious powder at the bottom of his cup.

He had gone pale. His breathing was rapid, shallow. He grimaced.

"Done with your wine?" Chanwa asked, feigning that she saw anything amiss with him.

"Wh—what?" He blinked rapidly. Tiny pinpricks of color returned to his cheeks. "More wine? No." He pushed back abruptly from the table as if he'd rise, but he went nowhere.

She took his empty cup. The tiniest pool of red sat in the bottom, with no evidence of the powder. He'd taken it all. Maybe the powder would kill him, or maybe it would simply make him uncomfortable for a while. Either way, she'd bought Oriz and those people who remained on the mesa more time. She might even be able to slip out if Muvumo fell unconscious, and send the guards to check on him, and while they were with their precious Most Worthy, she could return to the mesa.

"The riders have returned!" cried one of the guards from the stairs outside.

She froze, the empty cup still in hand. Oriz and the others had left just that morning. There was no way they could have reached the valley, asked for help, and returned already. In fact, they should have only just reached the valley. Her heart thumped. Something must have gone wrong. There was no help coming.

Muvumo chuckled. "That's what happens when a woman gives instructions," he said. "Things get messed up. Being a ruler is harder than you thought. Maybe after this little incident, you'll have greater respect for what I do."

Numb, she scrubbed the cup in the soapy water, then dried it slowly, methodically. Maybe Oriz had simply changed his mind. Maybe the others had changed their minds and overruled him. Maybe—

"Jeguduns!" cried the guard, fear tinging his voice. "The riders return with Jeguduns!"

She let out a short breath. Not quite a laugh, no. There was no way, as she had calculated a moment ago, that they had reached the valley, asked for help, and returned so shortly. They had to have come across the Jeguduns already in route to the mountains, which meant one of the servants had reached them. Her hand tightened around the cup. She'd done the right thing, sending the servants for help, and then Oriz. *She'd done the right thing.*

"Perhaps after this little incident," she said, placing the cup on the shelf beside the others, her back to Muvumo, "you'll have greater respect for what *I* can do."

There was a hitch of breath behind her, a shift of shoe against stone, a faint rustle of clothes, and the quick whisper of a blade against leather. She turned, stepping closer to the hearth as she did so, closer to the poker for the fire.

But Muvumo remained seated, his dagger sheathed. He might have drawn it and then thought better of it. He couldn't kill the woman who might be carrying his son, no matter how furious she made him.

"Did you do something to me?" he asked.

"Whatever do you mean?"

Sweat beaded along his forehead despite the temperate room. "I feel… odd."

"Perhaps you should go lie down. Perhaps your stubborn refusal to listen to the demands of at least half of your people has taken a toll on you."

His eyes narrowed. "Did you put something poisonous in my wine?"

She straightened. "I only gave you what you desired. There was no poison in your wine." She crossed the room. "Come. I'll help you to bed."

Before she could touch him, the white door covering brushed aside, and Delkis ran in. His gaze darted between Chanwa and Muvumo. "You heard the cry, Most Worthy?"

"I did."

Delkis hurried to his side and went down on one knee. "You look ill." He turned to Chanwa, scowling. "What did you do to him?"

"I was about to help him to bed. I've been sitting out on the mesa for days. What do you possibly think I could have done to him in the short time you left us? Unless you're prepared to give me far more credit than I deserve, planning a protest, planning to be grabbed and dragged back to my home, all so I could harm him."

Delkis put an arm around Muvumo. "Come, Most Worthy, you're needed."

"You can't drag him out there looking like that," she said. "Not unless you want someone to challenge him tonight for his position as Most Worthy. If you take him out there, you're guaranteeing his death." She paused. "Unless you mean for that to happen. Maybe you want to take it for yourself. Maybe *you* made him ill."

A dragon roared, very close outside. There was the sound of flames hissing in the air, followed by screaming. Footsteps hurried up the stairs. A crossbow twanged, and another, and another. There came an unusual scream, part animal, part human. It must have been a Jegudun. Chanwa had never seen one, save in some crude drawings she'd come across as a child. But she knew there was more to the story than what she'd heard.

Muvumo closed his eyes, leaning his head back. If not for Delkis holding him up, he would have fallen back into the pillows. "Who is out there? Numbers?" he said.

"The riders she sent out have all returned, along with at least a couple hundred Jeguduns. There are Taakwa riders with some of the dragons and Maddion. And Most Worthy, the servant you have been searching for is among them, I'm almost certain."

The words scooped out Chanwa's heart, leaving her hollow, and replacing it with a vast ache. Ankti had returned? But she was supposed to be in the Taakwa Valley, safe. Or even on her way home. Not here. No. No no no nononono. She let out an involuntary groan as she sank to her knees.

Muvumo's head came up, his eyes opening. He took a long, shuddering breath. "Help me up."

"No," Chanwa said. She got to her feet quickly.

Just as quick, Delkis was beside her. The stench of his unwashed body rolled over her as he grabbed her wrists and pulled her arms behind her. He half-walked, half-dragged her into the other room and sat her on one of her chests. Then he leaned over her, planting his hands on either side, his face only a few hairs' breadths from her. His breath stank, and his gray eyes darkened, like the storm clouds that had rolled through earlier that day.

"You did something to him," he hissed. "You made him sick. If you weren't carrying his child, I would rip you open." He pressed a finger against her breastbone and traced it down the center of her chest to her navel. Her stomach quivered, and she shrank from him.

He grabbed her by her chin and forced her to meet his eyes. "Instead, I will help him bring your lover back here, and we'll rip her open instead. We will disembowel her like a dragon would, and you will get to know her body more intimately than you could ever have imagined."

She trembled violently, going hot and cold and back again. Her hands clenched the edge of the chest, and she fought the urge to wrap them around his throat and squeeze. She would never win in a fight against Delkis, not like this.

"She's the one on a dragon, though, and you are the one who is grounded," Chanwa said, shocked that her voice was so steady. "She is the one riding teeth and claws, with more teeth and claws surrounding her. If anyone will be disemboweled tonight, it will be you."

"Brave words for a woman who talked people into something as simple and stupid as sitting around."

"And yet, that stupid sitting has grounded you for days."

"Delkis," Muvumo cried from the other room. "We must go now."

"You're a woman," he said. "You know nothing."

Delkis straightened and, without another word, left.

Chanwa swallowed hard, pressing one hand over her heart. It thumped hard and fast. She took a deep breath. In the other room, Muvumo grunted. There was the scrape of wood and stone as he or Delkis fetched his weapons from where they hung over the hearth, then murmured voices, and then the faint sounds of the fighting.

She crept across the room and peered out. A guard stood just inside the door. Muvumo and Delkis were gone. She stood in the center of the room and looked around. She had to figure out a way to leave, now, while there was only the one guard to worry about. Like the others, he must be scared, hungry, tired, frustrated. She had to figure out a way to use that against him. There had to be something in here that could help her, some sort of weapon.

She went through Muvumo's trunks and found nothing but clothes. She searched behind the tapestries in the faint hope that he might have hidden a dagger or some other such weapon. Nothing. She went through her trunks even though they held nothing but clothes, because she had to do something, anything.

And in the last one, she found the wooden fertility statue that Nyda had given her. That visit seemed such a long time ago. Chanwa didn't put much value in good luck charms or things like that, but had the little statue with the big cock helped get her with child? She hefted it. The balance was all wrong. She grabbed the statue by the cock and gave it a practice swing. That felt right.

She imagined what Nyda would say at the idea of using the fertility statue as a weapon. *Grip that cock tighter*, she'd probably say, and follow it with a smirk.

Chanwa let out a strangled little laugh, then swallowed it. She would have given anything for her sister to be here. The next best thing would be to follow through with the fight she'd begun. She gripped the statue tighter, took a deep breath, and headed for the other room.

Malia stood in the meadow with Cian as Jeguduns flew overhead, shadows against the dark night sky, their passage making the stars blink in and out of existence. Hundreds of wings beat at the air. The dragons' sides pulsed red and orange and russet, and then they were all past. The pack of Jeguduns who were going to immoblize those in the guardhouse were already well past the main group and headed up, circling around to avoid the dragons flying restlessly overhead. Malia silently wished them luck.

"We have to hurry," she said.

"We could leave," Cian said. "The others have this in hand. You don't need to put yourself at risk."

"What?" She shook her head. "People I care about are headed into a fight, and they need my help. You know what I feel. I can't hide it from you. You know I love Vedran and Enuwal, and Rasmus and

Ankti, and even Andrij. They are family. They are friends. I will not leave them to fight alone."

Cian's eyes swirled red-orange in the dark, like the sides of the dragons. "I do feel it. I just don't quite understand it."

"You've lived alone for too long. You've forgotten what it's like to care about somebody else."

"No," he breathed. "I remember all of it."

She grew dizzy with the sensation of standing at a cliff's edge, with no bottom in sight. Loneliness filled the space, pressed against her, and made it feel as though her skin couldn't hold her, and it, together. "Yes, I suppose you do, after all. That is what I feel for my family, my friends, my people, the Jeguduns." She braced herself, then closed the space between them and laid a hand lightly on his arm.

Cian flinched. She fought the instinct to jump back and kept her hand on his arm. "Help me to help them, and then I really will leave with you," she said. "We can go far from other people if that's what you want. All I ask is that I make sure that my people and the Jeguduns are safe. Then you can return to your self-imposed exile."

He stiffened. "Self-imposed exile," he echoed. A strange sentiment stirred in her mind, as if something had come together for him. She reached for it, curious, but he snatched himself back before she could make any sense of it. "Yes, of course. Well, stand back, Malia of Selu, and I will lend you power so we may both reach the dragons' roost quickly."

She let her arm fall to her side and waited. Cian held one hand up, and a red-orange flame blossomed to life in his palm. Part of it lengthened into a tendril and then snaked its way to her. It curled around her arm, and its touch made her skin break out in gooseflesh. It tingled, and the power began to course through her. All of her aches and fatigue fell away, leaving her body humming with potential. The power flowed through her blood the way it did when the Jeguduns held her hands and coaxed power from her.

The last of the flame in his hand traveled up her arm and disappeared within her, leaving his burning eyes dimished. "Straight up the slope," he said.

She turned, and with hardly any effort, bounded through the woods. Each stride was fast, and unbelievably long. More than her sudden strength and ease of movement was her sharpened vision. Although it was night, she could see details nearly as well as if it were day. She easily avoided roots and rocks, and she found animals in the brush, hiding from her passage. She passed a rabbit, a fox, and even a bear that seemed as if it couldn't make sense of a human moving so quickly and had thought it better to hide.

Cian's footfalls were light and steady behind her. Her breathing quickened a little, as if she walked at a brisk pace. She raced through the woods, the ground falling away behind her, the trees growing taller, changing from pine to aspen to fir to spruce.

A dragon roared in the distance to her left. A scream cut through the air. The fighting had begun. She spurred her legs on faster. She was halfway up the mountain now.

A sharp whistle pierced the air, echoing off the granite. High above, a dragon roared in reply. Another whistle, and another dragon's roar. The calls continued, and the beasts began to cut away from their frenzied circling to come down the mountain.

"Are the mesas clear? Can the dragons land?" Malia asked.

"I don't know," Cian said. "But even if they can't, their mere presence will cause problems for your people."

She climbed and climbed and climbed. She jumped over a deep gorge, cut away by spring rains. Dragons passed overhead, zipping down as she raced up.

A dragon loomed ahead, in the woods. Several dragons. She pulled up short, holding back the cry that rose to her mouth. Cian stopped beside her.

"Dragons," she whispered. Then she realized that they weren't moving, and that the one nearest her was lying with its neck at an awkward angle. It was dead, as were the others. The stench of rotting flesh struck her then. "It's a graveyard. But I thought they burned their dead."

"They usually do," Cian said.

She breathed shallowly as she walked around the dragons. They were not full-grown, nor were they younglings. "What's going on here? Did you give them the illness when you took it from the Maddion?"

"This isn't my work. This, I think, has been a while coming. Perhaps the Maddion were too preoccupied with their deaths to notice."

"I'm sure they've noticed by now," she muttered. There was no way they couldn't know, not with so many dragon corpses lying around.

She picked up the pace again, long strides eating up the steep slope, with Cian right behind her. More dragons flew overhead, headed down. The occasional roar or Jegudun whistle echoed off the rock.

Malia reached the base of a tall, steep cliff and waited for Cian. He stopped beside her, not even breathing hard, and craned his neck. His nostrils flared. "Their roost is up there. They have several entrances, but I'm sure they all lead to the queen sooner or later."

"So we climb?"

He studied her. "I think you're nearly out of borrowed power. I'll jump, and carry you with me."

"All right." She wrapped him in a tight embrace, and he did the same to her. His body was familiar, but the way he held her was nothing like the way Dalibor used to hold her. Cian's hold was strong, but there was nothing in it that threatened to overpower her, unlike the times Dalibor held her. Dalibor had seemed to relish the physical strength he'd held over her. Malia relaxed into the embrace. Cian counted down, and together they jumped.

Her stomach flipped, and her heart leaped into her throat. The cliff sped by. A few loose tendrils of hair whipped around her face, stinging her cheek. The rushing air bordered on cold, and she gasped. Then their ascent slowed. They weren't at the top yet. They would fall, and then—

But Cian stepped onto a wide, deep ledge and set her down gently. She took a few hurried steps away from the edge, willing her heart to slow. "That was close," she said.

"We made it just fine." Cian's eyes flickered between red-orange and normal eyes untinted by magic.

She looked around. The ledge was worn and smooth and bare, and it was large enough for several dragons to comfortably land or take off. Set back in the mountain was a wide, tall, dark opening, like the maw of some large underground creature waiting for an unsuspecting passerby. She shuddered. The brimstone and charred meat smell of dragon was unmistakeable here, and she could have sworn a low rumbling came from the cavern.

Malia remained rooted to the spot. She was about to go into a dark cavern, filled with dragons, in search of their queen, and have Cian help her understand the beast so she could control her, and thus the dragons. It seemed so tenuous all of a sudden.

A scream echoed below, followed by a dragon's roar. Each moment she hesitated, people and Jeguduns were dying.

"I need a light," she said.

Cian held out his hand, and a silent red-orange flame bloomed in his palm. Malia swallowed the hard lump of fear in her throat and nodded once. "Let's go."

CHAPTER TWENTY-SEVEN

At Enuwal's cry, Ankti's head whipped around. Malia was falling through the night. Ankti braced herself, ready for the man she rode with to toss her off. Oriz had betrayed them. But no, Malia was slowing, and in that meadow were the twin pinpricks of red-orange that meant Cian stood there. He was controlling her descent. Malia hadn't been thrown; she'd jumped.

Ankti wanted to howl with frustration. She rode on a loathsome dragon, with the beast's stench assaulting her nostrils, behind a man who would sooner see her bent over and scrubbing the floor of his home than carry her behind him. No, that wasn't quite true. A host of emotions had crossed his face when he'd learned he was to carry her, among them surprise and caution, but no distaste, no leering superiority. This was a new world, and a confusing one, but one that he seemed willing to at least try out.

Her hands clenched the saddle's pommel even tighter than they had the entire flight. The question remained… why did Malia jump? Cian might have coerced her into doing so. But she'd promised him she would go with him if he helped the Taakwa and the Jeguduns, and although Ankti had known her but a short time, she knew that Malia kept her word, and Cian would know it, too, since he simply knew whatever she was feeling. She would never be able to betray him.

Did Malia seek to put distance between her and the Maddion? Did she decide to abandon them to their fate? Ankti didn't think so, but she'd been disappointed by many people over the years. She risked a dizzying glance down.

Cian and Malia were a blur, running through the woods in the direction of the mountain peak, not away. Why in the name of the stars would Malia leap off a dragon to head in the very direction they were all going?

Unless she wasn't quite going to the same place. Ankti's stomach lurched. She recalled Malia's questions about the dragons, their roost, and their queen. *They do as their queen does.* Wasn't that what Ankti had told her? It had seemed like harmless information. But now Malia was headed right for the dragons' roost, most likely in search of their queen. Ankti's teeth clenched. She had Cian with her, but how much protection could he offer against all of those dragons, and *in their roost*? The dragons would feel threatened by anyone entering. *Malia, you damned fool.*

Then again, if Malia could pull it off… if she could get the dragon queen on her side, then Chanwa surely couldn't fail.

Tiny pinpricks of torch light shone at regular intervals along the stone stairs as the dragons reached the Maddion homes. More tiny pinpricks of light shone around the lower mesa, which was covered with people. With women. And a few men. Pride swelled within Ankti. Chanwa had done this. She had all but immobilized the Maddion to make her point. She hadn't needed weapons or brute strength, but determination and a quick wit. It was one of the many things that Ankti loved about her.

A shout arose from the stairs. The dragons, riders, and Jeguduns had been spotted. Only a handful of guards stood on the stairs, but as the cry went out, men poured out of their homes, weapons in hand. A crossbow twanged, and an arrow hissed through the air nearby.

"Are we landing?" she said, shouting to be heard over the wind's passage and the beat of the dragon's wings.

The beast banked hard to the right. She yelped and clung to the saddle even though her legs were well secured.

"We can't, not with people on the mesas trapped by those on the stairs," the Maddion called back. "And we don't want to clear the mesas, because then the others can land their dragons."

Plans had changed, then. It was probably best that the Taakwa remain on the dragons for now, rather than join the protestors. She scanned the people milling below. Shouts rose from the thick crowd on the mesa. Some of those on the stairs were pulling at them, apparently trying to get them to leave. "Do you think you could leave me on the mesa? They wouldn't have to clear the entire space if I jump."

He cast her a quick glance, brows furrowed. He was a young man, perhaps even younger than her, but with weary lines around his eyes. "The Most Worthy has sought you out. He killed a servant others had mistaken for you."

She shuddered, suddenly cold, and wondered if it had been anyone she knew. She sent a silent prayer skyward, asking for forgiveness for another's life taken in lieu of her own. "I must go, for my lady Chanwa."

"You'll do her no good if you're dead."

"I'm doing her no good sitting here. I can't work a weapon from dragonback like you." There was nothing hanging from the saddle, at any rate. No crossbow, no short axe. "There's not even a crossbow to load for you."

The dragon banked left. "We had to saddle quickly to get out of here." He paused. "We'll have to come in fast, or risk getting shot. Be ready, because I'm only going to do this once."

Jeguduns were darting close to the stairs, enticing men to loose their spears and crossbows, but after a few fell short, someone began shouting for them to hold. Other Jeguduns had landed on the mesa and were fighting with tooth and claw to protect the Maddion protestors. With a bottleneck between the stairs and the mesa, only a couple of fighting men could truly get close enough to do any harm. But those on the stairs were trained fighters, and most on the mesa were not. The crowd was being pushed back slowly, but steadily, from both sides.

Her heart leaped into her throat as they came in quick and high, diving at the last moment. The rider shouted back for her to unbuckle herself. Her cold fingers fumbled at the straps as they drew closer to the mesa at an alarming rate. People screamed below, and the rider shouted for them to make room.

She freed one leg and turned to the other. The rider yelled for her to get ready to jump. *But I'm not at all ready*! she thought. Her fingers tugged, and then she was free.

She looked up in time to see them coming in over the crowd, faces looking up at them in surprise and terror. Ankti whipped one leg over the saddle and sat with both legs together, balanced on the very edge.

Then she jumped.

The dragon's wings stirred the air around her, sending bits of tiny debris and dirt flying, stinging her eyes, whipping at her hair, her clothes. She was certain the beast was going to unintentionally strike her, and she made herself as small as possible.

She hit the mesa and half-rolled, half-collapsed to her side. Hands grabbed her, hauling her up. She blinked rapidly, trying to clear her stinging eyes of the debris.

A whistle rose from the stairs. Three short blasts, and one long. Other whistles rose, one after the other. The men were calling their dragons. And yet the mesa was filled with bodies. The beasts couldn't land.

One woman, young, petite, and rather round, held onto Ankti as she steadied herself and checked her over. The woman's movements were deliberate, not fueled by fear, although her time on the mesa showed in the lines around her mouth and eyes and the way her dress hung a bit slack on her. When she met Ankti's gaze, though, a spasm of fear crossed them.

"My brother, Oriz, was one of the riders sent for you," she said.

Ah, that explained the fear. Not for herself, but for her brother. "So far as I know, he is well. He's—" she bit off the rest. She'd held in her rage and terror for so long that it was hard to speak the words she knew she must. But if these Maddion could look to change, and if those riders could treat her with respect, then she could say what she must and make her people and her god proud. "He's very brave. You must be proud."

A smile flickered across her face. "Proud, and terrified." She sobered. "You're the one the Most Worthy has been looking for. Why in the name of dragon's fire did you return?"

Ankti held back her retort. As much as these people were seeking change, they still had to shake off their old ways, and that wasn't easy. Speaking to her in such a manner, as if she were stupid for being here, was an old habit of theirs. She took a deep breath as bodies jostled around them and said, "I came to help my lady Chanwa."

The woman's brow crinkled. "Why would you…" Realization spread across her face. "Ah. *Ah.* But you're in danger, and my lady Chanwa would be devastated if anything happened to you." The woman, strong for one so petite and unused to hard work, pulled Ankti deeper into the crowd. "Her sister was killed right in front of her."

An angry cry came from the stairs, followed by a high, piercing scream. Weapons clashed. Two Jeguduns passed just overhead, their passage stirring the air and whipping a few loose tendrils of hair around Ankti's face.

"What?" Her chest constricted. "Which sister? How? Why did he kill her?"

"He was raising his hand to strike at my lady Chanwa because she was charging him, and her sister Nyda stepped in between them, taking the blow instead."

Her heart thumped as fast as hummingbird wings. "And my lady Chanwa, where is she? Is she—" She couldn't ask, *Is she alive*, because if the answer was that she was not, Ankti wasn't sure what she would do. Either crumple in a heap, or grab a weapon and dive into the melee. The smell of iron was in the air. Blood. A man cried out on the stairs, the sound abruptly cut short.

"She's alive, or she was when the Most Worthy grabbed her a while ago," the woman said. "He took her away. What happened after that, I do not know." She grimaced. "His personal guard came out, claiming that my lady Chanwa ordered us to leave the mesas and return home. She would never have given up so easily and in such a short time."

"No," Ankti breathed. "She wouldn't."

The woman scanned the night sky. "Who rides with them?"

"A few Taakwa. They were already on their way here, along with the Jeguduns, when your brother came across us."

"And are there more coming?"

"Not immediately. But the men on the stairs cannot last against those on the dragons and the Jeguduns. They will have to give up, or too many will die."

The woman grimaced. "The Most Worthy's title should be 'most stubborn'." She glanced around her quickly, as if afraid someone overheard and would disapprove. Old fears never truly let go.

"But if he dies," Ankti prompted.

"Then I doubt there would be much fight left in those standing against us. Each day we've had more men join us. Others probably would, except they're scared."

A quick count of the bustling, shuffling bodies around them showed about one man for every ten women. Not all women would be out here, of course, but that still accounted for more men than Akti would have ever guessed would join the women.

"You should hide," the woman said. "You can stay in the cavern until the fighting is over."

The cavern's wide mouth led into darkness punctuated by a couple of torches. Inside she'd find saddles, empty living quarters for apprentices, food, safety. But Chanwa was out here somewhere, and had been for days, fighting, suffering, grieving.

Ankti's blood ran hot through her veins. How many times had she lain awake, wondering how she could escape this place? How many times had she bit her tongue when spoken to as if she were nothing but meat? How many times had she longed to fight against her captors? Too many, altogether.

The first of the riderless dragons swooped down, pulling up when they realized the mesa wasn't cleared for them to land. Their sides brightened and faded, in shades of red, russet, orange, yellow. They were like bloated, giant fireflies.

The crowd shifted, and several people screamed as the air from the dragons' wings buffeted them, and their talons came nearly close enough to touch. They jostled against Ankti, pushing her one way and then the other. Her foot came down on something hard. It felt like the shaft of a spear.

Ankti used her foot to lift it off the ground, then bent over to snatch it up quickly, before the crowd could shift enough to make her lose her balance. It *was* a spear, although the shaft had been broken. But the tip was still sharp. She clutched it tight.

"I will stay and fight," she told the woman. She would fight for Chanwa, for those who had braved the mesa, for those who wanted a better life, for herself. She jabbed it up with a yell, catching the dragon's foot with the tip.

Those around her followed suit, driving spears or blades up.

Ankti forgot all about the danger her life was in as rage took her over.

Lanterns burned in the front room of Chanwa's home, and the smell of oil and unwashed bodies filled the stale, still air. The guard Muvumo had left stood beside the door, occasionally peeking out. Footsteps ran past, most of them going up. Crossbows twanged for a while, and then fell mostly silent, but the men called out to one another. Jeguduns whistled and chirped rapidly, and people's cries echoed off the granite that rose high above them.

Somewhere out there was Ankti, and Muvumo. If Muvumo got to Ankti before Chanwa could… her stomach coiled at Delkis's threat, that they would bring her back here and disembowel her. She had no doubt that he meant to do exactly that.

She clutched the fertility statue by the impromptu handle. She held it behind her, trying to look casual. The guard probably loathed waiting in here with her while the real action occurred out there. She slipped into the main room.

"Is it very bad?" she asked in a tremulous voice. *Careful. Don't sound* too *scared, or he'll get suspicious.*

But he didn't seem to notice her much at all. He looked at the white door covering, gave a little sigh, and said, "Most of the fighting is up near the mesa."

Her heart lurched. "And… how is it going?"

He glanced at her with a smirk. "Not many have died. Yet. But the Most Worthy would like to keep it as bloodless as possible. No thanks to you."

As bloodless as possible. She believed that as much as she believed mountain goats would sprout wings and fly.

"How many Jeguduns?" she asked.

"At least a couple hundred." Something heavy and fleshy hit nearby with a thud. His hand tensed around the short axe he was holding, his knuckles going white, and his eyes narrowed.

"What was that?" she asked in a heady voice.

"Probably one of the Jeguduns falling."

"Are you certain? They probably weigh as much as people. Maybe it was another guard, or one of our fighters, or… the Most Worthy."

"Delkis would raise a cry if it had been."

"Maybe Delkis is dead."

He glared at her, the muscles in his jaw twitching. "Go back in the other room, and stay quiet."

"Only if you take a quick peek for me, just so I know it wasn't the Most Worthy. Please."

He studied her a moment longer, then muttered, "If it'll shut you up, then very well."

He flicked the door covering's edge aside. Chanwa stepped forward lightly, raising the statue. The guard peered out, and was already turning around. Gah, she wasn't ready yet. But she had to do this now if she wanted to escape this space and find Ankti before Muvumo did. She ran forward a couple of steps and swung the statue down as she'd seen Muvumo and Delkis do when they were practicing their fighting skills, as she'd seen her brothers do when they were all younger and the boys were pretending at being warriors while the girls were trying to find something proper to play at.

Her anger surged forward, unleashed at last, surprising her with its ferocity and its heat. The guard was twisting out of her way, the short axe starting to rise to parry, but she brought the wooden statue down hard on his temple before he could do much more.

He crumpled to the floor without a sound. Chanwa stood over him for a moment, breathing heavily. Then she checked that he still breathed. He did. Good. She didn't want to kill him, just get him out of her way. She hefted his short axe and frowned. Too heavy. She tried his dagger. It felt better in her hand, more maneuverable. She tucked it back in its sheath, straightened, and wrapped the guard's belt twice around her waist. She studied the wooden statue. Toss it aside, or keep it?

Keep it.

She slipped out of her home and padded up the stone stairs, toward the fighting and toward the brave people holding the mesa.

CHAPTER TWENTY-EIGHT

Malia took a deep breath and braced herself to enter the cavern where the dragons lived. Even with Cian beside her, knowing he wouldn't let harm befall her, her heart raced and she felt light-headed. The air coming out of the cavern was warm and smelled of brimstone and the musk of wild animal.

"You can hold onto me if you need to," Cian said.

"I'll be fine."

"I could walk beside you for a change. We could face the cavern together."

She let out a nervous laugh. "This might be the only time I allow you to do so."

She kept one hand on the hilt of her dagger. Not that it would do her any good against a dragon, but it eased her nerves a bit. She was halfway across the ledge when a frantic whistle sounded overhead.

Several Jeguduns were coming in fast. They landed, stirring the warm air. Some were from the large group that had traveled with them to the moutains, but two—

"Aru!" Malia cried out.

Aru and Releven, one of the other Jeguduns sent to gather more information about the Maddion, were among them. They were bedraggled, fur matted and feathers hanging askew, and after they landed, they stood with slumped shoulders.

Malia hurried to them. She threw one arm around Aru and the other around Releven. "I'm so glad you're safe. The others?"

Aru shook his head and trilled sadly.

She pulled both of them a little tighter. Releven yelped, and she let go immediately. "You're hurt."

Releven twisted his hand back and forth. He wasn't hurt bad.

Aru smelled of bird and beast, and also of something else that made her crinkle her nose and think of cramped spaces.

"You were captives," she said. She glanced at the other Jeguduns. "But they found you."

He nodded. Then he glanced at Cian and the cavern and chirruped inquisitively.

"We're going to find the dragon queen. She controls the dragons, and if I can command her, then we can at least take them out of the fight."

Fear flickered across Aru's wolfish face, and he flashed his teeth. He chirped and whistled rapidly. She shook her head.

"There's no negotiating. I'm going in."

He straightened, his head nearly reaching her shoulders at full height, although the apex of his wings, folded behind him, came even with her head. His tufted ears swiveled forward, and he chirruped, pointing to himself, then her, and then the cavern.

"You can't come," she said. "You've done enough already."

His hand sliced through the air. He took a couple of steps toward the cavern and crossed his arms.

"Ah, you've finally met your match in stubbornness," Cian muttered.

She narrowed her eyes at him. "Very well, Aru, come along." Truth was, Aru's presence steadied her. "But you stay close to us. And Cian will make sure you do not come to any harm. Won't you, Cian?"

"I suppose."

She narrowed her eyes further. Cian said, "Right. I won't let any harm come to him."

The others flew off quickly. Malia couldn't blame them for not wanting to stay close to the dragons' roost. If she had wings, she'd be tempted to fly away, too.

Cian held out his hand, and a red-orange flame came to life again. Despite the light, the cavern felt as though it was swallowing them. Cian walked beside Malia, and Aru on her other side. She grasped Aru's hand and squeezed. He returned the squeeze, and her racing heart slowed.

The dragons' caverns were crudely made, unlike the smooth walls and floors of the Maddions' cells or the Jeguduns' homes. She tried to distract herself by wondering if the caverns had been here already, or if the dragons had carved them out. There were no jagged rocks protruding that might tear at wings or feet, so surely they'd done some work to make the place more like home, whatever that might feel like for a dragon.

Cian had said they were simple minded. Would it really be that easy for her to bind her mind to the queen's and make her desires a reality? The magic she and her people shared with the Jeguduns was more of a give-and-take. With this, she was planning on merely taking. It felt wrong somehow, even though she was dealing with simple-minded beasts.

They came to a fork in the tunnel and stopped. "Which way?" she whispered. The place was eerily empty. She'd been expecting dragons at every turn, multiple fights, confrontations, not this… hollow silence.

Aru sniffed the air, then pointed left. They went that way, the cave leading them deeper and down. They passed room after room, some padded with pine needles and smelling strangely of forest and dragon, while others were padded with rags, and still others with fir or spruce branches. These were places to sleep, and no more, but made somewhat comfortable all the same.

They came to several more intersections, and at each, Aru told them which way to go. They found no dragons, which made the skin along the back of Malia's neck prickle. Were they all in the air? Or elsewhere, sick? She thought of the corpses in the forest and shuddered. If they were ill, could it pass to her or Aru? Too late now. They had been breathing in the dragons' air for what felt like days, but which had most likely been not very long at all.

Aru raised his head at the next intersection. His nostrils flared as he looked down the right branch, and he pressed himself a little closer to Malia.

"Is she down there?" she whispered.

He nodded.

It was a narrower opening, just large enough to allow a dragon through. The air this far down was sweltering, and sweat beaded along Malia's forehead and down her back, making her tunic cling to her. The queen's cavern was dark, and the darkness seemed to press out, unwelcoming and unyielding. She shivered despite the heat.

Cian's presence moved in her mind and brought forward waves of comfort and contentment, the same as she felt while making pottery, the clay slowly taking shape, or the feeling she had at the end of a busy day when the only thing she had left to do was watch the sun go down and eat warm bread with honey and drink tea, or the feeling she had when Enuwal held her close, the smell of crushed herbs and light sweat filling her nostrils. She let out a quiet sigh, renewed her grip on Aru's hand, and walked down a short hall and into the queen's lair before she could change her mind.

It was stifling, like sitting in the hottest spring in the Taakwa Valley, and the air was heavy with the stink of brimstone. Malia didn't need Cian's light, because the queen's sides pulsed brighter than any dragon's she'd encountered before.

She was not the largest dragon Malia had ever seen, but her muscles rippled as she raised her head to regard them, nostrils flaring. Spikes rose in a row along the back of her neck, small near her head, and increasing in size near her shoulders, continuing on to her tail, the end of which twitched. She let out a low rumble that vibrated the very air. Her sides pulsed brighter, so much so that Malia squinted. Aru clung to her hand. She pulled the Jegudun closer to her, though whether it was to keep him safe or make herself feel better, she wasn't certain.

"You won't be harmed," Cian said. "I can at least get us out of the caverns safely. Hold steady. Don't let her see your fear."

"I don't see how she could miss my legs trembling, or how fast my heart is going," she said.

"She notices that, yes, but she also notices that you don't run. Hold your ground."

There was movement around the queen. Four smaller dragons came into her light. They ranged from dull gray to brown to the black of a moonless night sky, and they were scarcely larger than Malia, and certainly incapable of carrying anyone.

"Are those the males?" Malia asked.

Aru trilled low and nodded.

"They have no fire," she said.

He nodded again.

Although they didn't have fire, they certainly had long talons on their feet, and teeth sharp enough to rend flesh. And given their size, they were still fully capable of ripping Malia and Aru apart in a matter of moments.

She took a deep breath. There was no time to stand around and talk herself into this. "Cian, what do we need to do?"

"I can make it so you understand her, the way I did for Ankti's language."

Her pulse quickened. "All right. Will it, ah, hurt as much as it did last time?"

"I'm afraid so."

Aru squeezed her hand. She returned the gesture.

"We have no time," she said. "Go ahead."

The smell of lightning strike filled the air. The dragon queen growled, baring her teeth. There were dark stains on some of them, and a bit of gristle stuck between two. Her rank breath competed with the smell of magic, and Malia choked back the bile that rose in her throat.

The dragon lumbered to her feet. She'd been lying on a nest lined with packed dirt, soft branches, and bits of forest detritus. Within, half a dozen dragon eggs sat tucked together, russet in color with light spots, each about half the size of Aru. It was a large nest, and so few eggs.

She drew back as the beast made her way across the cavern. She moved lightly for a creature so large, her footfalls like the soft padding of a wolf through the forest, but Malia held her ground. Aru moved slightly behind her, his free hand clutching her skirt, his talons pricking through the fabric and stinging her hip.

"Aru," she hissed. "Not so close."

He loosened his grip on her skirt but did not move. Cian held her hand, as steady as if he stood ready to greet a friend. The red-orange swirl of his eyes was slow, steady.

The dragon stopped a stride away from them. She stretched her head forward, sniffing the air around them. Malia held her own breath, waiting for the investigation to end.

The dragon sniffed in Cian's direction. She jerked her head back with a grunt as if she'd been smacked on the nose. Then she stretched her head forward tentatively and sniffed again. She let out a little growl, lifting one side of her lip, and drew her head back.

The dragon turned to her. Malia held herself still, willing her legs not to shake. The dragon's gaze was steady, searching… bright. She suddenly recalled how she had snuck up on Tuvin after he'd fallen, certain she was approaching a wild animal, only to discover he was as intelligent as her.

"She's not simple minded," Malia breathed.

"Apparently not," Cian said.

"I thought you knew them."

"I thought I did, too. Their queen must be different."

"Of course she is, if she controls them." It seemed so obvious now. "I can't just take control of her mind."

Cian frowned. "Why not?"

"It would be like taking control of Aru's mind and making him do as I want." She paused. "But… I could still communicate with her."

"You could. There's no guarantee she'd help, though. She's been loyal to the Maddion."

She thought again of the dead dragons littering the forest.

"Something's going on with them, though. Let's do it, Cian."

The dragon queen regarded them through lidded eyes. She sensed Cian's power, and she couldn't have been happy with their intrusion into her lair. The males had shifted so they stood between the eggs and Malia's group.

The smell of magic grew. Prickles of energy ran along Malia's skin. She closed her eyes and waited.

Cian's presence in her mind strengthened and loomed. Pressure built within her skull until she feared it might burst, and still it seemed that Cian hadn't done much more than begin the process, much less finish it. He abruptly retreated, and she opened her eyes, gasping at the pressure in her skull dwindled.

"What happened?" she asked.

"There's too much going on in there," he said, tapping her head gently. "Between the magic you share with the Jeguduns, and the repairs I made to your memory, and your ability to communicate with Ankti, I can't do much more to tweak things."

"So that's it? No communicating with her?" she asked with a jerk of her head toward the dragon queen.

"Not unless I shift things around. Otherwise I'd be working a major change like I did before, and I'm not certain what the result would be."

"What do you mean by 'shift things around'?"

"You would have to lose something magic-related. Then I could make it so you could communicate with her."

"Then take my ability to understand Ankti. I can figure that out on my own anyway. More slowly, but still."

"That wouldn't be enough, Malia. Speaking with another human is not as complicated as communicating with another species. It would be best if I exchanged the bond you have with Jeguduns for the ability to communicate with the dragon queen."

Aru took in a sharp breath beside her. "But," she said. "That would mean I could not do magic with them anymore."

Cian nodded.

"And they couldn't share memories with me."

Another nod. "I'm sorry, but it's the only way to make this work."

She thought of the skull-splitting pressure she'd just felt. She thought of the flights she'd taken through Jegudun memories, of how they'd shared their collective history with her. She'd be cut off from them.

"Would it be permanent?" she asked.

"Yes," he said.

"Aru, what do you think?" she asked.

He blew out his breath, the fur around his mouth fluttering. His green eyes held sadness. He nodded.

She didn't know how much time had passed. She didn't know what the fighting was like out there, but she could be certain it raged on. "Very well," she said. "Let's do this, Cian."

The sharp, pungent smell of magic enveloped her, and tingling ran along her arms, down her spine, down her legs. Cian's presence loomed in her mind again, and the pressure built. She closed her eyes and took a deep, shuddering breath.

Something shifted with an almost palpable *thunk* in her mind. Then another thing, and another, as if her mind were a series of shelves, and Cian was removing entire shelves and everything on them. The pressure dwindled.

There was another shift in her mind, and the pressure swelled again, pressing against her skull. She held back a whimper as the pressure bordered on pain and reminded herself that it was temporary.

There was a massive shift, and more pressure. Aru grasped her hand tighter, and the pain from it brought her back. She was gasping for air, struggling to breathe. Her head felt as though it might split open. She wanted to tell Cian to stop, but she couldn't speak. Her free hand reached for Cian but found something hard as stone and warm instead. It shifted beneath her hand, moving so that she could hold herself up.

A new presence stirred in her mind. The pressure faded, leaving behind a throbbing headache. Aru's hand was gone. But she was holding something, and that something shifted under her hand.

She opened her eyes slowly. She was holding onto the dragon queen's shoulder. The beast had turned her head around to study Malia.

The new presence shifted. *Greetings*, came a surprised thought in Malia's mind.

Her mouth was dry. She worked her tongue, trying to find some spit so she could talk.

You don't need to speak aloud, the dragon queen said. *Feel this*?

A tug came at her mind, like the one the Jeguduns used to ask if it was all right to share a memory with her. Malia returned the tug and thought, *Yes*.

The skin around the queen's eyes crinkled, and she let out a gentle snort. *I never thought I'd be able to speak with a human.*

And I certainly never thought I'd speak with a dragon, Malia thought.

It wasn't quite speaking, not in the sense that the dragon had a spoken language, but somehow, that was how the beast's thoughts came across. Malia could tug on the unseen line connecting them and speak with the dragon, or hear her.

This one was like the dragons' clan mother. She spoke for them all, made decisions for them all. Malia suspected she often chose who mated with whom. It was unsettling, realizing the Taakwa actually had something in common with the dragons.

The dragon tugged at Malia, and said, *What brings you here, human*?

She hesitated. Before, she would have demanded help. But now, she was speaking with an intelligent being who ruled her entire people. She said, *Queen dragon of the Maddion mountains, I and my friends have come to ask for your help.*

Another presence in her mind twitched. Cian. There was the feeling of surprised, pleasant warmth when she said *friends*, as if he didn't quite believe he was included in that statement.

What help do you need? the queen asked cautiously. She hunkered down, as if to make herself smaller, bringing her head eye level with Malia.

Malia explained all that had happened as quickly and succinctly as possible. She concluded with, *The Taakwa and Jeguduns are hoping to avoid bloodshed on all sides, including the dragons under your care.* That wasn't quite true. Malia had been prepared to let them all die, but that was before. Guilt gnawed at her. She shoved it away. She'd wallow in her guilt later, when she had time, and if she got out of this.

The queen's pulsing sides slowed, and her eyes grew heavy-lidded. Malia worried that she was falling asleep. She fidgeted and waited. It wouldn't do to hurry along a beast that could bite her head off.

The queen's eyes widened, and her sides brightened. She said, *I will help you if you will do something for me and my dragons.*

What is that?

We have been confined to this mountain for generations based on an old agreement with the Maddion. Our numbers grow too large to support us all, and we must go farther and farther to hunt.

The dead adolescent dragons in the forest had been culled from the population. It was like the Taakwa in their valley. If they never left, and they didn't keep their population in check, there would be too many to feed.

Malia said, *Is there no way to change the agreement?*

There is a bond between dragon queens and the Maddion's rulers. But I fear their rulers have forgotten about that bond, or the agreement, or they have chosen not to respond.

Or, it might have been detailed in their scrolls, and the scrolls were gone. She frowned at Cian, and his brows crinkled in perplexion. She shook her head.

So, what can I do for you? Malia said. She couldn't change this agreement. And if the dragons were bound, then they must feel something akin to what the Jeguduns felt if they traveled too far from the valley, or what Cian had felt when he traveled far from her initially.

Convey this information, the dragon queen said. *Let them know what is happening to us, because I fear they don't see it, and they won't until it is too late. I only want my dragons to thrive. Some of us need to*

"There's nowhere to land," she muttered through clenched teeth. But the dragons were territorial; they'd attack the Jeguduns.

The air was thick with the smell of unwashed bodies, and blood, and the sour stench of fear. Chanwa's heart galloped along. So far she hadn't spotted Muvumo or Ankti, which didn't make her feel at all better.

Most of the riderless dragons streamed by the mesa. Some turned on the Jeguduns, roaring, snapping at them. One let out a stream of fire, catching a Jegudun, who erupted in flames, letting out a piercing scream that abruptly cut short as the beast tumbled to the forest below. The smell of burnt flesh and feathers drifted on the breeze moments later. Chanwa swallowed the bile that rose to her throat. The Jeguduns broke their sweeping attacks and flew away.

Screams drew her attention back to the mesa. Some dragons were trying to land, despite all the bodies on the space. One dragon's sides were pulsing rapidly and ever brighter as it prepared to unleash its fire.

Chanwa clutched the statue to her and ran up the stairs. "No," she said. "No, no, no."

The crowd on the mesa broke. People ran up the stairs, or down, tumbling along like a waterfall, sweeping up anyone who got in their way. A body tumbled over the wall and into the darkness below. Somebody screamed, over and over, and abruptly stopped. Those above Chanwa turned and ran toward her, their eyes wide.

She looked around wildly. She'd be crushed if she stayed on the stairs. Home was too far for her to make it back there, and besides, she wasn't returning to what was essentially her prison. Instead, she ran down three steps and into somebody's home.

The main room was dark, and smelled of sweat, bread, and milk. A faint light outlined the sheet hanging over the door to the other room. A sniffle and a hushing sound came from behind the sheet. A baby fussed, slightly, but with the promise of full on wails to come, and a woman murmured.

Chanwa tried to recall how far she'd come before stopping. She took a few tentative steps into the dark room until her shin hit a low table. She hissed at the sharp pain. The murmurs beyond the sheet stopped.

"Tangie?" Chanwa called out softly.

Fabric rustled, and a corner of the sheet pulled back. Tangie, clutching her newborn to her, peered out, her eyes wide. "My lady Chanwa." Footsteps thundered down the stairs toward them, and screams filled the air. "It's a good thing you're in here."

Then the crowd was outside, running, feet slapping on stone, people breathing heavily, or sobbing, and one person keening. The sound tore at Chanwa's heart, and she was all too glad when the keening faded. A dragon roared, and she broke out in gooseflesh.

"What's going on out there?" Tangie said.

Chanwa could hear the unasked questions in the strain in Tangie's voice. Are we winning? Losing? Most important of all… was this all worth it?

"I don't know," Chanwa said, answering all questions spoken and unspoken.

Footsteps faded down the stairs.

"Stay here," Chanwa said.

The sheet fell back. The light behind it dimmed.

Chanwa crept back to the door. There was a scuffle outside. A grunt. The heavy sound of fist on flesh, then a moan.

"Are you hurt?" It was Delkis.

Chanwa's heart kicked against her breastone. She leaned near the door to hear better.

"No," Muvumo said. "She caught me by surprise, is all." Gruff, and slightly breathless. "But," he continued in a gloating manner. "I found her."

She bit back a moan. Muvumo could be happy about finding only one woman.

"Let's bring our prize to my wife," he said. "Help me."

A grunt, and then footsteps hurrying down.

Chanwa's pulse raced. She had one chance at this. When they found her missing from home, they'd as soon as kill Ankti and leave here there for Chanwa to find. She had to do something, now.

She crouched beside the door, grip tight on the statue, and waited. The footsteps approached rapidly. They'd be past her in moments. She waited, every muscle coiled, hardly breathing. They were at the door, just on the other side of the sheet. It stirred as they passed. She let out a long breath and slipped out.

She brought the statue down on the back of Delkis's head, twice in rapid succession, and as hard as she could muster. He grunted and stumbled to one side, precariously close to the short wall.

Chanwa pushed him over. He fell without a cry into the darkness below. She turned and met Muvumo's gaze.

He held onto a limp Ankti. One of her eyes was swelling, and there was a bump above it on her forehead. She blinked rapidly, and when she noticed Chanwa, a host of emotions crossed her face—relief, fear, and a fleeting tenderness that felt as though it might crack Chanwa's heart into pieces. Ankti wore Taakwa-style clothes, with her hair pulled back. She looked brighter, younger, more herself than she ever had in the drab, rough garments she'd worn as a Maddion servant. She was not subservient any longer, but a warrior, and she'd never been more glorious in Chanwa's eyes.

Muvumo, however, snarled at her, flashing teeth like a Jegudun might. A vein in his neck stood out, throbbing rapidly. He had one arm wrapped beneath Ankti's arms, and the other hand held a dagger to her throat. His hand shook slightly, then held still. A thin line of red appeared beneath it, and Ankti hissed.

"Don't," Chanwa said. "Please."

Sweat beaded along his forehead, and his face was flushed. Dragons and Jeguduns soared all around them, teeth and claws and screams, but Chanwa had eyes only for Ankti and the dagger pressed against her throat. Nyda had bled so much. Chanwa hadn't known one person could hold so much blood inside them. She did not want to see Ankti's blood spill on the stairs. That foolish, brave, wonderful woman. She should have stayed in the Taakwa Valley, where it was safe. Why had she come back here?

Chanwa shoved all of that aside. She had to focus on Muvumo. "You look ill. Let me help you home. Make you some tea."

He was breathing so fast. And the pulse in his neck throbbed… he couldn't remain upright much longer if his heart was beating that quickly. She had to distract him, wait for the right moment.

"You don't know your place," he said between clenched teeth. "You fell in love with a *servant*." He said the last as if describing dragon shit he'd found on his shoe rather than a person.

"Let's go back home," she said, taking a tiny step forward. "The mesa has cleared." So much noise behind her. Men shouting, running, dragons snuffling. She dared not turn around, but she was certain she'd find Muvumo's supporters saddling their beasts, getting ready to fly against her dozen men and the Jeguduns. So many cries in the air around her. *Focus*. "You've won, Muvumo," she said. "You have your people back, you have power, you have a child on the way."

Ankti's eyes widened at this.

A shudder went through his body. "It's not over. You need to learn, once and for all, who is in charge here."

The muscles beneath his tunic bunched, tightened. He was going to drag that dagger across Ankti's throat. Chanwa started forward, panic rising like a flood. Muvumo's eyes fluttered, and he swayed.

"Ankti, move," she cried out.

Ankti grabbed his forearm and yanked it down and away as she leaped forward. The dagger tumbled away. Chanwa reached for Ankti, to pull her up the stairs, but she jerked back.

Muvumo's eyes were clear, and his hands steady, filled with a fistful of Ankti's clothes. He shoved Ankti at the short wall. Ankti clutched at it, hands scrabbling for purchase. The fertility statue fell as Chanwa leaped for her.

Chanwa's fingers brushed against the skirt, against Ankti's leg, and then Ankti was over the wall and falling into the dark.

When Malia emerged onto the uneven ledge outside the dragons' cavern, she took a gulp of fresh, cold air, relishing how it burned her lungs and drove out the heat and stench of the caverns.

"I'll need a saddle," Malia said to Cian. She thought the same at the dragon queen, who was emerging onto the ledge.

There's no need, the queen said to her. *None would fit me, and you can sit between the ridges on my back.*

There are no straps to hold me in.

I will not let you fall. She was absolutely certain.

Malia eyed the ridges dubiously. She would simply be a passenger, holding on tight, at the dragon's mercy. The queen could turn upside down if she chose, and let Malia slide off.

But no, she wouldn't do that. The nice thing about speaking with someone the way she spoke with the dragon queen, or the way she received impressions from Cian, was that there was no room for dishonesty. The queen said she'd keep Malia safe, and she meant it.

Aru trilled and pressed closer to her. Malia put a hand on his shoulder. He shuddered.

"It will be fine," she said. "You find the other Jeguduns, or a safe place to wait for this to be over."

He shook his head, his ears pinned back, and bared his teeth.

"Aru, I insist." She didn't want him in harm's way again. He'd been through enough already.

He snuffled once, the fur around his nostrils fluttering, and then his shoulders slumped and he nodded.

"Thank you, Aru," she said, squeezing his shoulders. She turned to Cian. Before she could say anything, he spoke.

"I'm not waiting up here," he said.

His emotions were a jumbled mess, but mostly there was a sick, twisty feeling. He was worried. The red-orange of his eyes had faded quite a bit, and a hint of golden-brown peeped through. Dalibor's eyes had been an unremarkable brown.

"I'll be fine," she said.

"I'm heading down. To be near, in case."

She wanted to insist he stay behind, or that she didn't need him, but the truth was, his presence steadied her. Maybe it was just the magic binding them, but knowing he would be nearby settled her nerves immensely. She gave him a tight-lipped smile, and then turned to the dragon queen.

How do I get up? she thought at the queen.

The queen snorted softly, thin plumes of smoke rising from her nostrils. She crouched. Malia clambered onto her bent knee, and with a boost from Cian, swung her leg over the queen's back and in between two ridges. She settled on a spot at the dragon's shoulders and found that the ridge in front of her was better than a pommel at holding on. And hold on she did. Her mouth went dry, and panic swelled. She nearly jumped right back off.

Settle down, the queen said. *Maybe you'll even enjoy flying.*

Before Malia could reply, the queen spread her wings and charged for the end of the ledge. A shriek built in Malia's throat. The queen leaped off the ledge, and there was nothing beneath them but tall pine trees, and the ground so far away. Malia's stomach jumped into her throat where her heart already had already lodged.

The queen's wings caught, and their dive turned into a soar. Malia's swallowed her shriek, her heart thumping madly. She held tight to the ridge before her. She looked around them wildly. Trees, stars, the pulsing lights of dragons below.

They're listening, the queen said.

Malia took a deep breath, and another. *Cease fighting. Please. Put distance between yourselves and the Jegudúns and their allies.*

The pulsing lights rose to meet them. The dragons were like a thousand caresses in her mind, soft as cornsilk, and so surprisingly gentle.

A few had landed on the mesas and were being saddled. Malia called to them. They shook off their saddles and their handlers and lifted into the air. Their riders tried to call them back with whistles and shouts, but the dragons ignored them. A thrill went through her, and her hands tightened on the ridge. She could turn the dragons on the Maddion and end this.

By ending an entire people.

It was no less than what the Maddion sought to do with the

Taakwa and the Jeguduns. Kill them, and enslave the rest.

But it wasn't right. It wasn't truly what her heart desired. She was tired, all the way to her bones. She wanted this to end, but not with the death of an entire people.

The dragon queen flew down, and down. People had been running up the stairs in a panic, but some stopped and watched her, or pointed, or shouted. Could they tell, in the dark, that a Taakwa woman rode the dragon, and that this was the dragon queen?

They passed one mesa and approached the other. A dragon landed, and the rider slid off. It was Oriz. A woman ran out of the cavern beside the mesa, hesitated, and then threw herself at him. She gestured wildly as she spoke, pointing down the stairs.

Down the stairs, a man held a woman close to him, his captive by the look of it, and they faced another woman. The Most Worthy held onto Ankti, pressing a blade to her throat, and opposite them stood Chanwa, nearly unrecognizable with a wild expression on her face.

We must get closer to them, Malia said to the queen.

As they banked, Ankti slipped away from Muvumo. Malia leaned forward with a gasp, urging Ankti on.

Then the Most Worthy shoved her over the short wall.

Dive! Malia shouted just as the queen lurched, already anticipating what she wanted.

Malia held tight as the dragon folded her wings against her sides and plummeted. She began to slip off and tightened her legs around the queen's wide shoulders. Her hands found a notch in the ridge and she squeezed.

Somebody screeched. The queen's wings unfurled with a snap, and she grunted as their descent came to an abrupt stop. Malia was light-headed, and her entire body quivered.

Do you have her?

I must land to set her down. She's alive. Her heart beats so fast... Ankti's heartbeat, as heard by the queen, echoed in Malia's head, followed by the strong tang of blood, and the concentration it took not to squeeze tender human flesh too hard.

"Ankti, hold on," Malia shouted down. "You'll be on the ground in a moment, and safe."

A half-scream, half-sob answered her from somewhere just below the queen.

They descended through pine trees, the queen tilting this way and that to fit between them. Then her hind legs were down, followed by her forelegs.

Malia swung one leg over and slid down the queen's side. Her wobbly legs couldn't hold her, and she collapsed to her hands and knees on dirt and pine needles. She moaned, fighting the urge to vomit.

Strong hands grasped beneath her arms and helped her stand. Cian, brow furrowed, studied her. His eyes were no longer red-orange, but a steady golden-brown.

"Thank you," she gasped.

"That was close," he said. "I was about to try to catch her, but then you swooped out of nowhere and grabbed her."

"It was her," she said, with a nod toward the queen. "She was brilliant, knowing what I wanted before I did." She leaned against the dragon.

Cian's face softened. He allowed his relief to come forward as he laid a hand briefly on her arm. Then he walked to where Ankti had been set down.

The queen's side expanded with each breath. She was warm, bordering on hot, but it felt good in the cooling night. Malia leaned her head back against the queen, and a content rumble passed through the beast.

Cian emerged with one arm around Ankti. Her eyes were wide and focused on the dragon queen. Her hair had come undone and stood out in wild curls around her face, and a couple of bruises were forming, including one around her eye, which was swelling shut.

"Ankti," Malia said, pushing off.

Her eyes turned to her. "Stars above, Malia, what *is* this?"

She gave the other woman a quivery smile. "Meet the queen of the dragons."

"Oh," she breathed. "I wasn't so scared when I fell, but when the dragon grabbed me… I thought I was dinner. Or I was going to be returned and used against Chanwa." She struggled to stand straighter. "Chanwa!"

"Sit," Cian said. "You're in no shape to go running off to help anyone."

"Malia!" a voice cried in the distance.

"Enuwal," she said. Then louder, "Enuwal, here."

Footsteps crashed through brush, followed by a thump and *oomph*, and then he stumbled into the small clearing. Relief flooded Malia. She hurried to him.

"Thank goodness you're all right," she said.

"And you," he said.

She reached a hand for him and hesitated. His own relief had been replaced by a stiff bearing, one not inviting to touch. She'd have to sort through her feelings later. "Ankti's been hurt. Would you look at her?"

"Of course. But there's a dragon…" He trailed off, squinting. "She's different."

"She's the queen."

"So *that's* where you went. I suspected as much, but… that explains why the dragons suddenly stopped attacking us. But how did you do this?"

"I'll explain it all later. Right now, Ankti needs your help, and someone else needs mine."

"Malia." He grabbed her arm gently, then let go. The corners of his mouth turned down. "I thought I might never see you again. Before you leave for good, we need to talk."

The bone-deep weariness returned. "Yes. We do." She hurried back to the queen and clambered up, this time without help. She looked down at Cian. "Follow me up?"

"Of course."

She didn't miss the glare Enuwal shot at Cian.

Let's return to the stairs, she said to the queen.

It will be tricky getting out of here. Hold on tight.

Malia found the notch again and squeezed herself against the dragon as she lurched into the air. She went up, and up, catching against trees a couple of times. Then they were clear.

Cian's presence remained closer to the forefront of her mind. He was racing up the steep slope, although fatigue was setting in. His magic couldn't be limitless. There was a lot she still didn't know about it.

Malia and the dragon queen emerged from the trees. Rather than finding the Most Worthy and Chanwa on the stairs, or even finding the stairs empty, they were filled with people shoving, fighting, screaming. There was no way of knowing what was going on, or where Chanwa was, or if she was even still alive.

CHAPTER THIRTY

Chanwa ran to the wall where Ankti had fallen, wild thoughts spinning through her mind. Ankti might have landed on a small ledge. She might have grabbed something and held on, waiting for help. She might survive the fall. She might, she might, she might.

Muvumo grabbed her and yanked her close. He smelled of days' worth of sweat, and something else that reminded her of the days when the illness stalked them all. She shoved him, fought against him, but for a man who looked so weak just moments before, he was holding her so tight she could hardly breathe.

"We're almost done with this," he said, his voice ragged. "You will tell those who sat on the mesa that it's over. Everyone will return home, and tomorrow we will all begin anew."

She let out a sob, hating herself as she did so. Ankti was gone. Truly gone. Muvumo was still here, and tomorrow would be a day like any other, except without Ankti, and without Nyda, and she'd have nothing to do but sit around and grow larger and then watch her child grow into a yoke forced upon them by tradition.

She tried pulling away. Muvumo yanked her close. She could hear a rapid, broken thumping and thought it fighting at first. But the skies had cleared, and any fighting occurred far below or above them.

Muvumo's heart was not doing well. It was struggling, beating hard and unsteadily beneath his breastbone.

"You've broken my heart," she said.

"You'll forget all about her when you hold your baby," he said, dragging her down the stairs.

"And my sister? Will I forget her, too, or how you killed her?"

"That was your fault, not mine. In fact, all of this," he said with a wave of his arm, "is your fault. This is what happens when you try to lift yourself above your proper place." She stumbled down two more stairs, and then he added, "Their lives combined would never equal Delkis's, though. *His* loss is the one you should be mourning."

She hissed at the searing pain and anger of his words. She held back the wave of anger. Instead, she went limp. "I can't... I can't make it any further. You have to help me."

He stopped and sputtered. "*This* is exactly what I meant. You are weak, incapable of tolerating such a physical strain. I can only hope you haven't pushed yourself so hard that you've harmed the baby."

He crouched to lift her, releasing his tight hold on her for a moment. She let her wave of anger and grief rush forward into her arm as she brought it back and imagined it pouring out of her and into Muvumo as she slammed the meaty part of her palm into his chest. Something in her wrist and her elbow popped and stung. He froze, and she stumbled away from him, ready to flee up the stairs.

His mouth opened and closed, but no sound came out. He drew in a wheezing breath, and then crumpled to the stairs.

Chanwa stood over him, panting, hands balled into fists, waiting to see if he'd move. She'd struck out blindly, hoping to get away from him. She didn't expect him to just... collapse. When he didn't move, she reached down and placed a finger beneath his nose. No breath. She crouched and laid a hand over his heart. All was still.

She stood. About thirty steps down, three men stared up at her. She swayed on her feet.

They rushed up the stairs to her.

Malia and the dragon queen flew alongside the stairs. Cool night air swept past her, carrying hundreds of voices. The front end of the crowd reached the mesa. The crowd parted momentarily as people spilled onto the open space, revealing a pair of men holding onto Chanwa and hauling her to the center of the space. The Most Worthy was nowhere in sight.

She could land and hold them back with the dragon queen, and she could command the other dragons to back her up, or attack, and she could have the Jeguduns return and add their numbers, but it wouldn't truly change anything. She would simply be overpowering them for a limited period of time, and then this chaos would return.

Change. Chaos. Chanwa. The world spun as Malia considered her choices and what she was about to do. There was one way to bring about the change that Chanwa fought so hard for. There was one way to help the Maddion, the Taakwa, the Jeguduns, and the dragons.

"Cian," she said, pulling at his presence in her mind. To the dragon queen she said, *Land quickly, please.*

The queen snorted in reply but slid away from the crowd and the noise and into the forest. *I can land on the slope. It will be steep, but I can hold.*

Do it.

The landing was no worse than the previous one, and Cian was there immediately to help her down.

"What's wrong?" he asked.

"I want you to change something for me."

"Malia, I have no idea what will happen to you if I do this. Or to me. Our connection—"

"Please," she said. "I'm so tired of all of this. It has to end tonight, one way or another. Then, if I'm still here, we can leave. One more fix for me, Cian."

Shouts drifted down from the mesa.

"Cian," she said, laying a hand on his arm.

He closed his eyes. "What do you want me to do for you, Malia?" Flat.

She spoke to the dragon queen. *I'd like to give you the opportunity to speak with Chanwa as you do with me.*

Yes. Yes, that will do nicely.

Malia spoke to Cian. "Give the gift of communication with the dragons to Chanwa. Make it so she can speak with them as I can."

His eyes opened. Deep in the golden-brown irises, tiny pinpricks of red-orange flared. Magic prickled along her skin. "I will have to take much from you," he said.

"Do it," she whispered.

The tingling along her skin strengthened, bordering on pain. Malia's blood roared in her ears, like the voices of the crowd above. Power hummed through her, flowing from her to Cian as it might from her to a Jegudun.

Pressure built in her skull. She grunted and went down on her knees. She reached for Cian, but he was beside her on all fours, his skin rippling and changing already. The pressure grew in her skull. She would have screamed, but she was afraid the effort might cause her head to burst, it felt so tight, so filled with magic.

Cian screamed, though, and the dragon queen screamed. The sound was like nothing Malia had ever heard, part animal, part human, and raw, as if the sound surprised the queen. She dug her fingers in the dirt. She smelled earth and pine, magic and sweat. The coppery tang of blood filled her mouth.

The pressure eased. Sounds shifted. Her cheek was pressed against the ground. She was breathing rapidly, making an alarming wheeze as she did so. She forced her breathing to slow. She was still alive, somehow.

A figure stirred beside her. He moaned. She blinked against her blurry vision, and the man came into focus.

He was slight, with olive skin and dark, short hair that showed some gray at the temples. His features were jagged, his nose hooked, although in a different way than Dalibor's had been. Dalibor had looked like a bird of prey, whereas this man simply had an interesting face. He looked ordinary, and unassuming. He blinked, and his eyes blazed such a bright red-orange that Malia had to turn her head.

"Did it work?" she asked, the afterimage of Cian's eyes against her eyelids.

The men hauled Chanwa up the stairs.

"Feed her to the dragons!" called an older man, his back bent.

"Spare her," called another man. Chanwa jerked her head around. It was the same man who had betrayed her to Muvumo. The skin around his eyes crinkled as he silently begged her forgiveness.

A crowd followed, all of them shouting. It didn't matter any longer that she might be carrying Muvumo's child. He was dead, and no longer the Most Worthy. Another man would take his place. Unless she'd stirred things up enough to create a ripple effect after she died, then things would soon resume as they always had. It was useless. She'd wasted the opportunity the changer had given them.

They reached the mesa, where she'd spent several days and nights fighting the best way she'd known how. Fitting, that it should end here. The men shoved her to her knees, and one of them whistled.

"We'll let the dragons take you," he said.

"Don't think that just because you were first to bring her to justice that you should be Most Worthy," said another.

Already the squabbling began. She choked on a snicker, turning it to a cough. The sharp pain in her wrist and elbow had given way to an intense throbbing. People crowded the edges of the mesa, leaving room for a dragon to land.

"All of the women who sat out here should be fed to the dragons," another man said.

"You fool, that would leave a handful of women for hundreds of men. You should definitely *not* be Most Worthy."

A third voice spoke. "All of the women should be forgiven. Save for her. She started this uprising."

"No," a fourth said. "*All* should be forgiven, including her, otherwise the remaining women could rebel again."

"Let them," growled the first man.

Round and round the voices went. Maybe she could crawl to the low wall surrounding the mesa and leap off before they figured out what to do with her. She could die on her own terms.

Suddenly, her head ached. Pressure built in her skull, unlike any headache she'd ever had. She let out a startled moan. Was she dying?

"Where's the blasted beast?" muttered the man. He whistled again.

She winced at the piercing sound. She fell forward, catching herself before she face-planted on the ground. A foot caught her in the side, knocking her over.

"Get up," the man said. "You're not getting out of this by acting sick."

She moaned again. She wanted to tell him she didn't care what he did to her, that death would be a blessing at this point, but she couldn't get any words out. She feared her head was about to explode.

The pressure disappeared abruptly. A voice slipped into Chanwa's head, reverberating pleasantly around her skull. The voice said, *Greetings, human. I am the queen of the dragons. Your friend from the valley granted you and I the ability to speak with one another. Through me, you speak with the other dragons as well. You look to be in trouble.*

She curled herself into a ball and laughed. The Taakwa woman had given her the ability to speak with the dragons. Chanwa had no idea such a thing was possible, but if the changer was involved, then she shouldn't be surprised.

"Where *is* that dragon?" the man muttered. He kicked at Chanwa again, hitting her legs and arms which had curled protectively around her middle. "And what are you laughing at?"

A tug came at her mind. The queen said, *Follow this thread, and you'll be able to speak to me.*

She tentatively said, *Good evening, queen of dragons.*

A pleased rumble replied.

Chanwa said, *Please come to the mesa. I'm in some trouble, and I could use your help.*

My pleasure.

Chanwa pushed herself up to sitting. Wings beat the air. A few people cried out, and those on the mesa hurried out of the way. The queen was rather average in size, but her sides pulsed so brightly that Chanwa had to squint. Ridges extended from the back of her neck along her back, making her look like a great, armored beast.

By the way, the queen said. *Your woman is safe on the ground.*

It took a moment for the meaning to sink in. Ankti was alive. Alive! Joy flowed through her, giving her renewed energy. Chanwa pushed herself to her feet.

"That's not my dragon," said the man, staring with mouth agape at the queen as she came in to land.

"No," said Chanwa, calmly brushing the dirt from her tattered dress. "She's mine." To the queen, she said, *Grab him, gently as you can.*

The man's companions ran as the queen's head darted forward. She grabbed him around his middle and lifted him high. He screamed, the sound echoing off the granite.

Chanwa thought at the dragon queen, *Would you have the others herd my people back out here?*

Dragons swooped in from all directions, driving people back to the mesa with rumbles and roars and snapping teeth.

Would you mind terribly if I climbed onto your back? So people can see me when I speak?

Amusement, then, *Not at all. It* is *rather difficult being human, isn't it? You're all so delicate, with your flesh so exposed.*

The queen dipped one leg so Chanwa could clamber up. The smell of brimstone and charred meat did not bother her at all this time, not like the other times she'd been near a dragon, or riding one. She scrabbled up, aware that she probably looked ungraceful doing so. Then again, most people probably wouldn't notice, they were so terrified of the dragon queen. And Chanwa.

She stumbled. So *that* was what the Most Worthy felt. Control through fear. People driven by terror. It was disgusting, and it would stop with her. She grabbed a thick, tall ridge and pulled herself to standing.

People filled the upper mesa, the stairs. People watched from their doorways, including Tangie, whose eyes were huge. Very few shared the mesa with her and the dragon and her captive. All had gone silent, without even the shuffling of feet to break the stillness. Only the torches popped and hissed.

Chanwa cleared her throat, then began, "You should know, first of all, that the dragons are mine." Her voice echoed and carried. All eyes were on her. "They hear me, they obey me." She actually wasn't sure just how much they would obey her, or for how long, but nobody needed to know that. "You also know that many of us have been working to be heard for the past few days. But the Most Worthy did not want to listen or compromise. He is dead."

A few murmurs. She raised her hands, and they fell silent again.

"There will be no more people deemed most worthy," she continued. "No man or woman is more, or less, important than the other. Going forward, our rules, our laws, will reflect that. We will no longer live in fear, but in cooperation. We will show mercy."

To the queen, she said, *Please let him down.*

She stretched her sinuous neck and slowly opened her jaws. The man stumbled, caught himself, and stumbled again on his way to the crowd, never taking his eyes off the dragon or Chanwa.

"We have a long journey ahead of us," she said. "For tonight, the Maddion will all return home and begin putting our lives back in order. The servants will have no demands put upon them. They will all decide whether they will live here, with us, with rights, or whether they will return home. But that can be decided later. For now, everyone must return home.

"There will be no fighting for leadership or control. Anyone who has a problem, come to me. I will listen and mete out decisions appropriate to the problem." There was so much more to say, but now was not the time. "Good night." To the queen she said, *I'm getting down now.*

The queen bent one leg again. Chanwa climbed down a great deal more gracefully than she climbed up, and said, *Do you know where Ankti is? Er… my woman?*

I'll bring her to you.

People filed home slowly, many wearing stunned expressions. None approached her. The queen lifted off the mesa and dipped into the dark forest. Chanwa stood to one side and fidgeted. There was so much to do. They had dead they must send off, including Nyda, and they had to set up new laws. So many laws. And they had to take care of the servants who wished to go home, and figure out what to do with those who stayed. And they had schools to set up. And they had to speak with the Taakwa and the Jeguduns. And—

She let out a moan and leaned forward, burying her face in her hands. Well, she had wanted change. There would be plenty to go around.

Wings beat at the air. She straightened and stood, her heart beating wildly. The queen landed on the mesa. Ankti sat on her back, between ridges. She gave Chanwa a shaky smile.

Chanwa hurried to the dragon's side and caught Ankti as she slid down. For a moment she just looked at Ankti, wincing at the swollen eye and the goose egg forming above it. But otherwise she was all right. She was alive. There was so much Chanwa wanted to say.

Ankti leaned forward and pressed her lips to Chanwa's. Words could wait. Chanwa returned the kiss, pulling Ankti closer. She would never let her go again.

CHAPTER THIRTY-ONE

Malia was never going to get up from her comfortable spot on the dirt. She would be shaded by pine trees when the sun rose. The fallen needles released a pleasant smell, and they cushioned her. Yes, this was a good spot. She would just stay here and—

A face appeared over her. Enuwal, brows creased, looked her over. "Are you hurt?"

"I don't think so," she said.

"Then why are you lying in the dirt?"

"I'm done. I've done enough. I'm going to spend the rest of my life right here, resting."

His brows drew down even further. Then his face relaxed, and he let out a quick laugh. "You can spend the rest of your life resting, Malia, but this is not the spot for it." All traces of mirth disappeared. "Where's Cian? Now that it's over—"

"Here," Cian said. But he had a different voice. Masculine, but softer. Tired. Resigned.

Enuwal looked from Cian to Malia and back again. "You worked a change? For who? How?"

"For me," Malia said, struggling to rise to her elbows. "To give the ability to communicate with the dragons to Chanwa."

"But it could have killed you. Or worse. Or… what price did you pay this time?" Enuwal asked, horror slowly dawning on his face.

"I have no clue," she said. "Cian?"

Large wings fluttered nearby. Then a familiar chirrup called, and Aru came waddling into the small clearing with them. He crouched beside Malia and fussed over her with chirps and whistles, occasionally baring his teeth at Cian.

Cian sighed. "I only suspect what it is this time. When you severed your ties with the dragon queen, other things were severed, too."

"Severed?" she said, her voice rising. "Like what?"

His red-orange eyes met hers. "Do you feel my presence in your mind?"

She reached for him and found… only herself. "No."

"Aru," he said. "Share a memory with Enuwal, would you. Anything will do."

She bit her lower lip and exchanged a worried glance with Enuwal. While she was glad to have Cian out of her mind, she wasn't sure she liked where the rest of this was going. And the power he'd shared with her was gone. She was just Malia again.

Enuwal placed his hands in Aru's. A moment passed, and then Enuwal said, "There's nothing. No pull, no memories, nothing." He looked up at Cian. "You severed all of our connections?"

Cian nodded, the corners of his mouth turned down. "I know it means a lot to you, sharing the Jeguduns' memories. I am truly sorry, for whatever it's worth."

"What about the bond that kept them near us?" she asked. "And the bond that kept you near me? Was that severed, too?"

He nodded.

"So then you can leave any time," Enuwal said to Cian. "At this very moment, in fact."

The red-orange of his eyes swirled faster, and they narrowed. "If that's what you want."

"Wait," Malia said. "Before you go tearing off with your feelings hurt." She turned to Enuwal. "And before *your* feelings get hurt, let me speak."

He frowned, but said nothing.

She took a deep breath. "Cian, a lot of people do not like you."

Enuwal made a strangled noise deep in his throat. She ignored him.

"They misunderstand you. Your family and friends feared you and turned on you, and you've lived alone since then. Of course you're a little… odd."

"I… am not sure whether to thank you for your take on the situation or not," Cian said wryly.

"But you've become a friend. Yes, you initially stuck around because you had to, but I felt how lonely you were. Cian, you don't have to stay here, but I would like you to. I think we can all learn from you." She turned to Enuwal. "I thought I was going to have to leave this place and everyone I love. But now I don't have to. I can have a normal life, with you. We can have children. I can resume training as clan mother, if my mother will allow it." She placed her hands on either side of his face. "Will you marry me, Enuwal of Posalo? Will you become Enuwal of Selu?"

She'd asked a lot of him, from seeking him out the summer before and entrusting him with the truth about the Jeguduns, to the time she spent healing after she repaired the barrier, to asking him to follow her so many places, and to put up with Cian. He might have reached his limit.

He placed his hands over hers. "I love you, Malia. I will marry you and join your family and your village."

She smiled. Aru let out a happy trill and clapped his hands. Cian nodded once and slipped into the darkness of the forest.

She leaned forward and kissed Enuwal. There was no one else in her mind, no magic to interfere, nothing and no one but her and Enuwal. She sank into him, the bone-deep weariness slipping away.

EPILOGUE

Malia's mother, as clan mother, waived the remainder of her mourning period. Malia chose to marry Enuwal during the winter festival. As she told him, it was the shortest day of the year, and the longest night, and so they'd have plenty of time in the marriage bed. He thought that was a splendid idea.

She was the only one to marry during the festival, and so she waited alone with her mother at one end of the large clearing in her village. The villagers filled a good portion of the clearing, but their numbers were still sadly depleted from the Dragon War. Given the number of babies crying, though, they were working on alleviating that.

Jeguduns stood in the front or perched on the rooftops all around. Aru stood front and center, his wings shining like polished wood in the torchlight, and his fur clean and fluffy. He gave her a wolfish grin, his tufted ears pricked forward. When the Jeguduns had found out their unknown tie to the Taakwa had been severed, they had simply gone on living in the cliffs. Some of them made long journeys out into the world, but they always came back. They made it known that this was home, and the Taakwa were their friends.

A dozen Maddion stood to one side, dressed in thick robes lined with fur, and wearing fur-lined hats against the cold. Chanwa stood before them all, with a contingency of men and women behind her. Their dragons waited a respectable distance from the village. They were, Chanwa had assured Malia, well fed and content. Ankti stood beside Chanwa. Every time Malia looked her way, Ankti gave her a wide grin.

Ankti had not felt comfortable living among the Maddion, so she and Chanwa had taken up residence in the guardhouse at the mountainpeak. It was close enough that Chanwa could be among her people in moments, and far enough for Ankti's comfort. Many things had changed for the better for the Maddion, but Ankti remained ever cautious. Malia couldn't blame her one bit. Of course, Ankti and Chanwa would soon have another concern to keep them busy. Chanwa's round belly was evident even beneath the heavy coat.

Standing near the front was Cian. He hadn't changed his name when he'd changed his appearance. It would have been too confusing, he'd said. He was dressed in a traditional Taakwa tunic and pants, with a thick robe over it. He was growing his hair out, but had no plans to become a braided man. He was content to simply live among them. Not everybody had been happy to have an Outsider among them, and certainly not the *mutara*, but none challenged him or threatened him, especially when Andrij, who had a reputation as a skeptic, demonstrated acceptance.

She turned her attention to Vedran, who had loaned his shoulder to Rina. She leaned heavily on him, but smiled widely. She'd lost Ziku soon after the events in the Maddion's mountains and had finally acquiesced to Malia's desire to move back to the village. Her mother had been less than pleased, which had made the move all that much sweeter in Malia's mind.

Standing to one side was Rasmus, his hair grown out to his shoulders now, and beside him, his new bride, Jetati. They both wore the blissful beams of those newly wed. Rasmus had been accepted back into his old village at last, and based on the easy grin he wore, life among the Taakwa agreed with him. He and Jetati would never have been able to make it through the snow on their own and so had been picked up by the Maddion on their way to Selu.

A rustling began at the back of the crowd. They parted, slowly giving way as Enuwal made his way to Malia and her mother. She couldn't get a good look at his face until he neared the front, and when the last of the crowd parted, she couldn't hold back her smile.

Enuwal wore a long robe over a light, cream colored tunic and pants. Fine stitching lined the robe, sewn in the shape of a forest scene, with pine and spruce and aspen, and deer flitting in and out among them, and trout jumping out of a stream. It represented both his clan and hers. The light color looked good against his brown skin.

He joined her, taking her hand in his, and together they faced her mother, who was also dressed in her very best skirt and tunic, with a fine, thick robe over it all, with trout jumping out of a stream embroidered around the hems.

Her mother blessed their union, welcomed Enuwal to Selu and to Malia's clan, spoke a few words, and then invited everyone to celebrate the union. Gourds rattled, and drums beat, and people began dancing.

The rest of the celebration was a whirl of people congratulating her and Enuwal, and dancing, and food. Malia's heart filled until she thought it might burst. All the people she loved were together. Her people were, tenuously, forming a friendship with the Maddion. They were all at peace, and safe. It was all she could have asked for as a wedding gift.

When at last she took Enuwal to their home, the voices and songs were still echoing in her head.

The hearth was the only light. A fire burned merrily within. Someone had come up before they got here and added more wood. She would bet on Vedran. He was thoughtful, for a little brother.

"Wait here," she said, sitting Enuwal on the sleeping mat laid out before the fire. She went to the pantry and took down her gift for him, wrapped in cloth and tied with string. "For you," she said, sitting beside him. The fire warmed her skin and crackled pleasantly. She fiddled with the feather hanging from a leather strap around her neck. It was one of Aru's feathers, donated to make a new necklace for her as she resumed her training to become Selu's next clan mother.

He untied the string and carefully folded back the cloth. Inside sat a thick bowl the color of cinnamon, with tiny, sparkling flecks embedded in it. A painted deer frolicked beside a stream, where a trout had been caught in midleap.

"Malia, it's exquisite," he said. "It's lovely."

"It's the first piece I made after we came home this past summer. I could hardly wait to give it to you."

He gave her a lingering kiss. "Thank you." He set the bowl on the shelf she'd given him for his things. "And I have something for you." He returned with a small, wrapped gift.

She opened it eagerly. Nestled inside were six brushes, ranging from tiny to large, made with the finest bristles. She sighed as she ran one softly over the back of her hand. "These are perfect. Thank you." She hesitated as a new thought came to her. She ran one of the medium brushes lightly over Enuwal's arm and grinned at the gooseflesh that broke out. "And they are useful for more than painting." Her grin widened as he sputtered in reply. She put the brushes away. For tonight, her fingers and mouth would tease his body. The brushes could wait for another time.

"I'll remember this night for always," she told him.

"I as well," he said, drawing in a sharp breath as she kissed the hollow of his neck. His fingers buried themselves in her hair. "Even though it *is* the longest night of the season."

She chuckled. "We'd better fill this night with love, then. And memories."

She kissed him, and they filled that night, and every day after, with love.

ABOUT THE AUTHOR

Rebecca Roland is the author of the Shards of History series, The Necromancer's Inheritance series, and *The King of Ash and Bones, and Other Stories*. Her short fiction has appeared in publications such as *Nature, Fantastic Stories of the Imagination, Stupefying Stories, Plasma Frequency*, and *Every Day Fiction*, and she is a graduate of the Odyssey Writing Workshop. You can find out more about her and her work at rebeccaroland.net, her blog Spice of Life, or follow her on Twitter @rebecca_roland.

A four-story collection featuring Rebecca Roland's return to the Taakwa.

THE KING OF ASH AND BONES

AND OTHER STORIES

Rebecca Roland

An exiled man returns to his family and the life he left behind. A king is determined to avenge his people. A man doomed to die gives his wife her greatest wish. A suspected affair leads to a shocking and wondrous surprise. Roland works her magic again in this four-story collection of eerie and enchanting works, including Rasmus's story from after *Shards of History.*

Thank you for reading!
We hope you'll leave an honest review at Amazon, Goodreads, or wherever you discuss books online.

Leaving a review means a lot for the author and editors who worked so hard to create this book.

Please sign up for our newsletter for news about upcoming titles, submission opportunities, special discounts, & more.

WorldWeaverPress.com/newsletter-signup

DREAM EATER

A Portland Hafu Novel

K Bird Lincoln

Koi Pierce dreams other peoples' dreams.

Her whole life she's avoided other people. Any skin-to-skin contact—a hug from her sister, the hand of a barista at Stumptown coffee—transfers flashes of that person's most intense dreams. It's enough to make anyone a hermit.

But Koi's getting her act together. No matter what, this time she's going to finish her degree at Portland Community College and get a real life. Of course it's not going to be that easy. Her father, increasingly disturbed from Alzheimer's disease, a dream fragment of a dead girl from the casual brush of a creepy PCC professor's hand, and a mysterious stranger who speaks the same rare Northern Japanese dialect as Koi's father will force Koi to learn to trust in the help of others, as well as face the truth about herself.

OPAL

Fae Of Fire And Stone, Book One

Kristina Wojtaszek

White as snow, stained with blood, her talons black as ebony...

In this retwisting of the classic Snow White tale, the daughter of an owl is forced into human shape by a wizard who's come to guide her from her wintry tundra home down to the colorful world of men and Fae, and the father she's never known. She struggles with her human shape and grieves for her dead mother—a mother whose past she must unravel if men and Fae are to live peacefully together.

"A fairy tale within a fairy tale within a fairy tale—the narratives fit together like interlocking pieces of a puzzle, beautifully told." —Zachary Petit, Editor *Writer's Digest*

CHAR

Fae of Fire and Stone, Book Two

Kristina Wojtaszek

Fire is never tame—least of all the flames of our own kindling.

Raised in isolation by the secretive Circle of Seven, Luna is one of the few powerful beings left in a world dominated by man. Versed in ancient fairy tales and the language of plants, Luna struggles to control her powers over fire. When her mentor dies in Luna's arms, she is forced into a centuries-long struggle against the gravest enemy of all Fae-kind—the very enemy that left her orphaned. In order to save her people, Luna must rewrite their history by entering a door in the mountain and passing back through time. But when the lives of those she loves come under threat, her rage destroys a forest, and everything in it. Now called The Char Witch, she is cursed to live alone, her name and the name of her people forgotten.

Until she hears a knock upon her long-sealed door.

Interwoven with elements of Hansel and Gretel and The Seven Ravens, Char is the stand alone sequel to Opal, and second in the Fae of Fire and Stone trilogy.

CURSED: WICKEDLY FUN STORIES

Short Story Collection

Susan Abel Sullivan

Wickedly fun YA short stories featuring witches, werewolves, limericks that can change fate, and a sinister vine bent on murder and the destruction of Alabama! Inside quirky settings with creepy plots, characters discover new and unsettling powers as their worst fears manifest.

Let these stories draw you in with their lighthearted tone — then delight you with their wickedly sly sense of humor. You'll laugh, you'll shudder, you'll think twice about taking a deal from a bucktoothed woman.

FAE

Rhonda Parrish's Magical Menageries, Volume One

Meet Robin Goodfellow as you've never seen him before, watch damsels in distress rescue themselves, get swept away with the selkies and enjoy tales of hobs, green men, pixies and phookas. One thing is for certain, these are not your grandmother's fairy tales.

CORVIDAE

Rhonda Parrish's Magical Menageries, Volume Two

In Corvidae birds are born of blood and pain, trickster ravens live up to their names, magpies take human form, blue jays battle evil forces, and choughs become prisoners of war. These stories will take you to the Great War, research facilities, frozen mountaintops, steam-powered worlds, remote forest homes, and deep into fairy tales. One thing is for certain, after reading this anthology, you'll never look the same way at the corvid outside your window.

SCARECROW

Rhonda Parrish's Magical Menageries, Volume Three

Within these pages, ancient enemies join together to destroy a mad mommet, a scarecrow who is a crow protects solar fields and stores long-lost family secrets, a woman falls in love with a scarecrow, and another becomes one. Encounter scarecrows made of straw, imagination, memory, and robotics while being spirited to Oz, mythological Japan, other planets, and a neighbor's back garden. After experiencing this book, you'll never look at a hay-man the same.

SIRENS

Rhonda Parrish's Magical Menageries, Volume Four

EQUUS

Rhonda Parrish's Magical Menageries, Volume Five

The Falling Of The Moon

Moonfall Mayhem, Book One

A.E. Decker

In the gloomy mountains of Shadowvale, Ascot Abberdorf is expected to marry a lugubrious Count and settle down to a quiet life terrorizing the villagers. Instead, armed with a book of fairy tales, her faithful bat-winged cat, and whatever silverware she can pinch, Ascot heads east, to the mysterious Daylands, where her book promises she can find True Love and Happily Ever After, if she only follows her heart.

Determined to win the hand of Prince Parvanel, Ascot storms the Kingdom of Albright. With the book's guidance, she's confident she'll overcome any obstacles the imperious Queen Bettina Anna throws in her way, be they witches, evil stepmothers, or Big Bad Wolves.

Unfortunately, the book doesn't cover reluctant princes, wolves who read Dostoyevsky instead of blowing down houses, or a guild of Godmothers whose motivations may not be as pure as three drops of blood on a sweep of snow. Most annoying of all is the captain of the guard who swears he'll see the moon fall before she weds Prince Parvanel.

There are stories … and then there are *stories*, and if this parade of shifty shenanigans continues, Ascot might have to rewrite her own tale lest she end most Unhappily Ever After!

The Meddlers Of Moonshine

Moonfall Mayhem, Book Two

A.E. Decker

Something is rotten in the town of Widget, and Rags-n-Bones knows it's all his fault.

WORLD WEAVER PRESS
Publishing fantasy, paranormal, and science fiction.
We believe in great storytelling.

Made in the USA
Las Vegas, NV
24 May 2024

90322826R00164